Marc Alexander had h
when he was fifteen, a
1972 of both fiction and non-fiction. He is an established writer of horror novels under a pseudonym. He is at present working on the third title in the fantasy quartet *The Wells of Ythan*.

Also by Marc Alexander

The Wells of Ythan 1: Ancient Dreams

Magic Casements

Part the Second of The Wells of Ythan

Marc Alexander

HEADLINE

First published in 1989
by HEADLINE BOOK PUBLISHING PLC

ISBN 0 7472 3026 9

Typeset in 10/12½ pt English Times by
Colset Private Limited, Singapore

Printed and bound in Great Britain by
Collins, Glasgow

HEADLINE BOOK PUBLISHING PLC
Headline House
79 Great Titchfield Street
London W1P 7FN

For Pat Andrew,
the best of old friends,
whose puppets are worthy of Toyheim

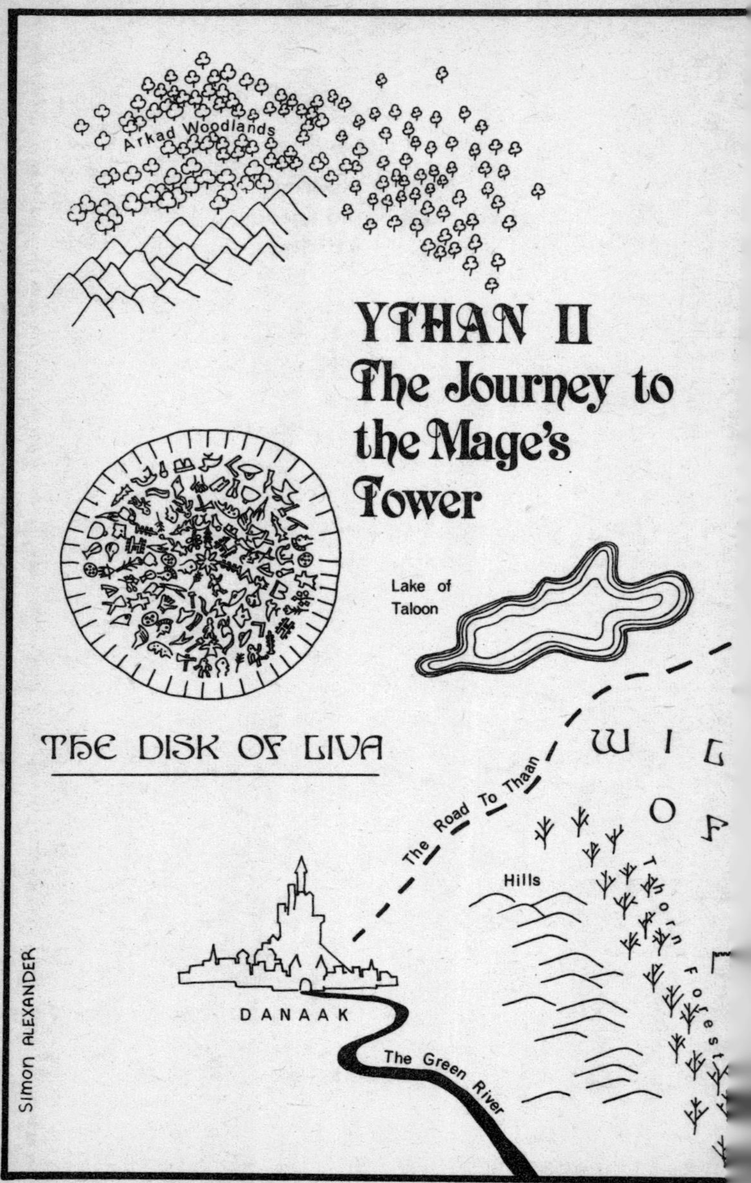
Arkad Woodlands
YTHAN II
The Journey to the Mage's Tower
Lake of Taloon
THE DISK OF LIVA
The Road To Thaan
W I L
O F
Hills
Thorn Forest
DANAAK
The Green River
Simon ALEXANDER

THE COLD SEA
The Mage's Tower
Northern Forests
THE RANGES OF DONO KARA
THE DESERT OF AKEA
e Domain of Olam
Giants' Circle
The Chasm
Subterranean River
The Blue Ranges
The Drakenfel
Plains of Thaan
THAAN
ights Towers
Fountains

Book One

It is time I ceased dreaming ancient dreams.

Since the crystal bird – that harbinger of parlous times – was glimpsed in the High Wald, marvels have come to pass that I never thought to see in the few years left to me.

Much has been terrible, yet I have an inkling that the vile shadow darkening Ythan since The Enchantment could be lifted at last.

Renewed is the quest for Livia!

And it was I *who sent two brave youths in search of the Princess lying bespelled in some secret place while the Lord Regent plays the tyrant beneath her empty throne.*

This day a missive penned in code from the courtesan Merlinda was brought through the forest by one of the Fey long friendly to my House. It tells that their adventure has met with more success than such attempts before, thanks, it would seem, to a most unlikely character for such an undertaking – an apprentice lad from Toyheim named Krispin. His ambition was no higher than to construct mechanical dolls, yet my news is that he survived the Land of Blight with Lord Alwald, and won the Esav from the forgotten god.

Alas, his sister still plays with my old doll like a child though she is a young woman of rare beauty whose likeness to Livia's portrait gives me much thought. When she alone escaped the Wolf Horde's destruction of Toyheim her mind sought refuge in childhood innocence and there it remains, perhaps for ever.

The Wolf King holds court in River Garde now, and the lands once protected by Lord Grimwald are ravaged by barbarians. At least the girl Jennet is safe with me for the mist I conjured still shields us from our enemies. How long they will stay before the lure of the Outland calls them back none – not even the Fey – can predict.

Yet it is an ill wind that blows nobody good.

Like me, Lord Grimwald, Hereditary Lord of the River March, was a secret follower of the Pilgrim Path and dedicated to seeking the return of the Princess. After he had been treacherously done to death I set his son, the fair Alwald, upon the quest. As his companion and guide I chose Krispin in whose receptive mind I hid directions for the journey.

The missive endorses my judgement, telling how the pair reached Danaak after following the River of Night. Soon they set out for the heretic city of Thaan in order to seek the only mortal left alive who knows the secret of Princess Livia, and who might barter his knowledge for the Esav.

May the Serene Mother grant that they travel swiftly because Merlinda also writes that the Lord Regent has sent forth a terrible army to punish Thaan for its blasphemy, or so it is declared. The real reason will be far more devious.

I am an old woman, the last of an illustrious line, living alone in the Peak Tower with retainers equally old. I have

Smoke the cat for company and for comfort I take a little too much wine, yet when I learned how the quest for Livia continues the yoke of years fell from my shoulders. All the hope I knew as a young girl returns, and it is with this joyous feeling that I inscribe these words . . .

– from the Commonplace Book of
Lady Eloira, Reeve of the High Wald

ONE
The Wilderness of Gil

An arrow flashed in a rare sunbeam.

Krispin's drong bellowed, reared, and flung him to the forest floor. Breathing hard, he hauled himself to his feet and drew Woundflame from its scabbard. His gaze roved over the dreary thorn trees that bounded the clearing for a sight of the archer who might be drawing a second shaft. Behind him the other drongs milled in terror while his companions clung to rein and saddle and shouted unheeded commands.

A slender bough trembled.

Krispin ran to the spot and glimpsed a dark figure disappearing in the hot gloom.

Ignoring thorns which clutched at him like witches' fingers, he plunged among the twisted tree trunks. His sword shone preternaturally bright as he used it to slice his way through barriers of pallid saplings. Behind him he heard the voice of their crouch-backed guide restoring the drongs to obedience, but this died as he ran further into the silent wildwood.

Suddenly he burst into a glade filled with thin shafts of light filtering through the canopy of tentacle-like branches above. Crossing it was the archer, bow in hand.

Krispin raced forward and tripped the enemy with an ease gained in playing the bladder game with his fellow apprentices in Toyheim. As he stood with his sword upraised he saw that the sprawled figure was bare-footed, tangle-haired and dressed in rags.

When it rolled over and sat up Krispin was shocked to see it was a girl who gazed at Woundflame with fearful eyes. Behind a mask of grime her features showed that she must have once been pretty but now her feral appearance chilled the young man even though it was he who held the sword.

'Why did you shoot my mount?' he demanded.

Seeming not to understand him, she raised her arms in supplication, then a crafty expression twisted her lips and reaching to the hem of the cloth that served as a skirt she pulled it up to her thighs. From a mouth which would have been attractive had it not been for her broken teeth came a laugh of lewd invitation.

With a deft movement Krispin swung Woundflame.

She screamed but the blade was merely aimed at her bow. As it was sundered Krispin turned and walked away in disgust, much of it against himself for the itch of lust he felt at the sight of her exposed limbs. Realising that he did not intend to harm her, the girl picked up one of her scattered arrows and ran after him.

Was it the crack of a twig that saved him or did Woundflame, with ancient sorcery forged in its iron, strike of its own accord? All he could remember afterwards was turning to face the girl raising the arrow like a poniard, and the sick sensation of his sword striking her side. Blood welled through her rags as she collapsed at his feet.

'Serene Mother, what have I come to!' he muttered aloud. He bent down to touch her but she lay as limp as a broken doll and he backed away in horror.

In the past Krispin had taken life when fighting nomads who had invaded the Wald; then it had been kill or be killed, but to bring about the death of a woman appalled him – because of her sex the fact that she had been as intent on his destruction as the nomads did not occur to him. There was nothing he could do. The blow he had struck could not be undone. And with his greenish eyes misted by anguish he left the huddled body.

On reaching the edge of the glade he cast a final glance behind him, and was ever grateful that he did so because he beheld his victim rise from her shamming and limp painfully into the trees.

He had not got her life on his conscience, yet curiously his spirits remained low. The last few minutes had in some way been a reminder of the bane which lay over the kingdom.

When Krispin returned to the clearing he saw that the injured drong was on its knees. Pink froth hung from its thick lips and its shuddering breath proclaimed that it was close to death. The other animals spluttered uneasily and watched mournfully as the guide, known as the Hump because of his crooked back, bent over it.

'Poor old beast,' he murmured gently, reaching out and rubbing the side of its head. 'Poor old Trailblazer, for many a season you have faithfully carried burdens for others' profit, and now . . .'

His voice dropped as he moved to one side of the kneeling animal and from his belt took his needle-pointed drong-rider's spike. Again he ran his hand over the animal's hairy skin, this time at the point where the arched neck joined the head. Then, having made sure of the exact spot, he raised the spike with both hands and drove it deep. The drong fell forward without a sound on a carpet of livid moss, its eyes glazing, its agony over.

The other animals gave forth a keening cry and backed away.

The Hump moved to where a couple of handspans of feather-tipped shaft protruded from Trailblazer's chest. Despite his great strength, it was with some difficulty that he drew out the bloodied arrow and held it up for the others to see.

'This was not crafted by a member of the Fletchers' Guild,' he declared. 'See, the tip is made of bone.'

'What does that mean, Master Guide?' asked Ognam, the tiny bells stitched to his red and yellow motley jingling as his mount moved restlessly beneath him.

'It is an outcast's arrow,' the guide replied as he began unstrapping the heavy saddle-bags from the dead drong. 'Thank the Mother it must have been a loner trying his luck more out of spite than hope of gain. If there had been a band of them we would be like targets in the butts – aye, stripped and robbed and, if there was breath left in us, tormented.'

'There was only one,' said Krispin stepping closer. 'And she – she fled.'

'You have blood on you – are you hurt?' asked the Lady Merlinda.

'No, my lady, but the thorns are cruel,' he replied.

'I did not think outcasts came so close to Danaak,' said Merlinda turning to the Hump.

'It is unusual,' he agreed as he buckled the saddle-bags to the harness of the baggage drong. 'I have not heard of outcasts in this great belt of thorn which divides the pastures and moors of Danaak from the Wilderness of Gil. Usually they haunt the wastes where, luckily, they can be seen by caravaneers before they can attack. But these are strange times and along trade route and in wilderness there is change.'

'There was no talk of outcasts in the Wald,' said Alwald. 'Who are these people?'

'They are all sorts,' the Hump replied as he remounted. 'Prisoners fled from the mines, heretics in fear of the Witchfinders, criminals who have somehow escaped the garotter's cord, madmen and rebels, but mostly the dispossessed . . . folk who have earned the displeasure of the Regent and his Council or who have been driven out of their villages and off their land to the advantage of rich favourites.

'At first those who are honest by nature try to support themselves in the barrens – I have seen their shrivelled patches of corn – but in the end they find the only way to live is by waylaying travellers and plundering caravans whose masters have not employed enough guards.

'But if they have entered the forest I fear them more than in the desert. Here they could be hid in the trees, drawing back their bows at this moment.'

At his words the travellers felt their backs tense as though expecting the impact of a bone-tipped shaft.

'Better we do not waste time in talk,' declared Gambal.

'Forward then,' cried the Hump. 'With luck we may clear the forest by day end. I suggest, Master Krispin, that you ride the baggage drong.'

He tapped the flank of his mount with the ornate bronze goad symbolizing his rank as a caravan guide, and swiftly led the party from the clearing.

No birds sang in the thorn forest.

No breeze stirred the leafless boughs.

No sound was heard save for the occasional snapping

of dead wood beneath the broad, horny feet of the drongs.

Bringing up the rear, Krispin was struck by what an oddly mixed company they were. At the head of the cavalcade rode the Hump in the voluminous black cloak he wore to cover his deformity. Sitting behind him side-saddle was the mysterious girl appropriately named Silvermane who spoke few words and whose gown was so long it hid her feet.

After her rode the noble courtesan Merlinda; then Gambal with the innocent face and thoughtful eyes, the youthful Revel Master who had arranged their escape from the Regent's dungeons. Crowding him in his anxiety to leave the forest was their fellow prisoner Ognam in his multi-coloured garb of a member of the Guild of Jongleurs.

The next rider was the Lord Alwald, with whom Krispin had journeyed from the Peak Tower in the High Wald. Once heir to the River March and now dispossessed, he retained his aristocratic bearing and was careful of his appearance with his blond hair carefully parted in the middle so that it fell on each side of his handsome face and his moustache still neat from a recent trimming.

What a curious lot we are, Krispin thought, not for the first time. *Curious, and yet despite our different stations we are becoming comrades – I even find my Lord Alwald less of an ache in the fundament than I did early on.*

The heat hung heavy, seeming to stifle the riders. Although there were no mires in the forest, there were flies – black flies which formed clouds about their heads, a myriad of tiny vampires crawling on exposed skin and invading ears and nostrils in search of blood. Added to this irritation was the danger of the finger-length thorns which clustered the springy limbs of the trees.

'You! You with the crooked back!' Alwald suddenly shouted as a branch left its claw marks across his face. 'You are supposed to be our guide – cannot you find us an easier path?'

At his harsh words Silvermane turned and looked hard at the young noble, but the Hump replied evenly. 'This belt of thorn forest stretches for a score of leagues either side of us. To avoid it we would have had to follow the high road to Thaan which lies to the north but, as you know, the Regent's army is already marching along it.'

'He speaks true,' said Merlinda. 'Our only hope of reaching the city before it is besieged is to cross the wilderness.'

'That I know,' muttered Alwald. 'But it seems to me there must be a better way through these accursed trees.'

'If there was, the Hump would know it,' Gambal told him quietly. 'Not only is his body freakish but there is something strange about his mind. He has an instinct such as homing birds possess which enables him to find the right route no matter what land he is passing through. He cannot explain it himself, yet this talent has made him sought after by caravan captains all over Ythan.'

Eager to be clear of the depressing trees, the flies and any lurking outcasts, the company followed the Hump without further talk.

Krispin rode with Woundflame unsheathed across the pommel of the heavy drong saddle. It was the sword which Lady Eloira had retrieved from the mausoleum of her ancestors as Alwald's quest gift, but thinking it no more than a mere tarnished relic he had passed it on to Krispin, not then aware that in times of danger its blade gleamed as though newly wrought and honed for combat. The fact that Krispin refused to return it once Alwald had an inkling of its inherent power had been a cause of friction between them. From time to time Krispin glanced at the blade which had resumed its dull appearance, and he was reassured to see that there was no sign of the crimson Death Dew which beaded it as a warning when blood was about to be spilled.

When they came out of the forest the desolate landscape before them could not dampen their elation at having escaped from the ugly thorn trees.

'Behold the Wilderness of Gil,' cried the Hump.

It stretched with slight undulations to the rim of the world. No trees grew to break it and sandy earth showed in bald drifts through the covering of low spikey bushes and purple-leafed sage.

'Do you know it well?' asked Merlinda.

'I should,' replied the Hump with a rare smile. 'It was out there that I was found as a baby. In a sense you could say it is my home.'

'Have you any idea how you came to be there?' Ognam asked.

'None. The caravaneers searched for those who might have been my parents – travellers who had lost their way mayhap – but nothing was found, not even a footstep in the sand. I am a mystery.'

'And so, I understand, is your sense of direction,' said Merlinda.

'I hope you will find it so, my lady. The wilderness takes a cruel toll of those who cannot find their way. But it was not always thus. I have heard it told that in the days when Ythan had kings there was a highway across this waste with towers set up at each twelve hours of travelling, and in each was stationed a wayside knight and his retainers dedicated to the protection of travellers.'

'And where did this road lead?'

'To Thaan. But after The Enchantment the knights were disbanded, the road forgotten and the few who ventured to Thaan went by the northern route. But by crossing the wilderness directly we should reach Thaan several days ahead of the Regent's army, after which my contract to guide you ends.'

He glanced at Gambal who nodded.

'That was the agreement,' he said.

'To arrive at a city which is about to be besieged by the Regent is a perilous undertaking but that, of course, is your affair,' the Hump continued, 'but I must warn you that the journey we are now about to undertake may be equally perilous. Be on your guard at all times.'

'Against outcasts?' said Krispin.

'Perhaps. And other things.'

'Such as?'

'That I cannot say. All I know is that among the men who travel the trade routes the Wilderness of Gil has an evil reputation. Sometimes caravan masters, driven by greed or need, sought to cross it and some – such as the one which found me – did succeed. But others have vanished out of the ken of men as though they have been magicked into another world. These days there is not a merchant in Ythan who would risk such a journey.'

'Thank you for the warning,' said Merlinda. 'But I doubt if there could be anything on the plain as evil as the dungeons of the Citadel.'

There was a mutter of agreement at this and Alwald said, 'Be not faint-hearted, Master Guide, for my companion and I are no strangers to danger and our swords have always had the final say, eh Krispin?'

The Hump made him no answer but said simply, 'I am going to follow the ancient trail so we may find nightly shelter in the Knights' Towers.'

He urged his drong forward and the others fell into line behind him. No one felt like talking, and for a long time the only sound was the swish of the drong's broad feet parting the miserable bushes. Until they had reached the wilderness the excitement of escaping from Danaak's Citadel, followed by the misery of their journey through the thorn forest, had given them no time for introspection, but now as their beasts bore them steadily over the empty plain each became the prey of memories.

To be free from enclosing walls lifted Silvermane's heart and her thoughts returned longingly to her wild homeland of Arkad; Merlinda pondered on the treachery which had led to her arrest in her house of pleasure and suddenly, as though she had solved a puzzle, she cried aloud, 'Urwen!'

Alwald's mind returned to the Vale of Mabalon and the Lady Demara, his beautiful young stepmother whom he loved with a guilty passion and who would soon birth the child of his murdered father.

Krispin's thoughts sped to the Peak Tower where his beloved Jennet remained in the thrall of a false childhood. It was for her sake he had undertaken the quest and yet, with male perversity, his thoughts shifted to the Vale of Mabalon and the maid Margan who had sweetened his last night there.

Only the thoughts of the Hump did not fly back into the past. All that mattered to him was his dream of the future when, having conveyed his mysterious party to Thaan, he and Silvermane could seek some far corner of the kingdom where there would be none to utter the word 'freak'.

So the leagues passed.

The dun landscape remained flat and barren but if the terrain was dreary, the sky compensated for it. During the afternoon it was a delicate blue across which sailed clouds in the form of shining ships and fantastic castles. As evening drew close and the sky traded its delicacy for the crude colours of a flaming sunset, the Hump pointed ahead and they saw the outline of a tower silhouetted against a backdrop of coral.

'The Knight's Tower,' he called with a hint of triumph in his voice. He urged his drong into a fast loping stride so they would be able to make camp before nightfall.

Time had taken its toll of the tower. The structures which had once surrounded it – walls, stables, storehouses and cisterns – had dwindled to half-exposed foundation rubble; the tower itself was so wind-weathered it looked more like the dead trunk of a gigantic tree than something which once had the precise lines of dressed stone. Its wooden floor had collapsed long ago but a circular staircase still spiralled within its walls to the roof of buttressed slabs.

As soon as the party arrived in its long shadow the Hump supervised the hobbling of the drongs while Gambal carefully ascended the staircase.

'We can lay out our sleeping bags up here,' he called. 'The roof is still solid and we can take turns as sentry on the stairs.'

'As you say,' the Hump replied cheerfully, 'but first let us enjoy our supper. I shall soon have the cooking pot bubbling.'

He was true to his word and soon a lively fire was crackling beneath a small cauldron. The travellers, well content to let him do the work, rested with the firelight flickering on their faces. The stew smelled delicious, the Hump produced a wineskin and they smiled upon each other as old friends. A simple contentment filled them. Many days would pass before they knew it again.

TWO
'Alas, my poor master.'

Late afternoon sunshine bathed the spires and towers of Danaak with a mellow luminosity which from a distance appeared like holy light. To the peasants of simple faith, toiling on the fertile plain which surrounded the great capital of Ythan, it seemed a mark of divine approbation – a mighty army was marching to bring retribution to the accursed heretics of Thaan who refused to acknowledge the divinity of the Serene Mother.

One labourer summed up the feeling of many when he leaned on his spade and, wiping the back of a begrimed fist across his brow, muttered, 'Mayhap for once the Lord Regent has done right.'

'Aye,' said another whose features – like so many born into servitude – were age-lined before his time, 'if them green-cloaked whoresons of Thaan be put to the fires the Mother may lift the burden from the land.'

'Pray it be so,' said a third. 'Meantime if sundown comes without this meadow cleared I would rather meet the Dark Maid than the master.'

He raised his mattock wearily and the others resumed their labour.

Such pious and popular expressions were not echoed in the mind of the Lord Regent who dozed fitfully on a balcony set high on the central tower of Danaak's Citadel. A page in sable and silver, whose long fair hair reflected her master's penchant for young female attendants, stood at the head of the ivory couch, ready to wipe his pallid face or ease his cushions if he woke gasping for air which, at this height, was free from the taint of the city. Another page in similar livery stood at his feet. The only other occupant of the balcony was a bodyguard, a Companion of the Rose, who, with visor lowered, stood as rigid as one of his master's automatons.

'He sleeps restlessly,' whispered the page at foot of the couch. 'Alas, my poor master!'

The page at the head of the couch sighed.

'It seems there is naught that can be done by the physicians,' she said. 'The poison he received in his hand came from something unnatural – or so I have heard it rumoured – and therefore it cannot be cured by natural means.'

'Do you know what this . . . this unnatural thing was?' The question was asked in a hushed but avid whisper.

'I have heard . . .' the answer was even softer. 'I have heard that it was some sort of mannikin, the creation of the old man who lives alone in the topmost room of the topmost tower. It was a blasphemy because only the Serene Mother can bestow true life, and now our master pays for old Leodore's gramarye . . .'

'Alas, my poor master.'

'There are few in Ythan who would echo your words – if the secret got abroad,' said the page at the head.

'I care not for that,' the page at the foot declared. 'All I know is that I would have become brothel meat had not my Lord Regent dispatched his Revel Master to bid for me in the slave mart.'

'May you never regret it,' said the other with a smile that

gave a cynical twist to her bright lips. 'But, hush, he stirs in his dream . . .'

The Regent uttered a low moan and his bulky body moved on the couch as pain from his bandaged arm increased. His eyelids opened to reveal adamantine eyes which appeared to the pages more than usually awe-inspiring in a face drained of the habitual ruddiness which gave him an air of rough good humour – a look belied at close quarters by those bleak eyes.

'What is the hour?' he muttered.

The page at his feet crossed to a water clock and told him.

He moved to sit up and then fell back against the cushions of cinnamon samite. 'Go now, my children, it is time for the Lady Mandraga to visit me.'

Gratefully the pages bowed and withdrew. Such was their fear of the ancient Lore Mistress that they hurtled undecorously down the winding stairs once they had quit the damask-draped chamber behind the balcony.

On his couch the Regent turned his leonine head and raising himself on his sound arm gazed past the balusters at the city below, the roofs of which shone as though gilded.

'If only those ants down there guessed the truth,' he muttered aloud, 'how long would it be before a rabble was hammering on my gates?'

'There is no need for them to know, my son,' came a reed-like voice. 'Do not my potions give you strength enough when you must appear before the subjects of the Empty Throne?'

The Regent lay back and his eyes swivelled to the bent form of the Lady Mandraga who had arrived in silence, being the only person in the Citadel permitted approach to his apartments without being challenged. She stood close to the couch, supporting herself on a T-shaped crutch.

'What I need is a cure, not some foul drug that revives me for an hour only,' he retorted. 'Look, look! It is worsening.'

He tugged at the bandages and when they fell away Mandraga saw his words were true. The poison from the bite of the homunculus made inflamed paths up the Regent's veins from wrist to shoulder, but worse was the state of his hand. It had enlarged to twice its normal size, the fingers were swollen into repulsive shapes and the nails had thickened into talons. It was a hand similar in appearance to that of the creature created in the alchemist's jar which had sunk its needle teeth into the Regent the moment before he hurled it into the fire.

'See!' said the Regent harshly.

'I see, my son.'

'Then how long will it be before the rest of my body takes on the shape of that abomination Leodore concocted? He claims a cure may be found in the elixir which animated the manikins, but he needs many times the original amount because the size of the homunculus was a fraction of that of a man. To that end I have supplied him with blood by the barrel from the Hall of Execution but still he demands more.

'And you, Lore Mistress of Ythan! With all your arcane wisdom, the best you can do for me is to give me only brief respite from this accursed affliction.'

'Be thankful for that. At least my potions help you to remain Regent of Ythan until the remedy is found –'

'Remedy! I begin to think there is no remedy.'

'Assuredly there is. Water from the Wells of Ythan.'

'They are long gone; indeed, they may have been no more than a fable.'

'No more a fable than the vanishment of the Princess

Livia, and you believe that she still lies englamoured in some hidden place.'

'If the Wells are no fable why cannot they be found?'

Mandraga gave a rare laugh – a laugh that some privately compared to the cry of a raven.

'Because none cared to look for them. For three generations the Pilgrims have searched for the sleeping princess because they believed she would restore Ythan's golden age, but since The Enchantment only a fool would risk the dangers of travel to seek some forgotten wells. *Once* it was believed that they held the waters of life and were a panacea but such belief is forgotten with so many things of the old time.'

'Yet *you* believe that the water from the Wells could restore me.'

The old woman straightened above her crutch and nodded.

'Of that I have no doubt.'

'Then the Wells must be found. Surely in your scrolls of ancient lore there is some hint of their place.'

'When the Guild of Witchfinders was established such knowledge was held to be magical and was thus destroyed in the Burnings – thousands of scrolls and maps were cast into the cauldron fires. Yet there is still a library where mayhap such knowledge has survived.'

'Where?'

'In Thaan. The heretics have the largest library left in the kingdom.'

'Then I shall send a message to the commander of the army that every scrap of parchment in Thaan must be saved and read by my scribes.'

The Lore Mistress nodded her approval.

'Do not delay. It is necessary that you are cured soon

because the path of the future is about to divide. It is foretold and there have been harbingers such as the crystal bird, yet no bygone prophet could predict which path will succeed. It depends on you to ensure that it is *our* path the world will follow, and for this you must be strong and resolute.'

'And what does your mirror foretell?'

'Little at the moment but I shall spend the night in watching. I hope to glimpse the Pilgrims you allowed to escape for I feel in my bones it is they who will lead us to Livia.'

The Regent actually managed to laugh, a curiously high-pitched sound for one deep-chested and broad-shouldered.

'Little do they realise that through their efforts the Empty Throne is likely to remain empty forever. The princess will only wake from her trance to enter the eternal trance of death. Meanwhile it is time I turned the treachery of Lord Odo to account.' And he laughed again despite his pain.

Lamps glimmered along the ramparts of the Citadel when a young man in a remote chamber there slowly awoke from the exhaustion of love-making. His hand slid across a sheet of finest spider silk seeking the young woman whose passionate demands had drained him more than any of the great ladies who discreetly called upon his special talents.

'My lady –' he began.

'She is gone.'

Opening his eyes, he almost cried aloud in fright. Beyond the ebony pillars of the vast bed stood a crone leaning on a T-shaped crutch, a crone with scanty white hair floating about a face which had been etched by time into a hundred wrinkles. Only her slate eyes had a suggestion of life as she regarded the dishevelled youth whose nakedness showed none of the prowess which had made him so sought-after since a pander had found him herding goats and, having taught him to wash, brought him to Danaak.

'Go now,' said the old woman. 'Here is your fee.'

She tossed a number of heavy bronze coins on to the bed.

'But the lady –' the youth began as he sought to protect himself with the sheet from the gaze of the beldame. 'She had such fire. Tell me her name.'

'Such a question could bring you sore punishment in the Citadel. Go now and be thankful to have earned so generous a fee so easily –'

'So easily!' exclaimed the youth indignantly.

' – and boast not how you came by your money.'

Although she was feeble there was something so inherently imperious in the nature of the old woman that he merely bowed his head and said, 'Of course, my lady.'

'Dress, and then the mute will conduct you down the secret stair.'

'Yes, my lady, but will I –'

'No questions. Should it be the wish of . . . my mistress . . . to dally with you again she knows how to summon you.'

'Yes, my lady.'

She gave him the ghost of a smile and as she did so the youth on the bed almost cried aloud as a wave of nausea engulfed him. On one of her blue veined fingers, taut on the crosspiece of her crutch, he saw a spiral ring in the shape of a serpent with eyes that glinted as though they held sparks of cold fire. The beautiful young woman whom he had serviced so recently had worn such a ring, and when he had admired it she had replied absently that it was an heirloom and there was none like it in the kingdom.

Serene Mother!

The whispered rumour of an ancient sorceress who could briefly regain youth by witchery sprang to his mind, filling him with horror and a blind desire to flee the Citadel before he should pay the penalty for this insight. Fortune favoured him in that the old woman had turned away without noticing the disgust and fear that crumpled his beautiful features.

Walking with painful slowness she left the apartment with its hanging silks and perfume lamps of silver and crystal, its musical fountain and floor of erotic mosaics, while the youth remained on the couch wishing he was back on a far hillside with his goats. When he had struggled into his hose and tunic a dumb servant woman came and nodded for him to follow her.

As he passed through the door of the chamber metal hands were clamped upon his shoulders – the gauntlets of a pair of Companions of the Rose.

'Time you had a rest, lad,' mocked one through his visor.

Meanwhile the Lore Mistress of Ythan entered her special sanctum and with a weary sigh settled her aching body into a comfortable chair before a large mirror of silvern crystal suspended between two pillars of antique workmanship.

The only light in the room came from a lamp of amber horn which cast a soft glow upon the old woman so that she saw her reflection in the looking-glass. Though her features remained as age-ravaged as ever, the image in the mirror was of a young woman of spellbinding beauty.

'Spirit of the mirror, I command, show the secrets I demand,' intoned the Lady Mandraga.

But only the false reflection gazed back at her.

Next she recited a couplet in Old Ythan, the ancient tongue only remembered by rare scholars since the

Witchfinders had proscribed it as the language of sorcery. The image held in the mirror became indistinct, a curtain of pale smoke rippled upwards behind the glass. Satisfied, Mandraga leaned forward, her chin resting on her bloodless hand, until the smoke steadied and took on the hue of an evening sky. In it glittered eight points of light which the Lore Mistress recognised as the Constellation of the Griffin.

In the background the outline of a tower pointed like a giant finger to these stars, then became hidden as the silhouette of a human form came into view against the darkling sky.

'Good, good!' murmured Mandraga.

Then she saw something move in the shadows behind him, something with gleaming eyes and shining fangs. She uttered a futile croak of warning before the figure was dragged from view. For a ghastly second a bestial face peered at her before the mirror went black; or so it seemed to Mandraga as she toppled into a swoon.

THREE
Night Walker

It had lain for many seasons in its buried cave, neither asleep nor dead, but waiting as though in a trance. Sometimes it dreamed; dreamed that there had been a time when the world was different, when it had known others of its kind and there had been no need for them to hide away in secret fissures of the arid wilderness.

Sometimes the dream was about the one with whom it had walked in the harsh light of the moon, and when the moon had followed his nightly path beyond the earth's end they had lost themselves in the ecstasy of mating . . . long ago, long ago.

Now it stirred.

Only the faintest echo from the upper world reached it but it was enough – it was what it had been waiting for so long, so long.

The trance ebbed and slight tremors rippled through it; a pulse began, eyelids slid back to reveal eyes golden in the dark, and with a shuddering gasp air was inhaled through its flat nostrils.

It hungered.

Conscious now, it knew not what it was but it did know what it wanted.

Guided by instinct, it raised its taloned fingers and began to scrabble at the earth which filled the shaft above its resting place. As it worked, first on its back, then in a sitting position and finally upright, it wondered if the same echo had reached the one who had been its mate, if she too would be digging her way out of her own tomb-like sanctuary. The thought made its talons claw frantically at the soft soil above so that it poured in dry streams down the elongated body. It must be the first to reach the prey!

Suddenly its hands could find nothing more to dig. It had broken through the surface. In a matter of moments it enlarged the hole, and cool night air began to replace the fetor in which it had existed. It grunted with satisfaction as it looked up and once again the moon was mirrored in its eyes.

Eagerly it snuffed the breeze. With power once more vitalising its limbs – dangling arms so pitifully thin and yet so terrifyingly strong – it hauled itself into the upper world and the immemorial hunt was on.

While the Hump bent over the stewpot, the firelight increasing the grotesquerie of his misshapen shadow, Krispin left the group watching him and, entering the tower, cautiously made his way up the circular steps to the flat roof. Here he leaned against an eroded merlon and gazed across a plain which appeared like a sea of shadow beneath the purple twilight. His lips still burned from the ordeal of the quicklime in the nether world beneath the Citadel, yet it was hard to believe so little time had passed since Gambal had taken them to freedom beneath a death cart's hideous load.

There had been the dawn journey along the Green River to the spot where the Hump, hired by Gambal, waited for them with drongs to carry them speedily through a smiling landscape of fields and copses to the old drovers' road. This wound through low hills to the thorn forest which was the natural boundary between the countryside surrounding Danaak and the barren wilderness beyond.

Only now that he was alone was he able to reflect on how remarkable their escape had been from such well-guarded dungeons far beneath the rock on which the Citadel was built, and to ponder the fact that he and Alwald were once more on the quest which would doubtless lead to perils as great as those that lay behind him.

'A copper piece for your thoughts,' came a musical voice behind him and he turned to see the Lady Merlinda in the gloaming.

'You would be over-pricing them, lady,' he replied. 'My mind was filled with what lies ahead.'

'I only wish I was better dressed for our journey,' she said. 'The gown in which I was arrested is hardly suitable for drong-riding across this miserable plain.'

'You are welcome to borrow what spare clothes I have in my pack.'

'What, dress as a man and risk being sent to the cauldron as a witch?' she laughed. 'Yet I must admit that in my time I have donned stranger costumes than that for the pleasure of my special patrons. But I think you know little of such whims and practices – the conceits which follow disillusionment. At your stage of life the act of passion must be enough in itself. You are to be envied.'

In Toyheim such a conversation with a member of the opposite sex would have brought the blood to Krispin's face but there was something so straightforward in the manner of the courtesan that he only felt a keenness to talk further with her.

'Lady, you have so much more knowledge in . . . in certain matters . . . than I, and therefore I have a . . . a favour to ask.'

'Favour? There is only one sort of favour that men come for to such as I, and while you are a likely young fellow –'

Krispin was shocked and spluttered a protest.

'Take not offence, toymaker,' Merlinda said with a laugh. 'If I mistook your meaning it is because for years I have been under no illusion as to the kind of regard in which men hold me. Lady I may be – even the fact that I was sold in the slave mart could not rob me of my hereditary rank – but to most men I am a whore, albeit an exceptional one. So, Krispin, what is the favour?'

'It is just that I wanted to ask you something, but it is of little importance.'

'You are still young enough to sulk.'

Now Krispin laughed.

'There is something that bothers my mind, lady, because the ways of love are still new to me,' he said. 'Only twice have I lain with a girl. That must seem strange to you, but . . .' He raised his shoulders and dropped them in a characteristic gesture. 'The first time was with someone I loved so deeply that when it happened it was as natural as breathing for both of us – or so it seemed. It was for her sake that I undertook the quest at the behest of Lady Eloira, but when I was in Mabalon I spent a night with another, one who I did not love but whose companionship I learned to value when we travelled through the Land of Blight . . .'

'And you enjoyed that, too, so now you doubt the strength of your feeling for the first maid.'

'You are right. Sometimes I fear that if my heart was true I would not have allowed myself to relish Margan's caresses.'

'Be easy. If you did not care for your first love the question would not come into your mind. Sometimes companionship alone inspires enough warmth to bring two people into each other's arms – to bring them comfort as well as pleasure – though it is not strong enough to bind them in the ways that real love does.'

'Do you still believe in love?' asked Krispin. 'I mean, after the life you have known?'

'Oh yes, Krispin,' she replied. 'Because the love I longed for has not been granted me it does not mean that it does not exist. It is curious: you choose your friends with care and thought yet when it comes to love' – she sighed – 'it can come with no more reason than the flight of an arrow fired by a blind archer, and have the same impact when it strikes.

'But as for you Krispin, I think you have little need for remorse, that you are still heart-whole and –'

Her words were cut short by a shriek which rose from somewhere in the gloom beyond the Knight's Tower.

A feeling of pleasant lethargy descended upon the travellers as they sat in a semi-circle and watched the Hump preparing their meal. That the camp work should be left to him was taken for granted; unlike them he was used to spending all day perched high on a drong saddle, and also he was *hired*.

As a wraith of steam danced above the pot, Gambal stood up and, stretching his arms wide, said to the company, 'Excuse me while I take a little stroll.'

'Do not wander far,' the Hump warned him. 'We must keep close together for protection.'

'I think you will thank me not to remain too close,' Gambal replied with a rare grin lighting his young yet solemn features.

Ognam, in loyalty to the latrine humour which was the stock-in-trade of the strolling buffoon, cried, 'After the delicacies of the dungeon we pray you to stay out of earshot as well as rearshot.'

The sally was greeted with silence and he muttered in mock sadness, 'There was a time when that would have at least earned a titter. It is the way you tell them, and it seems I have lost that talent since my incarceration.'

'The Regent has a lot to answer for,' said Alwald drily.

Gambal walked away and was lost to sight behind the tower. Ignoring the tethered drongs whose jaws were grinding their evening corn ration, he hurried over drifts of sandy soil and through patches of dwarf furze until the tower dwindled to an indistinct column above which the Griffin constellation had begun to glitter.

'The time is right,' he murmured to himself.

Reaching a shallow declivity, he sat down with his arms outstretched and his palms turned inwards. Long moments passed while he remained without movement and if there was the softest sound of a footfall on soil nearby he did not hear it.

He was only conscious of danger when something heavy fell upon his back, when two sinuous arms imprisoned his chest and the air he gulped was poisoned with a charnel stench which brought vomit to his throat.

Turning his head he beheld the face of his attacker – a high-domed head devoid of hair, fleshy ears ending in feline points, slanting eyes which, without pupil or iris, shone gold, a lump of a nose with gaping nostrils and, set in simian jaws, teeth like long ivory spikes. The skin of the creature was as white as that of a sea-bleached corpse.

Gambal's scream echoed through the dusk.

At the camp-fire his companions leapt to their feet. The Hump, his drong-rider's spike appearing in his hand as though by conjuring, leapt beside Silvermane to protect her from attack. Ognam seized a blazing brand and then dropped it with a howl while Alwald drew his sword and raced away in the direction taken by Gambal. Seconds later Krispin came bounding out of the tower, Woundflame in hand.

'Where – ?' he began.

Ognam pointed to the path taken by Alwald and he sprinted after him. In a few moments he saw his figure ahead of him and then, as he drew up with him on the brow of a declivity, both gasped as they saw a tall, spindly creature – vaguely manlike in the shadows – dragging Gambal after him at unbelievable speed. When it turned its head, they caught a flash of golden eyes and gleaming teeth.

'Serene Mother! What can it be?' gasped Alwald.

'We had better find out or Gambal will be welcoming the Dark Maid,' Krispin answered. Without another word they plunged down the slope in pursuit.

As Krispin ran he felt the grip of Woundflame come alive in his hand in the way an iron chisel had once responded to a sudden lightning storm that burst over Toyheim in the High Wald. This tingle running up his arm had an exhilarating effect on the youth; as he pounded beside Alwald he had little in common with the mild apprentice who had grown up in the village of Toymakers. His experiences since the Wolf Horde overran the Wald had brought forth an aspect of his character which he had tried to ignore since his mysterious childhood.

But now such thoughts could not have been further from his mind; all he wanted was to catch up with the sinister figure and let it feel the sword's bite through flesh and sinew before Gambal, his new companion who had saved him from the limepit, came to harm.

Despite the weight of its victim, the tall intruder kept ahead with an easy loping stride thanks to its unnaturally long limbs.

Krispin became aware of someone running beside him and then surging ahead of both himself and Alwald. With her long hair streaming behind her in a manner befitting her name, the silent girl who had ridden with the Hump was overtaking them. In one hand she held high her skirt the hem of which normally swept the ground; in her other there was what appeared to be a wand of silver which they later realised was the Hump's long cooking knife which she had snatched up when Gambal's cry had broken the evening stillness.

Suddenly the creature vanished as though swallowed into the earth. When Silvermane reached the spot where they had last seen it she stopped abruptly and beckoned them to hurry. With hearts thudding against their ribs and breath burning their throats, the two young men reached her and saw that the creature had stumbled down a bank into the remains of a dry water course. He stood his ground in the shallow ravine, his victim slumped at his feet and his golden eyes blazing up at them.

Then, in a ghastly gesture of defiance, he seized the limp Gambal by the head and raised him so that his feet swung free. A low-pitched grunting issued from the creature – a monstrous form of laughter – and with a sick fascination they saw that he was about to bite through Gambal's neck.

Alwald sprang down the bank and, with the skill which was a legacy from his military training at River Garde, managed to land on his feet. At the same time he made such a skilful sword thrust that, while it missed the dangling Gambal by a hand's breadth, the point of the blade slid into the creature's breast. It dropped its victim to the ground and, hissing fury, swung a long arm so that its talons ripped the sleeve of Alwald's doublet.

Again he lunged and again the sword entered the elongated body but with little success. Driven back by the terrible bone-tipped fingers, Alwald used his fencing skill to plunge his sword again and again into the loathsome white body. Amazingly the wounds appeared to have no effect upon it.

As he backed away from the creature's onslaught, Alwald's heel slipped on a loose stone and he tumbled backwards. For a moment his adversary reared above him, then it turned and began to shamble down the dried-up river bed. The fact that he could not run with its previous speed suggested that Alwald's sword may have done it some hurt after all.

By now Krispin had clambered down the bank and, passing Alwald as he struggled to his feet, he ran grasping Woundflame with both hands. As he caught it up, the creature turned and, with teeth bared and dagger fingers outstretched, it flung itself at the youth – and into the hissing arc of Woundflame as Krispin swung the sword with all the strength he could summon.

As though in retribution for what had been intended for Gambal, the shining blade struck the head from the gangling body. It rolled for several paces along the sand and then lay with eyes glaring and jaws champing.

'It is unbelievable!' cried Alwald as the arms of the decapitated body made jerking movements as though it would raise itself up. 'I must have stabbed it a dozen times and there is not a drop of blood on my blade.'

'He had no blood,' came the voice of the Hump. 'It was blood that he wanted. To such as he blood is the essence of life. Is it not written in some holy history "the life of all flesh is the blood thereof"?'

'What is – that thing?' Krispin asked.

'A dhrul,' the Hump answered somberly. 'I have heard tell of such creatures in lonely places.'

'A vampire?'

'I think not. Legend says that vampires were once living men and women – a dhrul was never human. Some think they were spawned by the All Father after he fell from grace, others say that long ago they were an accursed race roaming the wastelands until most died out – or went into endless trances underground – through lack of . . . sustenance.'

The Hump shivered.

'Now I know why those old caravaneers spoke of them in such whispers.'

'Let us get Gambal back to camp,' said Alwald. 'The fellow is in a swoon – and who can blame him?'

'Will the head die?' Krispin asked. 'Its eyes still stare at us.'

The Hump replied, 'I know little of such things but –'

He picked up a large rock in his powerful arms, raised it until it was poised high above his head and then cast it down upon the face of the dhrul. The others winced at the sounds which issued from what lay beneath the rock, but at least it was hidden from sight.

The three men lifted Gambal as gently as they could and carried him up the incline to where Silvermane had been joined by Ognam and Merlinda.

And as the small procession walked back to the Knight's Tower, Ognam gave a cry and pointed to the north. The others saw a distant shadow among the shadows, a spindly figure running away with a loping gait.

'It must be the mate,' said the Hump.

'Serene Mother, preserve us from the abominations of the night,' Merlinda prayed aloud.

FOUR
Brother Mias

The fingers of the old man appeared as white as the ancient parchment scroll he handled so reverently. The cowl of his plain robe of dark green, the traditional garment of the heretic priests of Thaan, was thrown back revealing thick silver hair cut short above ascetic features. His dark eyes shone with enthusiasm which seemed out of place for one burdened with his years - perhaps because he did not find his years a burden but a gift from his creator in which a life of learning had been transmuted into wisdom.

He sat at a stout wooden table, whose surface had been polished by the sleeves of generations of men such as he, in one corner of a vast hall known as the Great Library. Its walls were shelved to hold hundreds of tomes bound in hide which gave forth a special odour, an odour that warmed the old man, as though it was the rarest perfume, whenever he entered. Across the floor of the hall were ranks of muniment chests and ancient terra-cotta scroll jars, and at the far end several priestly scribes sat at ink-dyed tables copying texts and rebinding old volumes threatened by decay.

Behind the old man, flooding his reading table with warm light, was a wide mullion window through which it was possible to see the high-gabled roofs of the city below, and beyond them the grassy plain stretching to a range of bare, lion-hued hills in the distance. Once, to give relief to his cramped body, he stood up, flexed his thin muscles and turned to the window. From this angle he could see streets between the pantiled roofs; streets abustle with men and women, many of whom wore the dark green habiliments of their faith.

He had just reseated himself when a slender, robed figure appeared and stood respectfully in front of his table. It was only the slight swell of her breasts beneath her grey novice's habit that indicated her sex, her deep cowl hiding her raven hair and most of her pale, finely drawn face.

'May I interrupt you, Brother Mias?' she said in gentle voice. 'Important news has just reached us.'

Although Mias was the spiritual leader of Thaan, he had no other title than 'Brother' after the custom of the heretics who believed that the trappings of authority were unnecessary as the importance of those whom the All Father had destined to lead was self-evident.

At her voice Brother Mias looked up with a warm smile and said, 'What is it you have to tell me, Sister Lorelle?'

'This message has arrived by a homing bird from Danaak,' she said, holding out a tiny scrap of vellum. 'On it is written "The Regent's army has set forth." '

'So, at last, what we have been expecting has begun,' Brother Mias murmured with a sigh. He rose and turned back to his favourite window.

'Look down there,' he said. 'In one street there is a marriage procession – in a moment we shall hear the ceremonial chimes – and in the next there is a cortège as someone whose spirit has returned to the All Father is borne to the Cavern of the Dead. The life of our people goes on in its multitudinous ways, daily tasks, joys, sorrows . . . It is hard to imagine that in a few days we will be under siege and such everyday scenes as those lads playing kick-bladder in that little square will be replaced by those of carnage.'

He returned to his seat while the girl watched his calm face intently.

'May I ask, Brother Mias, why at this time it should be the wish of the Regent to destroy us?'

'It must suit him politically,' he answered. 'A crusade against so-called heretics will steer the people's minds from their discontent - for a while. It is ironic that those who regard us as enemies of their faith are the real heretics. It was their priests who made the false claim that the All Father fell from grace and his daughter - she whom they call the Serene Mother - replaced him as the deity.'

'This I know from my studies,' said Lorelle, 'yet it has puzzled me why this change of belief came about.'

'There are always those who profit from change,' said Brother Mias. 'The faith we follow was ancient and men were ready to embrace something that was less demanding and "in accordance with their time", for the truth is like a sword - though it may shine like a mirror, its substance is hard and its edge unrelenting. The truth was - and is - that the All Father created *everything* so that not only are the Three Worlds his inspiration but equally the Past, Present and Future are as one to him.

'It is almost impossible for mortal comprehension because the divine decree was that we have the illusion of always moving from the past into the future, whereas the future without end and the endless past are a whole in the consciousness of the All Father. Therefore our petty destinies are foreordained, though we only conceive of them second by second in what we term the present.'

He paused, smiled at the girl.

'Forgive my lecture, Lorelle. I know that all this will have been made known to you by studying the Book of Precepts.'

'But not so clearly,' she murmured.

'It follows, then, that the All Father is not limited by our human notion of time. His creation is complete, for if it were subject to alteration he would not be omnipotent and Chaos would be the real inspiration of Time and the Three Worlds.

'Such austere truth brings little comfort to those who seek to better themselves by demanding of God that he alter his whole timeless concept for their profit, or to those who seek comfort in nursery tales. So, to make life more acceptable for such, unorthodox priests and prophets preached a new doctrine in which the All Father was said to have become the enemy of his own creation, and was supplanted by his daughter. In the mythos created around her she exemplified the virtues of motherhood: caring for her earthly children, ever ready to listen to their prayers and on occasion altering the universal scheme for their benefit.

'The attractions of having a *merciful* deity – one who could even be persuaded by her priesthood to act in advantageous ways – were obvious. Everywhere men and women turned from the All Father to worship the Mother, and a powerful new priesthood developed, fearful only of the ancient truth which some continued to hold. After The Enchantment the doctrine of the All Father was coupled with sorcery and the Guild of Witchfinders was established to destroy both magicians and priests of the All Father. Only in Thaan, remote from the rest of Ythan, were the followers of the true faith too strong to be suppressed.'

The novice said quietly, 'There is one question that has of late been much on my mind and perhaps I shall not have the chance to ask it again.'

'Then ask. I shall answer – if I can.'

'It is this: If everything in the Three Worlds is predestined, if there can be no alteration of the Great Cycle – why do we venerate the All Father, for what is the point of veneration without free will? And if the moments of our birth and death, and all that goes between, are immutable, why do we strive to alter our lot?'

'That is the Great Question, Lorelle, and the answer is because it was so ordained. We act with the illusion of freewill having been given that illusion by the All Father.'

'Then – and I mean no disrespect, Brother – would it not be better for people to have the illusion of a more comforting deity?'

'To your fresh young mind that might be so, my dear,' said Brother Mias, 'but it is an old tenet of those who wear the green robes that truth is to be valued above all else.'

The old man smiled at her.

'Of course you will say that we were destined to believe such a tenet and you would be right, but there is more to it than that. The truth allows us to adjust to the inevitable. For example, a warrior is destined to die in battle. Nothing can alter that fact, yet the warrior does have a choice – he can face his fate with a warrior's pride or as a coward. Whatever the outcome of this approaching siege, we have the choice of how we accept it.'

'But surely even that choice must be predetermined,' Lorelle argued.

Brother Mias frowned and his fingers traced the edge of the vellum sheets on which were newly drawn diagrams. He felt a guilty sense of relief when a man, wearing a soldier's leather surcoat, crossed to his corner and saluted.

'Brother Mias – sir,' he said. 'The captain asks if you would come to the roof, sir, to calculate the angles of reflection.'

'Of course,' said the priest, gathering the loose pages.

'I must go, Lorelle, there is vital work afoot,' he added kindly. 'We will continue our conversation in some quiet hour.'

'Thank you. I shall pray for enlightment and acceptence.'

She turned away with downcast eyes and hands folded piously in the sleeves of her robe.

The travellers were hollow-eyed when, soon after sunrise, they drank the sour milk which the Hump had brought and broke their fast with travellers' bread.

After the attack by the dhrul the hours of darkness were like a nightmare as they sought safety on the roof of the tower with Krispin and Alwald taking it in turns to guard the entrance with drawn swords. Nothing came near the tower but from time to time they were shocked into wakefulness by a wild keening sound floating across the waste – a cry that was both frightening and poignant. They knew that somewhere out there the female dhrul was mourning her mate.

Gambal had revived soon after they had brought him back to the tower. His body ached and there were black, coin-sized bruises where the creature's talons had pressed mercilessly into his flesh. His neck was so swollen that he could only speak in a low husky voice when he told his companions how the dhrul had leapt upon him.

He could remember in frightful detail the creature's arms encircling him like iron bands and – inured as he was to evil smells after years spent in an underground abattoir – the stench of its breath; it was the latter, he believed, that had caused him to faint.

When he had been laid on the softest fur rugs on the flat roof of the ruined tower the Hump had tended him with surprising gentleness, giving him sooma seeds to numb his pains and rubbing a pungent salve on his neck, a salve which, the Hump claimed, caravaneers swore by as a universal panacea.

'It will cure saddle sores and belly ache from fouled water – in fact most things except the Red Death,' he declared as he continued to massage Gambal who muttered his thanks.

'I seem to remember you doing the same for me during the Festival of Fools,' the guide said with a rare smile. Of them all he seemed the least upset by the encounter with the dhrul.

He must be hardened to such perils through travelling in outlandish places, Merlinda thought. *He is rather outlandish himself, though he could be described as handsome in a rugged way if he were not such a great crouchback. Ugh! His spine must be like a fully-drawn bow. I wonder what that pretty little thing with the silvery hair sees in him. She hardly ever takes her huge brown eyes off his face. Well, no one forced me to follow the Pilgrims' Path so I should not complain, but what would I not give to be back in my bed this night. Such a beautiful bed, but I suppose I shall never see it again . . .*

Serene Mother, protect thy daughter in the realm of sleep . . .

Merlinda, like the others on the roof, had been wrenched from the realm of sleep by the wordless lament which filled the chilly night about them. There had been little repose after that and, now that the sun was rising and clearing the terrors of the night, all were anxious to quit this ill-omened place.

As soon as the Hump had checked the last drong girth, he told them to mount and with the beasts grumbling in their throats they swayed away from the tower with relief.

Alwald slowed his animal so that he fell abreast of Krispin who was bringing up the rear.

'It is good to be on our way again,' said Krispin. 'I think that dhrul was worse than anything in the Land of Blight. At first it seemed impossible to kill it.'

'I suppose that it is difficult to kill something that is not properly alive,' said Alwald thoughtfully. 'Again and again I ran my sword into it but nothing seemed to happen. Strange how your sword did so much more damage than mine –'

'That was because I cut its head off,' said Krispin quickly.

'Mmm,' said Alwald. 'I think I made a great mistake when I entrusted Woundflame to you –'

'You gave me Woundflame because your own weapon was so much better; bright, bejewelled and honed. Woundflame is a dull relic from a bygone age.'

'Some relic!' commented Alwald.

'It is a relic I intend to keep so let us not go over it again.'

For a moment Alwald looked sullen, and then said, 'Did you notice anything strange last night – apart from the dhrul?'

Krispin shook his head.

'Why do you ask?'

'Because I think we travel in very odd company. What do we know of any of them? An ex-harlot –'

'At least there is nothing false about her,' declared Krispin hotly. 'It was she whom the Lady Eloira planned we should meet.'

'Of course,' Alwald said hastily. 'I spoke more harshly than I intended. Whatever she has been, she is still a woman of rank – and beauty.' A faint flush came to his handsome face, a face which itself had the subtle lines of ancient aristocracy imprinted upon it. 'Only one woman have I seen who is fairer . . .' His voice trailed away as his memory took him back to Mabalon where the Lady Demara, his step-mother, waited to birth the child of her husband who had been slain by the shape-changing Wolf King.

Oh, Demara! My desire for you still fills me with shame and yet . . .

'. . . and as for the others,' he heard Krispin saying, 'we need not worry over much about them. Ognam came with us only to escape the dungeon. At times I think he is simple but, like the humpback, he will be parting from us once we have crossed this wilderness. As for Gambal I see nothing strange about him. Without his aid I should be dead – or worse – by now. At first, I must say, I wondered why he took such a risk in helping us, but when I saw he wore the Disk of Livia and realised he followed the Pilgrim Path . . .'

'There is one you have not mentioned,' said Alwald. 'The girl with the silver hair who rides behind our guide.'

'Odd that one so fair should be the companion of one whose body is bent, though I doubt not that his heart is true.'

'Have you noticed that she rarely speaks a word, and when she does it is strangely formed? And have you noticed that she wears a skirt that hides her feet?'

'What I have noticed is that she can run like the west wind,' said Krispin. 'She overtook us both when we were chasing the dhrul.'

'Ah yes,' said Alwald, lowering his voice unnecessarily as they had dropped behind the others. 'Her running . . . last night, when she passed me, I saw that she had lifted her skirt –'

'She could hardly have run with it trailing on the ground.'

'– and in the moonlight I am sure that I saw her feet – or what should have been her feet. I swear that she did not have feet of humankind but *hoofs – silver hoofs*.'

A gust of laughter burst from Krispin's lips.

'She was probably wearing silver slippers. Ever since the Shallows you have had weird fancies.'

'I know slippers when I see them, toymaker, and I have heard of creatures that are abominations to the Mother.'

'Certainly you could call the monster that came in the night an abomination, but Silvermane! – there was nothing of an abomination about her when she ran to Gambal's aid with a cooking knife in her hand.'

'Then keep your eyes open,' said Alwald darkly and he urged his drong forward to end the conversation.

Alone at the rear of the small column of riders Krispin glanced back over his shoulder. Already the Knight's Tower had dwindled and he felt oppressed by a sense of desolation that brooded over the empty landscape. The others seemed to be equally affected, for hardly anyone spoke during the long, uncomfortable morning.

In every direction the view was equally monotonous; dun-coloured land rolled to the horizon, unbroken by tree or boulder and only partly covered by patches of dull vegetation which, as though lacking the strength to rise on its stalks, appeared to crawl over the hot sandy soil. No breeze stirred their flaccid leaves and towards noon the still air became so heated it trembled, giving the illusion that the horizon was rippling.

The only signs of life were the occasional flick of a lizard galvanised by the heavy approach of the drongs, and a dot high in the harsh blue vault above which reminded Krispin and Alwald of the eagle which had circled above them when they had crossed the mountains from the Vale of Mabalon to the plain of black lava.

The only sounds were the creak of harness and the soft crunch of drongs' feet pressing the barren earth, so that when the Hump halted the small cavalcade at noon it seemed as though they had entered a kingdom of silence.

With relief they climbed down from the high saddles and stretched stiffened limbs while the Hump tethered his animals and then measured water into their leather nose-bags. Silvermane followed him from drong to drong, patting their necks while they gurgled away their thirst. Remembering Alwald's words when they had set out, Krispin could not help gazing at her legs but her long skirt continued to brush the ground as she walked.

When the animals were watered the Hump produced a wineskin and a long length of sausage from a saddle-bag while Silvermane spread rugs of raw wool on the ground for the party to rest on.

'No wonder the Regent had no wish to send his army across this plain,' said the Lady Merlinda as she endeavoured to chew delicately on the hard sausage. 'They would have no fight left in them by the time they reached Thaan.'

'And you can see now why we were not pursued here,' said Gambal, his voice still hoarse. 'It is a matter of honour with the Dungeon Master that none escape the Citadel. You can be sure that his patrols are scouring the countryside round Danaak, but none would dream we had entered this Mother-forsaken waste with no shelter or water.'

'It was not always thus,' announced Ognam unexpectedly. 'Once it was not known as a wilderness but as the Land of Gil – then it was a smiling land, fertile with groves of trees bearing sweet fruits and great pastures and fields bright with corn.'

The others looked at him in surprise. There was a certain timbre in his voice that they had not heard before.

'If you know about this Land of Gil tell us, Master Jester,' said Merlinda. 'I love to hear stories – if they are well told.'

'And I,' said the Hump in his low voice, 'I long to know the histories of the lands I travel, and this waste where I was found as a babe has more than usual interest for me.'

Ognam glanced round at the circle of his companions, each holding a leather cup of wine and lengths of sausage while behind them the tethered drongs stirred restlessly as though the monotony of the plain had filled them with boredom. Carefully placing his cup beside the rough blanket on which he sat cross- legged, the ex-jongleur raised his hand in the gesture of the professional story-teller.

'Listen,' he said.

FIVE
Ognam's Story

'Listen,' repeated Ognam. 'Long before the high days when Ythan became one empire reigned over by benevolent kings, the land was divided into many small kingdoms, and the fairest of these was the land ruled by King Gil – the very land that surrounds us now. How different it was then, when Gil sat upon his throne in a palace that – if it could be found – would now be no more than heaps of stones.

'Oh, my friends, if you could have seen it then with silken banners flying from every turret and markets beneath its protecting walls where good folk traded everything fair that came from their land, fruits of the earth and fruits from the orchards which grew like forests.

'Perhaps once, in this very place where we are sitting, trees heavy with fruit cast their shadows, or perhaps vineyards were laid out in rows as straight as Companions of the Rose on the parade ground. For the land was not only famous for its abundance but also for the quality of its wine, which the people consumed in great quantities, declaring that it had a special quality which preserved them from plague.

'And in those days there were shallow meres teeming with wildfowl and forest domains whence hunters brought fresh game to the markets.

'There was plenty for everyone and, because the laws

were strict but fair, none walked in fear but enjoyed life. There was always music in the air and the fame of Gil's land spread and became the envy of the other kingdoms so that the subjects there became discontented with their lot.

'Gil was proud of his kingdom and he knew that envious eyes were cast upon it, and therefore he kept an army in which every man had armour of bronze and the finest weapons, and such was the prowess of each soldier that none dared to cross Gil's frontiers except in peace.

'As well as being proud of his kingdom, Gil was proud of his only son and he was content that when the time came for him to follow the Dark Maid, as every king and pauper must in the fullness of their time, the prince would sit upon his throne. If the old tales be true this throne was fashioned out of rare stones that came from the mines of Thaan – onyx, jet, porphyry and adamant. And though such a throne would be taken for granted in the Citadel today, at that time it was regarded as a wonder of the age.

'The prince who some day would inherit this wonderful chair – and the happy kingdom with it – was a handsome, dashing fellow who was known to be generous in taverns when he caroused with the officers of his father's army; but he had one fatal flaw and that was a tremendous admiration of himself.

'When he looked about the prosperous Land of Gil he saw it as his birthright – as his due! – though the fact was that he had done nothing to enhance it. That it was the result of his father's life's work never occurred to him. He was the heir to the kingdom and that was enough; he need not do anything further to prove himself.

'Because he doted on his son, old Gil was blind to his arrogance and strove to make the kingdom even more secure for the day when the prince should become king. His only regret was that the prince had not yet found a wife, for it is the wish of every king to see his House perpetuated, and naturally Gil hoped that he would live long enough to dandle a grandson.

'He suggested several noble ladies of the land as suitable consorts for the prince, but with each the youth found something to criticise . . . this one had no humour, that one laughed too much, this one was too thin to bed and that one would smother him. And none were worthy of his bloodline.

'Then Gil sent ambassadors abroad to kingdoms where there were eligible princess, but though they came back with the most flattering portraits – and promises of profitable trade agreements – the prince declared that there was not one in whom he could feel the slightest interest.

'Old Gil became a worried king. He feared that perhaps the prince found it impossible to be interested in the opposite sex, and therefore he was relieved when the prince came to him one day and demanded a marriage be arranged for him.

' "You have said that you would only marry the fairest princess in the known world, so I am eager to know how you have decided upon your future wife," said Gil as he sat upon his marvellous throne.

' "I saw her in a dream," said his son. "Such was her beauty that I fell in love with her instantly . . . and naturally she returned the feeling."

' "Naturally," agreed Gil. "Yet, my boy, a dream is one thing and flesh-and-blood another."

' "She is of beautiful flesh and the most noble blood," said the prince. "When I awoke from my dream I went to the hall of paintings and I discovered a miniature portrait of her . . . I have no doubt that in some magical way she shared my dream, for it seems that destiny has decreed that the most beautiful princess of all the kingdoms should be the bride of the prince with the fairest birthright, not to mention a certain personal charm."

' "Then tell me the name of your dream love," said Gil, a trifle impatiently.

' "The Princess Mia of Bram," the prince replied. "And it is only she that I shall marry – ever!"

' "Alas!" sighed Gil's chamberlain. "The daughter of the King of Bram is already betrothed."

' "What?" cried the prince. "If that be so she must be un-betrothed."

' "Her future husband – the King of Hex – would have something to say about that."

' "I care not," cried the prince, stamping his foot. "I know Mia loves me and that tyrant of Hex is ugly and thrice her age. And his army is a joke compared to ours."

' "And I like not such talk," said Gil, "You have a dream about some princess you have never seen, and because she is no doubt happily promised to some other man you begin to talk about armies. Why cannot you marry some pretty girl from one of our local families? After the first night you will find that the degree of her beauty is of little importance compared to a sense of humour. Companionship is what is needed in this world."

'The prince gave his father a withering look and quit the throne room in terrible silence, and immediately old Gil felt remorse.

' "Today's young people are far more sensitive than when I was young," said Gil. "Why, I remember when I married the prince's mother – may her shade be at peace – she was shaped like a tun and had a wen on her nose but – by the Mother! – she made up for it in . . . in . . . other ways. And laugh! She always saw the funny side. Made a far better queen than some stuck-up beauty too noble to fart." '

Ognam paused to drink some wine while his tiny audience laughed. For a few minutes his words had taken them away from their surroundings and their secret misgivings about the future. Once more they were children listening to a folk tale.

Having wiped his lips on his bright sleeve, the jester continued, ' "We all remember the humour of Her Late Majesty with great affection," said the chamberlain. "I am sure the prince will get over his infatuation. After all, it was only a dream."

'But the prince did retain his infatuation, and he complained bitterly to his father for not forcing the King of Bram to change his plan for his daughter's nuptials. Gil was bowed by guilt because he was unable to bring about what his son desired and he even sent secret envoys to Bram. They returned saying that the king had told them that, while he was flattered that the son of such a distinguished king as Gil could look with such favour on his daughter, he feared the consequences if he broke his word to the King of Hex, especially as the princess had already left in a royal caravan for her bridegroom's kingdom.

'In order to prevent his son pining for the impossible Gil called for the prince and told him that he must forget the Princess Mia.

' "You may as well tell me to forget my name," said the prince. "I met her again last night in a dream. If you were a real king nothing would stop you making Mia my bride, especially as our army outnumbers that of Hex several times over."

' "The King of Hex may not have many warriors but he is

feared as a sorcerer,'' said the chamberlain. ''Who needs warriors when you can summon avenging spirits out of the air?''

'The prince said something under his breath that was very wounding for Gil who had loved him ever since he rocked his cradle after his mother had died as a result of his birthing, but the king could do nothing – except feel sad and old.

'Now it happened that the cavalcade taking the Princess Mia to the Kingdom of Hex followed a route which at one point ran close to the frontiers of Gil's land, and the prince – who had been sending out his own spies – called together the young captains who were his boon companions, and with a number of picked horsemen they raided the royal caravan when it had encamped for the night and the sentries were half asleep.

'Like the hero of a folk tale – as indeed he was – the prince spurred his horse straight into the royal pavilion, seized Princess Mia and galloped with her into the night.

'Looking up at him in the moonlight the princess cried, ''I have seen you in my dreams!'' And was delighted that she would not have to marry the King of Hex who from all accounts had some rather unpleasant habits.

'The prince and his companions returned to his father's kingdom and before dawn had crept across the land had bribed a priest in the main shrine to marry them. Then, when Gil was sitting down to his breakfast, the prince introduced him to his new daughter-in- law . . .

'Poor Gil found himself in a difficult situation. He could not send the Princess Mia back as he did not wish to be at odds with the prince – and anyway, who would want her now that she had been deflowered after the ceremony at the shrine!

'He sent envoys to both Bram and Hex with offers of generous compensation but they were stoned by the populace and ordered back by the royal servants. Although the King of Bram had no stomach for war, his people demanded revenge and reluctantly he formed an alliance with several other kings who were willing to send troops to his aid in return for a share of the spoils when the Land of Gil was overrun – the King of Halt sent five regiments in return for an undertaking that he should have Gil's remarkable throne.

'King Gil had to defend his realm against his enemies, and many a battle was fought on his borders but each time his troops won the day, though the war brought a change to the kingdom. The trade routes which had been so profitable were cut off, taxes were raised to keep the army supplied, and young men were taken from the land to replace those who had been killed, so that many fields fell fallow and only half the harvest was brought in.

'And the Land of Gil was no longer a smiling land. So many families had lost sons and fathers that music was no longer heard in the streets, and even the news of yet another military triumph on a far frontier was received in silence.

'But in Gil's palace courtly life continued with pageants and masques as the prince wanted his new bride to be happy in her new kingdom, though many was the curse muttered against the prince and princess when sounds of revelry drifted from the palace casements.

'As for Gil himself, he sat on his wonderful throne and even when news of his latest victory reached him his expression of sadness never changed. Since the arrival of Princess Mia his hair turned from glossy black to swan white, and the courtiers whispered that it would not be long before there was a new king on the throne. They became even more deferential to the prince as they devised more extravagant entertainments to amuse his dream bride who, it must be admitted, was inclined to become bored if a day passed without some event taking place.

'When the other kings found that they were no match for the defenders of the Land of Gil truces were agreed, and the King of Bram congratulated himself on having got out of it without having to provide a dowry – but the King of Hex still burned with anger and he alone refused to make peace.

'King Gil's chamberlain had been right when he said that the king had the reputation of a sorcerer, and now he turned to gramarye. First he laid a curse on the land so that just when the people were rejoicing that peace had returned their crops withered in the fields as though they had been sown with salt. This was followed by a curse upon the kine and the flocks so that the animals fell and became putrid where they fell.

'Starvation drove the peasants from their holdings and villagers from their homes, and they wandered away so that the once abundant land became a waste where no smoke rose and no birds sang – and only round the palace did life continue. Here there were storehouses still full, and guards to keep the starving peasants away, and within the palace there was music still for the prince and princess to dance the nights away while old Gil sat on his throne as though entranced.

'And then the King of Hex had his final revenge.

'He sent an army of creatures against the palace, creatures which were like beings from a madman's nightmare. I know not what they were called but they were created by magic, spawned from cauldrons of unspeakable elixirs. Manlike in shape they were, and male and female but without the spirit that animates humankind. Cruel they were, eager only to rend their master's foes; a band that not knowing true life did not fear death.

'In the night they came, when the chambers of the palace were filled with dancers and wine flowed so freely that even the guards were drunk at their stations . . . in the night they came like spindly shadows which climbed over the palace walls and broke the necks of the sentries before they could even grope for their weapons.

'And then this terrible throng, naked and armed only with tooth and talon, flowed up the steps and into the great hall where the musicians stopped dead and the dancers shrieked and the terrible carnage began. Many fled along corridors seeking places of refuge, but the intruders played fearful games with them, and when dawn came the creatures left off feeding. They slipped away into shadowed places, for the light made them uneasy, and the palace of good King Gil was nothing more than a silent tomb.

'And so Gil's land became what it is today.'

There was a silence as all secretly thought of their experience the night before, and then Merlinda said, 'You weave your words well. I had no idea buffoons had such art.'

'To be accepted into the Guild of Jongleurs one had to be able to tell tales as well as throw somersaults, lady,' Ognam replied.

'Tell me, Master Jongleur, is what you told us true or is it a legend?' asked the Hump earnestly.

'Who can say?' said Ognam, his voice returning to its customary flippant tone. 'There is truth in legend – and legend in truth.'

SIX
Beneath the Griffin

The stars which made up the Constellation of the Griffin glittered with cold light in the northern sky as the Lady Eloira stood on the flat roof of the Peak Tower. Beside her was a beautiful young woman with spun-gold hair flowing to her waist, cradling an exquisitely gowned doll in her arms. Below the tower a sea of mist stretched in the starlight to dark shadows against dark sky, the mountains which ringed the High Wald and provided a natural barrier between its forested slopes and valleys and the outer world.

'The magic holds,' said Eloira, more to herself than to the girl. 'None of the Wolf King's nomads can find their way through it to our gate – nor any Witchfinders from Danaak for that matter.'

'Could Krispin find his way through the mist?' asked the girl in a voice which, while it was mature, had a disturbing childish quality about it like an adult mimicking a child; though in this case there was no mimicry.

'When he returns there may be no need for the mist, Jennet, but if there is there will be a Fey path for him to follow as there was when he left.'

Jennet gave an exaggerated sigh of impatience.

'I have been waiting for Krispin for ages. Sometimes I dream about him.'

'And what do you dream?' asked Eloira with sudden interest.

'Running. We are always running through trees. And I am very scared.'

'What are you running away from?'

'The little house.'

'Whose little house?'

'The old woman. We ran away . . .'

'What had the old woman done to make you run away?'

Jennet did not answer for a moment and then said defensively, 'It was only an old dream.'

That I shall know soon enough, muttered Eloira. *I owe it to Krispin to solve the mystery of who you really are – and to myself to know how you come to be like a portrait of Princess Livia come to life. Could there be a drop of bastard blood royal in your veins, I wonder. If only your mind had not fled back to childhood what might I have learned!*

'Tell me the names of the stars, please.'

'Up there is the Griffin, my dear. When I was a girl I used to wish on the Griffin . . .'

'When I was a girl I used to wish upon the Griffin,' said the Lady Demara – now better known in the Vale of Mabalon by her bestowed name of Star – as she stood in the garden of the small house which had been given to her after her arrival by the kind folk of the valley. The air was filled with the scent of apple trees and when the fitful breeze blew petals floated down about her like snowflakes in the starshine.

'And I am still wishing upon it,' said Margan who had been her maid at River Garde and who now lived with her as a friend. 'I wish for you an easeful birthing . . .'

Demara smiled as more petals fell about them and ran her fingertips over the graceful swell of her belly.

'Today he was so restless . . .'

'He?'

'I am sure it will be a son – the Mother will surely grant that after his father was so cruelly done to death. But tell me what it is that you wish for yourself. Are you not content in this peaceful haven?'

'Content I am,' replied Margan. 'And my wish is that, whether it be boy or girl, it be well formed . . .'

'Margan! My dear, you mean . . .?'

'I am sure. And today the conjure man agreed that there is new life within me.'

'This is a joy,' exclaimed Demara. 'Our children will grow up together but the father . . .?'

'I lay with Krispin the night before he left to continue the quest.'

'I thought I heard you creep past my door,' laughed Demara. 'You chose well, there is much to that young man, but –'

' – but he is far from here and probably I shall never set eyes upon him again,' Margan sighed. 'And believe me, I love him, for it was love and not lust that took me to his chamber. I am delighted that I carry his seed, yet sad that he will never know.'

'Perhaps, when the quest is over –'

'The quest! Such quests never end. They are things of dreams. And if it were to end – if he were to survive the perils – it would not be to me that he would return.'

'Hush, my dear, you cannot say.'

'I *must* say,' said Margan almost fiercely. 'I am happy that I shall birth his child – more than that I cannot expect.'

Demara looked up at the pattern of stars.

'My wish for you, Margan, is that someday Krispin shall return.'

'With Alwald,' said Margan.

'Alwald, poor youth,' murmured the Lady Demara.

The Lady Merlinda said, 'When I was a child – in the good times before my family was ruined by the machinations of our Lord Regent – I always wished on those stars up there.'

Standing with Alwald on the top of the second Knight's Tower to which the Hump had led them unerringly at sunset, she pointed to the Constellation of the Griffin.

'Even in the faraway Wald, where my father was River Lord, the forest folk had special reverence for the Griffin,' Alwald said. 'But what did you wish for when you were small?'

'That Princess Livia might be found – you see, even at that age I was a Pilgrim. In my family it was impossible to be anything else.'

Below a spark of flame appeared in the darkness, then grew as the Hump lit the fire for the evening meal.

'At least my belief in the Pilgrim's Path is the one thing I have been able to keep over the years.'

She leaned forward on the eroded parapet where long ago watchmen had kept a look-out for the travellers they had vowed to protect.

'Master Alwald,' she said in a mock serious voice. 'Of this party only you and I have noble blood, unless the horse-maid was a princess in some unknown land –'

'Horsemaid?'

'Yes, that girl who rides behind our guide and cannot take her eyes off him – surely you have noticed something odd about her.'

'I thought I did last night. I could have sworn that when she ran I saw that she had hoofs –'

Without thought he made the protective Circle of the Mother.

'Of course you saw hoofs,' said Merlinda. 'Her limbs are like those of a horse from the waist down, or so I understand. There was a lot of talk about her when the merchant Azrul brought her to Danaak from some far distant place. But – unlike me – she never reached the auctions. Our friend Gambal secretly purchased her for the Regent.'

'I have heard tell of his collection of freaks.'

'Do not use that word within the hearing of the guide. He is mad about her, and he only agreed to take us across the wilderness on the condition that Gambal arranged for her to come too. A strange love story, is it not? But then, are not all love stories a little strange?'

At her words something within Alwald seemed to give, the dam that pent his emotions was swept away in a torrent of words. In an ecstasy of relief he described how he had fallen in love with his father's new wife almost from the moment she arrived at his castle on the River of Night, of the evil desires that had risen within him after his father had been murdered and how, after having rescued the Lady Demara from the nomads who had invaded the Wald, he actually believed he was making love to her – until to his disgust he found that he had been bewitched by one of the succubi who haunted the Shallows where they had camped. The horror of his experience was compounded by the guilty realisation that he was eager to make love to Demara even though she had been widowed only for a few days.

In his confession he made no excuses for himself. Indeed he listened to his own words in amazement; never in his life had he been able to open his heart like this, and when he faltered the Lady Merlinda would murmur some word of encouragement which enabled him to continue his recital to the point where he left Demara in the Vale of Mabalon. In the silence which followed he wondered what it was about Merlinda which had enabled him to speak so freely, and then he realised that apart from the natural warmth that she radiated he was at ease with her because, no matter what strange paths destiny had forced her to take, she was one of his class.

These anguished young men! thought Merlinda. *Had they lived in Danaak a few nights in my establishment would have given them a more clear-witted understanding of the Old Game.*

Aloud she said, 'I am honoured that you have chosen to tell me your sorrow. I sense that you have spoken to no one about it before.'

'No one.'

'But does not your companion guess?'

Alwald exhaled in a humourless laugh.

'Krispin? Of course not. I admit that he has proved himself to be a fine fellow on the quest, but at heart he will always remain what he is, an apprentice toymaker. What notion can such as he have of courtly love . . .'

His words died as a wail – a sound of ultimate despair – reached their ears.

'Serene Mother!' muttered Alwald. 'The dhrul – the mate of that thing we slew last night – she has followed us.'

'I have learned that there are many forms of love other than that what you term "courtly",' said Merlinda as a second doleful cry echoed across the wasteland. 'Even out there.'

* * *

Day after day the companions continued their journey into the heart of the wilderness; each day was as monotonous as the last and it seemed that they had been travelling on the backs of the swaying drongs for weeks. The flat scenery never altered, no colour – not even a lone flower – broke the drab hues of the scrawny vegetation that rustled no more than knee-high across the impoverished soil. It was a barren land beneath a brazen sky which, once they had penetrated deeper into the waste, no longer provided the cloud effects which had delighted their eyes on the first day.

'Clouds, like birds, do not cross the wilderness,' the Hump explained. Only he seemed at ease, and the others realised it was an ease borne out of his years spent on Ythan's far flung caravan routes.

'Besides,' Ognam remarked one evening while their guide and Silvermane were settling the animals, 'he should feel at home here, it's his birthplace. No wonder he carries such a burden on his back – what chance is there of anything whole coming out of such a desert? It is as dismal as a carnival in a rainstorm.'

But their respect for the guide continued to grow. His sense of direction never failed and towards the end of each afternoon they would see the distant pillar of a Knight's Tower break the line of the horizon, proving that they were following the route taken by travellers journeying to Thaan in olden times.

Every time such a tower was glimpsed relief filled the hearts of the party. Since the dhrul's attack they had no wish to spend a night in the open. No matter how uncomfortable it was to sleep on cracked stone paving, they passed their nights on the flat roofs of the towers with the men taking it in turns to stand guard.

And each night their blood was chilled by the unearthly

lament that reached them from the wilderness. Though they saw no sign of her, there was no doubt that the dhrul's mate was haunting them with her grief.

After Ognam's tale of how the Land of Gil became the Wilderness of Gil, they could not rid themselves of images of dhrul-like creatures holding their unspeakable feast in the halls and passages of the king's palace. Could it be possible that a pack of such creatures might suddenly overwhelm them?

'Ognam, you must tell us the truth,' declared Gambal finally. 'Is the story of King Gil true or did you make it up?'

The jester looked puzzled and scratched his stubbled head beneath his cowl with its cockscomb crest.

'There must have been a Gil or this charming stretch of countryside would not be called after him, so that much must be true. As for the story of the prince stealing another king's bride and the curses he laid on the kingdom . . . well, I did not exactly make it up though it was not a tale that I had heard before. It came into my head as I spoke – it sometimes happens that way, as though there is a something of the past waiting in the air to be put into words.'

'That is no answer,' said Gambal. 'You are just trying to make yourself sound important.'

A sullen expression crossed Ognam's moon face and he walked away, the bells sewn to his costume tinkling with indignation.

Towards midday of the seventh day after they had escaped from the Citadel, Alwald, who was riding close to the Lady Merlinda, rose in his saddle and gave a great cry of excitement.

'A city! Ahead! A city!'

The others, roused from the almost trance-like state in which they rode, followed the line of Alwald's outstretched arm and saw a city above the horizon . . . crenellated walls with high-gabled houses huddled beneath them, towers, buttressed halls and shrines each with a curious symbol atop its spire. All was built with reddish stone which, in the bright light of noon, took on a roseate cast. Even at this great distance the amazed travellers were conscious of a quality of age which softened its outlines.

What was most remarkable about it was the fact that it appeared to be floating in air.

They reined up round the Hump, demanding an explanation.

'Yonder is Thaan,' he said. 'Not the city itself, of course, but a vision of it – the real city is still more than a hundred leagues to the east. It is not unusual for such illusions to occur in empty places – often in the driest deserts travellers are tormented by visions of lakes of shimmering water but when they rush to slake their thirst they find only dry sand. Such wonders I cannot explain. Look, it fades.'

As he spoke the city which had appeared so magically before them began to lighten, its walls grew transparent and then it was gone.

'A wondrous city,' murmured Ognam.

'Once it was,' said the Hump. 'It is older than Danaak, and is built before a great mountain named the Drakenfel, for in fancy it is said to resemble a sleeping dragon. Great galleries were cut into it when Thaan grew rich through mining rare stones and marbles and even precious gems. It is said that there is not a shrine in the land that does not have its altar carved out of stone that was once carried from Thaan – even though the people of the city were called heretics for they venerated the All Father.'

'That is the Regent's excuse for sending his army against it,' Gambal said. 'But it seems the city is long past its days of fame for few spoke its name until the army assembled.'

'True, for after The Enchantment the caravans ended and the men of Thaan ceased to mine the Drakenfel – perhaps there was no demand for such beautiful stone or perhaps the mines were worked out.' He shrugged so that his crooked back moved uneasily beneath his loose cloak. 'Whatever the cause, Thaan became one of the forgotten cities. Its glory faded, as did its image just now.'

The visionary glimpse of their destination had lightened the hearts of the travellers. So far they had been inclined to ride in silence, each doubtless busy with his or her own thoughts about what the future might hold, but now they even laughed when Ognam felt inspired to make a joke. Krispin was inwardly surprised at the change which had come over Alwald; since he had taken to conversing with the Lady Merlinda in the evenings his manner had become almost light-hearted.

She could coax a smile out of a statue, Krispin thought. *If my heart was not pledged to Jennet I could make a fool of myself over a woman like that even though she is in her middle years and no doubt thinks me a yokel.*

That night the silence brooding over the wilderness was unbroken. The eldritch cries which had snatched sleep from the travellers and left them with pounding hearts did not ring out, and when dawn lightened the sky with a brief flush of saffron the Hump went to the base of the Knight's Tower where Krispin sat with Woundflame across his knees and said cheerfully, 'It follows no more.'

'Thanks be to the Mother,' said Krispin. 'But where can it have gone?'

'Perhaps back to its lair; perhaps it has found a new mate out there, perhaps it died from grief . . .'

'Surely not – it is inhuman.'

'Grief and love can be felt in breasts that are not human,' said the Hump and he walked to where the drongs had been tethered in ruined stables.

Krispin burned with embarrassment. He had grown to respect their guide and the thought that the Hump might think that he regarded all non-human creatures in the same light – the dhrul and Silvermane! – made him want deny such any suggestion. He rose to follow the Hump, and then wondered if he might not be making matters worse with his protestations.

His quandary was cut short by a deep-throated cry of anguish.

'Master Guide, I am coming,' he shouted and sword in hand he ran to the ragged stable walls.

He beheld the Hump standing in the gap – once the gateway – with his arms raised as though trying to claw the air above him. Krispin was also aware that no curious drong heads on their tall curved necks were visible above the stonework – usually they turned with grunting affection to greet their master. Next moment he was beside the Hump and he saw why.

Amid vast pools of congealing blood the drongs lay on their sides as they had fallen when their throats had been torn out.

The Hump's cry ended as abruptly as it had begun. He walked forward and laid a hand on the nearest carcass.

'Cold,' he said. 'The dhrul had her revenge before you went on guard.'

By now the others had arrived from the Knight's Tower and stood gazing with horror at the dead beasts. At first they were appalled by the slaughter, and then by the awakening realisation of what it meant to them.

Without drongs –!

'How could this have happened without someone hearing?' demanded Gambal in a fury. 'Who was on guard?'

'As we did not know when it happened who can say?' said Alwald, angered by the young man's words. But Gambal disregarded him and turning to Ognam, he cried, 'You, fool! You took the midnight shift. That is when it must have happened and I'll stake a fortune that you slept. I should have never allowed you to come.'

The jester turned his round face to Gambal and said quietly, 'It was curious, Master Gambal, that when I came to relieve you, you were not to be seen –'

'I was merely relieving myself,' retorted Gambal.

'A double relief!' cried Ognam, unable to restrain his penchant for a quip. 'And as I be a fool of a fool, Master Gambal, perhaps you can tell me why a mirror was necessary –'

Gambal's face suddenly returned to its habitual paleness beneath the tan acquired through days of riding in the open; he raised his hand to strike Ognam who comically held up his wand with its carved jester's head to protect himself.

'Stop!' thundered the Hump. 'If we fall out among ourselves we are lost. What matters it how this happened, we shall have to make the best of it. And it is my belief that there is no blame.'

They looked at him in puzzlement.

'If the drongs had been attacked in a normal way they would have made such an uproar that we all should have been awakened as well as the sentry if he was sleeping. No, there is the taint of ancient evil in this. Who knows what powers the dhrul have? Perhaps the dhrul could lay a glamour over them or perhaps she possesses the same power as the cockatrice and can numb beasts with a look.'

'We must thank the Mother that it was not us that the monster bespelled,' said Merlinda.

'Accursed I am for not guarding the animals better,' muttered the Hump, 'but usually drongs are as good night-guards as geese and I believed that we would have soon heard if anything had been amiss with them. Idiot! Idiot!'

Silvermane caught his arm in a tight grip. Her command of the Ythan tongue, mainly learned during her stay in the Citadel, was limited but she struggled to put her ideas into words.

'You not . . . to blame!' she told the Hump breathlessly. 'Not your fault . . . wilderness bad . . . bad place . . . you good person . . . you still take us to Thaan . . . we walk, we walk now . . . only you find way . . . only you save us . . .'

In her frustration at not being able to speak fluently she burst into a monologue of musical sounds which the Hump knew was the language of her kind.

The others saw tears glisten in his eyes as he turned to her, tears that seemed so out of place on his weathered features which would have suggested hawkish good looks in a well-formed man.

'You are right,' he said to her. 'Later I can mourn the animals, first Trailblazer and now the whole drove! All that matters is that I lead you to safety.' He faced the others. 'We have covered most of our journey, and if we still had drongs we might have sighted Thaan in two or three days. Now we must go on foot and it will take much longer, so let us start at once.

'Each of us will carry a waterskin, a blanket and a bag of traveller's bread. What other possessions you take is your decision but remember that water will become more precious than silver.'

He went to the pile of baggage which had been unloaded from the drongs the previous night and began fixing straps to full waterskins so that they could be worn like rucksacks.

Silently the others began to pack food and a few belongings in blanket rolls. Krispin went to the pack containing his possessions and from it he took the leather cylinder which had been made for him by the tanner in Mabalon, and this he placed carefully within his blanket roll along with a spare pair of shoes.

Swarms of flies were performing aerial dances above the pools of drong blood when the party left the Knight's Tower in single file.

SEVEN
A Walk in the Sun

All through the hot, dry-throated day they toiled behind the Hump. He allowed them to rest each time he reckoned they had covered a couple of leagues, but only for a very short while. He feared that once they settled comfortably or began to doze he would find it hard to rouse them and their tempers would become even more sullen.

One of the most trying aspects of the march was the sandy soil which shifted beneath their soles with every step and painfully packed their shoes. Krispin and Alwald, toughened by their long trek from Mabalon to Danaak, found no difficulty in keeping pace with the Hump who strode ahead with a tireless gait but Ognam, Gambal and the Lady Merlinda, being unused to walking, soon began to suffer. As for Silvermane she hoisted her skirt so that it no longer trailed on the ground and walked easily beside the Hump, leaving delicate hoofprints behind her.

Each time they rested the first thing they did was to untie the necks of their waterskins and drink, ignoring the Hump's warning to merely take a mouthful and hold it for as long as possible. By noon Merlinda was swaying as she tried to keep up with the party and Alwald and Krispin took turns in carrying her waterskin and blanket roll.

As night fell all were exhausted as they stretched their aching bodies out in a sandy hollow and within minutes they fell into slumber, apart from Krispin who had offered to stand guard until the Griffin reached its zenith. Thankfully the night remained silent and in order to stay awake he cast his mind back to the making of his mechanical dancer for The Choosing, recalling in sequence every piece he had carved and each mechanism until he had arrayed her in one of Jennet's outworn dresses. He remembered that Jennet had been so much on his mind that his automaton bore a resemblance to her . . . but that was before the nomads invaded the Wald.

He sighed, and then to stop his mind dwelling on the tragedy he began to plan his next automaton, should he ever be able to return to his craft. This, too, would be a dancer, a dancer with such grace and movement that when she was offered to the Regent he would be unable to resist adding her to his fabled collection of mechanical figures. And she would dance for the Regent, oh yes, how she would dance, and what a surprise she would hold for him before her clockwork ran down . . .

The next day a burning wind moaned across the wilderness, plaguing the travellers with thirst and whirling sand grains into their eyes. With cloths tied to cover nose and mouth, they hardly uttered a word to each other, each intent that he or she should not be the first to fall behind or give in to the siren desire to lay down and rest.

The moon was rising when they reached the next Knight's Tower, the journey to it having taken twice the time that it would had they been mounted. The ancient walls gave them protection from the wind while they chewed their hard bread and – alarmed at how light their waterskins were becoming – moistened their lips.

Suddenly the Lady Merlinda began to laugh. The others looked at her uneasily, afraid that she was in the grip of hysteria.

'If the nobles who came to my house to be entertained to wine and music – and easy love – could see me, the elegant mistress of it all, as I am now . . .' she rambled, 'see me in this dirty gown, perfumed by my own sweat. And my skin! My skin was toasted as the fairest in Danaak . . . My skin! – blotched by sun and wind, and my hair! Serene Mother! *My hair*!'

For a moment no one spoke, not knowing how to answer her. Then Ognam rose and, with a theatrical flourish, said, 'Gracious Lady, in my profession we are creatures of illusion – we costume and paint our faces so that in the light of the flares we look as we would wish, comical, handsome, beauteous. But the truth is that behind the masks of powder and coloured grease we are just poor players, creatures without substance, mouthing the words of others.

'You are the opposite. The more you lose *your* mask, the more the real Lady Merlinda appears.'

Next morning they felt reluctant to leave the shelter of the tower.

'You see the well is blocked with rubble,' the Hump cried. 'We must press on while we still have some water in our skins. If my reckoning be right we should be coming to the edge of the wilderness by nightfall, and then there will be proper countryside again with streams . . .' And so he cajoled them into setting out.

Before long Alwald raised the neck of his waterskin to his peeling lips, and then threw the empty bag away with an oath.

'Come, Master Alwald, have a mouthful of mine,' said the Hump, but Alwald shook his head.

'Why should you suffer for my greed!' he said. 'Would that I had heeded your words when I gulped it down.'

The party moved forward again, aware that their water-skins were almost as light as Alwald's.

At noon they were staggering as they followed the Hump who, hand-in-hand with Silvermane, plodded on with his piercing eyes fixed on the horizon. The wind still teased them, and the endless rustle of the withered sage sounded in their ears like the surge of waves washing a distant shore.

Then Ognam, the oldest and least hardy of the party, gave a groan and dropped to his knees.

'Cannot go . . . another step,' he murmured. 'Leave us . . .' Here he ludicrously held up the staff with its jester's head. 'Leave us to rest and then we'll catch you up. Just need to rest a while.'

The others looked at each other.

'I should have left him to rot in the dungeon!' Gambal muttered. Ognam, now sunk full length amid ragged grey-leafed herbs, heard his words and said, 'No, Master Gambal, you did right. Here at least I can meet the Dark Maid as a free man. Go on, my friends.'

Krispin looked at Alwald who nodded. Together they bent, seized the jester by the arms and lifted him to his feet; then, with him reeling like a drunk between them, they resumed the march.

Silvermane, whose need for water had been greater than the others, was the next to collapse. The Hump poured the last of his water into her slack mouth and then he lifted her across his shoulders so that it appeared she was resting on the deformity which gave him his name.

Holding her securely he set forth once more, but now even his step was far from steady. Ognam, to add to the impression of drunkenness, began to sing deliriously one of his stage songs about a little dancing girl, and he kept entreating a long vanished audience to join in the chorus.

With a stab of fear Krispin realised that his tongue was swelling. Soon it would fill his mouth, choking him.

Gambal and the Lady Merlinda lagged behind, their eyes glazed like sleepwalkers.

To make matters worse the terrain became more undulating – a sign, the Hump lied, that they were almost at the end of the wilderness – but climbing the wave-like slopes of soft soil robbed them of the last of their strength.

They reached the top of one slope and then, with hearts pounding, began to go down the other side but they were unable to control their limbs. Their steps speeded up with the steepness of the descent, balance was lost and they plunged forward, rolling together until they reached the bottom of a dried water course. For a while they lay as they had fallen. Only Ognam made a sound.

He sang deliriously:

> ' "Dance for me," cried the kind old king,
> "Dance once more for a silvern ring."
> "Sire," she cried "I'll dance for joy
> And give the ring to my darling boy."

No one had been hurt in the tumble because of the softness of the soil, but that made little difference – they were too stricken by thirst, too exhausted and disheartened to continue. All they wanted was to rest where they had fallen, and if the Dark Maid should come she would come as a friend in this hostile region.

Only the Hump was driven to continue, by what he did not know, but greater than his desire to slip into the easeful shadow of unconsciousness like his companions was a relentless force that made him get to his knees and – having straightened Silvermane into a more comfortable position – begin to shuffle up the next incline on them.

That it should end like this, he thought bitterly. *I have betrayed the only one who has ever loved me. I reward her with death. Surely I was cursed from the moment I was found in this wasteland. If there be a deity – why?*

But, as ever, there was no answer and he continued to edge upward on his knees, sometimes falling and lying prone for a score of fluttering heartbeats and then shuffling forward again like some penitent approaching a miraculous shrine. The cloth of his breeches wore through at the knees, and he left little damp patches of blood behind him as the sharp grains of sand rasped his skin. But the main physical pain he endured was in his back, in the disfiguring hump where it seemed that there was agonising movement. To his disordered fancy it felt as though he was sharing his misshapen body with something alien. Finally he reached the top of the rise, falling forward with his eyes closed and the tip of his swollen tongue protuding from between his lips, the penalty of having surreptitiously replenished Silvermane's waterbag at night as he guessed that the need of the horsemaid was greater than that of the others.

Surely, when he opened his eyes he would have his vision of the Dark Maid approaching . . .

So, open them and welcome her.

With difficulty he forced his dry eyelids apart, and when his sight came into focus he tried to shout but only achieved a croak.

'Water!'

He tried again and this time his voice reached the six sprawled below him. They raised their heads painfully and made out the bent shape of the Hump against the skyline; as though infused with new energy he was beckoning them with wild gestures.

'Water!'

The word floated into their benumbed minds like a ray of sunlight through smoke. Being the most hardy, Krispin and Alwald began to move up the incline, sometimes crawling, sometimes managing to get to their feet for a few staggering steps, until they reached the top of the incline and fell to their knees beside the Hump.

Before them was a sight that was like their feverish dreams come true: a balustraded terrace of white and grey marble rose from the ground a score of paces away. Flowering creepers trailed from tall urns mounted at each corner, curved seats of white stone had been placed at regular intervals and in the centre stood a graceful rotunda composed of marble columns supporting a circular dome dazzling in the sunlight. But it was not the unexpected architecture which sent a bolt of joy through them, it was the glittering sprays which plumed from a row of fountains, a myriad intermingled jets of pure water in which rainbows shone and flying droplets sparkled like a fall of diamonds.

'It cannot be,' Alwald muttered, afraid that it would vanish like the mirage of the rose-coloured city; but this was no illusion he realised as the endless plash of water falling upon water filled his ears.

Charged with new energy by the mere sight of the fountains, the three rose to their feet and took several steps before they halted, turned and went back down the slope for their companions.

When the reeling band approached the crest again Alwald felt a terrible fear that, when they breasted it, all he would see would be wilderness, empty and barren, and that the fountains had been a cruel illusion created by evil spirits haunting the wasteland to torment them in their final hours. He laughed aloud when once more he saw the fountains playing and, as they broke into a shambling trot, felt drops of water carried by the wind bring little sensations of coolness to his burning skin.

They reached the short flight of semi-circular steps leading to the terrace and, half-pushing and half-pulling each other, they reeled on to its marble paving.

Everywhere they looked there was water. It gurgled into shell-shaped basins from the stone mouths of mythical beasts; it flowed in gleaming curves from ewers held by bending naiads, it lay still in ornately shaped pools reflecting the blue of the sky and it bubbled spring-like in shallow wells of greenstone ashlar.

Through the fine mist drifting from the fountains they saw the old man. He sat on a stone bench in the shadow cast by the rotunda. A dark cloak was about him and his long staff rested against a veined column. Beneath his broad-brimmed hat his features were a combination of age, authority and a hint - just a hint - of sly humour. He raised his hand in a casual salute, a gesture inviting them to drink.

Laughing despite their swollen tongues and parched lips, the travellers flung themselves to the nearest fountain, sprawling over the rim of its basin and plunging their heads into the bubbling foam as they gulped away the torture of thirst. And when this began to be allayed they lowered themselves into the pools where the chill of spring water revived their exhausted bodies.

With the relief came a strange somnolence. Slowly they left the pools and stretched themselves in their dripping tatters on the marble benches and, while the old man looked on with a slight smile, they fell into trance-like slumber.

EIGHT
Drumbeat

Boom . . . boom . . . boom . . .

The measured notes of the drum echoed with increasing power between the steep walls of the valley. At its approach the spy roused himself from the languor which had resulted from hours of waiting on a sun-warmed crag. After taking a tablet and inkstick and a silvered mirror from his pouch, he carefully eased his body forward so that he could look along the valley to the point where it curved from view.

It was deserted; the road of cracked paving that ran down its centre – the long-neglected highway that skirted the Wilderness of Gil to link Thaan with the capital – was as empty as ever. Not even a bird stirred from the branches of the oil-berry trees which grew in clumps on the valley floor.

Only the remorseless beat of the unseen drum heralded the approach of the Regent's army.

The spy turned on his side and raised his mirror so it caught the sun. He was immediately reassured by the sight of an answering speck of light from a peak of rock two leagues to the east, and he knew that, by mirror flashing to mirror over the rough terrain, within a few minutes Thaan would be alerted to the approach of the enemy; soon his work would be to send precise details of the force with coded flashes as it passed beneath his eyrie.

He laid aside the mirror and waited, his eyes straining along the empty valley, his ears filled with the drumbeat which in his imagination had become a harbinger of doom.

Boom . . . doom!

Boom . . . doom!

And then, round the bend in the valley, appeared several lines of armoured riders, visors down, gauntleted hands holding lances from which fluttered regimental ribbons. They rode at a smart trot, an élite advance guard of knights whose role was to ensure that the way ahead was secure for the main body of the army. By the time they were below his vantage point and he had counted them, six ranks of four horsemen, the van of the army appeared.

It was led by a rider on a richly caparisoned drong holding aloft a banner of Ythan, a blank banner of yellow silk for it had been decreed by King Johan at the end of his life that the royal emblem of the black rose should not be displayed until his daughter returned to claim the throne which he was leaving empty.

Behind the standard bearer marched a company of slingers, each with the muscles of his right arm developed to such an extraordinary degree from constant practice at his deadly art that by comparison his left arm looked withered, with the result that they were nicknamed 'crabs'.

They were followed by ranks of infantry marching to the throb of the still unseen drum, their halberds sloped over their shoulders; then a company of drong-riders with iron-toothed whips coiled over their left shoulders, their chain mail glinting; and then the drum – the pulsebeat of the army – came into view.

It was the largest drum that the spy had ever seen: too heavy to be carried by man or beast, it hung from supports on a wheeled platform. Beside it stood the drummer, one of a team who worked in short shifts to prevent tiring muscles slowing the tempo.

Behind the drum several staff coaches lumbered over the broken road escorted by a number of mounted men whose attire suggested they were officers and field commanders. Then into view came more formations of soldiers marching behind the gilded symbols of their companies.

Now came drong-drawn baggage wagons, wains of hay and corn for the animals, endless carts of meal and wine for the men, wheeled siege-engines and catapults and homely ploughs which the spy knew were for the Regent's practice of sowing salt in the pastures of the vanquished.

As more and more enemy forces came into view the spy's inkstick scrawled symbols and numbers on his tablet, but he paused with mystification when he beheld a huge, many-wheeled vehicle, drawn by two long lines of grunting drongs. It was painted entirely in black and the guards who walked beside it wore black robes with cowls that hid their faces. Each had the silver symbol of the Mother embroidered over his heart, and the spy realised that this was the garb of Witchfinders. The great wagon must be the fabled travelling headquarters of the Witchfinder General. To confirm this several carts came into view, driven by similar black-habited figures, on which were mounted huge cauldrons of brass.

Despite his training the spy could not repress a shudder.

More troops appeared so that it looked as though a river of humanity flowed along the valley. The banner of Ythan had long passed the watcher when the last ranks of the column came into sight.

At a long distance behind them appeared a wagon draped with red cloth. When a gust of wind whirled along the valley it partly raised one side of the crimson covering and the spy gained a fleeting impression of bars as though it could be a huge wheeled cage. He was further puzzled by the driver who was muffled from head to foot in red raiment and who appeared to be wearing a mask. Several men swathed in the same manner walked at a distance from the vehicle, cudgels swinging in their hands.

When this final conveyance was safely past, the spy, appalled that such a formidable army had been sent against his city, began translating his symbols into mirror code, so many long flashes, so many short. He picked up the mirror and was about to angle it to the sun when a languid voice behind him said, 'Put down your mirror, fellow, and you may live a little longer.'

With a sigh the spy did so, rolled on to his back and sat up to see a young officer standing a few steps away. Beside him was a crossbowman, his weapon loaded with a fearful crescent-bladed bolt.

'We seem to have caught our first prisoner, bowman,' said the young man. 'Should be worth a few extra flagons in the mess tonight.'

'Sir!' said the soldier in agreement.

'You, heretic. Were you so foolish not to realise that our commander would send scouts along the heights in case of ambush? On your feet.'

The spy slowly obeyed, his eyes fixed on his captors.

'Why do you want to attack my city?'

'Do not ask me,' said the officer. 'Regent's orders.'

The spy nodded.

There was movement in the rocks behind them. The crossbowman gave a grunt and fell transfixed by a javelin. The second missile brought down the officer. He fumbled for the grip of his sword but was unable to draw it more than half way out of its scabbard.

'Were you so foolish not to realise that I would be protected?' said the spy. He picked up his mirror and began to signal. He did not pause when one of his comrades cut the throat of the wounded officer.

Coming out of a dream of wondrous fountains and cooling waters, Krispin opened his eyes and gazed without comprehension at a sky of bright blue across which a flock of small clouds was being harried by a high wind. Filled with bodily content, he remained watching the clouds for some time while memory returned. How good it had been to feel the pure water surge down his throat, how good to lower his racked body into that cool pool and then stretch out to fall into blissful sleep on that marble bench . . .

Marble bench?

If he had gone to sleep on a marble bench, what was he doing lying on the barren soil of the wilderness?

In shocked bewilderment he sat up.

Close by, his companions lay as they had fallen asleep, but of the terrace with its fountains, wells and rotunda there was not a sign.

'Wake up,' he shouted. 'We are bespelled.'

Yawning and stretching the others roused themselves from slumber; with the realisation that it was the earth beneath them they voiced their amazement together, then fell into silence.

'Master Guide, you warned us of the evil of the wilderness . . .' began the Lady Merlinda.

'But, lady, whatever has happened to us, it was hardly evil,' said Gambal. 'I was near dead with thirst and now I feel I could not drink another drop of liquid, not even of the wine from Ronimar. Let us try and remember exactly what happened.'

'I saw fountains,' said the Hump.

'They played upon a beautiful terrace,' said Alwald. 'It was like a garden of water.'

'And we drank *real* water like it was the milk of the Mother,' said Ognam.

'Perhaps it was,' said Merlinda. 'Perhaps we have been granted a miracle.'

'I am sure I saw an old man sitting on a bench,' mused Krispin.

'How long . . . we sleep?' asked Silvermane.

'The sun had taken her path past noon when we drank,' said the Hump, 'but now she is in the quarter of the morning.'

Gambal rubbed his hand across his face. Conscious of his appearance he liked to be clean-shaven and each day made a point of coating his face with scented grease and shaving with the help of a small hand mirror; now he felt a heavy growth of stubble beneath his palm and cried in astonishment, 'We have been sleeping for two days or more.'

'Yet we have come to no harm,' marvelled Merlinda.

Ognam stood up and brushed the soil from his breeches, one leg of red cloth, the other of green.

'I cannot comprehend what happened but this poor buffoon is suitably grateful,' he said in his well-modulated voice. 'At some time in the future we can speculate on the nature of the beguiling, but now let us press on before we get thirsty again and while our bodies are still refreshed.'

'Wise words from the fool,' said Alwald, climbing to his feet. 'Are we close to the edge of the wilderness, Master Guide, or did you lie to encourage us?'

'Perhaps I was a little in error,' said the Hump with a laugh, 'but see the clouds up there – that is a sign that the waste cannot stretch much further.'

'Then on to Thaan,' cried Alwald.

'Can we still reach the city ahead of the Regent's army even though we have been slowed by having to walk?' asked Merlinda.

'That, lady, I cannot predict because there is also time that passed uncounted while we slept,' answered the Hump. 'Best we follow Master Ognam's advice.'

He looked round the monotonous landscape and suddenly raised his arm and declared, 'That way lies our path.'

He set off with an eager stride, Silvermane walking on her delicate hoofs beside him.

'Great heart,' she said. 'We owe you . . . life. You kept walking . . . found water.'

'Hardly walking,' he answered in a tone softened from his usual drong-rider's voice. 'My knees feel worn to the bone with my crawling.'

'You and I . . . what happen when come to Thaan?'

'If we can enter the city you and I shall be wed at the first shrine we come to – I give not a curse if they are heretics – and then with the silver Gambal has promised I shall buy drongs and, as you wished, we shall set out for Arkad where our contentment lies.'

She sighed with pleasure.

'What joy . . . to journey home . . . with you!'

Behind them Alwald walked with the Lady Merlinda.

'You will know who to seek out in Thaan?' he asked.

'A man named Mias. He is a priest and it is he who we hope will agree to direct you and Krispin on the next stage of your journey to the Mage.'

'Just Krispin and I? But you –'

'My task ends in Thaan. After that I should be a burden to you.'

She laughed at the crestfallen expression on her young companion's face.

'All the world lies ahead of you, Alwald. I am old enough to have mothered you . . . well, almost. So, because you entrusted me with your confidences and I honour you for travelling the Pilgrim Path, do not place more account on our friendship than that. To do otherwise would be a grievous wrong.'

He looked at her with a dark flush of anger beneath his sunburnt skin.

'. . . to me,' she concluded.

NINE
Crabs and Manikins

From every ivied tower, from every weathered spire and turret, from barbican and battlemented wall, even from housetops, fluttered flags dyed in the heretic colour of green. Each flag was emblazoned with the golden insignia of an open eye – the traditional symbol of the All Father. Beneath these brave signals of defiance the citizens of Thaan crowded every vantage point to gaze at the Regent's army which had encamped a league away in what until that morning had been meadows of browsing kine.

Along the city battlements archers and javelin-throwers stood elbow to elbow while without the walls, behind entrenchments and barricades of huge balks of wood protecting the overspill of timber-framed dwellings, spearmen nervously fingered their weapons as they watched the approach of a black coach escorted by a detachment of knights.

The vehicle was reined up a hundred paces from the main city gates. Such was the silent tension of the watchers that when a skylark swooped overhead its trilling notes were clear to every ear.

The silence was broken by a universal hiss of detestation as a knight opened the door and a tall figure in a black habit descended and raked the city with bleak eyes.

'The Witchfinder General!'

The words whispered by thousands sounded like the surge of an angry sea along the cliff-like walls, and the temptation to pull back bowstrings and see their shafts hurtle into his body was almost too much for the archers. But orders had been given that not a blow was to be struck nor a missile fired until the enemy opened hostilities, and master archers glared at their men to remind them that orders were orders.

A knight handed the Witchfinder General a long tube of bronze, the end of which flared wide like the mouth of a bell. Raising this to his lips he cried in a tone devoid of human quality, 'People of Thaan, by the authority invested in me by my lord the Regent of Ythan and in the name of the Serene Mother, I call upon you to renounce this day your adherence to false doctrines and the practice of profane and obscene ritual, and to abjure the heresy that the All Father did not fall from grace, as is told in official scripture.

'If you heed my words the Commander of the Host will show undeserved clemency. You will be allowed to join the congregation of the true faith, and your city shall remain standing.

'Pay heed to me. Do not reject the mercy which flows from the Holy Heart but pull down the banners of your heresy, open your gates and deliver up the false hierophants and prophets who have so long deluded you.

'If you refuse to do this by noon the might of Ythan shall descend upon you and not a stone will be left upon a stone nor a measure of heretical blood unspilled. I await your answer.'

He lowered his tube. For a moment there was silence, then the voice of an uncouth man-at-arms roared from a crenal: 'Coddocks!'

* * *

'Too late!'

The Hump uttered the words with the bitterness of a curse.

He had just forced his bulk through a thick hedgerow which had been planted as a windbreak along the brow of a hill, and was gazing down a slope of rough pasture towards the verdant plain from which Thaan towered.

'The army?' Gambal demanded from the other side.

'The army! It cannot have been here long because men are still setting up camp a league from the city.'

'Are they fighting yet?'

'No, but they soon will be by the look of things.'

There was a snapping of branches as his companions tunnelled their way through the tightly entwined branches, then silence as they gazed in awe at the city they had travelled so far to see. From this high spot they had a breathtaking view of Thaan, whose mellow stonework was caught in a dramatic shaft of light which pierced the cloud unfolding across the sky like a funeral pall for those about to meet the Dark Maid. Every aspect of the city was so weathered, so gracefully time-worn, that its architectural lines blended to give it an organic effect of something living but gnarled which had grown out of the plain rather than been built upon it.

Behind the city rose the sombre bulk of the Drakenfel. It was a low mountain whose fantastic shape could be imagined as that of a long dragon resting on its coils against a background of blue ranges whose snow-tipped summits filled Krispin with nostalgia for the peaks which had looked down on his now-lost Toyheim.

Under ordinary circumstances only the dullest eye could fail to be captivated by the romantic scene but the eyes of the travellers were held by the warlike preparations taking place nearer at hand. Small groups of cavalry fanned out from the sprawling camp to take up skirmishing positions, while along the old highway leading to the city gate marched a long column of troops among whom wagons moved like debris caught in a river of glittering humanity. Awaiting it on the defences hastily erected to protect the houses huddled outside the walls stood the soldiers of Thaan with green plumes waving, breastplates agleam and long-bladed spearheads bright with honing.

From the rear of the column the great drum began to beat and from now on its changing rhythms provided the tempo for the attack. Men marched to it; soon they would advance in double time to a quickened tempo, then lunge and parry with devastating precision to its *boom-boom boom-boom* . . . and gasp their last to its remorseless tattoo.

'Too late,' muttered the Hump again. 'A few hours earlier and we might have gained entrance . . .'

'By the look of that army I am thankful we are on the outside looking in rather than other way round,' Ognam declared.

'Hush, fool,' said Alwald who, having done martial training as part of his education, was fascinated by the military manoeuvering on the plain below.

Before long the column, just out of bowshot from the barricades, divided to form long battle ranks right and left of the field commander and his staff mounted on drongs draped with mesh armour, the tall beasts providing them with a much better view than if they had been on horseback.

Boom. Boom. Boom.

As one the infantry began to move towards the barricades in front of the city's barbican as the drumbeat quickened.

Boom. Boom. Boom.

To the ears of the travellers peering from the hedgerow came the sound of cheering, exuberant, almost joyful, above the mad rataplan.

'Idiots!' exclaimed the Lady Merlinda.

Boomboomboom.

At that moment the advancing soldiers came within range of the archers positioned on the battlements. A flight of arrows hissed in a high arc and fell among them like dark rain. Suddenly there were gaps in the ranks but even before the second flight was sleeting towards them the soldiers used their free arms to raise small circular shields above their heads – reminding Merlinda of the fashionable silken shade she had used in happier days to protect her creamy complexion.

The archers had time to release a third flight and then the first rank of the Regent's army burst like a roller on the seawall of the barricades. The spears of the defenders rose and fell, rose and fell, and those axemen who managed to clamber up the untidy barrier of beams and carts scored only a few blows before they were hurled back as though they were stocks of hay flung from farmers' forks. But, like the waves of the sea, they flowed back spent only to sweep forward again.

With each assault they were repulsed by the spearmen skilled in driving their slender-bladed weapons past shield and through chain mail and, seeing that he was losing more men than the defenders, the commander gave a sign and immediately the drum was silenced – the signal for the attackers to fall back, no longer in ranks but as a vast crowd of men eager to get out of arrow range as fast as possible. As they retreated the defenders jeered them, and a number of spearmen jumped down with daggers to dispatch the fatally wounded left behind like mortal litter.

‘How quickly they turned tail!’ cried Ognam exultantly.

‘It was an exercise to test both the strengths and the weaknesses of the defenders,’ declared Alwald. ‘Our friends with the green plumes will not have it so easy the next time.’

Ominously, the drum began to sound again.

The men who had been summoned back formed up under the shouts of their officers, those with wounds limping to carts which would take them back to camp.

‘The commander is going to give his crabs a turn,’ said Alwald almost with relish. ‘Now you will see what war is about.’

As he had predicted groups of slingers came forward, each with a mantle of chain mail over his head and shoulders and a net of lead shot hanging from his neck. These men, looking lop-sided with their overdeveloped arms, even from a distance, ambled forward without the discipline of the axemen; it was not their job to stand and fight in ordered lines but to run to any spot which gave them even a brief firing advantage.

While still beyond the range of the archers on the city walls the crabs unfolded their slings and, having placed the heavy missiles into their straps, began to whirl them with all their specially developed strength. The swish of the slings came distinctly to the ears of the hidden watchers until, on a sudden double beat from the drum, every man released one of his thongs and a hail of leaden balls whistled over the barricades. Screams and curses testified to the effectiveness of the simple weapons. Laughing in triumph, the slingers darted forward a number of paces and the loaded straps of their slings spun again.

The archers of Thaan, judging the enemy to be in range thanks to a system of markers disguised as innocent-looking stones, sent a curtain of arrows over the slingers. Several fell but in most cases when a shaft with its extra-heavy head did hit a slinger it was deflected with little harm by his mantle, the links of which had been coated with goose grease.

Meanwhile roofed wagons were driven in the wake of the ever-advancing slingers who maintained such continuous fire that the Thaanites had to remain crouched behind their defences while shot whistled above their heads.

'I cannot understand the wagons,' Alwald muttered. 'They are covered with metal plates against arrowfire, yet what can they hold?'

He was soon to know.

At a change in the drum rhythm the drivers lashed their horses towards the barricades, swinging their long vehicles round to face the opposite direction when they were about fifty paces from the makeshift walls. They halted with dust swirling round them, and from the rear of each fell a wooden ramp down which surged tiny figures.

'Serene Mother! They use children!' cried Merlinda in horror.

'No, it is the Manikin Company,' said Gambal. 'In the Citadel I heard that at the Regent's command midgets and dwarfs were brought from every quarter of Ythan to form it.'

They watched in sickened fascination as hundreds of manikins scurried forward on twinkling legs, each brandishing a curved sword little longer than a normal dagger. Reaching the barricades beneath the covering barrage of leaden shot, they began to climb with simian agility. The slingers ceased their fire for fear of hitting the little men. At this the spearmen rose, expecting to meet an attack by troops of their own size; for a moment they held their weapons in puzzlement, then the manikins appeared, shrilling war cries.

For several moments the defenders were paralysed by the notion that the Regent had sent children against them. Realisation of the nature of the foe came with the ferocity of the attack; no children could fight with the bitterness the midgets harboured against the 'giants' as they termed men of natural stature.

Throwing their small bodies straight for the spearmen, even dodging beneath their shields, the manikins were difficult targets for the long-hafted spears. Several were transfixed and flung high from the reddened blades, but most were among the defenders before they could drop their spears and draw their short double-bladed swords.

Stabbing upwards into genitals and slicing hamstrings, the manikins scuttled about the barricades in blood-letting ecstasy while the spearmen began to fall back in panic which was added to when – perhaps as a humorous touch by the Regent's Commander of the Host – a force of huge warriors from the the Land of Anak appeared.

All along the barricades these brutish men, each a head taller than the average soldier, swung their two-handed slashing swords with ghastly effect, driving the men of Thaan along the alleyways of the houses they had sought to protect.

With the Anakians romped the manikins, shrieking, stabbing, slipping in gore with maniac laughter, tormenting the wounded.

The slaughter was horrendous to behold and even Alwald turned his head away.

TEN
The Commander of the Host

In dismay the men on the walls of Thaan watched the defeat of their fellows among the buildings clustered below; many were for going to their aid but their captains ordered them harshly to stay at their posts. On the barbican a horn was sounded, summoning the spearmen to fall back to the main gateway where the massive doors of bronze-plated oak were thrown open for them.

Shocked by the debacle, bloody from wounds, the defenders of the barricades flooded in until the last of them appeared, fighting a rearguard action with the great men of Anak and the manikins who continued to scuttle among the combatants, using their curved swords to cruel effect.

As soon as the rearguard reached the portal and backed through it an iron portcullis clattered down and the gatemen winched the doors into position, trapping about a dozen of the enemy who had followed the spearmen too closely. Several of these were manikins whose eagerness turned to terror the instant they realised they were caught. Squealing with fear they clambered to the shoulders of the Anakians who made no attempt to surrender but continued to advance until a volley of arrows cut them down.

Now that the archers were able to rain arrows down on

the victors below without fear of hitting their own men, the Regent's troops responded by setting the barricades alight so that smoke billowed up to blind the bowmen. The drum ceased to beat, and at this signal the slingers and Anakians trooped back to their lines while the manikins, many reeling under the weight of loot from the houses, jostled to climb into their roofed wagons, their shrill voices carrying to where the travellers watched from the cover of the hedgerow.

Merlinda and Silvermane buried their faces in their hands as a score of heretic prisoners were hanged from portable gallows in sight of the city.

'So much for the Mother's mercy,' muttered Krispin in disgust.

'You cannot blame the Serene Deity for the evil men do in her name,' said Ognam with uncharacteristic seriousness.

'I did not know you are a believer,' said Gambal.

'Of course I am – only I wish I knew what it is that I believe in.'

Much of Thaan was now obscured by smoke rising from the barricades and the timbered buildings behind them. Dancing flames appeared through it and before long ash and smut drifted over the plain like black snowflakes. While the main force marched back to the sprawling camp in time to the renewed beating of the great drum, pickets were set up at various points round the city and cavalry patrols continued to circle it.

'That drum . . . I hate,' said Silvermane. '*Boom* in my head . . . go mad.'

'Will there be more fighting?' Merlinda asked.

'I think not,' said Alwald knowledgeably. 'Tomorrow the business will begin in earnest with siege engines. That skirmish was to test the mettle of Thaan and make the citizens fear the ruthlessness of the Regent's army – hence the hangings.'

'Mayhap that will firm the resolve of the citizens,' said Krispin.

'Aye, better to die swordhanded and free than bow surrender to the Regent,' said the Hump. 'But such matters are not our concern at the moment. I have brought you to Thaan as I agreed, Master Gambal, but too late to enter the city.'

'Perhaps not too late,' said Gambal.

'After dark we might . . .' began Merlinda eagerly.

'If we got past the patrols, how would we get into the city?' demanded Alwald. 'Every gate will be sealed and sentries will be ready to shoot shadows on sight.'

'After braving such dangers so far for the quest I am amazed at your words,' declared Merlinda.

Alwald made no reply.

'Master Alwald spoke sense,' said Ognam. 'And even if we get into the city, I doubt if we would ever get out alive.'

'We cannot go back to Danaak, if we stay here we will be found by the enemy, and our crusts are nigh finished, so what are your suggestions, my lords?'

No one answered and then Ognam said, 'Master Hump, cannot you guide us to some safe region . . .'

'Not without drongs,' said the Hump, his frustration making him sound unusually sour-tempered.

'Krispin, what do you say?' Merlinda asked.

'Yes, let us hear the wisdom of the toymaker,' sneered Alwald, hurt over Merlinda's reaction to his words, despite their apparent truth.

'We must put our trust in the quest,' Krispin answered quietly. 'We have come so far on the Pilgrim Path that our hope must be to continue on it, and that path goes through the city.'

'Brave words, but how –' argued Alwald.

'The toymaker is right,' said Gambal unexpectedly. 'At this moment I cannot say how we may enter Thaan but let us wait until nightfall and mayhap the way will become clear.'

In the pavilion of Lord Mandal, the Commander of the Host, his lieutenants rose to their feet as he appeared to give them their evening briefing. The commander was a bulky man with cropped hair, a manner of studied calm belied by restless eyes; a soldier who had risen from the ranks and won his present exalted position by his ruthless suppression of those who dared to rebel against the Regency.

With him came the tall, sable-shrouded Witchfinder General and two men in armour whom the officers recognised with suspicion as Companions of the Rose, the curious name given to members of the Regent's élite bodyguard.

'Good to smell smoke again, eh?' said Mandal as he seated himself at a long folding table on which lay a vellum map of Thaan and the surrounding district. The Witchfinder stood behind him, his face half-hidden by his cowl, a figure of menace.

'It started well,' he continued. 'The midgets gave those heretics a surprise. Keep the little turds in their own camp or they'll be chopping off our dangles next . . .'

Respectful laughter.

'Right then, I must tell you that we are going to have our work cut out. Thaan is well fortified and is defended by fanatics – do not be misled because we managed to burn a few houses today. To take a city with such walls could be the work of many weeks, but these gentlemen' – he nodded to the Companions of the Rose – 'have arrived in haste from Danaak with an order from the Lord Regent that Thaan must be taken without delay no matter what the cost, so do not expect to settle down to a comfortable siege with starvation doing your work for you.

'Our tactics must be to dishearten the heretics, give them no rest day or night, fill them with fear of the unexpected, wear them down with every trick we know and then –'

He drove his right fist hard into the palm of his left hand.

'I have also received special orders that when the city falls only the Companions and the scholars who have accompanied them are to be allowed into the Great Library. This is by the express command of the Regent, so tell your lads that if anyone goes near the library after Pillage Permission punishment will be crucifixion.'

'Your words have been noted, my lord,' said one of the Companions.

Not by the twitch of a muscle did the Commander of the Host give the Companions the satisfaction of showing the irritation they caused him.

'You should have no trouble,' he continued in his usual soldierly tone. 'Our fellows will be more interested parting heretic thighs and pouring heretic wine down their gullets than reading scrolls.'

More respectful laughter.

'The scryer tells me that after midnight a steady wind will come from the west so we will be able to give the heretics a surprise . . .' His blunt forefinger began to move over the map.

'Now, this where I want you to deploy your men, and make sure that each has tinder . . .'

'Master Guide, I trust your talent at wayfinding works as well by dark as day,' said Merlinda as she rose with the others who had been resting behind the hedgerow. It was still an hour before moon dawn and night pressed heavy on the world, stars hidden by cloud and air acrid with smoke still drifting from the charred ruins below the walls of Thaan.

'My lady, what talent I have is for finding trails for caravans to follow,' responded the Hump, 'not paths between enemy bivouacs.'

'From now on no more words,' said Alwald who, anxious to regain Merlinda's favour now that it was settled that they should attempt to reach the city, had drawn his sword and was the first to push his way through the hedgerow.

From their vantage point on the brow of the hill the travellers saw the lights of the Regent's camp twinkling in neat rows to the west while to the east a fume-dimmed glow gave them the position of the city. Lights scattered across the plain indicated the outposts of the besieging army.

Ognam whistled between his teeth as though trying to keep his fears at bay by this show of bravado – until the others hissed him to be quiet.

The trek down the slope was easier than expected. There was no sign of the enemy and the smooth surfaces of the pasture-land with its cropped grass caused them no difficulty. Their only misadventure was to stumble into a cow chewing its cud.

Gradually the slope flattened out and after passing through a gate in a farm fence they found themselves on one of the many paths that meandered across the plain in the direction of the city. By now their night sight had improved and they experienced less difficulty than they had anticipated in following the rutted track. Often they would stop and listen for the creak of cavalry harness or clink of weapons indicating an outpost, but only the night sounds of the countryside came to their ears, the lament of an owl, the squeak of some tiny animal, the rustle of leaves, the murmur of a rill.

When they had been looking down on the plain it had appeared deceptively flat but once they had reached it this illusion was dispelled. Their path, often sunken by centuries of use between high banks, wandered through spinneys and along along farmers' hedges which seemed to enclose them. If it had not been for the glow of the city they would have lost all sense of direction.

Suddenly the sounds of marching men made them freeze. Lights danced into view on a road which crossed their path a little way ahead. As one they threw themselves into a ditch which flanked their path and waited with thudding hearts as the procession came nearer, reached the crossroads and thankfully continued on its way.

Raising their heads and peering through a fringe of adderweed, Krispin and Alwald could make out the soldiers clearly in the light of lanterns swinging from the ends of poles. What was puzzling was the fact that apart from regulation short swords they did not appear to be armed; instead, each man carried a flat triangular-shaped object which in the uncertain light appeared covered with material, perhaps silk from the way in which the lantern light sheened it.

Long minutes passed as the column passed silently over the crossroads and when the last rank had vanished the companions remained in the ditch for several more minutes before even daring to speak.

'What were they carrying?' asked Gambal finally as they stood up.

'Kites,' said Krispin.

'Kites?' Gambal. 'They are not children going to play.'

'Be that as it may,' said Krispin, 'they were carrying kites. I know a kite when I see one. I have made enough of them in my time.'

'What are . . . kite?' asked Silvermane.

'Hush. Let us move on before more come with or without . . . kites,' said Alwald.

The moon was edging over the distant ranges when the path straightened and joined a cobbled road which ran straight across a common; ahead of them loomed the city in its halo of smoky light. They followed it in single file, Alwald leading the way and Krispin guarding the rear.

Several times in the distance they saw moving lines of lights which suggested that other columns of men were on the move.

'They must be getting into position for a dawn attack,' Gambal suggested.

'Then we must hurry before the lines close,' said Alwald, and they pressed on with renewed rigor.

To their surprise they saw little more of the enemy other than distant lights, and only twice they heard the creak and jangle of unseen cavalry patrols.

'Once the siege proper begins, with its entrenchments and palisades and saps there will not be enough room for a rabbit to pass by,' said Alwald. 'For us it is tonight or never.'

Suddenly Merlinda gave a choked cry.

Right in their path stood a tall tripod structure constructed from long ashwood poles, and hanging from its apex – in the same manner as the Hump's cooking pot had hung from its portable tripod – was a dead spearman, one of the prisoners who had been put to death in sight of his comrades. For a moment shock paralysed them while the body, head on one side, turned until the purpled face was visible, the mouth emphasised like that of a clown by blood from the tongue bitten through during the slow process of strangulation.

That mouth, even more than the protruding eyes, struck horror to their hearts; it seemed to be giving them a friendly grin, a grin that said, 'Welcome to the world of the dead.'

Krispin's memory treacherously brought to mind the picture of the first hanged man he had seen, on the shining path on the mist-shrouded night when he and Alwald had set out on Lady Eloira's quest, the first of the many horrors that he had to learn to stomach.

'I must cut him down,' he said, and for the second time Alwald ordered him not to.

'If a patrol finds him unhaltered they will begin a search,' he said. 'And it matters not to him – his troubles are over in this life.'

ELEVEN
The Regent's Rain

That smell!

That sour smell of burned homes!

It made Krispin gag as for the second time this night memory revived a scene of horror, this time the sight of his razed village.

To their relief, and surprise, the travellers had reached the charred barricades without a single challenge being shouted from the darkness, and now they picked their way between the burnt houses towards the great gate of the city. In the smoky shadows embers still glowed and winked at them, fine ash whirled upwards with every step and on several occasions they tripped over lifeless forms which were the detritus left by the tide of warriors which had flowed up to the city walls and then receded.

Sometimes there were rifts in the smoke and, looking up, they could see the bright battle lanterns set above crenellations and the gleam of helmets. Their fear now was that they might be mistaken for enemy scouts and become targets for nervous archers without a chance to explain their plight. Their hope was to reach the tall bronzed doors undetected and call the gatemen in the manner of travellers – the defenders *might* realise that this would not be the normal action of an enemy. Suddenly Alwald, who was still in the lead, paused with his sword raised. A voice sounded feebly from a black alleyway.

'*For the love of the All Father . . . water.*'

They froze.

'*Is there anyone there? Please help . . .*'

The words turned to sobs.

'Poor thing,' muttered Merlinda. 'Perhaps we can –'

'Leave him be,' said Gambal. 'He may be one of the Regent's men.'

'Whatever he is, he is a man,' declared the Hump, and without another word he turned into the alley.

Gambal savaged a fingernail in frustration.

'To have come so far –' he began.

The Hump reappeared, a grotesque figure with a soldier held in his strong arms. Despite its bloodstained condition, they could see that the man's garb was that of a Thaanite spearman. He begged for water but they had none to offer.

'We will take you to the gate,' said the Hump in a whisper.

'It was the dwarfs,' the spearman muttered on the edge of delirium. 'I fell and they . . . *cut* . . .' He sobbed harshly.

'Listen, fellow, do you have a watchword for the gatemen?' hissed Alwald. 'Your life depends upon it.'

His tone appeared to pull the man back from the brink of delirium.

'I know the word.'

'To the gate then.'

A minute later the sentries watching from the crenellations of the barbican raised their bows and drew the strings to their ears as in the glare of battle lanterns they saw a ragged group of figures hurry out of the shadows.

'Halt. Password or we fire!' the master archer challenged.

The figures below looked up and the watchers saw that one – a crookback, it seemed – cradled a body in his arms.

'We have one of your wounded,' he called.

'And you may have other surprises. Name me today's creature or you will be butts by my count of ten.'

An archer snickered.

'Try *hedgehog*, mates,' he called.

'The word – give him the word,' cried the Hump.

For a moment no sound issued from the spearman though by the contortions of his mouth he was fighting to say something, and then a cry burst from his parched throat, a terrible cry born out of agony.

'*Grimalkin*!'

There was a rattle of chains as the portcullis was raised and then the bronzed doors opened just wide enough for the Hump to carry his burden through.

The captain of the guard appeared with several soldiers bearing flambeaux. When their light fell upon the spearman they cursed to cover their revulsion at the mutilation wrought by the playful knife-swords of the manikins.

'To the chirurgeon with him,' ordered the officer. 'And gently.'

Turning to the little party he said, 'His meeting with the Maid is close, but my thanks for bringing him in.'

He regarded their wild hair, sunburned skins and tattered clothing. 'Now you must prove who you are.'

'Travellers,' said Alwald.

The Lady Merlinda stepped forward, her voice charged with confidence bestowed by her noble blood.

'We are travellers who desire to speak with Brother Mias. We have come from Danaak to see him.'

'So has the Regent's army,' said the captain.

'But not across the Wilderness of Gil,' she retorted. 'That is why we look like outcasts but it should also prove the importance of our errand. I ask you to take us to the honoured Mias.'

'You may have observed that we are at war,' said the captain. 'Brother Mias has much on his mind, he is old and now he sleeps. When I know that you are not mad people or the Regent's assassins I will see that he is informed but . . .' He shrugged.

'Sir, there is something I wish you to know,' said Krispin. 'When we were crossing the plain an hour back we saw troops – the Regent's men – on the march . . .'

'So? We expect them to attack with the dawn.'

'But they were armed with kites.'

'*Kites?*'

'Kites. Like the toys children fly on strings . . .'

'You are certain?'

'In Toyheim I made kites.'

The captain glanced upwards to where a green banner rippled from its staff.

'The wind is rising,' he said turning to his men. 'Nab, get them to sound the water bell.' He turned back to the bewildered party.

'If you are right, Master Kite-maker, I have no doubt Brother Mias will want to thank you for the warning. Until then you may eat, drink and rest though I regret your accommodation will hardly be that of an inn.'

He gave hasty orders, nodded and hurried away leaving half a dozen of his men with naked swords to escort the travellers across a small square. By the time they reached the opposite side they heard the clamour of a mighty bell. Lights appeared in windows of houses, doors were flung open and as though by magic there was as much bustle in flambeau light as in a daytime market.

The guards hustled them into a tall, keep-like building and

up stairs to a stone chamber lit by an oil lamp set behind a grille; another grille was set across a window which overlooked the city ramparts. There was straw on the floor and in the corner a basket of loaves and a water pitcher.

'Home again,' said Ognam.

'What do you mean?' asked Merlinda.

'My lady, in my years as a theatrical I have from time to time – due to completely unjustified circumstances, often the result of spite on behalf of fellow artistes who envied my talent – found myself incarcerated . . . in a word, gaoled, and therefore I am a connoisseur of such accommodation.' He sniffed. 'This is high class. Fresh straw. No chains. Good view.'

'Certainly better than the dungeon I took you from under the Citadel,' said Gambal biting into a loaf. 'They make good bread, these heretics.'

The others followed his example and then sank down wearily with their backs to the walls. Now that the long journey was over, now that they had gained the beleaguered city, a great fatigue filled them and despite the urgent reverberation of the bell throughout the city their eyelids drooped.

Out on the plain long lines of widely spaced men stood with their backs to the wind that blew fresh from the west. Many laughed, for the moment boys at heart as they followed the orders of their officers and raised the silken kites they had carried from their camp. Fixed to the tail of each was a small oil lantern which had been crafted to stay alight in a fierce draught.

Orders were shouted to each company.

'On the word of command, you will take your tinder boxes and ignite the wicks of your lanterns, after which you will close your lanterns. Upon the word of command you will launch your kites in the approved manner and feed out the line to the third knot – any man who fails to get his kite into the air will be fined a crown. Upon the word of command you will cut your lines.

'*Ignite!*'

Still laughing the men fumbled to get the wicks alight, and shouted in triumph as all along the ranks little flames flickered into life, a score, a hundred, a thousand, thousands . . . A soft glow spread across the plain.

'*Launch!*'

Carefully holding the tail lanterns clear of the fabric, the soldiers raised the kites above their heads and allowed them to be snatched away by the wind. Lines burned through fingers which clamped tight when the third knot rasped against their skin.

There was still laughter and cries of delight at the effect of six thousand kites riding high above them, each with a lighted lamp swinging at the end of its tail, a myriad yellow fireworms.

From his seat beneath the canopied entrance to his pavilion the Commander of the Host gazed eastwards at the spectacle.

'Very pretty,' he said to the Witchfinder General. 'Whoever said there can be no beauty in warfare! Should give your heretics a surprise when they wake up to find it raining fire.'

'A taste of things to come, by the Mother, a taste of things to come,' murmured the Witchfinder General.

'Ah, there they go,' said the Captain. 'At least it will show our rosy companions that we are not sitting with our thumbs up our fundaments.'

On the plain the order had been given for the lines to be cut and the wind whirled the kites towards the city. Without their string to keep them up they lost height as they were borne along, and so well had the height and distance been calculated that most fell within Thaan's walls, their lanterns breaking on impact so that the oil they carried flamed up. But, thanks to the tolling bell, the folk of the city were prepared for what they dubbed 'the Regent's rain'. They stood watching the ember shower fall towards them with leather buckets of water, wet sacking and ladders.

As the lanterns dropped about them their flames were beaten out with the sacking or doused with water, and when fire was seen to flicker on the roofs of timbered houses men raced up ladders to extinguish it. So many lanterns fell on the city that despite the vigilance of the people, led by their green-robed priests, not all could be dealt with and fires did break out fanned by the strong wind. First a row of market stalls blazed, then a number of houses caught alight and wains piled high with straw for the cattle brought into the city at the approach of the invaders became infernos with sparks fountaining into the night air.

Curiously, the effect on the people was the opposite to what had been expected by the commander and the Witchfinder – every fire extinguished was seen as a tiny victory against the Regent, and when the last of the kites had fallen and major conflagrations were put out with water from the city's cisterns the crowds were too excited to return to their beds. In main thoroughfares and squares musicians began to play and, linking hands, neighbours and strangers danced. Even the priestly brothers and sisters joined in with laughter and flying robes.

To the travellers watching the spectacle through the bars of their prison chamber it seemed that the aerial fire had provided Thaan with an impromptu festival.

Book Two

Piper, piper, pipe us a tune,
Make us dance beneath the moon,
Pipe us up and pipe us down
And pipe us out of this old town.

Out of the town the piper pranced
And the children laughed and the children danced
Up the road and under the hill –
And there, folk say, they've living still.

– *Old Ythan children's rhyme*

ONE
The Jewel from the Stars

Brother Mias looked up from his scroll-littered table in the Great Library and surveyed the seven strangers through the green-tinted pebble spectacles he wore when weariness inflamed his eyes. He had been informed of their arrival during the night and now he was curious to see what manner of persons they were, and if it was true that they had crossed the Wilderness of Gil.

Behind the glasses his eyes looked from face to face . . . a woman in early middle years from whom he received a hint of warm sensuality, a woman well experienced in the wilful ways of the flesh doubtless but behind that there was an elusive something else.

Interesting, he thought. *She is the one who will demand most from me*.

Beside her a much younger woman whose tattered dress swept the floor, beautiful and with the most amazing hair, a mane of flowing silver . . . and yet again there was more to her than met the eye, something alien that inspired uneasy thoughts.

Is she a child of the All Father? he wondered.

The humpback holding her hand was also curious, a simple soul by the look of him and yet again there was something . . . perhaps a talent not at first apparent.

The other men? A young man of nobility which his

begrimed clothing could not hide, naturally brave and endowed with the traditions of his House . . . another young man with scheming eyes behind his innocent expression, and a youth with auburn hair and the honest looks of one brought up in some far place free from the shadow of Danaak. Probably he was the young noble's body servant.

And the older man in green and red motley, a Fool and a fool.

But what an odd collection!

'Welcome to Thaan,' said Mias with a sweet smile. 'And I thank you for the warning which enabled us to be prepared to meet the fire-kites. We had expected fire to be used against us in the siege so our cisterns were full but it came sooner than I expected. Again, my gratitude to you.'

He paused and wiped his spectacles.

'Now tell who you are and why you have come to a city under threat of destruction. Who will speak?'

'I,' said the Lady Merlinda. 'I am Merlinda once of an illustrious House – alas no more – and my companions are . . .' After quick introductions she continued, 'I speak because I was entrusted to see that Lord Alwald and Master Krispin came to you for they have travelled far on a perilous enterprise and it is believed that the knowledge which they need to continue can only be found in Thaan.'

She paused and Mias asked mildly, 'And the nature of their quest?'

'Like me, they follow the Pilgrim Path.'

'The Pilgrim Path . . . the search for the fabled sleeper. It is many years since a Pilgrim came to Thaan, many years, and then we had no clue to offer him, and he went on his way – and perished beyond the ranges no doubt. It surprises me that the quest continues.'

'The quest will always continue until Princess Livia has been found and restored –'

'– and the Golden Age returns –'

'– and the Golden Age returns, Lord Mias.'

'*Brother* Mias. In Thaan we who don the green of our faith renounce worldly titles. As children of the All Father we are all brothers and sisters, though' – and he nodded to the window beyond which they could see the plain and the distant camp of the Regent's army – 'not necessarily good brothers and sisters.

'But tell me, noble lady, why you think you have any more chance of success than that poor fellow I just mentioned?'

'There has been a sign, Brother Mias, which makes us believe that one who was involved in the Enchantment still lives.'

The priest gave a gentle laugh though his eyes narrowed behind the green glasses.

'There is the stuff of a folktale here. What makes you think that this person still lives?'

'Because he has released his wondrous crystal bird which for the last three seasons has flown across the face of Ythan as a portent.'

'Even more like a folktale . . . and for such a fable you braved the wilderness?'

'But the crystal bird is no fable,' declared Krispin. 'I have truly seen it in the Wald, like a bird made from rainbow when it flies in the sun.'

'And who is it that has released this marvel?'

'I only know of him as The Mage.'

Mias did not allow his benign expression to change though a remote memory of something read long ago stirred in his mind.

'And supposing you did find this ancient personage, how

can you be sure that he will give you the truth you wish for?'

'We cannot – it is one of the many risks of the quest,' said Merlinda. 'But I take heart from the fact that he released the crystal bird. That must have significance.'

Mias made no answer, then asked, 'How am I to know that you are truly Pilgrims and not in the employ of the Regent?'

'We gave the warning,' said Alwald.

'It would not be beyond the wit of the Regent to mount the fire raid just so that you could win our trust by revealing it.'

'Show him,' Merlinda said to Krispin.

He nodded, and pulling the chain from about his neck he handed the disk, with its indented spiral of rune-like symbols, to the priest.

'This I do recognise from old studies,' he said. 'The Disk of Livia.'

'It has been said that when the disks were secretly wrought after The Enchantment for the Pilgrims a spell was worked into the metal so that none could be copied exactly, and that if they were stolen or got into hands for which they were not intended the metal would lose its lustre,' said Merlinda.

'That I have heard also,' Brother Mias said. 'Who bestowed this upon you, young man?'

'I – I think it was Lady Eloira, Reeve of the High Wald – what I mean is, I found it round my neck after she had entranced me.'

'I think,' said Brother Mias, 'that you should tell me of your part in this undertaking from the start, but much as I enjoy such tales I must ask you to be brief for there is much happening today.'

He glanced at his window lit by brilliant sunlight and a smile of satisfaction played on his thin lips. 'My commanders have told me that there is a great stirring in the Regent's camp so we can expect to be under attack before long. Please begin.'

Alwald and Krispin glanced at each other, not knowing how or where to start, so Merlinda began the narration from what they had told her, with them filling in where necessary.

'So you were the Wayfinder?' said Brother Mias turning to Krispin.

'Yes, my lor . . . brother. When Lady Eloira entranced me she put knowledge into my head which later I remembered bit by bit, as necessary.'

'There are still things hidden in your memory?'

'That I cannot say . . . brother. I only know of it when I see something which awakens my memory, for it is like suddenly remembering something that I once knew well.'

When the story reached Krispin's essay into the City Without a Name the priest's interest quickened.

'You found the Jewel from the Stars?'

Krispin looked puzzled.

'You may know it as the Esav; it had that name in the Third Book of the Arcanum. As I recall it, it was said to have been brought to this world by a messenger from the stars and, not being of this world, had certain unique powers.'

Normally caution instilled into him by the Lady Eloira would have held Krispin back but, sensing the need to impress the high priest of Thaan with the truth of the quest, he felt inside his jerkin, brought forth the heart-shaped crystal which he had taken from the eidolon, and carefully placed it before Brother Mias.

The old man made no move to touch the flat stone; rather he drew back as its swirling opaline colours suggested a living force held within it.

'I doubt not that this is it,' said Brother Mias with admiration in his voice. 'In the old days of high magic what would a sorcerer have traded to gain it! Take it back, youth, for it holds too much temptation for those who have studied esoteric doctrines.'

Without a word Krispin picked it up and replaced it in the soft leather bag, which hung from his neck by a thong, such as were used by Wald folk as purses. As he did so he was aware of the effect the jewel had upon his companions, especially those to whom it came as a complete surprise.

'No wonder the dhrul came for the drongs and not for us when you wore such a talisman,' whispered the awed Hump.

Gambal spoke not with his tongue but with his eyes; it was as though the beauty of the stone had overwhelmed him.

'Please, continue you account,' said Brother Mias.

Alwald was recounting the journey from the Vale of Mabalon when a slim, cowled figure entered the chamber and approached the priest.

'Brother Mias, the tower commander sends word that columns of men and siege engines are advancing across the plain,' she said. At the sound of her soft voice Alwald and Krispin looked at her with curiosity, surprised that heretic priests could be women and – from what they saw of her grave face beneath her cowl – beautiful.

'I shall hear the rest of your epic at a later time – I must go and see to the defence,' said Brother Mias. 'The war resumes, and the next hour will be a crucial one. Go with Sister Lorelle who will find what fresh apparel you require and then bring you to the tower – for it seems that you deal in wonders and today you may see another.'

Half an hour later Lorelle, her head bowed slightly beneath her grey hood, her arms folded demurely across her breast with her hands hidden in the wide sleeves of her novice's robe, led the travellers up a wide staircase which spiralled to the roof of Thaan's tallest tower.

Merlinda was attired in a dress of soft undyed wool, something that only her humblest servant might have worn in her house of entertainment but which now overjoyed her; Silvermane was grateful that the gown Lorelle found for her was long enough to conceal her hoofs. In the chamber where the women changed, Lorelle was surprised at the modesty of this girl with shining hair who put on her new garment before removing the old skirt whose hem was ragged from sweeping the floor.

Alwald, Gambal and Krispin had changed their tattered tunics and breeches for clothing which came from Thaan's military stores, but the Hump retained the jerkin which had been tailored to fit his curving back while Ognam only gave up his motley on the promise that it would be laundered and given to a seamstress for repair.

When the novice led the companions out on to the broad, sun-drenched roof they were amazed at the panorama it provided. Directly below were the roofs and spires of Thaan; beyond the city walls to the east rose the sculptured bulk of the Drakenfel and the blue ranges behind it. To the west rolled the pleasant green plain over which moved ant-like columns of troops while on the old highway long teams of drongs and heavy horses pulled an array of siege engines – catapults, battering rams, fire-carts, wagon loads of scaling ladders and nets.

In the middle of the siege train rolled the wagon bearing the great drum to whose beat the advancing army marched.

Beneath their golden-eyed banners the people of Thaan watched the approaching might of the Regent in silence. For the first time they saw the extent of the besieging force and most tried to hide the expressions of dismay on their faces.

'What is that, sister?' asked Gambal, indicating a vast, canvas-swathed structure which stood on massive tripod legs in the centre of the roof, beneath which Brother Mias conferred with his military commanders and a number of anxious priests holding parchments which fluttered in the breeze.

'I would find it difficult to explain its mechanics,' replied Lorelle in her low, sweet voice. 'It is something secret that has been constructed since news first came that the Regent was going to campaign against us. But you will see soon enough.'

From the belfries of Thaan the rolling peal of a hundred bells enveloped the heretic city, and everywhere people, priests and soldiers fell to their knees and, with arms raised in the heretic attitude of prayer, entreated the All Father to give them the power to destroy the evil horde which had come against them 'until not one be left to draw breath'.

At the same time on the plain the drum fell silent, the marching columns halted and a priest who had accompanied the army from Danaak mounted a tall scaling platform and, while the men bowed their heads, made the holy sign and intoned, 'Serene and merciful Mother, fill us with courage that we may cut down the blasphemers who deny your authority in the Three Worlds, strengthen our arms and harden our hearts that we may spare not man nor woman who kneel to the false one.'

Both sides thus having taken care of their devotions, the hostilities began.

TWO
The Burning Glass

'That accursed drum,' muttered the Lady Merlinda as she watched the approach of the besiegers from the parapet which surrounded the tower's flat roof. 'It is like the footsteps of doom.'

'I am sure that is the idea,' said Alwald. 'And if it is not doom's footsteps, it is the heartbeat of the Regent's army. You cannot escape it. Look at the effect it is having already.' He nodded to where their guide, the novice Lorelle, stood by herself watching the great engines of war lumbering towards her city. The wind had disarranged her cowl and they saw that a tear glistened on her pale cheek.

Gambal moved towards her and said something the others could not hear. She answered one word and turned away. The young man shrugged and looked discomfited but the eyes of his companions were fixed on the plain where the siege train was being drawn up just out of bowshot of the city. Soldiers crowded round a line of wagon-mounted catapults, mangonels and trebuchets, positioning them to the orders of weapon-masters and securing them with chains and massive wooden props.

To the watchers there was a sense of unreality about the scene – the men from Danaak were going about their work in the manner of everyday workers; their laughter and curses as they struggled with the heavy beams of their engines floated up to the towers of Thaan and sounded no different than if they had been carpenters erecting houses.

'Do you think the old man will help us?' Alwald asked Merlinda.

'I know not but I believe we have convinced him of our sincerity,' she answered, 'thanks to the sight of the Esav. But I fear that while his city is under siege there will be little that he can do. We are trapped here.'

Boom . . . boom . . . boom.

The beat of the drum slowed and the watchers saw the siege crews time their ritualistic drill to it, winching the heavy arms of their engines into position and loading their missiles – heavy spears with broad metal heads in the catapults; nets of stones, to burst murderously on impact, in the 'spoons' of mangonels, and boulders to batter down the city's gates in the slings of the huge trebuchets.

'Any moment now,' muttered Alwald. On the battlements the defenders sought to protect themselves behind merlons, some throwing themselves flat, as they awaited the missile barrage.

There came a sound of activity from behind the travellers and turning round they saw the canvas drapes pulled away from the structure in the centre of the roof to expose a colossal mirror of highly polished electrum mounted on a framework of metal rods. To Alwald there was something familiar about its outline, reminding him of the Eye at River Garde which enabled him to see for great distances, though this was at least twenty times larger. A polished crystal, at least an armspan across, was mounted before the curved mirror and, as with the Eye, there was a device for taking aim and a complicated system of gears controlled by a soldier to turn and tilt the reflector.

The companions were suddenly blinded as the sun's rays caught the electrum and were focused on to the crystal. When they could open them again they saw a searing beam directed from the crystal to the plain below. Founts of steam burst from the earth where the beam touched it and its moisture boiled, and when the beam caught a tree it exploded into flame.

Deftly the soldier turned his geared wheels and directed the brilliant shaft towards the enemy; a charred track traced its progress over the ground. For a moment the enemy troops stood dazzled and speechless; the sudden appearance of the shining ray had the quality of a miracle. But as they heard the hiss of broiling soil and felt the very air heat up they broke ranks and stampeded across the plain. Mounted officers, drawing their ceremonial whips, tried to stem the panic but as the ray came closer like the white-hot wrath of a vengeful deity they spurred their horses after the fleeing multitude.

Faithful unto death one man remained at his post behind a trebuchet. He slashed at the winch ropes with his sword until they parted and a boulder hurtled in a high arc to crash just short of the city wall, throwing up a cascade of ash from blackened ruins beneath it. On the central tower the soldier made an adjustment and the probing ray swerved to catch both man and trebuchet. He staggered for several steps before collapsing like a smoking scarecrow while the siege engine was outlined in fire.

The incandescent finger moved again, weaving a smouldering trail past the engines until it reached the abandoned drum wagon. Within moments the wagon became a pyre and the drum a cloud of flying sparks.

In Thaan the astonished citizens found voice, rejoicing that the menacing drumbeat would never again fill their hearts with dread. Bells pealed wildly overhead and everywhere the green sleeves of the priests rose in thanksgiving.

On the plain the siege engines were ignited one after the other, and when the last one flared the soldier controlling the mirror moved its angle so that it lost the sun's rays and men rushed to cover the precious electrum.

'What would the Regent give to learn the secret of such a weapon!' Gambal exclaimed.

'Ah, if I was the poet I had yearned to be in youth what a paean I would pen to such magic!' cried Ognam. 'What chance has the Regent against a city of enchanters!'

'There is nothing magical about our Speculum, my friend,' came the calm voice of Brother Mias behind them. 'An ancient treatise on the power of reflection has been in our library for generations – it is said that in mythical times the King of Taloon had a sun mirror to protect his harbour. It came to my mind when I had tidings that the gaze of the Regent was upon us, and night and day our priestly scholars made the necessary calculations and our finest craftsmen laboured in secret to construct it in time. Now they see the reward for their efforts.'

'Would that we'd had such a device at River Garde,' said Alwald. 'The enemy will not be able to come nigh your walls.'

'At least not until sunset,' said Brother Mias drily.

From the platform of the hastily constructed observation tower beside the commander's pavilion the Commander of the Host, the Witchfinder General and the two Companions of the Rose gazed eastwards to Thaan. Above them masts used for signalling flags thrummed in the wind.

'Accursed heretics,' the Witchfinder General said bitterly. 'What evil wizardry have they summoned to defeat us . . .'

'I doubt if it is wizardry,' said Lord Mandal, 'but it is

certainly a most remarkable weapon, and now I faintly recollect a legend of an ancient king who had such a mirror. A pity, mesire, that after The Enchantment your guild burned so many books for, by seeking through the old lore, we might have discovered how to fashion such an artifice for our own use. At least when the city falls we may gain the secret.'

'And do you think the city will fall?' asked one of the Companions of the Rose.

'Of course. It may mean that we have to attack by moonlight, for I doubt if a reflected moonbeam will do us much hurt.'

'Remembering the words of the Lord Regent, it had better be soon,' said the Companion grimly.

'Already my engineers are building new machines,' said the commander. 'What a pity it is not the good old days when every army had its enchanter – a powerful weather spell and Thaan would be covered by cloud.'

'Perhaps there is a weather witch somewhere in the countryside who could be persuaded to help us,' suggested the second Companion.

'Magic is the abomination which led to The Enchantment,' declared the Witchfinder General. 'Pilgrims, sorcerers and heretics are the enemies of Ythan and their destruction is the duty of my guild . . .' He paused. 'However, sometimes, fire is fought by fire and if the recognition of a little weather witchery will lead to the quick fall of a heretic stronghold I would have no objection.'

'Excellent logic, mesire,' said the commander. 'I shall send out patrols to the villages in the hope of finding a beldame who can weather spell.'

'Let my finders ride with them,' said the Witchfinder General. 'They can *smell* a witch.'

'And when she has conjured up clouds for you, you can reward her with the cauldron,' laughed one of the Companions.

Late that night the novice Lorelle went to the Black Cat Inn where the travellers were permitted to lodge after Brother Mias had accepted the explanation of their singular arrival. Still exhausted by their passage of the wilderness they had retired early to sleep, and the novice sent a potboy to rouse them urgently.

Bleary-eyed, Krispin and Alwald were the first to come down the stairs. Their weapons had been returned to them and now both were still buckling on their sword belts in the belief that an attack was taking place.

'Sorry I am to break your slumber,' said the girl, 'but Brother Mias would see you in the Great Library.'

'A pity it could not wait until morning,' grumbled Ognam appearing in his refurbished motley. 'It was a rare dream I was enjoying. Never have my sallies been so fast or so witty. Would that I could remember them.'

'Brother Mias has little time,' explained Lorelle in her low voice.

'Then let us not keep him waiting,' said the Lady Merlinda.

Within a few minutes they entered the library which was filled of the sweetish smell of old parchments and bindings of leather. Apart from a pair of candles throwing soft light over the priest's table, it was a place of friendly darkness. Brother Mias rose as they approached and gestured to a semi-circle of clerk's stools which had been arranged for them, a courtesy which Merlinda took as a good omen.

'Thank you, Sister Lorelle,' he said. 'You may retire

now, unless it is of interest to you to hear what I am to tell these good folk.'

The novice inclined her cowled head.

'I would learn from your words,' she said and seated herself in the shadows. Spying her exquisite features lambent in the candle glow, Gambal was aware that something unique was occurring within him. In his dreadful past his heart had only raced through terror or – just occasionally – through well-concealed triumph; now it was as though a trapped bird fluttered behind his ribs but for neither of these reasons, and as comprehension came he felt he was going to faint.

'I have pondered on what you told me,' Brother Mias began. 'When I listened to you at first it sounded more like a fable, but when I saw the Jewel from the Stars I knew that you were telling the truth. As a priest I must say that I detect the hand of the All Father in your arrival at this time.'

They remained silent. Brought up in the belief that the Mother was the Queen of the Three Worlds, they felt ill at ease with the heretical suggestion.

'Since The Enchantment our city has been isolated from the rest of Ythan, by distance, by religious belief and by the breakdown of trade, yet we were aware of how the bane of the Regency spread across the kingdom – much more so since the bane has finally reached us.'

He paused. Although the candle light was soft and flattering, his hearers were aware of the fatigue that pressed upon him by lines which were etched deeper into his worn features than when they had seen him that morning. He sipped from a silver goblet.

'An infusion of wine and mandrake root,' he said with a slight smile. 'It helps. Now, to return to the rule of the Regents . . . I understand it is the belief of those who follow the Pilgrim Path that only the restoration of Princess Livia to the Empty Throne can end this malignance. On the possibility of this belief being correct – and in the present circumstances anything that could bring harm to our enemy is welcome! – you may expect all the help I can give you.'

Merlinda expressed gratitude and inwardly felt a warm sense of relief that she had succeeded in her appointed task.

'Do not expect too much,' continued the priest, raising his white hand in caution. 'Even if we manage to find the knowledge you require the problem remains that you are in a city ringed by enemies.'

'When the siege is over –'

'We may all have been gathered to the All Father by then. Though we shall fight to the last man – and woman! – I doubt if we can resist the might of Ythan forever. But the All Father moves in mysterious ways, and perhaps a way will be revealed by which you can continue your quest. But, as I understand, the quest now only concerns two, Lord Alwald and Master Krispin.'

'That was the original idea,' said Gambal, 'but if they agree I would like to journey on with them.'

'I thought your interest was merely to escape Danaak with us,' said Alwald.

'You forget this,' Gambal replied. From his tunic he drew out a coin-sized talisman. 'I, too, wear the Disk of Livia and after crossing the Wilderness of Gil with you I would be honoured to continue.'

'And, my good sirs, as I have no immediate engagements, I too –' began Ognam to everyone's surprise.

'It seems that this is something you must decide among yourselves,' said Brother Mias with an amused smile. 'Meanwhile tell me what it is that you hoped to find in Thaan.'

‘Yours is the last ancient library in Ythan and must hold many secrets,’ said Merlinda. ‘It is thought that it might contain a description of the place where the sorcerer known as The Mage worked his magic at the time of The Enchantment, and the route by which it may be reached.’

‘It is true that here there is much arcana stored on our shelves from olden times, and such knowledge that you want may well be among it, though it is our scriptures with which we are most familiar,’ said Brother Mias. ‘But come daylight I shall set scribes questing through vellum and tablet. May the All Father grant them enough time.’

THREE
'A pox on you!'

Time passed slowly for the besiegers and the besieged. Each day the sun shone brilliantly, for which the people of Thaan raised paeans of thanksgiving to the All Father. Each night small forces from the Regent's army approached the formidable walls of the city to fire flaming missiles from portable catapults to keep the inhabitants in a state of alarm.

After a week the Commander of the Host sent forward a trebuchet which had been built by his siegemen to have extra long range. During the day a team of drongs dragged it to a spot short of the scorched trail which had been left by the burning ray. Its crew hastily loaded it with an iron ball and aimed it at the Speculum. At that moment the covers were pulled from the shining electrum of the reflector and a shaft of dazzling light raced across the plain with swirling vapours marking its progress.

At the sight of it coming towards them the soldiers fled, and only just in time as the terrifying incandesence reached the engine. Its winch ropes were the first to ignite with the result that the sling beam was released, hurling the iron ball so that it whistled within a few armspans of the enormous mirror.

The Commander of the Host watched the trebuchet blaze from his observation tower.

'Promote the aimer,' he told one of his lieutenants. 'It was a close shot.'

'Sir, we need something more than close shots,' said a Companion of the Rose. 'The impatience of my Lord Regent still rings in my ears.'

'How many witches have we found?' the commander asked.

'Five were brought in,' answered the Witchfinder General. 'Not one could raise a puff of cloud. Curing warts is the limit of their powers.'

'Then we must pray for rain – natural rain,' said the commander.

'I have questioned peasants,' said the Witchfinder General. 'They say that at this time of year clear skies can last for weeks.'

'Then we must wait for weeks,' said the commander testily. 'I cannot get men to march into that.' He nodded to the dazzling beam playing over the plain.

'There is the alternative – in the red wagon,' said the Witchfinder General.

The Commander of the Host frowned.

'That is a weapon which does not distinguish between friend and foe.'

'True, but there is no need for troops to face such a weapon,' said the Witchfinder General. 'Your task is to destroy the accursed city and the heretics who dwell within, and if this is done without entry so much the better – it is the Companions of the Rose who are charged to enter with their scribes.'

The commander nodded.

'It will be a test of your fabled courage,' he told the Companions and, smiling, went to his apartment in the far end of the pavilion where his courier awaited him, still dust-stained by the long ride from the capital.

'Well, Hans, how goes it?' the commander said, slapping

the courier on the shoulder. As young men they had campaigned together and though Mandal had risen to an exalted position it was part of his character never to forget old friends.

'The dispatches, my lord,' said the courier formally and held out a sealed satchel.

The commander took it with a grimace.

'More potton-cursed parchment-work,' he complained. 'The clerks can deal with it. I'll wager a month's pay that most of it is about the wine ration. Those poxed commissaries in Danaak – who have never seen an arrow fired in anger! – are trying to get it reduced by two cups a day per man. It is bad enough for my poor sods in this fundament of the kingdom, on stale rations and being fried by the heretics' infernal mirror, without their daily rotgut being halved. If it has to be, let the quill-pushers in Danaak come out and make the announcement – and sort out the mutiny that would follow it.'

He laughed.

'Sit down, Hans, and – talking about rotgut – I have some pretty reasonable Ronimar here.'

'Thank you, my lord.'

'Forget the "my lord" bit, we're not on parade. It was Mandal and Hans when we were with the Regent's Own Lancers. By the Milk of the Mother, I miss those days. Good honest soldiering it was. Now I may have an army but I am surrounded by witchfinders and Companions of the Rose and captains of gentle birth who sneer at me behind my back because I was once a coarse ranker – and I am still coarse.'

The courier's travel-grimed face split into a grin as the commander called an orderly to bring wine.

When the two old comrades sat opposite each other with

their leather campaign cups full of black wine Mandal said, 'Tell me the latest scandal in the city.'

'Danaak is agog with the assassination of Archpriest Gregon,' replied Hans with the pleasure of one imparting dramatic news.

'Old Gregon? Who would want to risk the cord for him - and why?'

'Ah,' said Hans and looked knowing. 'Who indeed?'

'Come on, you are dying to tell me. You love intrigue, which is why you made your career in the Couriers.'

'Only rumours mind, but the story goes something like this: Lord Odo disappeared mysteriously on the night of the last Re-election Feast, and the belief of many is that he has a dungeon to himself after leading a plot against my Lord Regent, though none know for certain - trust our master to stoke the fires of uncertainty - but Odo's fellow conspirators are in a state of terror in case they are implicated.

'Putting together what I have picked up here and there' - the courier gave Mandal a sly grin - 'I would wager that the archpriest, who has always envied the temporal power of the Regency, was in the plot with Odo, which no doubt Odo confessed when he was embraced by the Iron Maiden or lowered into the rat pit.'

'Interesting,' said Mandal reaching for the wine jug. 'Even the Lord Regent could not have the Serene Mother's earthly representative publicly arrested. Did he have Gregon assassinated then?'

'He was too crafty for that. He worked out a plan to kill several birds with one bolt, which is one of the reasons you are out here, old friend. He sent this army against Thaan and then put his Whisperers to work spreading the false rumour that Archpriest Gregon had come to him with an offer - he would betray Odo in return for the destruction of the heretics.

'You can imagine the effect of this on Odo's friends – in their minds not only did Gregon trade their leader for Thaan but he was a threat to them. There was only one thing they could do . . .' Hans drew his finger across his throat.

'What method?'

'A very spectacular one. The archpriest was conducting the Spring Festival ceremony in the main shrine and when he drank from the chalice he toppled frothing on the altar steps. Dead in a minute. The sacred wine had been laced with essence of nightshade by a discontented acolyte who had been bribed by the conspirators, and who confessed it publicly the moment the Witchfinders got their hands on him.'

'You have to admire the Lord Regent's cunning,' Mandal said. 'He has rid himself of the scheming archpriest and Odo's conspirators without appearing to be involved himself. He let his enemies do his work for him.'

'He may be in need of more than cunning. I have heard that he suffers from some incurable malady . . .'

'Such stories always abound. Wishful thinking!'

'I hope you are right,' Hans said. 'He has been a good master to the likes of us.'

'I hope it will stay that way,' responded the Commander of the Host, and for the first time since he had known him the courier saw a look of anxiety on his face.

Within the beleaguered city life took on a monotonous rhythm; men – and the younger women – took their turns on the walls, and slept; the older women cooked continuously or minded the children, and the old men worked their fingers raw making arrows. The many priests of the city, conspicuous in their green, worked alongside their lay brethren when not conducting religious ceremonies in the many shrines to invoke divine aid – the tenets of predestination were now ignored by the apprehensive population. The use of shrine bell was restricted to warning of attack, but the melodious litanies sung by the priests hung in the air like a constant benison.

Time hung heavily for the travellers. Although they knew that in the Great Library Brother Mias had set scribes sifting through thousands of scrolls and manuscripts devoted to history and ancient lore, they felt ineffectual for not being able to contribute to their own cause. Alwald and Krispin went to the priest and offered their services on the battlements but the old man, while gently thanking them, pointed out that it would only take one enemy arrow to jeopardise the whole quest.

'Although Thaan is like an island bright with the true faith in a dark sea of false belief, it may be that in the fullness of time your quest will be of greater import to Ythan than the defence of our city,' he said.

'I wish I had his confidence,' muttered Alwald as they returned to the Black Cat. 'Although I have beheld marvels that I would have never credited when I dwelt in River Garde, I still find it difficult to believe that the princess can be alive after a hundred seasons.'

Apart from guilt that they were not involved in the defence of the city, the travellers suffered from a psychic weariness as though there had been some unseen element in the wilderness which had sapped them of both strength and will. As a result they spent much of their time sleeping.

The novice Lorelle had been given the task of taking care of them, and she spent much time at their inn, where her presence produced conflicting emotions in Gambal. His heart had become independent of his mind; it beat faster when the robed girl with the face of pale tranquillity appeared while his mind raged that he could be so affected by someone who knew nothing of the outside world and who had sacrificed the prospect of an emotional life on the altar of heresy. He had to struggle to control his impatience when waiting for Lorelle to arrive – for Gambal was the Gambal of old and his deceptively innocent features gave no indication of his inner feelings. And when she did come he felt like cursing her because of the power she unknowingly exerted over him.

At night on his pallet he would wake uneasily with Lorelle's image in his mind, and he would try to fathom the reason for his feelings. It was not – he told himself – that he wanted to bed her; when he had begun to rise in the Citadel he had enjoyed the charms of women whose passion reflected their ambition. In a short period there was no mystery of the couch that he had not plumbed, and with such experience he knew that there was much more in his passion than the stirring of his loins.

So what was it?

There was one answer that he could not face, an answer of one word – *love*!

One day the Hump took Lorelle aside and, encouraged by the fact that her clear grey eyes had never lingered in curiosity over his deformity, he told her that it was his wish to marry Silvermane in one of the city shrines.

'Would that I had taken my vows so that I might perform such a joyful ceremony, Master Guide,' she said, 'but I shall take you to Brother Davon in the shrine across the square. He is kindly and his voice is musical, which is important.'

When Brother Davon invited the Hump to sit with Lorelle in his private chamber adjoining the shrine and offered them refreshment, the guide agreed that his voice was musical and he was kindly.

While the Hump sipped straw-coloured wine with threads of tiny bubbles, Lorelle explained his situation.

'You are one of the heroes who crossed the wilderness and warned us of the fire-kites,' Brother Davon said. 'It will be an honour to call down the blessing of the All Father on you and . . . who is the lady you wish to marry?'

'Silvermane,' said the Hump. 'She is known as Silvermane.'

'Ah yes,' said Brother Davon in a voice that was not quite so musical. 'She is one of your party, is she not?'

'That is true, but I learned to love her long before we quit Danaak.'

'Quite. The problem is, Master Guide, that I have heard that there is something – shall we say – *unusual* – about the . . . lady.'

His words hung in the air.

'Unusual?' said Lorelle finally.

'Is it so?' Brother Davon asked the Hump. 'It is something I must know before I can agree.'

'She is a horsemaid,' said the Hump quickly. 'She was taken from her folk in the distant woodlands of Arkad, many hundreds of leagues from here.'

'A horsemaid?' mused the priest. 'And what sort of a . . . person is that?'

'It is simply that from below the waist her limbs are like those of a young horse.'

'Then marriage in Thaan is out of the question.' Brother Davon turned to Lorelle. 'I am amazed that you, a postulant, should embarrass me with such an impossible request.'

'Brother, I saw no evil –'

'No evil! Have you not learned your scripture? Is it not written: *In the first time the All Father rose from the chasm of Chaos and blew forth his breath so that the void was filled with mist, and the All Father took some mist thereof and fashioned the Three Worlds, and from more mist he clothed our world with water in the deeps and herbs upon the high land, and with the last mist of his breath he fashioned beasts and men, and he said, "I shall raise Man from the Beasts by his understanding, and his understanding is that his time is limited so he shall seek to raise himself in his span, but the brutes will not have this understanding and will be content not knowing their days are numbered, and being content they will not rise themselves, and this is the difference between Man and Beast and must be ever so, and thus it will be an abomination in my sight for Man to mate with Beast for both will be accursed and twice cursed will be those who do not cry, 'Hold, for this is an abomination* . . .' "'

'I know my Credenda,' said Lorelle, her voice softer than ever, 'but it seemed to me that there could be nothing of the beast about such a beautiful person as Silvermane.'

'Then answer me this, Sister, for this could hold the solution to the problem and all may be yet well: are her limbs as they are through accident or deformity?'

At the last word there came the sound of knuckles cracking as the Hump locked his fingers painfully and tried to stop himself putting voice to his anger.

'Silvermane is not malformed,' said Lorelle.

'Then she cannot be wholly human if the shape and texture of her limbs is natural to her, and if she is not human . . .' He paused, then, resuming his mellow tone, quoted: '. . . *it will be an abomination in my sight for Man to mate with Beast* . . .'

Under his enveloping cloak the Hump fingered the cold comforting metal of his drong-rider's spike, and feverishly imagined it delving into the smug heart of the heretic.

'But Silvermane is a child of the All Father –' Lorelle protested but the Hump heard no more. Alarmed by the rage that consumed him, afraid of how it might make him act, he rose so abruptly that his chair crashed over and ran into the sunlit square.

People passed to and fro with their burdens, soldiers marched to take up their positions and shrieking children raced through a swirl of startled pigeons in pursuit of a bright inflated bladder.

'A pox on you all,' growled the Hump. 'A pox on you all!'

In an attempt to keep the minds of her charges occupied, Lorelle told them tales of Thaan's past when they met for meals, describing the glories once known by the city.

'There has been little traffic with the outside world since the mines were closed,' she said at supper ten days after the travellers had arrived at the city gate.

'Was that because there was no call for marble in Ythan after The Enchantment?' asked Gambal who, to his own disgust, found himself trying to impress the novice by his interest in her words.

'That is partly true,' she answered across the table. 'For centuries the men of Thaan mined the Drakenfel for its wonderful stone; marble, adamantine, porphyry, starstone, serpentine, aventurine . . . all were taken from the mountain leaving huge galleries and chambers. As generation followed generation, the miners had to delve deeper until they finally came to one of the great subterranean waterways which weave through the underworld like the veins beneath our skin.'

'That is something that I have not heard of,' said Ognam, adding with a sigh, 'but then there is much that I have not heard of. Alas, my education was restricted; prat-falls, juggling, voice-throwing, comic mime . . .'

His voice trailed off as Gambal cut in, 'Tell about this underground river.'

'The miners named it the River of Varah after the first of their company to come upon it,' Lorelle continued. 'It was planned to explore it and a special vessel was constructed underground, but soon afterwards the deepest galleries were abandoned.'

'This was before The Enchantment?'

'Just before it.'

'So why . . .?'

A frown appeared on the high brow of the novice.

'Something came. Today it is not known for sure – the history of that time became confused – but there are tales that the greed of the miners took them too deep and malefic beings came to haunt the lower workings so the priests of the city ordered them to be sealed.'

As she continued speaking Krispin tried to imagine the world beneath the Drakenfel; huge man-hewn halls whose walls gleamed with rare stone and the black river flowing mysteriously through caverns without measure – a world below the world. Could it be possible that somewhere in such a maze the Princess Livia lay entranced?

His thoughts were interrupted by the panicked footfalls of folk fleeing past the inn. For a moment all feared that the gate had been breached and the enemy were upon them – then a worse fear grew as above the screams and curses a desperate chant came to their ears, 'The Red Death! The Red Death! The Red Death!'

FOUR
The Red Death

Master Archer Ulban gazed across the moonlit plain from his turret on the city wall. His bowmen sat nearby, backs against the weather-sculpted merlons, watching as several of their number played Toup, a gambling game which involved spinning coins. Their occasional bursts of laughter irritated him as he strained his ears as well as his eyes. Some soldierly sense warned him of danger. During the day the enemy had been too quiet. Apart from a few cavalry patrols galloping at a safe distance round the walls to exercise their mounts, there had been no activity. Admittedly, since the Speculum had destroyed their siege engines the Regent's forces had been reluctant to come within range, but each day they mounted some action to keep the defenders' nerves on edge.

Yesterday – beyond the reach of the Speculum – they had staged a mass execution of peasants; the day before the westerly breeze had brought clouds of mephitic smoke . . . but today not an arrow had been fired.

If it had not been for the distant knocking of hammers on wood – the army carpenters doubtless building new siege engines for when the weather changed – there was nothing to suggest the conflict between the adherents of the Mother and the devotees of her celestial sire. Now the moon was high on his sky path. Below him the world was a mystery of black and silver, and suddenly Ulban's sharp eyes perceived a movement. On the plain two teams of drongs moved from shadow into moonlight. One team pulled a mangonel mounted on a wheeled platform, the other pulled a heavy wagon which, as it drew nearer, the archer saw was draped with crimson cloth. Figures with masked faces and swathed from head to foot in red habiliments led the drongs and marched beside the lurching vehicles.

'Fangal, run to Brother Mias and tell him that the idolaters are bringing up a mangonel,' Ulban ordered. 'Tell him the strange thing is that they are without infantry support so he might consider sending out a mounted troop to welcome them.'

The two wagons crossed the charred path left by the Speculum's beam and halted just out of bowshot from Thaan's walls. The mangonel was chocked and aimed, and then the watchers noticed activity round the red wagon though in the moonlight it was hard to make out exactly what has happening.

Suddenly the counter-weighted beam of the mangonel was released, and a large object hurtled towards the city. It crashed on to Ulban's turret and to their disgust the archers found themselves splashed with blood and ordure. Their first thought was that one of their comrades had been struck by a boulder, then in the light of a battle lantern they saw the shattered corpse, its arms and legs trussed, which had been fired at them.

'All Father protect us,' they croaked as they crowded back from the burst horror.

There came the familiar thud as the mangonel fired again. Another body was launched towards the city. This time it cleared the wall and fell upon a crowd in the square behind the barbican. Packed together for a special torchlight procession to invoke the aid of the deity, their bodies broke the fall of the human missile and when they looked upon her they saw that she was still breathing and muttering in agony; they also saw that she had been stripped and her once fair skin was blotched with patches of scarlet.

'The Red Death!' someone screamed. The cry was taken up and men and women fought to back away from the dying woman. Those on the edge of the crowd turned and fled through cobbled thoroughfares and alleys.

Out on the plain the shrouded figures brought another screaming victim from the red wagon with its bars and coverings; their gloved hands quickly set him upon the specially-crafted sling and within seconds he vanished in an arc over the city wall. Again and again the mangonel shuddered as it dispatched its terrible shot at the heretics.

'Last one,' muttered one of the men bearing a naked form towards the mangonel. 'Looks like the turd has died on us.'

'No matter,' said the mangonel master. 'He'll carry our message just the same.'

The corpse with its ghastly plague marks was dispatched, the men in red – criminals who had escaped the garotter's thread by agreeing to this vile work – set the infected wagon ablaze, tore off their veil-like masks and started back to their lines.

In the city men and women ran to their homes and bolted their doors; anyone who had been close enough to the corpses which had been flung over the walls to have stained garments – even a splash of blood – was shunned as a pest-carrier. Everywhere locks were turned against them.

Within minutes every street and square was deserted, and from the shrines came the tolling of bells to implore divine aid against the terror. It was as though the Dark Maid herself and her skull-faced outriders were stalking the city.

Only on the walls did men remain uneasily at their posts,

their eyes fixed with hatred on the far lights and bonfires of the enemy camp. Although they were soldiers who had become hardened to mutilation and death in the last few days, they found it almost impossible to believe that fellow professionals could resort to such a horrendous act.

At the Black Cat Inn the landlord barred his door and shuttered his windows as soon as it was known what had happened.

'Not that you can lock out the Red Death,' he muttered. 'They say the contagion pollutes the air you breathe.'

Lorelle made the sign of the All Father.

'Have any of you seen it?' she asked, her face even paler than usual in the lamplight.

'Once,' said the Hump somberly. 'I was with a caravan returning from the Silver River. We came to a village where the Red Death had visited. Only a few folk were still alive and they all had the marks upon them . . .'

'The . . . the marks?'

'Scarlet stains on the body but especially on the face. That's what gives the distemper its name. It begins with blood oozing through the pores, then dizziness, delusion, flux, agony and death within the day.'

'But a few victims survive,' Merlinda said.

'Yes – so hideous of feature that they wear veils,' muttered Ognam. 'But must we talk of such –'

'What I cannot understand,' said Alwald ignoring him, 'is that if death comes so quickly how could the victims which the enemy catapulted upon us have lasted on the long march from Danaak?'

'When I was in the Citadel I heard a secret whisper that the Regent planned to make the Red Death his ally,' Gambal said. 'At first I thought it impossible, but then I learned that there are a few who can carry the distemper without actually dying of it, and such as they must have been brought with the army.'

'Only the Regent could have devised such evil,' Krispin declared.

'Was it knowledge of this secret which endangered you in the Citadel?' Merlinda asked.

Gambal narrowed his eyes and drew back his lips as though wincing at some evil memory.

'Forgive me, but even now my time at the Citadel is something I have no wish to talk about,' he said.

The landlord came over to their table.

'If you wish to drink you may drink free,' he said. 'What use is silver when the Red Death is upon us. I am opening my best cask of Ronimar –'

'Ronimar, eh?' said Ognam. ' 'Tis a long time since I savoured its dark smoothness. Strolling players can rarely afford such pleasure, so thank you, mine host, let us drink our healths while we still have them.'

'Well said, Master Fool,' said the landlord and he began pouring the black wine.

'Thank you, sir,' said Merlinda. 'A good wine is balm for the troubled heart.'

The only ones not to accept the landlord's desperate hospitality were Lorelle, the Hump and Silvermane. The novice sat back in the shadows while the guide and the horsemaid climbed the stairs to a warren of tiny bedchambers beneath the gambrel roof of the inn. By an unspoken agreement they passed his room, which he shared with Ognam, and entered the tiny garret which Silvermane had to herself. Through the leaded panes of the casement they saw the moon riding high above one of the city spires. Its light was enough for them and for a while they sat in silence gazing at it. Here the cries of alarm which still sounded in the city seemed remote, and calmed by the serene beauty of the silver disk they allowed themselves the illusion that the world with its terrors had ceased to exist outside the little room. Here they were the world.

At last the Hump said, 'I had wished that we might have been wed here but . . .'

'Priest no marry?'

He shook his head.

'We would have to share their heretic belief in the All Father,' he lied.

She gave a little laugh.

'No matter. I not believe in mother or father gods, only in life spirit . . . that everywhere, in trees, in animals, in everything that grows or breathes . . . even in horse-maids.'

She laughed again.

'And in men?' he asked.

'Oh yes, but they forget it when they make . . . gods like themselves. They worship . . . own image.'

The Hump said nothing. He had little faith in religion because he could have scant respect for a deity who had created him so misshapen. If there was a god, the Hump had decided on long caravan journeys where men are free to give rein to their thoughts, he or she must be a joker – a joker who got some lunatic amusement from playing tricks on his or her creatures until boredom set in and they were discarded like the toys of a petulant child. Had not their adventures since Danaak been typical of this – an obstacle overcome, elation, and then a greater obstacle! Now, after all the perils they had survived, they found themselves locked in a city with the Red Death.

Who, in their right mind, gives worship to a joker? the Hump wondered. And the only answer was: *the desperate.*

And yet, the Hump had to admit, at times of stress he had cried, 'Serene Mother!'

Silvermane yawned, placing the back of her hand across her mouth and the Hump was once more awed by her delicacy, both of gesture and body. He took her slender hand and gazed at it in the moonlight. It was strong yet finely formed, like the rest of her body, and though her lower limbs might be non-human they too, in the Hump's eyes, were part of her beauty.

'So tired,' she murmured, 'but not afraid . . . with you.'

Moving her arm, she traced her fingertips over the ungainly curve of the Hump's spine. This gesture of affection made his heart race. Although there had been no doubt of the bond between them, there had been no physical intimacy since they had begun the journey together. It was something that was never put into words but both understood the need to be entirely on their own when the barriers of restrain were lowered – secretly both feared that they might become figures of amusement to their companions. They remembered half-heard jokes about the mating of freaks when they became friends on the caravan journey from the Arkad woodlands.

Now, as she caressed the crooked back, the Hump suddenly thought: *You are my goddess.*

'No fear with you,' she said sleepily. 'Whatever happen . . . we . . . together.'

Her eyes closed and he sat holding her through the night, only moving to give himself sooma seeds when his cramped position added to the habitual pain in his back or to gently stroke the long hair, doubly silver in the moonlight, which inspired her name.

From below came the sound of talk, and at midnight there were stumbling footsteps in the passageway outside as tipsy guests sought their beds. Two came together and the Hump recognised the voices of Alwald and Krispin. They paused outside the door before going to their respective rooms.

'Would that I had never left Mabalon,' Krispin was saying in wine-weary tones. 'Mabalon . . . that was the place where a man could be happy. I should have stayed with . . . never mind. Too late now.'

'What price the quest . . . and that girl you left in the Peak Tower?' Alwald slurred.

'As it has turned out I have been no help to Jennet, and it seems to me the quest ends here –'

'Mabalon! Mabalon, I often think of it –'

'And the Lady Demara! We will never know if she births a son or daughter . . .'

The Hump was surprised to hear a racking sob.

'Sorry, Alwald, I did not mean . . .'

'Not your fault . . . so much you do not understand . . . no matter now . . . remember the old saw? The Dark Maid solves all problems. At least we tried . . .'

'We tried,' Krispin declared with the solemnity of intoxication.

'You know, Krispin, you are not such a bad fellow,' said Alwald with a sudden turn of mood. 'For a toymaker you have ac-ac-quited yourself well.'

Krispin laughed.

'I am honoured by your words, my lord.'

'Lady El-Eloira said . . . said there was more to you than met the eye when I said it seemed odd to have a toymaker on the quest.' They mumbled goodnight.

Silence fell on the inn, and in the city – as a chronicler later wrote – the Red Death held dominion.

FIVE
The Last Days of Thaan

Three terrible days had passed since the plague victims were catapulted over the walls of Thaan, and in those days the Red Death had danced through the city bringing suffering and oblivion to all it touched. The most common gesture among the citizens who had so far escaped the contagion was the compulsive glancing at the palms of their hands. Blood seeping through the pores of the skin signalled the death sentence – and abandonment by one's fearful neighbours.

The bloody warning affected the victims in many different ways. Some ran to the shrines where the tireless green-robed priests offered them the comfort of prayer and a place to lie until the process of dissolution was complete; some locked themselves away to meet the Dark Maid alone; others wandered the deserted streets in a vain search for friends to help them until they collapsed in doorways and gutters, and a few saved themselves the final agony by seeking the Dark Maid themselves with the aid of a sharp knife, a deadly potion or a leap from the city walls.

Among the hundreds who developed the pest symptoms every hour were a perverse few who, realising they had but a short time to live, endeavoured to revenge themselves against fate by passing on the infection to the healthy. These wretches stalked the streets or hid in alleys waiting for their prey, and when a victim appeared they would rush forward to deliver the contagion by seizing him or her and forcing a bloodied kiss upon them. Such was the fear of these unholy plague-spreaders that patrols of archers, their lower faces in swathed in veils saturated with spirits of wine, were sent forth to shoot on sight any they could find.

At the Inn of the Black Cat, its door stoutly bolted and its landlord resolutely depleting his cellar, the companions obeyed instructions – given to them by Lorelle before she departed – to remain indoors but be ready to leave at a moment's notice. She promised to return but could not say when. They tried to pass the dragging hours by telling stories – here Ognam did his best to entertain – or playing the board and dice games that the inn provided. But a time came when a story would die mid-sentence or a hand let the dice cup fall and they would relapse into silence and lethargy.

The only one who remained active and restless was Gambal who feared that the novice might be lying somewhere with her ethereal beauty transformed into the hideous pest blotches. He prowled from window to window, gazing out on the deserted square in the hope of seeing her slim grey-robed figure gliding towards him. At times he bitterly cursed himself for allowing her to have this effect upon him, and at other times he was in despair at the thought he might never see her again. Frequently the sight of a novice's robe aroused his hopes, but only for a moment.

Yet his patience was rewarded. On the morning of the third day he saw her approaching the inn between two archers with arrows notched on their bowstrings. He raced down the stairs and had flung open the door before the landlord could prevent him.

To his relief he saw that there was no plague mark to disfigure her almost translucent skin, and when she spoke her soft voice was as steady as it had ever been.

The pottons take her! he thought viciously. *Why do I behave like a moonstruck buffoon over this chit who probably never once numbered me among her holy thoughts!*

But as usual he masked his feelings and responded politely when she said, 'Forgive me for not returning before but much has been happening in the city and I had to be with Brother Mias. Now he wishes to see you immediately and has sent these two good men to protect you.'

'I did not know you could shoot the Red Death with arrows,' said Ognam.

'Worse than the Red Death are those who spread the Red Death,' Lorelle answered. 'Come now, and bring your belongings.'

A few minutes later – to the consternation of the landlord – they left the inn and found themselves in the dismal streets of the plague-stricken city. On every corner braziers gave off sulphurous smoke to combat the contagion, and as the fumes burned Krispin's nostrils a far distant memory was half-recalled, a memory of childish terror in which he clutched an unknown adult hand and in turn his other hand was held by a little girl who sobbed as they passed huddled bodies of grown-ups. He tried to force himself to remember more. Was Jennet, the child who had stumbled along beside him, his sister?

It was the hope that the mystery of their origins might be solved by the Lady Eloira that had led him to undertake the quest at her behest.

He shrugged. Little had he dreamed that it would end in this far heretic city. The memory faded, overtaken by other impressions, as they hurried towards the Great Library.

Nearly every door they passed had the protective eye symbol of the All Father daubed upon it, and in some of the doorways beneath it lay still forms with contused features. When the fumigatory smoke was briefly lifted by a fitful breeze from the west the travellers were conscious of an underlying charnel miasma that made them hold their breath behind their wine-soaked veils.

Thaan was dying.

When they had last been in the streets they had been teeming despite the siege, perhaps more so because of it; now, apart from groups of men and women in green habits hurrying on errands with the dedication of the priesthood, the only people they met were staggering plague victims or, once, a ragged procession of penitents swinging chains across each others' backs to atone for whatever wickedness it was that had caused the wrath of the All Father to fall upon the city.

'Heretics!' exclaimed Lorelle with unconscious irony.

When she led them into the Great Library they found it silent and deserted by the scribes. In a broad beam of light from the window above his table Brother Mias sat in his accustomed place, his table as ever littered with scrolls. Fatigue had reduced his fine old face to the likeness of a skull and he clasped his hands together to prevent them trembling. Only his voice retained its timbre of authority as he thanked the novice. She bowed and left the library.

'You will see her again,' he said. 'She has much to do . . .' He paused. 'Sit please. I have much to tell you and there is so little time.'

They seated themselves in a row of heavy wooden chairs normally used by the scribes at their trestles.

'I have to tell you that Brother Peto – may he rest in the Father – found something that will be of great interest to you before the sickness fell upon him.'

Brother Mias nodded to a stained parchment lying on the table before him.

'As I promised I had my scribes at work night and day seeking some reference to The Mage for you. They read through hundreds of manuscripts which referred to gramarye, prophecy and history but, apart from some references to his mysterious powers, they found nothing that would assist you to find him should he be alive today.

'It was Brother Peto who thought to seek through the cartography collection, and here is the result of his research. It is a map, torn from an ancient grimoire I should think, which shows his island situated close to a piece of coastline which there has not been time to identify.'

'We thank you for your efforts,' said the Lady Merlinda. 'Alas that this chart came to light too late.'

'It may not be too late,' said Brother Mias mildly.

'But the city is ringed by the Regent's army, apart from the plague . . .' began Alwald impatiently.

'Listen, my son. There is a chance that you and your companions may escape the city in the next few hours, so heed well what I tell you.'

The priest raised a glass of liquid to his lips, an elixir to revive his flagging strength.

'Do you know about the mines in the Drakenfel?' he asked.

'Lorelle told us something of them,' said Gambal.

'And the great subterranean river that flows beneath them?'

They nodded.

'Good. That will save some explanation, and time presses.'

He glanced at a waterclock.

'There is no way that our city can be saved since the

enemies of the All Father set the Red Death amongst us,' he continued. 'At the rate the infection is spreading it will only be a matter of days before there are not enough of us to man the walls. Perhaps it is the inscrutable will of the All Father that his city should reach the end of its span – it is impossible for mere mortals to comprehend the workings of the divine consciousness, for how can we who are bound by the human concept of time begin to conceive a creator who is timeless, to whom the past and future are as the present is to us. All we can do is follow our destiny as we believe it was intended.'

Krispin and Alwald shifted in their chairs, uneasy at the thought that Brother Mias was about to lecture them on heretic theology.

'I must not disgress,' the old priest went on, sensing their apprehension, 'especially as you do not share our religious beliefs. As I have said, the people of this city are doomed if they remain within it, and there is no chance of them escaping from it with the Regent's army without. Therefore they have harkened to the priests who have moved among them and agreed to take part in a gesture which will not only wreak vengeance upon their enemies but will, in the history of Ythan, remain an enduring testimony of Thaan's dedication to the True Faith.'

Again he raised his glass to his lips.

'At the sound of the noontime gong – in two hours time – the gates of the city will open and every man and woman who is still capable will set out against the enemy.'

'But that is suicide,' declared Gambal. 'From the first your fighting men have been greatly outnumbered by the Regent's troops, and now there is plague amongst your people. What chance will they have?'

'None,' said Brother Mias. 'But we believe it is better to

die together in defence of our belief than to succumb one by one to the Red Death.'

'But you spoke also of vengeance?' said Alwald.

'Of course. Our enemies unleashed the Red Death upon us. Now we shall carry the contagion back to them. I doubt if many will return to Danaak, and those who do will hardly be welcome there. As in old folktales, the Regent has released an evil spirit from its bottle but no one will be able to put it back.'

'Serene M –' the Lady Merlinda began but checked her exclamation in time. 'Surely *your* religion teaches compassion!'

Brother Mias smiled.

'Alas, we have no time for theological debate,' he said, 'but what may appear a lack of compassion in allowing the Red Death to spread in Ythan may lead to a greater compassion – those who believe the blasphemous lie of the fall of the All Father may awaken to the truth, proclaimed by our example, in their extremity.'

'But your children . . .'

'That, my lady, brings me to the other part of the plan. A number of children – many of them orphaned but all so far free from infection – will be taken from the city to find sanctuary in the mines of the Drakenfel. Their flight will coincide with the opening of our main gate when we pray that the ensuing conflict will draw the enemy patrols from the eastern quarter of the city. In time, when the children are grown to men and women, it may be that they will reclaim their city and in order to prepare them for this they will be accompanied by teacher-priests – and you.'

'Us?'

'Certainly. I told you it is our hope that the Regency may be overthrown, and therefore if there is the slightest chance of your quest succeeding it has the blessing of all of us. You will leave Thaan with the children and by entering the mines with them you will escape the enemy.'

'But will not the enemy commander send his men into the mines when he realises what has happened?' said Alwald.

'That will be impossible for him,' said Brother Mias. 'You will see why in due course.'

'But if we are to hide in the Drakenfel how can we continue with the quest?' Alwald persisted.

'You say that Lorelle has told you about the great river that flows through caverns far below the mine galleries. When it was discovered it was believed to be one of the great underground waterways as described long ago by the great sage Omgarth in his *Geographia of the Underworld*. The miners of the day thought that perhaps this river could be used to transport stone which was quarried from the mountain and which was so laborious to send to far cities by caravan. In order to see if it was feasible a stout vessel named the *White Dragon* in honour of the mountain, was constructed far below ground to follow the river. Its timbers were of the strongest oak bound by brass and it was fitted with masts and spars so that, if it reached open water, it could sail like a normal craft.

'Before its voyage could begin the lower workings were closed and then came The Enchantment, and the mines of the Drakenfel were abandoned. But the vessel has remained in good condition and is ready for you to use to continue your journey.'

If the priest had expected a chorus of thanks from his hearers he would have been disappointed. While each experienced relief at the possibility of being able to quit the doomed city, the prospect of a voyage along an underground waterway cancelled out any elation – especially as several members of the party wanted no involvement in the quest.

'You cannot tell us where this river emerges?' asked Alwald.

Brother Mias shook his head.

'Then it may lose itself in the bowels of the underworld?'

'According to Omgarth's *Geographia* all subterranean rivers eventually flow into daylight.'

Alwald looked unconvinced.

'While thanking you for your generosity in allowing us to use this craft, it must be well over a century old if it was built before The Enchantment . . .' said the Lady Merlinda.

'Have no fear as to its condition,' interrupted Brother Mias. 'When we first learned that the Regent was turning his thoughts in our direction a presentiment – mayhap divinely inspired in the light of what has happened – made me order that the old galleries of the mines be stocked with provisions and that craftsmen should descend to the river and re-rig and repair the *White Dragon*. You need have no fear of her water worthiness.'

'But if we come out in some unknown place how can we use the map to seek the abode of The Mage?' Merlinda asked.

'The map is drawn in relation to certain formations of stars,' Brother Mias explained patiently. 'I understand that you, Master Guide, have great experience in taking caravans across unmapped wastes.'

'That is so,' said the Hump.

'Then you must have experience in using the heavenly bodies for your wayfinding.'

'All caravan guides learn to use stars as signposts.'

'Then you will have no difficulty in relating the map to your position when your subterranean voyage is completed.'

'But I am not . . .' the Hump began to protest but as

second thoughts followed his initial intention to declare he had no interest in the Pilgrim Path, he stopped himself mid-sentence.

'Yes, Master Guide?'

'I . . . I was about to say that perhaps I am not . . . as skilled in wayfinding as you may believe.'

'After bringing your party across the Wilderness of Gil no one could doubt your ability,' said the priest. He glanced again at the waterclock. 'Time presses. Soon it will be time for you to leave Thaan. To whom shall I entrust the map?'

'As Hereditary Lord of the River March –' Alwald began.

'Give it to Krispin,' said the Lady Merlinda. 'He is already the bearer of the Esav.'

'As you say. Go now.'

Brother Mias raised his hands in blessing and as they rose to leave he asked Krispin to remain behind.

'I have a favour to ask you.'

'Yes, my lor . . . brother?'

Brother Mias sighed.

'You see in me an old man at the end of a long life dedicated to the faith of his fathers, a man who has got more pleasure from this collection of scrolls than any worldy pursuit, and yet though my blood is thin and my time is short a remarkable thing happened – love came into my heart like a flower blooming in snow. To you alone I confess that a girl, young enough to be my granddaughter, has presented me with the priceless gift of knowing what it is to love.'

Krispin said nothing, not knowing how to respond to this unexpected confession.

'Of course she has no inkling of my feelings. I had no wish to lose my dignity in her eyes when we were together and strangely I did not desire any response from her even in my most secret dreams – to have at last experienced the sensation of love was enough. I was happy for her to be near me, I enjoyed our conversations, I . . . no matter.'

He glanced at the waterclock again. For a moment its regular drip was the only sound in the library.

'Because of my concern for her welfare I have arranged for her to go with you, though she will not guess that such was the motive behind my order. And the favour I ask of you is that – while you tell her nothing of this conversation – you will act as her secret protector unto death if necessary. I can meet the Dark Maid with a contented heart knowing that my dear love is in safekeeping. Her name is . . .'

'Lorelle?'

'Lorelle. Will you make me this promise, Krispin Tammasson?'

'I shall do my best, my lord. But what of you when we leave the city?'

Brother Mias smiled a slight, humourless smile, held up his hand and opened it so that Krispin saw a smear of blood seeping through the skin of the palm.

SIX
The Drakenfel

Perhaps it was a morbid fancy but it seemed to the people of Thaan that when the note of the noonhour gong floated over their doomed city it sounded like a vast groan.

Immediately all the bells of the spires rang out madly in order to attract the attention of the enemy. In the archway beneath the barbican the portcullis was winched up and the brazen doors of the city were opened to allow a band of riders – the green-and-gold banners of the All Father fluttering from their lances – to thunder out in the direction of the enemy camp.

Behind them surged an army of city folk, jostling each other in their determination to wreak revenge upon those who had brought the Red Death upon them. Soldiers in mail, priests in green, ordinary citizens in commonplace attire. Their weapons reflected their trades – a tailor carried his shears, a housewife her kitchen knife. Chanting a hymn of heretic praise, they flowed like a multi-coloured river across the plain. Most carried ghastly pest-marks upon their features, some were so ill they could only creep towards the foe, and some fell in their tracks and died before they could throw themselves upon the Regent's troops.

At the unexpected clangour of the bells and the thunderous voice of the mob which continued to stream out of the barbican gate, the enemy cavalry detachments patrolling the city walls spurred westward to be confronted by the amazing sight of the citizen army advancing towards the Regent's camp. Here trumpets sounded the call to arms and formations of infantry hastily assembled and marched forward to halt the heretic wave with a wall of shields and spears.

Meanwhile the cavalry charged straight into the crowd, the troopers swathing lanes with their curved swords until the very press of humanity halted them and they were dragged from their saddles by a forest of clutching hands. Expecting death, they screamed when they saw the blotched faces of the plague-stricken materialise above them, felt the harlot kisses of the Red Death upon their lips as they struggled in the grip of their captors.

A company of drong-riders sped across the plain from the camp with their metal-bladed whips making hissing circles, but they halted abruptly when they were close enough to make out the scarlet stains on heretic skins. Realising the horror that was approaching them, they wheeled and carried their panic to the main army.

From behind the uneasy lines of foot soldiers, archers unleashed arrow flight after arrow flight to halt the approaching rabble but, while hundreds fell, scores came through the hissing curtain to hurl themselves upon the shield wall, triumphant in the knowledge that the very spilling of their blood would bring agonising death to their foes.

On his tower the Commander of the Host watched waves of heretics immolating themselves against his infantry and cursed the Companions of the Rose who had demanded a quick end to the siege. Orders had been issued for the companies which had not come into contact with the plague-stricken to retreat along the old caravan road before the infection could reach them – a retreat led by the black coach of the Witchfinder General. The commander dreaded the terrible days ahead and, though the idea of using the Red Death as a weapon of war had come from the Regent himself, he knew that it would be he who would pay the penalty for this military error.

Who could have foreseen that the heretics would have had the spirit to turn the weapon against us! he thought yet again. His hand tightened on the hilt of his dagger. It was his only comfort.

Meanwhile Krispin and his companions followed the slender figure of Lorelle through the crooked streets of the oldest part of Thaan to a cobbled square. Three sides of it were made up of half-timbered houses, now blind-looking since their windows had been shuttered, and the fourth was a stretch of the city's east wall in which was set a small gate. In the centre of the square a fountain splashed pleasantly, and round this, under the direction of a number of green robed men and women a couple of hundred children fidgeted in frightened silence. By the gate a score of men-at-arms waited to escort them to the dragon mountain.

'They are ready,' said Lorelle. 'The Eastgate will be opened any moment now.'

Krispin, still pondering on the words of Brother Mias, noted that of all the people in the square the novice appeared to be the most calm. Her voice remained as quiet as ever and her beautifully formed face – its skin so fine there was a hint of blue veins traced across her high forehead – held its usual pensive expression.

A minute later there came a creaking of massive timbers and a screech of rusted metal, and the gates opened to reveal a view of the dark Drakenfel and a road of ancient paving running for half a league to its coil-like slopes.

'The way is clear,' called Brother Nahon, an elderly priest with a white beard covering his chest, who had ventured through the gate with the men-at-arms. 'Bring the children. And hurry. We cannot be certain that the patrols may not return.'

The teacher priests marshalled their charges four abreast into a column which they escorted through the gate into the open. At first the children moved obediently but the moment they were outside the city their courage failed and they stood as though paralysed.

'Want to go home!' a small boy yelled.

Despite the anxious hushings of the adults, his anguished protest was taken up by others; tears streamed down small faces and there were frantic calls for mothers many of whom, when they saw the mark of the Red Death upon themselves, had hastened from their children lest their very breath infect them.

'We must hurry!' Brother Nahon repeated. 'For the love of the Father, get those children to move.'

But the more they were coaxed the more adamant the children became. Many sat down on the road to demonstrate their determination to stay put and several were caught trying to duck back through the gateway. Desperation changed the coaxing tones of the teacher priests to angry commands, with the result that the children cried louder and became even more disobedient.

Alwald caught Krispin's eye and raised his eyebrows as much as to say, 'What a way to go questing!'

A frown even appeared on Lorelle's face as the sounds of childish rebellion increased and the men-at-arms scanned the pastures on either side of the road and muttered how *they* would soon get the little brats on the way given half a chance.

Then they saw the figure of Ognam go calmly up to the head of the ragged column. He raised the short staff, which was topped by the carved head of a jester similar to his own, and Krispin noticed for the first time that it had been hollowed to make a pipe. Ognam placed the end to his lips, his fingers moved over the holes which had been bored along the side, and a shower of silver notes floated through the air.

The crying faded as the children turned wide eyes towards the figure in green and red. The tune became more and more jolly, daring them to stand up and skip, to forget their fears and follow . . .

A little girl laughed, and then a ripple of mirth ran along the column. At its head Ognam gave a leap with his legs twinkling beneath him and then, without looking back, he began to caper along the road.

Jumping, hopping, leapfrogging, the children followed. Hands reached out to hands and a group of children formed a moving ring round the piper. On and on went his tune and the procession behind him tripped gaily in time to its promise of good times to come, of sunshine and games, of puppies and kittens waiting to play, of wonderful stories soon to be told, and always, always the dance . . .

'Serene Mother! There is magic in his pipe!' exclaimed Alwald as he watched the laughing children go past.

'I feel I want to dance with them,' said the Lady Merlinda. 'We have underestimated Master Fool.'

The men-at-arms grinned at each other and several self-consciously tried to mimic Ognam's cavorting steps. A smile even lit the careworn face of Brother Nahon.

'Keep playing,' he cried to Ognam. 'We will soon be there at this pace.'

As Krispin walked at the rear of the procession he was

awed by the way the Drakenfel appeared to rear higher and higher above them. Ahead he saw that the road ended at a huge tunnel mouth among a massive formation of rocks which had been sculpted by wind and weather into a fantastical gateway. It was from this entrance, he realised, that long ago the stone wealth of Thaan had been transported. If he let his imagination rove he could see that it appeared like a dragon's gaping mouth – the dragon's body making up the bulk of the mountain with its head resting beside its lowest coils like a sleeping serpent.

As rank after rank of children pranced from sunshine into the shadow cast by the mountain none wavered. Ognam's tune still filled them with merriment and the rock-framed portal was merely a gateway to all it promised.

Walking beside the procession the teacher priests were blowing into tinder boxes to light tar-soaked torches when a cry went up from one of the men-at-arms. Turning, Krispin saw a troop of enemy cavalry racing after them. He drew Woundflame from its scabbard and once again felt a tingle run up his arm as though some mysterious power inherent in the blade had awoken.

Ognam, alerted by the shouts of the men-at-arms, played faster and faster so that the skipping of the children became almost a run as they sought to keep in time to his bewitching tune. Into the dragon-mouth tunnel he went and the dancing children followed him while Krispin and his companions remained on the road.

'Hasten inside,' cried Brother Nahon. 'I must seal the entrance.'

'Do as he says,' said Lorelle, 'for you are about to witness an act of theurgy.'

At that moment a very small boy emerged from some

roadside bushes about a hundred paces away and began to toddle towards them.

'Run, Kemi,' Lorelle cried as several riders with faster horses drew ahead of the main body of enemy cavalry.

'Come quickly.' Brother Nahon's voice was urgent.

'Tell him to wait a moment,' said Krispin and he raced forward. Seeing three strangers – for Alwald and the Hump were at Krispin's side – coming towards him so fast the child yelled with fright and fell on his bottom. A moment later the Hump swept him into his muscular arms and began his ungainly run back to the black opening amid the rocks. Krispin and Alwald followed, looking over their shoulders at the galloping riders until they had to turn and face them or be ridden down.

The leading rider sighted his outstretched sword on Krispin's breast in the same way that an archer would squint along his arrow shaft.

Krispin held the grip of Woundflame in both hands and as he did so he felt the same magical surge as he had when he used the weapon against men of the Wolf Horde on the first day of the quest. Now, as then, time seemed to slow to Krispin, seconds stretched into minutes, and he was able to move to one side in an almost leisurely way so that the trooper's sword missed him by a handspan. He then brought up Woundflame in a deliberately aimed stroke and saw the blade part the fabric of the man's legging, slice the skin and then flesh, deeper and deeper until bone shone briefly before blood filled the wound and flowed over the horse's flank.

The shriek of the trooper went on and on in Krispin's ears as he turned to face the next rider who was almost upon him. He saw Alwald crouching low to hamstring the horse, and he raised Woundflame to deflect the enemy's weapon but before steel smote steel the enemy flung his arms wide and reeled back in his saddle under the impact of a javelin flung by one of the men-at-arms. At the same moment Alwald severed the animal's tendon and both mount and rider toppled to the road.

The next two riders drew rein as more javelins were launched in their direction.

Then time returned to normal for Krispin. He was aware of Alwald tugging his arm, of shouts and screams and the voice of Brother Nahon reverberating from the rock entrance. He turned and ran to it.

Krispin and Alwald were the last to enter the shadowy interior. They could make out Brother Nahon standing further along it with his arms raised as though about to perform a benediction. Sonorous words rolled from his lips, words that had no meaning for the two young men as they hurried past him, but which a scholar of Old Ythan would have recognised.

Outside, the reminder of the cavalry reached the entrance and dismounted. Several troopers had entered the tunnel when there came a sound that froze everyone except the old priest who continued his incantation – it was the sound of rocks stirring, a great grinding as stone moved upon stone, a screeching as formations which had stood for aeons suddenly slid into rubble.

For those inside the tunnel the daylight beyond the entrance was extinguished as an avalanche of rock sealed it, burying the troopers who had been on the point of pursuing the fugitives. A cloud of dust rolled along the passage which continued to echo with groans of mighty rocks which had split and tumbled to the old priest's conjuration; the floor worn smooth by generations of miners shuddered spasmodically as the mountain stirred and settled.

Torches began to flare and Krispin, conscious of his promise to Brother Mias, looked about for Lorelle. He saw her comforting Kemi, the little boy whom she had taken from the Hump, the latter's deformed figure having frightened him more than the sound of the rockfall. Gambal had materialised by the girl and, satisfied that he had no need to be concerned over her welfare, Krispin turned to the jubilant priest.

'You people work powerful magic,' he said.

'Not at all, my son,' Brother Nahon responded. 'I merely invoked a spell that had been set upon this place before The Enchantment. Then the idea was to seal something in . . .' He stopped and then said quickly, 'All Father be praised, we have brought the children to safety without loss, thanks to the Fool and his pipe. Someday today's exploit will be told as a folktale.'

SEVEN
Old Ythan

The firelight in the long gallery gleamed on the purplish-red walls of clean-hewn porphyry while here and there crystal deposits glistened. The children sat round several fires which had been lighted, mainly to keep them cheerful in their strange new surroundings. Thanks to the forethought of Brother Mias wood for these fires had been stored along with a mountain of provisions in a dry side gallery prior to the siege, and a steady draught of air bore the smoke away through the maze of galleries and passages which honeycombed the Drakenfel.

Outside it would be night, and the adults knew that the moon over Thaan would be shedding his light on a dead city. Stoically, those in the green robes of the priesthood tried to conceal feelings of loss and regret – it was their duty to bow to the will of the All Father and it was His will that Thaan had come to the end of its time.

And there was hope in the children!

Later – when the Regent's army had departed and all that remained of the Red Death was a scattering of bones – they would lead them out from this subterranean world and with the blessing of the All Father they might begin a new cycle in the history of the time-worn city.

In the meantime the children had to be comforted and cared for. Several times there had been outbursts of weeping and then the Fool would put his pipe to his lips and another merry tune echoed through the gallery. And when he was not playing he sat with the firelight flickering on his motley and told wondrous folktales.

One he was called upon to repeat over and over was about Princess Tig who was changed into a cat by a jealous step-mother with magical powers. But Princess Tig enjoyed being a cat so much that when the traditional prince came to give her the traditional kiss which would restore her to her human form she ran away.

'So when you see a cat be kind to her because she may be the Cat Princess,' Ognam would conclude.

'I wonder when any of them will see a cat again,' murmured the Lady Merlinda. She was seated in a corner of the gallery with the rest of her party.

'I wonder when *we* will see a cat again – let alone a princess,' said Alwald. 'For myself the river voyage through the Land of Blight was enough for a lifetime, but at least our boat was in the open air! Now we shall be travelling along some great sewer to an unknown destination.'

'You will, my friends,' said the Lady Merlinda. 'I shall be staying here. There is no more that I can do for the Pilgrim Path – indeed I would be a hindrance – so now I am going to do something for myself.'

They looked at her in astonishment.

'My lady, not in this darkness . . .' Krispin began.

'Yes, Krispin, in this darkness. My old life is gone forever and now I want to stay and help look after the children. Motherhood is among the many things that have been denied me. Perhaps I shall find this the next best thing.'

'You are tired. When you have rested . . .'

'It is true, I am tired. But it is a tiredness of the heart rather than the body. You, Krispin and Alwald, you have seen my house in Danaak full of riches and music and beautiful young women and dedicated to pleasure, and perhaps you thought "How rich that noble-born courtesan must be". And how rich I was if riches be measured by silver. Yet I knew that though I wore spider silk and samite, and my lineage went back to the early days of the kingdom, I was just as much a whore as some poor drab who hoisted her skirt for the porters in a back alley in the caravanserai.'

'My lady, that is not so.' Krispin sounded shocked. 'I well remember you telling Lord Alwald and I how you purveyed dreams . . .'

'That was true, for anything can be made into an art and I made an art out of whoring.'

'It is not my concern,' said Alwald, 'but I could not help wondering how it was that a daughter of a noble house' – he paused and gave her a smile to indicate that he was speaking as a noble himself – 'came to enter into your chosen calling.'

'That is something for which I must thank our Lord Regent,' said Merlinda. 'It goes back to when he had just become the protector of the Empty Throne thanks – if the rumours of the day were true – to the help of that hag Mandraga, the Lore Mistress who still spins her web in the Citadel.'

'How was that?' asked Gambal with eager interest.

'I know not whether it was her viperherb or sorcery which introduced the Dark Maid to the last Regent so that her protégé – the present master of Ythan – could take his place. The new Regent believed that certain of the old noble families who had ancient ties with the Kings of Ythan posed a threat to him so he planned to destroy them one by one, but in such a way that it could never be proved that he had engineered it.'

'I know,' cried Alwald. 'My ancestor was Good King Johan's Champion, and now my father lies murdered and my domain is held by the Wolf Horde which could not have invaded the Wald had it not been for secret help from the Citadel.'

'The House, of which I am the only daughter, was the first to fall to the Regent's scheme though years were to pass before I saw his hand in the affair. The actual work was done by the Guild of Witchfinders who accused my father of practising necromancy. In his library there were many scrolls on gramarye which our family had owned in the days before The Enchantment when high magic was openly studied.

'Those scrolls were enough to condemn him, and the Court of Heresy and Treason found him guilty which meant that his estates were forfeit and he would be put to death. At this point the Regent pretended to use his influence to save his life and the sentence was changed to one of slavery in the mines of Endor.'

She paused as old pain returned with her recital.

'My mother, unable to endure life without her jewels and maid servants, took the hemlock draught and, as my brother fled to where I do not know when our father was arrested, I found myself alone and homeless. It was then that the Regent befriended me. His agents sought me out and took me to the Citadel where he told me of his regret that he had not been able to do more for us but he had no control over the powerful Witchfinders. Because he had saved my father from the cauldron I was full of gratitude towards him and could not believe my good fortune when he suggested that I reside in the Citadel "as a poor compensation for the over-zealous acts of the Witchfinders".

'I admit I was naïve to accept this but I had barely reached my fifteenth season and my life had been a secluded one in our manor on the bank of the Green River. But I did not remain naïve for long – within a month I was raped.'

'The Regent?' cried Gambal.

'No, not the first time. His sensual pleasures are more subtle and perverse than for something so crude, and besides he had his pages if he merely wanted young flesh. What he savoured in me was my aristocratic blood, and his pleasure was in *watching* my humiliation . . . perhaps he was curious to see how much I could stand before madness claimed my mind or I embraced my degradation – what he did not understand was that degradation can only come from within.

'You, Master Gambal, must know that in a remote part of the Citadel the Regent has his menagerie and that is where I was led on an innocent pretext for my introduction to venery. I found that the menagerie did not house wild animals but the Regent's collection of *freaks* . . .'

Merlinda stopped mid-sentence. She dared not even glance at the Hump and Silvermane who were sitting on the edge of the group. She had become so used to them that she was no longer conscious of their physical oddities. To apologise would, she knew, only make matters worse so she continued, 'Even now I have no wish to talk of what followed; suffice it to say that when the Regent grew tired of his games with me he had me auctioned and a brothel-keeper bought me.

'Unbeknown to me, I had an admirer. He was a noble, a member of the Regent's Council, who had glimpsed me in the Citadel.'

'Lord Odo?' Gambal demanded.

'Yes, you may have heard the story in the Citadel. There must have been something about me which stuck in his memory – my youth, I suspect – because when the word reached him the Regent had discarded me, he searched the pleasure houses of Danaak until he found me and bought me out with a silver crown.

'He kept me for several years. Although his tastes were odd, he was generous and taught me much. At that time my interest in the Pilgrim Path – our family had always followed it – and the thought that through the quest the rule of the Regent might be ended filled me with hope.'

'Did he know?' Gambal asked, a picture in his mind of Lord Odo being carried to the dungeons by the Companions of the Rose after his forlorn attempt to usurp the Regent.

'I never told him because I believed him to be a man more interested in gaining personal power than seeing Princess Livia returned to the throne. But, as I said, he was generous and when he tired of me he gave me enough silver to start my career as a courtesan with my own establishment which, in time, became the finest house of pleasure in Danaak . . . until I was betrayed.'

'Odo was betrayed by the girl he loved,' said Gambal.

'Urwen! I had come to the conclusion it was her,' cried Merlinda. 'I gave her shelter when Lord Odo disappeared. She must have set the Witchfinders on to us.'

Gambal said nothing but his silence seemed to confirm Merlinda's suspicion; then she shrugged and said, 'What matters it now? I have done what was expected of me as a Pilgrim and now I shall remain here with the children. I have spoken to Brother Nahon and he has agreed, but there is a sadness as well as happiness in my decision. I shall miss you, my companions of the wilderness. For the first time in my life I learned the meaning of comradeship and it is something far more valuable than so-called love which grows like a flower in the heat of summer and dies at the first touch of frost.'

'It seems to me that not all love is like that,' said Krispin.

'Perhaps not to you,' replied Merlinda. 'We can only judge by our own experience. Perhaps the love you have known was mingled with comradeship.'

Krispin said nothing. He had a vivid mental picture of running past the houses of Toyheim with a laughing Jennet sitting in the wheelbarrow he was pushing just as they had done when they were children.

Gambal drew a deep breath. Knowing that he was about to give up all that he had schemed for ever since he left the slaughterhouse in Danaak, knowing that he was foolish beyond his own understanding, he still went ahead and said, 'Of course, I shall be staying as well.'

'What?' said Krispin and Alwald together.

'But you wear the Disk of Livia,' Merlinda protested.

'I fulfilled my obligation to the Pilgrim Path by getting you out of the Citadel,' he said. 'And I fulfilled my obligation to myself in escaping the wrath of the Regent.'

'But why stay here – in the dark with these heretics?' demanded Alwald.

'Better than going into the unknown,' he said and tried to sound convincing.

Will she ever know the sacrifice I am making so that I can remain near her? he thought. *And would she care if she did*?

'I prefer the thought of the unknown to the thought of staying in a cave like a potton,' declared Ognam.

'But you had no interest in the quest, only getting away from Danaak,' said Alwald.

'Now I am interested in getting away from Thaan,' he retorted.

'Perhaps you should stay and play your pipe,' suggested

Krispin. 'You enchanted the children with it today.'

'I wish to come with you,' said Ognam, his own expression almost childish in the glow of a nearby fire. 'Please.'

Krispin looked towards Alwald and Alwald said, 'You have already come a long way with us so I suppose we can put up with your foolery a little longer. And we may be glad of an extra pair of hands on that wretched craft.'

'And you can count on my hands,' came a soft voice and the slender hooded form of Lorelle stood above them.

'You mean you want to go with them!' Gambal almost shouted.

'My last instruction from Brother Mias was to accompany you on the *White Dragon*,' she said.

'But why?' Gambal asked brusquely.

'Master Krispin, take out the map which Brother Mias gave you.'

As Krispin took the map from the flat wallet which he wore on a thong round his neck, the novice raised the candle lantern she was holding so that the yellow light fell upon the folded parchment.

'Have you looked at it closely?' she asked as Krispin spread it out.

He shook his head.

'I have hardly had a chance.'

'Then look now.'

They craned forward to see a sepia map of what appeared to be a coastline and an island with columns of words and numbers below and formations of stars – they easily recognised The Griffin – above it.

'Who of you can read Old Ythan?' she asked.

No one replied.

'It is one of the subjects a novice must learn,' she said. 'The instructions on the map are in Old Ythan. Brother

Mias has sent me with you so that I can read the map when the time comes and translate the configurations of the stars for you, Master Guide.'

So that is how the old priest made sure she left Thaan, thought Krispin. *He could surely have had it translated for us, but this way he was certain she would come with us . . . and with me as her guardian*!

'Now it is time for me to meditate and I suggest you get some rest,' she continued. 'In a few hours Brother Nahon will lead us down to the boat.'

With a swish of her robe she walked into the shadows.

EIGHT
The White Dragon

In the light of the torches held by the men-at-arms the pure white vessel was a thing of beauty.

Krispin had expected to find a barge-like craft on the subterranean river but with her high prow and poop the *White Dragon* had the lines of a ship designed to ride the billows of the ocean. Twenty paces in length, she had two masts and yard-arms complete with sails which, Brother Nahon explained, would catch the air which blew through the endless caverns to give her steerage. She was moored beside a quay of natural rock. Above her mast-heads stalactites caught the torchflare and glimmered like pale jewels, but of the river all that could be seen was a slow-moving body of black water whose surface was patterned with arabasques of reflected light.

'If the roof does not hold its height we shall lose our masts,' said Krispin.

'The same thought occurred to her builders all that time ago,' said Brother Nahon, still panting from the long climb down passages and ramps and spiralling steps which after an hour had brought them to the river. 'The masts are stepped so that they can be lowered if necessary. You will find stores aboard – I saw to that, as Brother Mias put me in charge of preparing the mines should they be needed. You can cast off as soon as you wish.'

'Tell me, what was the evil which came to the mines before The Enchantment?' asked Alwald. 'I saw that the entrances to the lower galleries had been sealed with great slabs until recently.'

'I cannot say but there is no evil now,' said the priest. 'We found the lower galleries to be safe but to be certain I held a ceremony of exorcism.'

One by one the party crossed the gangplank to the bleached deck lit by lanterns hanging in the rigging.

'I thought you had decided to stay,' said Alwald as Gambal came aboard.

'I changed my mind,' he retorted defiantly. 'I . . . it occurred to me that on such a journey as this you will need all the help you can get so I felt I could not desert you.'

'Nobly put,' declared Ognam. 'Those are the words of a hero.'

Gambal looked at him sharply but could detect no hint of mockery on his moon face.

Silvermane came next; below her long skirt her hoofs tapped the wood in a way which made the men-at-arms stare. The Hump followed her and as he was the last of the party the men-at-arms heaved the gangplank over the bulwark and began to release the mooring lines. As the current slowly edged the *White Dragon* away from the rock Brother Nahon invoked a blessing upon them and the Lady Merlinda, her eyes unusually moist, called, 'Protect the Path!'

Krispin, who had gained some experience in steering the Fey boat along the River of Night, took the tiller and swung the craft into the current. The torches, casting vivid streaks upon the oil-like water, dwindled to embers and then vanished as the white craft was carried round a curving bend. With candle lanterns hung in its rigging and torches blazing in metal sconces fore and aft, the *White Dragon* was lit like a votive tree at the Festival of Rebirth, yet its lights were of little help to Krispin at the tiller. Unable to see beyond the nimbus surrounding the craft, it seemed to him that he was piloting a boat in a void.

'Take the helm,' he said to the Hump who, with a nervous Silvermane close beside him, was standing on the high poop.

Krispin then opened the light pack in which he had brought his most essential belongings and brought out a tube of thick hide. From it he extracted a slender object carefully wrapped in spider silk, and as he unwound it brilliant light gleamed through the folds. He and his companions were dazzled when he revealed the wand which he had taken from the eidolon in the City Without a Name. Although it generated no heat enough light flowed from its tip to light up the vast cavern through which they were sailing.

Holding it carefully, Krispin climbed up the rigging of the foremast and tied it to the mast-head.

His companions gazed in amazement at the wand above them and a score of questions were raised to which he replied that he had no more knowledge of its secret than they. It was a wonder from the ancient days which he had brought out of the Land of Blight along with the Esav.

'Why did you wait until now to use it?' Gambal demanded. 'It would have been of great use when we entered the mines.'

'It would have been cruel to the children to let them have such light only to take it away again and leave them in the shadows,' he replied as he returned to the tiller.

The light gave him confidence. He could now see ahead and could judge his distance from the rock walls whose veins of quartz sparkled diamond bright. It became clear that the water did not flow along a tunnel but rather through a series of connected caverns some of which were so large that the river was transformed into lakes whose banks stretched far back into shadows which even the wandlight was not powerful enough to penetrate. Here and there on these banks were fantastical configurations of stone which, at first glance, suggested stunted trees. Garnet crystals embedded in the stone branches glowed like lustrous berries.

'A land beneath the land,' mused Ognam as the *White Dragon* passed such a numerous collection of these formations that they gave the impression of a petrified wood. 'And if there are stone trees – why not people of stone?'

'Stone people!' laughed Gambal.

'If you had been in front of some of the audiences that I have you would believe in stone people.'

'When I was small my grandmother used to tell me a tale about an army that was turned to stone beneath the Drakenfel,' said Lorelle. 'It was a punishment for some evil they had done, and a spell was put upon them. And my grandmother always ended the story with, "And if you are not a good child you will turn to stone just like those soldiers – first your heart and then your body and lastly your face." I used to lie in my bed at night and wonder what it would be like to feel my body slowly hardening.'

She laughed.

'What strange tales they tell children.'

'There is much truth in children's tales,' said Ognam.

'Such as stories about enchanted princesses,' suggested Gambal. 'Sister Lorelle, do you believe the princess can still be sleeping after a hundred years?'

'Anything is possible if the All Father wills it,' she replied piously.

'Like the Red Death!' muttered Gambal.

'That, too, has its place. Excuse me please. I calculate it must be midday above so I must attend to my noon devotions.'

She crossed the deck and went into the cabin which had been allocated to her in the forecastle.

Gambal leaned over the bulwark and gazed moodily at the shoal of eyeless fish which swam beside the *White Dragon*.

Yet again he reviled himself for becoming obsessed with a girl who cared only for prayer and meditation – a cold heretic! – and yet as his anger seethed his inward eye held a vision of her tranquil face, downcast eyes and glossy hair which, when glimpsed beneath her hood, contrasted the paleness of her skin.

Serene Mother, why did I quit Danaak? he thought, but he knew the answer perfectly well.

Hours passed as the *White Dragon* was carried with the grace of a swan through the endless caverns and the travellers, wearied of watching rock walls sliding by, rested and slept fitfully. Each had a fear that none dared to put into words and which they expressed by surreptitious glances at the palms of their hands in case they carried the plague from Thaan.

The Hump was taking his turn at the tiller when he first heard it – a sound so low and distant that at first he thought his hearing was playing tricks after the prolonged silence which had only been broken by the creak of the vessel's cordage or the occasional plash of one of the pallid fish that haunted the dark waters. He strained his ears and through the rhythm of his pulse he caught it again – a moaning which rose and fell in forlorn cadences.

In his travels over the far-flung caravan trails and in

wastes where only the most intrepid caravan captains ventured, the Hump had encountered his share and more of the mysterious – of the unexplained incidents and unearthly portents that caravaneers only dared to put into words when safe and full of wine in caravanserai inns – but there was something so dolorous about the wordless dirge that it raised the fine hair on his neck.

'Lord Alwald, Master Krispin,' he called.

Krispin appeared, combing his fingers through his auburn hair which now reached his shoulders.

'What is it?' he asked sleepily.

'Listen,' said Alwald who followed him on to the deck.

'Serene Mother, protect thy child,' Krispin muttered as his ear caught the sound.

'I wish we knew what it was that made the old miners seal off the bottom galleries,' said Alwald. 'It would not surprise me if that wailing had something to do with it.'

'Lorelle,' Krispin called she emerged from her cabin. 'Brother Mias told us that when the miners delved too deep an evil came upon them, and they had to abandon the lower workings. Do you have any idea what that might have been?'

She shook her head.

'All I ever heard was that childish tale about a petrified army,' she said. 'And I do not think that lament could be made by men with throats of stone.'

'We shall soon know the answer,' said Krispin, 'for it seems to me the current is going faster.'

'That is true,' the Hump said. 'The waterway is becoming more and more narrow so that it acts like a mill-race.'

'Rouse the others,' ordered Alwald. 'We must be armed and ready to meet whatever awaits us.'

Krispin half drew Woundflame from its scabbard. As

usual it looked in need of refurbishing by a weaponsmith, with its surface dull and its edge unsharpened, and to Krispin's relief he saw that there were no blood-like droplets on the blade to warn of forthcoming conflict.

The river that bore the *White Dragon* was no longer like black oil; as it speeded up miniature whirlpools spun over its surface and bubbles seethed silver in the all-pervading light of the wand. The walls continued to narrow and this had the effect of funnelling the air current so that the sails became taut as though blown by a wind. Several times the yard-arms grated against rock and Krispin helped the Hump to steady the tiller.

As the craft raced on the moaning grew louder, an embodiment of despair that filled the travellers with corresponding emotions; honest fear would have triggered reserves of energy and courage but this filled them with a sense of doom against which it seemed they had no defence.

On and on raced the *White Dragon*, rocking and slewing in the current so that the travellers had to cling to rope and bulwark as they gazed ahead, trying to make out what lay beyond the light cast by the masthead light. Often, when the bow struck a crossflow, spray would fly over the deck like a cascade of pearls. Out of the gloom emerged twin columns formed like a huge gateway which seemed too symmetrical to be natural, but there was no time to speculate whether they had been shaped by unknown hands – or what manner of hands . . .

The white craft shot between them and emerged into a vast stretch of water with such velocity that, suddenly freed from the current, she whirled round and round until the men at the helm managed to get her back on to a straight course. The moaning filled the air about them and immediately they saw whence it issued.

Close to the opening from which they had emerged with the thrust of wind and current was a rampart of black rock upon which was set a row of skulls – but skulls such as the travellers had never imagined. They were so huge they could have only belonged to giants, and it was the subterranean wind, forced through the narrow tunnel, which caused the moaning as it blew through empty eye sockets and grinning jaws fringed with teeth the length of dagger blades.

NINE
The Pilgrim

Amazement and apprehension filled the travellers as they stared at the row of huge skulls which continued to sound their dirge in the subterranean wind.

'Giants!' muttered Ognam as the *White Dragon* glided past on the calm surface of the vast lake. 'But where could they have come from. This is hardly giant territory – not a beanstalk in sight, if I remember my nursery tales correctly.'

'Pox on your nursery tales,' said Gambal who was constantly irritated by the jester's attempts at levity. 'The point is – who put them there?'

They looked across the dark water as far as they could see in the wandlight but, apart from the skull-topped groyne and a dim shoreline beyond it, there was nothing but shadow.

'Do you know anything of this?' Alwald demanded of Lorelle.

'As I told you, all I know was my grandame's story about the petrified soldiers,' she replied. 'Perhaps those remains go back to the age when there were giants in the world.'

'In some places there still are,' the Hump said under his breath. 'In the land beyond the Cold Sea, I have been told.'

'Let us hope you are right,' said Alwald to the novice. 'They give me the feeling that they could have been there a long time.'

'But we shall not take chances,' said Krispin pulling over

the helm so that the bows turned towards the centre of the lake. Now that the *White Dragon* was free from the racing river current her momentum slowed and it was some time before the skulls began to dwindle astern and vanish into darkness.

In a halo of white light the vessel continued her slow course, riding her reflection upon the black water, until the Hump – whose eyes were the sharpest – called from the rigging, 'There is something ahead. It looks like an island.'

A dark mass loomed up out of the unnatural dusk, and as the wandlight spread towards it, it was seen that the Hump was right. There was indeed a rocky islet with more tree-like formations rising from its black shoreline.

'There's something else,' the Hump called as Krispin piloted the *White Dragon* round the left bank. 'It looks like . . . a boat! Yes, a proper upper world boat. It is moored up. Get alongside if you can.'

A few moments later those on the deck below saw it for themselves, a craft about half the size of theirs and without masts. A cabin rose from the decking at the stern and thole-pins set along the gunwales suggested that it was a small galley. It was held against the bank by a rusty mooring chain running to the bole of a stone tree.

'Anyone there?' Alwald shouted but the only reply was the distant moan of the skulls.

As Krispin ran the *White Dragon* alongside, Alwald, sword in one hand and a mooring line in the other, jumped over the strip of gleaming water which separated the two boats and made the *White Dragon* fast.

In the light from the mast-head he looked about him and called back, 'It is a long time since this craft was sailed. The woodwork is decaying and the deck is deep in dust. But we may as well look inside.'

The others crossed over holding candle lanterns and saw, as Alwald had described, that the decking was covered in a thick patina of grey dust which over many years had drifted down from the roof of the cavern. Carefully they walked the length of the galley to the stern cabin where Alwald had no difficulty in opening the double doors – they merely fell from their brass hinges at his touch. Raising his lantern he looked inside and uttered an exclamation.

Sprawled across a table lay a figure in clothing which might have been fashionable in Danaak fifty years earlier but which now hung in tatters. The travellers crowded into the cabin and looked at the skeletal body, its flesh desiccated by time and cold air and its skin like parchment.

'No sign of anyone else,' said Krispin. 'No single man could manage a boat like this so he must have lost his friends by the time he moored up here. I wonder what brought the Dark Maid to him.'

'Starvation I expect,' said Ognam somberly. 'But where did he come from?'

'Certainly not the Drakenfel mines,' said Lorelle. 'Brother Nahon unsealed them for the first time since the days of The Enchantment.'

'Brother Mias told us that rivers like this flow through the earth like the veins in a body . . .' Krispin began.

'So wrote the Sage Omgarth in his *Geographia*,' added Lorelle.

'. . . so he could have come from anywhere in Ythan, or beyond, if he had found a way of entering the web of waterways. Remember how the River of Night disappeared under a mountain in the Vale of Mabalon?'

'I remember Mabalon,' said Alwald and sighed.

'Most like he got carried in by accident,' the Hump said.

'Who in their right mind would enter this underworld with no star to guide and no sun to give life.'

'Unless he was seeking something,' Krispin mused. 'Yet another riddle to which we shall probably never get an answer.'

He held his lantern close to the dust-shrouded table and his eye caught a tiny glint. He leaned forward and from the brittle fingers of the unknown he detached a chain from which hung a coin-like talisman of yellow metal.

'The Disk of Livia!' Krispin exclaimed. 'He was a Pilgrim and must have been seeking the princess all those seasons ago.'

They all looked at the disk closely and found it identical to those worn by Krispin and Gambal. The fact that the skeletal form was a long-ago victim of the same quest upon which they were embarked made their spirits plummet. The improbability of success – and the possibility of ending like this luckless Pilgrim – filled their minds.

Krispin laid the disk and its chain across the fingers which had held it for so long and they filed out of the cabin.

Gambal was the first to climb back aboard the *White Dragon*, intending to help Lorelle over the bulwark but he forgot her at the sight of wet footprints on the deck.

'Serene Mother!' he muttered. 'What has left those?'

The prints were vaguely human in shape but the toes were unnaturally elongated and *webbed*.

Alwald and Krispin bounded across and Woundflame hissed out of its scabbard, no longer tarnished but glittering with its edge as keen as a barber's razor and the moonstone mounted on its pommel bright as though a light glowed within it.

'Look,' said Alwald pointing to the wet track. 'It has gone into the forecastle – and it has not come out!'

With their swords held out in front of them the two young men advanced cautiously past the masts while the others remained beneath the poop. They halted in their tracks when the door of the forecastle swung slowly open and the intruder appeared.

'A pikemaid!' exclaimed Alwald and he made the circular sign of the Mother.

The naked creature before them walked upright and was about the size of a half-grown child. Her skin was as pallid as that of a drowned corpse; her head was spherical with hardly any neck, and had a growth of short spikes in place of hair. The mouth was filled with fine teeth which curved back like those of a fish, her nose was a flap of flesh covering her nostrils and her eyes were round luminescent orbs the size of silver crowns. Her breasts were small and flat but as though to compensate their nipples were distended and black – the only non-white parts of her body. Like her legs, her arms were pitifully thin ending in large hands with webs of skin between exceptionally long taloned fingers.

At the sight of the humans she raised her hands in front of her and uttered a sibilant mewling. From the open mouth came a stench of decaying fish.

Krispin felt Woundflame vibrate; the silver wire that bound the grip burned his skin and it seemed as though the sword was eager to cleave the monstrous being. He raised the weapon . . .

Silvermane's hoofs thudded on the deck as she ran forward and stood in front of the creature.

'You not . . . hurt,' she cried.

'Get back,' shouted Krispin, alarmed for her.

'No . . . she not bad.'

Alwald reached forward and pulled Silvermane by the arm. At this the Hump pushed Alwald roughly to one side, then he picked up the creature and flung her far over the side.

'How dare . . .' began Alwald.

'You humans . . . hate those not like you,' said Silvermane breathlessly.

'She could have killed you,' said Krispin easing Woundflame back into its scabbard.

'She is a pikemaid,' declared Alwald, remembering the folklore of River Garde.

'I horsemaid . . . why not sword me?'

'Look,' said the Hump pointing to where the creature now swam on the edge of the wandlight. She raised her spindly arm as though in farewell and then the black water closed over her. 'She is harmless, only looking for food.'

'You could have said that about the dhrul,' muttered Krispin.

Without a word Ognam cast off from the galley, and soon the *White Dragon* was on her way again across the lake. For a long time no one spoke. Finding the remains of the unknown Pilgrim, coupled with the antagonism which had flared over the lake creature, lowered the spirits of the travellers. The Hump and Silvermane stood alone on the forecastle, silently gazing into the darkness ahead and emphasising their sense of alienation from the rest of the party. Only Lorelle seemed to be unaffected. She sat beneath the main mast, her hands tucked into the sleeves of her novice's robe and her face tranquil as her lips silently repeated an orison.

An hour later a sheer wall of rock reared up in the wandlight ahead as the craft was borne slowly towards it by the current.

'It seems we have crossed the lake,' said Krispin who still stood at the helm. 'But how do we get out of it? There is no sign of a tunnel mouth.'

'Perhaps the flow continues beneath it,' said Alwald with a shiver. 'And that would mean . . .'

'I know. We would be here for eternity – like that galley.'

As the *White Dragon* came close to the cliff Krispin swung the tiller to bring the vessel broadside against it and thus prevent the bowsprit being snapped. Held against the rock by the pressure of the current, the hull chafed gently against its wetly gleaming surface.

'Now what?' asked Gambal from the deck below.

Krispin raised his shoulders and let them drop.

'This accursed quest,' muttered Alwald. 'Hardship after hardship and each time it gets worse . . . Why did I let that old dame talk me into it!'

Krispin made no comment. He knew that, like him, Alwald had set off from Lady Eloira's high castle with more in mind than the search for the Princess Livia – in his case the rescue of Demara from the Wolf Horde. It was ironic that they had come so far on a quest that neither had originally believed in, though as the journey had progressed he become more and more convinced of the need to find the mysterious princess.

'Master Guide,' he called to the Hump. 'Does your sense of direction tell you where the river flows out?'

The Hump turned, his face looking haggard in the shadowless light that fell upon him.

'For the first time since I found my talent in the wastes I have no idea of where I am,' he answered in a voice whose muffled tone indicated deep distress. 'That talent left me when we entered the mines.'

'The air still blows,' said Ognam. 'There must be an opening somewhere for the draught.'

'That's easy to say, but how do we find it while the current holds us here?' demanded Gambal.

No one could think of an answer.

At last Ognam said, 'My stomach does not share the fears of the mind and makes its regular demand. At least let us end our hunger.'

At his words the others realised that they too were in need of food.

'I shall see what provisions were stowed for us,' said Lorelle rising.

'Look,' said Alwald quietly to Krispin. He pointed to where the glow cast by the wand dissolved into dusk. Krispin made out several dead-white forms half-emerged from the water, their round heads turned towards the *White Dragon* and their big eyes silver with mirrored light.

'They are waiting,' said Alwald.

He said no more and deepening gloom filled the *White Dragon*.

TEN
Waterhorse

Krispin set aside his empty bowl, drained his cup of light white wine – a luxury which had been included in the stores of the *White Dragon* – without relish and stood up.

'Never say die until a dead horse kicks you,' he said.

'Does that philosophical gem come from Toyheim's treasury of wisdom?' asked Alwald sourly.

'It is a popular sentiment that die is never to be said,' said Ognam, 'but there are times when such a sentiment has a hollow ring – for example when you are in boat on a lake without egress in the gut of the earth . . .'

'There has to be a way out because of the way the air moves through the caverns,' said Krispin. 'At least we can try moving the boat on the chance of finding it.'

'I agree,' said Gambal. 'We may as well try anything rather than sit on our . . .' He paused out of respect for Lorelle's sensibilities.

'The point is, Krispin, how do we move the *White Dragon* when the current holds it against this wall?'

'We push,' said Krispin. He went over to the gunwale, braced himself and putting his hands against the rock, pushed with all his young strength. For a moment nothing happened, then the Hump joined him and pushed with his powerful arms and the *White Dragon*'s clinker hull grated along the natural wall for several handspans before he and

Krispin doubled up panting with the effort of moving the vessel against the force of the current.

'You need levers,' said Gambal. He looked about the craft, then vanished into the cabin beneath the poop deck. A moment later there came the sound of rending wood, and then he reappeared with table legs under his arm.

'Use these,' he said, and himself used one of the legs to thrust against the rock. Following his example, the other young men heaved on the improvised props and the craft began to move a trifle more easily. Although the air above the water was chilly, sweat was soon pouring down the faces of the men. Other pieces of wood were found and soon everyone was pushing against the rockface.

The Hump remembered how, on one of his longest caravan journeys which had ended at a seaport, sailors chanted as they hauled up sails or turned capstans.

'One, two, *heave*,' he began, and as the others caught the rhythm the craft did move easily; yet it was slow work and at the end of half an hour they reckoned that they had only moved the *White Dragon* a couple of hundred paces.

' . . . and the tunnel might be a league away, if there is one,' said Alwald as he licked his blistered palms.

'Then what do you suggest, Lord Alwald?' asked Krispin.

'Look, there are more water creatures about us,' cried Gambal who had crossed to the opposite side. 'Would that we had thought to bring shotbows.'

The others crowded the gunwale and saw that the merfolk who had been watching them from the periphery of the wandlight had swum close to the hull of the *White Dragon*, and every moment more round, pallid heads broke the oily surface. Several had taken hold of a mooring line which hung from the bows.

Krispin's hand closed on Woundflame's grip.

'They want to climb aboard,' he said. 'Be ready for them, Alwald.'

Alwald's bright sword was already unsheathed and he raced to the forecastle ladder with the idea of cutting the rope.

'No . . . you not!' cried Silvermane. 'See what they do.'

At her words all paused in their preparations to repel boarders and looked beyond the bows to where at least a score of the merfolk had seized the rope.

'They . . . help.'

As the horsemaid spoke more of the merfolk held the rope and as the creatures began to swim with powerful leg strokes the craft swung away from the rock which had inhibited its progress and then began to move steadily forward.

'Mistress Silvermane is right,' said Ognam.

'Provided they are not towing us to some place where they can do us mischief,' muttered Alwald who had vividly recalled the chilling tales of pikemaidens – told in the Wald by his father's rivermen.

As though in answer to his doubts a strange sound floated up from the water – the creatures were *laughing*. More and more had appeared, gambolling round the vessel, their eyes goggling in the light which appeared to throw them into ecstasy, and there was great competition among them to get handholds on the rope. Seeing this, Ognam seized a coil of rope and, after making one end secure in the bows, threw it over the side. It was immediately seized by more merfolk and as they surged forward with the thrust of their webbed feet, the vessel picked up speed.

As the minutes passed by to become an hour even Alwald and Krispin lost much of their suspicion, realising that it would have taken them the length of a day at least to move the *White Dragon* so far by poling it along the rock wall. And they noticed that the current of air which moved across the face of the subterranean lake was gradually increasing in strength.

'Thanks to our fishy friends we may yet get away from here,' said Ognam. 'It is lucky that Master Guide saved the one that . . .'

His words were lost in a sudden babble of high-pitched cries which rose all round the vessel. Looking over the side, the travellers beheld a scene of confusion as the merfolk, abandoning the two towing lines, splashed wildly in all directions. Into the circle of inky water illuminated by the wand there appeared an ever-lengthening furrow of foam.

When it had almost reached the nearest swimmer the furrow became a vortex out of which reared a monstrous horse-shaped head. Everything happened so quickly that those looking down from the deck were left with a sickening impression of a heavy black body, huge luminous eyes and an enormous gaping mouth from which protruded tusk-like teeth. In the few moments that the intruder was visible the watchers saw the long jaws seizing a frantic merman, crushing his chest and the terrible teeth scoring his flesh. Then bloodied froth closed over both hunter and victim. Of the other lake creatures not a sign remained, only the two ropes dangling beneath the bowsprit.

Tears coursed down Silvermane's cheeks and the others were too sickened to speak. It was only after some little time that they noticed that the *White Dragon* was being borne along by a new current and a natural arch appeared in the rock wall.

Krispin seized the helm and steered the vessel into its centre to prevent the spars being snapped against its curving sides. Once more they found themselves in a narrow cavern which appeared to stretch ahead endlessly in the mast-head light; above it stalactites sparkled while layers of metallic ores gleamed in the walls. The current in the narrow passage was so strong that the water, usually so darkly smooth, was foam-flecked while the cold air was filled with its rushing echo.

Hour after hour passed.

Krispin remained at the helm to keep the *White Dragon* in the middle of the fast-flowing stream while the others, mesmerised by the endless rock walls, slumped on the deck. The Hump and Silvermane remained by themselves on the forecastle; since the incident when Krispin had unsheathed Woundflame on the mermaid they had withdrawn themselves from the rest of the company. Nothing had been put into words but it was as though the guide and the horsemaid were conscious of being alien in the eyes of the others even though Krispin admitted he had misjudged the merfolk after they had come to their help.

Again the Hump told Silvermane that if they reached the upper world all he wanted was for the two of them to journey to some remote place, such as the Arkad woodlands, where they could live out their lives free from the jeers and interference of arrogant men.

On the deck below Lorelle sat demurely, her dark violet eyes downcast and her expression one of contemplation. Yet when Gambal leaned on the gunwale close by she turned to him and with a simple gesture invited him to sit beside her.

He obeyed with alacrity, and at the same time sneered at himself for that alacrity. He was behaving like some lovesick swain, but then . . .

'I have watched you, Master Gambal, since you all arrived in Thaan,' she said in her gentle, slightly melancholy, voice. 'The others I think I begin to understand, but there is something about you which has a touch of mystery . . . Forgive me if I talk boldly but we have all been through strange times together and I have not yet been able to quell the imp of curiosity in my nature. Of you all, you are the one who has the deepest nature; you are not what you seem and that intrigues me. Tell me about your life in that terrible city where they blaspheme against the All Father.'

'I know naught about blasphemy, nor care,' said Gambal, 'but for the poor and those without favour Danaak can be a terrible place.'

'It was so for you?'

He nodded, and then found himself describing his life as a child after his father had been sent in a slave convoy to the mines and his mother was more out of life than in it through her addiction to Moon Bloom leaves. He went on to tell how from boyhood he laboured twelve hours a day in one of the city's underground slaughterhouses until the Regent's Revel Master noticed him and took him as an unpaid servant.

At first Gambal spoke from the heart. To unburden himself was a hitherto unknown relief for him and now he was able to describe his early hopes and terrors to the young woman who, for some reason he could not fathom, was the first person to affect him emotionally. But as he continued his narration he became more aware of the effect his words could have on the novice who listened in such sympathetic silence, and he began to tailor the tale to create a favourable impression.

He naturally omitted the way he brought about old Wilk's downfall by pandering to his vices and, knowing the hatred felt for the Regent by every citizen of Thaan, he did not describe how he had found favour in the Regent's cold eyes; rather he weaved a romance in which he played the role of a Pilgrim dedicated to restoration of the old monarchy to the Empty Throne.

Lorelle listened gravely. Occasionally she asked a question but her eyes never left the pale and innocent features of the young man, and sometimes a sigh escaped her.

And so more hours passed.

The *White Dragon* continued to race on its subterranean voyage 'like a toy boat in a drain' as Ognam put it. The jester offered to relieve Krispin at the helm, and to the young man's surprise he was an apt steersman.

'Timing, everything is a question of timing,' he replied when Krispin congratulated him. 'As any old trouper will tell you, unless you deliver the nub of a joke at exactly the right instant you will be rewarded by a resounding silence; so it must be with the tiller, a little too soon or a little too late and there will be a resounding crunch.'

'Tell me, if – *when* we get back to the upper world, do you still want to follow the quest with us?' Krispin asked.

'Yes.'

'But why, when – unlike Lord Alwald and myself – you are under no obligation?'

'Curiosity,' Ognam replied. 'Burning curiosity. It will be impossible for me ever to return to my chosen profession. As an escaped prisoner from Ythan, if I performed again sooner or later a spy or Witchfinder would remark me. So, if the Mother decrees that I must wander for the rest of my days I will wander with some purpose. If Princess Livia is to be found and awakened it will be the greatest happening in the history of Ythan and I shall be there, I shall feel the heartbeat of destiny . . .' He chuckled. 'That last line was from a tragedy I played in as a youth. I wore the mask of a nobleman who fell for a shepherdess. Ah, happy days.'

'I hope your curiosity will be satisfied,' said Krispin drily.

From the bows the Hump – who had spoken to no one except Silvermane – gave a shout.

'Light. There is light ahead.'

At his words there was a scramble to the forecastle in which Gambal helped Lorelle up the ladder and somehow forgot to release her hand.

At first they found it difficult to see beyond the radiance cast by the wand, then far ahead they began to discern a tiny half circle of silver. Minutes later the *White Dragon* swept out of the tunnel into moonlight.

ELEVEN
The Chasm

The moon was riding high when the *White Dragon* surged out of the cavern. His beams were so brilliant that those on the deck had little difficulty in seeing that they were following the river along the bottom of a vast chasm. Dizzy precipices of shadow and silver soared above them on either side while half a league ahead the river once more plunged into the mouth of another subterranean passage. Through some fault of nature the river was permitted this brief contact with the outside world before returning to the underworld.

At first the travellers were so elated at the sight of the moon amid a scatter of stars in the strip of sky between the cliffs – so delighted to breathe air that was not redolent of sunless water – that they were not at first aware that within minutes they would be carried back into endless night.

It was the sharp-eyed Hump who perceived the danger and shouted a warning. In alarm, they gazed about them. The steep banks between water and cliff were composed of boulders and screes of stones which had been rounded into perfect spheres by aeons of rushing water. There was no possibility of running the vessel aground.

Alwald and Krispin leapt up the ladder to the poop deck where they unfastened the anchor with desperate haste and hurled it over the stern. There was a clatter as it was followed by a length of chain which became taut as one of the anchor's flukes caught in the stones of the riverbed.

The vessel halted so abruptly the travellers reeled and had to grip the gunwales as it shuddered against the stony shore.

'Get off as quick as you can,' cried Krispin. 'The anchor may not hold her for long in this current.'

As if to emphasise his words the vessel lurched forward for several paces before the anchor was caught again. Ognam looked down at the strip of silver water between the hull and the black bank, closed his eyes and leapt to land painfully on his hands and knees. The Hump followed him with Silvermane in his arms, and Gambal jumped and turned to catch Lorelle.

'What about our supplies?' Alwald cried.

'Get ashore. We can come aboard again if she holds,' retorted Krispin. As he spoke the *White Dragon* shuddered alarmingly.

Alwald made a graceful leap on to shore and turned to see Krispin desperately climbing the fore-mast rigging.

'He's trying to get the wand,' said Ognam as he hauled himself to his feet.

'The boat is moving!' exclaimed Lorelle.

'Leave it! Leave!' the others shouted.

For a moment Krispin hung motionless, caught between the need to retrieve the precious wand and the fear of being swept away with the craft. There was a loud crack as one of the rusted links in the anchor chain parted and the *White Dragon*'s stern began to swing back into the current.

'Kris, for the Mother's sake, jump!' cried Alwald, his voice betraying unusual concern.

As he felt the craft move beneath him, Krispin slid down a rope to the deck, ran to the bows and took a flying leap towards the shore. The gap between boat and bank was too wide and the young man landed waist deep in the raging water. Round stones slide beneath his feet as he struggled forward and a moment later he lost his balance.

'Take hold,' cried Alwald who, wading towards him, held out his scabbard.

Krispin managed to seize the end before he was swept away, and, with help from the Hump, Alwald hauled him to safety. He waved aside Krispin's spluttered thanks and, with the others, watched the erratic progress of the *White Dragon* along the moonlit river. Without steerage the craft revolved in the current, crashing against boulders and rasping her keel on submerged rocks where she remained locked for a few moments before the surge of the water raised her enough to be spun away again.

Soon the mast-head light illuminated the entrance through which the river plunged to continue its subterranean course. The *White Dragon* was hurled against the granite side of the natural arch and splintering spars sounded above the rush of the water; then the once graceful craft was swept away with the current. For several minutes the travellers could see the glow of the wand dwindling until it was nothing more than a white ember.

They turned away in silence.

The *White Dragon* had carried them safely through the underworld and now that she was gone once more into the realm of endless night they were struck by a sense of loss.

'The wand,' Krispin muttered between shivering teeth. 'Another minute and I would have had it. There was a time in the Land of Blight I would have been rid of it but now I realise that a treasure beyond price has gone for ever.'

'It would have been useful now,' said Alwald. His words brought them all back to reality. Not only had the abandoned craft carried away the wand but also their food and shelter. They looked about them, aware that because of the narrow nature of the chasm the moon would soon cease to cast his light upon them. The prospect of spending the night in darkness on a narrow strip of pebbles was unpleasant at the best and dangerous at the worst. And when the sun rose high enough to fill the narrow gulf with her light would they find any way out?

They gazed about them uneasily.

The Hump's eyes travelled up the shadowed precipice which soared so high above them that it gave the illusion of reaching the stars glittering overhead; one star appeared as though it was balanced on the very rim of the rocky wall. There was something about this star which caught the Hump's attention. Unlike the others it did not twinkle, and as he screwed up his eyes to focus on it more closely he saw that whereas the light of the others was as pure as diamonds this had a definite reddish tinge.

'Unless I am fooled by a ghost lantern or will o' the wisp I swear there is a light on the edge of the cliff,' he said. 'Perhaps it is the beacon of some watchtower or even a lamp in a shepherd's hut, but it means there might be someone from whom we can seek shelter.'

'Provided it is not one of the Regent's outposts,' said Alwald drily. 'And there is just one other point – how are we to reach your light?'

'Oh, that is simple,' said Ognam who had crunched for some paces along the pebbled strand to view a section of the chasm hidden by an overhanging curve of the cliff. 'We just go up the stairs.'

'One day his jokes will be the death of him,' declared Gambal sourly.

'They nearly were, when I mocked the Regent,' Ognam replied. 'But this time I do not joke. Come and see for yourselves.'

They moved to where the jester was standing and saw by the moonlight that a line of steps, hewn in the living rock, ran zig-zag up the cliff-face.

'I wonder who cut this stairway,' said Alwald.

'Whoever it was did it a long time ago,' said Krispin approaching the spot where the flight of steps began. 'They are worn and weathered and I would think many a season has passed since anyone climbed up or down.'

He shuddered and it was not just caused by the cold of his wet clothing but also the memory of climbing down a steep trail with Alwald and the old soldier Emon when they set out to rescue the Lady Demara. Krispin had to admit that he had no stomach for such parlous pathways.

'The moon will soon pass out of sight, so if we want to reach the upper world we should hurry,' said Ognam.

'Lead on then,' said Gambal. 'And if you fall off we will know that a treacherous step lies ahead.'

Ognam felt a surge of apprehension at Gambal's mocking words and it was with reluctance that he approached the first step. Small pieces of rock debris lay upon the steps, which had been eroded more by water than by feet, so that instead of being flat they slanted alarmingly.

'Follow me,' said Ognam making a brave attempt to sound confident. 'Up we go.'

He had climbed several steps when rock fragments rolled beneath the soles of his soft leather shoes and he measured his length before sliding painfully back to the pebbles at the base of the precipice.

'On second thoughts, you had better come last,' said Gambal. 'If that had happened half-way up you would have carried us all with you.'

'Enough foolery – I'll lead!' Alwald said decisively. 'If we do not hurry the moon will be gone.'

He began to ascend the rock stairs with the confidence of youth and strength, and when he encountered dangerous debris on them he sent the fragments plummeting into space with a sweeping kick. The others followed, Gambal close behind Lorelle while the Hump, a grotesque shadow as he leaned forward, kept his hands on Silvermane's waist for fear her hoofs might lose their purchase on the rock. Krispin and Ognam went through a ritual of 'after you' which was won by the youth who finally brought up the rear.

The steps were so narrow in places that the travellers had to turn sideways in order to continue climbing. When Krispin reached these parts he sweated beneath his soaking shirt and, with eyes closed and outstretched arms pressed affectionately against unyielding stone, shuffled from step to step one foot at a time with the result that the others were soon far ahead of him.

As they climbed the moon reached the rim of the opposite cliff so that the lower part of the chasm began to fill with darkness, and Alwald realised that to reach the top in safety they must race the shadow which was creeping up the rock-face. All were panting now and they gasped protests as he urged them to greater effort.

'If the dark overtakes us we will be stuck here until dawn,' he told them.

At times Krispin found himself in the penumbra of the moon shadow and he had to force himself to move faster even though it was becoming more difficult to see where to put his feet. Above him Ognam panted and groaned, but he too was filled with a fear of being left like an insect on a black wall in an unlighted room.

'Soon be there, soon,' Alwald shouted encouragingly. He was now too high to be worried by the creeping shadow and he was able to see clearly where the steps ended at a cleft in the edge of the precipice. Several minutes later he hauled himself out of it and threw himself full-length on hard ground.

'Six hundred steps!' he gasped as his chest rose and fell like a bellows.

One after the other his companions appeared out of the cleft and collapsed, too breathless to talk. Finally Krispin appeared and, walking a safe distance from the edge of the chasm, sat shivering with his head in his hands.

When the travellers regained their breath they began to look about them. The enormous fault out of which they had climbed was now a gulf of black from which came the sound of the river reduced to a murmur, but the rest of the scenery was sharply defined by moonlight. Stretching away from the chasm the table land appeared like a sea that had been magically petrified. Towards the horizon rolled undulating ridges of sand from which formations of stone appeared like islets.

They realised that they had emerged from the underworld to find themselves in a desert, but all their attention was given to a long, graceful building on a rocky elevation overlooking the chasm. From its arched windows of rose-tinted panes shone the light which had caught the Hump's attention. Beyond its colonnaded terraces were sloping gardens in which fountains played and both flowering and fruit trees grew in profusion. In turn these were surrounded by a curving wall of dressed masonry.

'A palace!' exclaimed Ognam.

'In a desert?' said Gambal in his usual mocking response to the jester.

'It might be a palace of the Fey,' said Krispin remembering his experience of the Fey folk in the Wald. 'Surely it could be raised only by spellcraft in such a place.'

'Fey or not, it will provide better hospitality than this barren ground,' said Alwald, and with his hand on his sword hilt he marched in the direction of the mysterious building.

As they drew near Lorelle said, 'What beautiful perfume wafts from the garden.'

'And if I believe my ears I am sure there is music,' said Ognam. 'I expect that it will vanish any moment like that vision of Thaan we had in the wilderness.'

But when they reached the wall they found that it was no mirage; it was higher than it had appeared at a distance and was topped with spiked railings of age-greened bronze.

'There must be an entrance,' said Alwald and led the travellers along the wall for several hundred paces to where they found a gate of metal in which was set a large grille. As they pressed close to gaze through the lattice Lorelle exclaimed, 'It is something in a child's nursery tale. Look at those coloured lanterns hanging from the trees, and those statues . . .'

Her view was suddenly obscured by the face of a handsome youth.

'How can I serve you?' he asked in a musical voice.

Alwald drew himself up.

'I am Alwald, son of Grimwald the Seventh, Hereditary Lord of the River March of the Lower Wald, and with my companions I require shelter for the night.'

'I regret I have not heard of the Lower Wald but I can tell that you are of gentle birth,' responded the youth who wore russet livery. 'I have no doubt that Mesire Florizan will be happy to welcome you. When I announce you may I tell him how you have come to reach his door?'

‘We came by the river,’ said Alwald. ‘We lost our vessel and ascended the stone steps.’

The face behind the grille looked at them in astonishment but its owner was too well trained a servant to express his incredulity. There came the sound of rarely used bolts being drawn and then the gate swung inwards.

The youth said, ‘Welcome to the Domain of Olam.’

Book Three

Have you despaired of it, that remote land?
  Mayhap it lies beyond a northern sea,
Shrouded in mist behind some icebound strand,
  Guarded by fearsome waters flowing free.
  Maybe 'tis but a dream within the city,
  A phantom formed by plenitude of mind;
Perchance you'll find it never, great the pity,
  Until such time this world you leave behind.

– fragment from the works of
Ronal, court poet in the Domain of Olam.

ONE
The Domain

'I think you may have guessed right, Master Krispin,' said Ognam as the party passed through the gate. 'This could be the Land of the Fey.'

A path bordered by fragrant bushes meandered up the sloping gardens towards the building with its luminous rose windows; on either side large birds trailing iridescent plumage strutted across swards of trimmed grass; beneath flowering trees parchment lanterns glimmered in rainbow colours and fountains splashed musically into marble basins in which gold-scaled fish trailed veil-like fins.

'Mesire Florizan and Lady Sylva are enjoying a Night of Scents,' said the youth who, having introduced himself as Gifon, led them along the moonlit path. 'Being thus occupied he will doubtless wait until tomorrow to hear your narration.'

Alwald looked at Krispin and mouthed the word 'Fey?'

Krispin raised his shoulders and let them drop.

'Your domain is a truly beautiful place,' said Gambal. 'Is it close to a town or city?'

'You would need to travel a hundred leagues to find such,' answered Gifon with a laugh. 'And certainly you will not find the Domain of Olam on any map.'

The Hump had been scanning the sky, marking the position of the constellations.

'I would think that Thaan lay to the south,' he hazarded.

'My master will tell you – if he deems it fitting.'

When they reached the end of the path they ascended a flight of marble steps to a colonnaded terrace which ran the length of the building, and their nostrils were filled with a delicate perfume wafting from within.

'Come,' said their guide and led them through an arched doorway into a circular hall lit by silver lamps hanging from silver chains. By now the travellers were too fatigued and bewildered to take proper note of their surroundings; they merely received impressions of a series of chambers, each furnished with extravagant yet artistic taste and each hung with draperies of a different colour . . . blue, green, yellow. And on the walls, between the draperies of the finest spider silk which sometimes billowed as though caught by an exhalation of scented air, were bright tapestries depicting scenes so fantastical that the minds of the newcomers were startled when they caught sight of them in passing.

Finally they entered a large chamber hung in purple. Amber lamps glowed dimly, shedding just enough light for the newcomers to see that several richly clad people lay at ease on divans spread in a semi-circle. In the centre was a small brazier mounted on a tripod of silver by which stood a woman in a white robe with a table of flasks and caskets before her. From the brazier drifted a faint haze of smoke which carried the haunting perfume which they had first noticed outside the palace – for such it must surely be. There was something so sensuous about the aroma that the men at least, had they been honest enough to admit it, enjoyed fleeting images of the erotic despite their weariness.

In a corner, beneath an exquisitely crafted tree of begemmed silver, sat an old man drawing his fingers across the strings of a lute. The notes died as he saw the strangers enter.

'Mesire Florizan, I bring strangers who have just arrived weary at your gate,' announced Gifon. 'Their spokesman, Lord Alwald, tells that they came here from the river.'

From the central couch rose a tall figure. He was dressed in a doublet and hose the colour of dark wine over which he wore a lounging robe of black damask in which was woven a pattern of fancy-wrought flowers. When the light caught his face they saw that he was a man in his middle years; his thick black hair was brushed back from his broad forehead beneath which his face narrowed from prominent cheekbones to a narrow jaw decorated with a small triangular beard. His skin was pale, a condition emphasised by the crimson of his full lips, and his grey eyes appeared filmed as though his mind was focused on mental images rather than the reality about him.

'I shall be happy to entertain you,' he said in voice which despite its weary timbre held surprising sweetness. 'Alas, we have begun our Night of Scents and it would be discourteous to my Mistress of Perfume if the sequence she has devised was interrupted. Sup and then rest and tomorrow we shall meet again.'

He gave them a charming smile and sank back on to his divan with a sigh. Slow notes of the lute filled the chamber again and the lady by the brazier measured a dark powder on to the charcoal it held. Gifon bowed to his master and led the travellers from his presence.

'He was kindly but brief,' muttered Alwald who felt that if Mesire Florizan really was of the aristocracy he would have spent a little time conversing with him – perhaps away from his companions who, despite their qualities, were commoners – as noble to noble. After all he, Alwald, was now the Hereditary River Lord which meant much more than a lordling of a tiny domain in the middle of barren wasteland. For the moment he forgot that since the Wolf Horde had crossed the River of Night he was a homeless wanderer whose only possession was his sword.

'Fret not if my master was occupied,' said the youth. 'Here in Olam time is slave not master; there is enough time to encompass everything and the master will be just as interested to converse with you at his leisure as if you had been able to tell him your tale while you still dripped river water.'

He led them back through the succession of chambers to a long narrow room whose tall many-paned windows were open to a balcony whose balustrade overlooked the chasm from which they had so recently escaped. A long table of wood of a deep reddish colour stood in the centre and Gifon gestured them to be seated in chairs carved from similar timber. A young woman with a grave face, dressed in the same rich livery as the youth, appeared with a tray on which were bowls of clear broth.

While the others began their supper, Gifon took Alwald and Krispin into an antechamber where unseen hands had laid out dry apparel for them.

'What sort of a place is this?' said Alwald quietly to Krispin when they returned to the dining chamber.

'When we reached Mabalon after the Land of Blight it was so . . . so *wholesome*,' Krispin replied. 'But it seems to me that this time we have reached a very different haven. There is more than a touch of strangeness here.'

'I agree, yet it is not necessarily evil. Do you think there is sorcery in the air?'

'Only perfume,' said Ognam, 'but I would wager my motley that some powerful drug was mingled with it.'

The servant brought platters of parboiled fish and fowl

in rare sauces with servings of steamed vegetables.

'How do you get such delicacies in the midst of a desert?' asked Alwald with more than idle curiosity.

'The Domain – it provides for all our needs,' was the reply.

The final course was fruit served with yellow cream, which, though all agreed was delicious, no one could name. As they were finishing it the quiet servant brought in a tray of cups from which floated aromatic vapour.

Remembering Ognam's words, Krispin asked the nature of the drink.

'It is an infusion of dried leaves from an aromatic shrub which grows in the Domain,' the servant explained. 'It is soothing when one has been stressed and will comfort your bodies.'

The first mouthful of the hot liquid tasted slightly bitter to the travellers, but the next they took made their palates tingle pleasurably and by the time they had drained their cups they felt that the servant had not exaggerated.

As soon as the repast was completed Gifon reappeared and conducted them up several flights of stairs – which demonstrated that the building was much larger than they thought when they first beheld it – and along a passage with ornate doors which opened into sleeping apartments.

As the travellers muttered their goodnights and entered the rooms they found them to be as richly furnished as the rest of the palace. Lamps of scented oil burned on tables of black wood inlaid with ivory scenes of courtly life, and in the soft light the rich hues of tapestry appeared to glow on the walls. Pale furs of extraordinary lightness lay on each bed. In the far wall of every apartment was a door in which were set panes of the rose-tinted glass. These doors opened on to a broad terrace which was decorated with flowering shrubs in urns between which were set benches of snow-white marble.

Gratefully Krispin removed his borrowed robe, lay down with Woundflame unsheathed beside him and covered himself with the fur.

In the next chamber Gambal remained fully dressed. For a while he sat on the bed like one deep in thought and then he crossed to the door where he listened for at least a minute. The only sound which reached his ears was the faint notes of a lute, probably issuing from the purple chamber where Mesire Florizan dreamed on his divan while perfume after perfume drifted on the warm air.

Satisfied, he walked out on to the terrace which was brilliantly lit by the moon still high in the western sky, and leaning his arms on the balustrade he gazed over an area of the Domain made up of dark copses with a stream coiling like a leaden snake between them. The trees ended abruptly at the wall beyond which desert undulated in alternate stripes of silver and shadow.

Somewhere in the park-like woodland a night bird sang. From his pocket Gambal removed a small mirror.

For a long time his pale reflection stared back at him, then gradually the glass clouded as though by warm breath. This opaqueness began to ripple like ascending smoke and through it appeared a series of indistinct images, each materialising for a heartbeat and dissolving again to take on another shape.

Hardly blinking, Gambal gazed at the ever-changing shadows with apprehension as though the glass he held had a mysterious power over him, a power to penetrate his expressionless mask and abstract his innermost thoughts, enslave him . . .

The swirling slowed, reforming into a suggestion of a

face, a face so lined and worn by the years that he could not tell whether it was fully delineated or still partly composed of smoke. For a moment the image melted into another – Gambal cried aloud as for a second the features of a beautiful young woman stared from the glass. The picture hazed and the ancient face was back, the face that Gambal knew so well that he shuddered.

Mandraga!

He felt her slate blue eyes bore into his. The lips began to move . . .

From the end of the terrace came the sound of a door closing.

In one rapid movement Gambal thrust the mirror back into the pocket of his jerkin, then moved so that he was hidden by a tall urn from which cascaded creepers with myriads of carmine flowers. Gazing from the shadows he saw a grey figure pace slowly along with cowled head bent.

Lorelle passed the urn and a short distance further on she turned and stood looking up at the moon with her hands resting on the balustrade. Suddenly she raised them and with an emphatic gesture threw back her hood.

Gambal had never seen her without it, and the sight of her gleaming black tresses flowing unruly to her shoulders startled him – he had always judged her to be beautiful from her face but how beautiful he only just realised and a breathless excitement overlaid his concern about the mirror.

An expression to describe her floated into his mind: the Lily Maid.

Silently he drank in the picture of her in the moonlight. Her lips were compressed and her features, alabaster in the cold radiance, showed no expression – until he noticed a tear was glittering on her cheek.

Impatiently she rubbed it away with her slender fingers, but another appeared and a single sob racked her.

Gambal walked forward softly and placed his hand lightly on her shoulder. She did not start but turned and gave a slight melancholy smile when she saw it was him.

'You came out to weep alone,' he said. 'If you wish I shall leave you to your tears.'

She shook her head slowly.

'I felt the chamber was closing upon me,' she replied. 'I had to come out into the open.'

'Mayhap that was caused by our underground voyage,' he said, 'but it does not explain your sadness.'

'No. My sadness has been with me for a long while.'

'Yet you gave no hint of it. You have always been so calm, so . . . so like someone completely sure of everything.'

She gave a bitter laugh.

'How I wish that were true. All I have is doubts – and discontent. Much of the latter is your fault.'

'How can that be?'

'When I first met you, after you had come to Thaan by night, I realised that you were different to the others. It was something deep inside you, and at the time I could not define it.'

'You always seemed so devout I did not think you even noticed me.'

'I was devout – or I was trying to be – but being a novice did not blind me. It was only when we talked on the *White Dragon* that I realised what it was about you that affected me so. *You try to shape your own destiny*. When you told me how you refused to spend the rest of your days in the slaughterhouse where fate had placed you, how you became the Revel Master and then arranged the escape of the Pilgrims from the Citadel . . . then I admired you for your determination to alter the scheme of things. And in the light of this I saw that my own life is nothing but a failure.'

Gambal, for all his cynicism, felt genuinely shocked at the vehemence of her words.

'But you had your faith –'

'Faith!' exclaimed Lorelle. 'I tried to have faith – no one will ever know how hard I tried to believe, but . . .'

Her voice trailed away.

'Then why did you become a novice?'

'Ah, I had belief then. I did not know my parents; they died when I was a baby and Brother Mias became my guardian, so perhaps it was natural that my thoughts should turn to the green robe. That was quite usual in Thaan: the priesthood was not apart from the people as it is with those who believe in the false doctrine of the Mother. You must have noticed that there were hundreds and hundreds of men and women who were in the priesthood, many of them doing ordinary work as well as their religious duties.'

Gambal had a sudden picture of a thoroughfare in Thaan in which a quarter of those thronging it wore green.

'I suppose as a girl I was very anxious to become holy. I studied hard and was rewarded by working close to my guardian Brother Mias, but even he could not help me when I found I could no longer accept the doctrines. He was patient but he could not convince me . . .'

She looked thoughtfully over the trees.

'You see, the scriptures taught that the All Father made everything, including Time, which means that for mortals everything is decreed for their terms of life. I found that hard to accept as I want to feel it is I who am responsible for my fate.'

To Gambal such questions had never entered his

head – he had never had time for the luxury of abstract thought – but he could see that the question was of supreme importance to the young novice and, because of the attraction she held for him, he listened with sympathy.

'I tried to come to terms with it through prayer and meditation,' she continued. 'But even as I meditated it occurred to me that I was following a course which had been intended since the beginning of things. And then, with the Red Death, came my blasphemy.'

'Blasphemy?'

'Yes. Our belief is that we are children of the All Father, but I could not help thinking that only a cruel madman would torture his children – his very own creations – with plague and warfare as a reward for venerating him.'

'Did not your elders have an answer?' asked Gambal.

'Oh yes. "Who are we to question the divine will?" A question answered by a question.'

'If, long ago, people felt as you do I can understand how they wanted to believe in a merciful Mother. But why let these questions trouble you so?'

'Because since I was small I wanted to lead a devout life. I dedicated myself to the All Father, I tried to have faith without proof, I vowed to renounce the flesh and . . .'

Such was her emotion that her voice choked.

Gambal, half amused and half touched by her distress, tightened his arm about her and felt a sensation of delight at the closeness – a sensation that he had never known in the Citadel with the studied eroticism of his would-be mistresses.

'Forgive me,' she said. 'I have no right to inflict my sorrows upon you. Tell me, Gambal, what do you believe in?'

'Myself,' he replied without a moment's thought.

She turned her face to him, and he saw that there was a new light in her violet eyes and a faint flush on her normally wan cheeks.

'That is wonderful. You have given me the answer I needed to hear. I was right when I thought there was something special about you.'

Gambal, amazed and gratified at the effect of his single word, could think of nothing further to say.

'*Myself*,' she murmured. 'From this moment no more devotion to an uncaring god; I renounce my unnatural vows, and I shall live for . . . *myself*.'

She stepped back from Gambal and for a moment stood still, her hands unfastening the girdle of her habit. With a soft rustle the material slid to the marble paving; beneath it she was naked and Gambal stared in wonder. There had been moments in his obsession with her when his carnal fancy had tried to picture what she was like under her novice's gown, but he had never thought he would ever see her so revealed.

In the searing moonlight she appeared like a slender statue of alabaster, except for the darkly aureoled nipples of her childish breasts and the luxuriant hair which for Gambal brought humanity to the statue; that and the new expression in her eyes which had been downcast for as long as he had known her.

Without a word Gambal went on his knees before her, his arms embracing her thighs, his face turned up to hers with an expression that no one who had known him would have recognised – tenderness. He rose, lifting her as he did so, and she laughed softly and twined her fingers cruelly in his hair.

'My room,' she murmured. He altered his hold upon her so that she was cradled in his arms and thus he carried her along the terrace to where her door hung open. Inside the sleeping apartment he laid her on the soft fur coverlet.

'The light,' she said. 'Later, if this should happen again and if it is your wish you may leave it burning but tonight . . . for the breaking of my vow I need dark.'

He blew into the lamp and the acrid smell of the extinguished wax filled the room, reminding her of the times she had extinguished altar candles. But that fleeting memory had no effect on her determination.

'Gambal,' she said while he undressed in the dark, 'I fear there will be little pleasure in this for you for I renounced the flesh before my cycle came and I have been true to the vow. But at least you will earn my gratitude at freeing me from what I was unsuited for.'

'All will be well,' he said as he lay beside her and felt her warmth against his skin. 'We have the night.'

TWO
Florizan Entertains

The following evening Gifon led the travellers on to one of the palace terraces where a long banqueting table had been set. Goblets of rose crystal, exquisite white porcelain, spoons of silver and burnished knives with handles of rare black amber sparkled and gleamed in the light of beeswax candles set in elaborately wrought candelabra. Their flames hardly flickered in the still air which was filled with the faint lament of the river rising out of the chasm.

'Mesire Florizan will join you in a few minutes,' Gifon told them. 'Meanwhile may I suggest you sample the wine which comes from our vineyard.'

Servants appeared with trays from which they proffered the guests cups of pale sparkling wine. Krispin took one and sauntered to the balustrade from where he gazed into the chasm. It was the same hour at which they had entered it in the *White Dragon*; the moonlight shone into its depths and the river appeared like a thread of quicksilver.

When Krispin had opened his eyes towards noon that morning a servant had conducted him to a bath-house where he washed away grime and fatigue in steaming water redolent of perfumed oils. Then a barber trimmed his reddish beard – which had only begun to grow since he had set out on the quest, as though the ordeals through which he had passed in some way conferred manhood upon him.

His new clothing was the most costly he had ever worn; shoes of softest leather, breeches of black velvet, a tunic of the same material on which was worked a geometrical pattern in crimson thread beneath which he wore a shirt of dark green spider silk. When he had tried to express gratitude for such generosity Gifon brushed his thanks aside with the words, 'The master would expect you to be suitably dressed at his table this evening. On such matters he is highly sensitive.'

During the afternoon he had wandered at will outside the palace, exploring the paths that ran among woods and orchards, across flowered meadows and through formal gardens sweet with the scent of flowers and herbs. In a walled garden he had sat on a stone bench beneath a lichened satyr and dozed and dreamed, the first time in a long while that he had felt free to do so. In his mind he wandered again in the High Wald with Jennet. Yet again he wondered whether the Lady Eloira would solve the mystery of their origins and be able to one day tell him whether Jennet, with whom he had been found wandering in the forest as a child, was indeed his sister or whether they would be able to marry.

Now as he gazed over the chasm a hand fell upon his shoulder. He turned and saw Alwald, and felt a twitch of amusement that he – presumably because he was the Hereditary Lord of the River March – had been provided with even richer clothing than the others. His blue doublet was richly embroidered with golden thread and he had lace at wrist and throat. Like Krispin he had had the services of the barber; his moustache was trimmed as it had been when he lived in River Garde and his fair hair had been washed and oiled.

'I sought you this afternoon but without success.'

'I wandered in the Domain,' Krispin replied.

'Did you learn anything about it? I tried to question the servants but while they remained respectful they managed to tell me nothing. Where do you think we are?'

'I expect Mesire Florizan, the prince of the palace, will tell us in his own time, but there is no doubt that it is a marvel. Today I saw trees and animals that I have never seen before yet beyond the wall there is a waste of rock and sand far more barren than the Wilderness of Gil.'

'I wonder if this Florizan is a sorcerer,' mused Alwald.

'Whatever he is, he is generous. Although he knows nothing of us, we are treated like honoured guests. Look how he has arrayed us.'

He nodded towards their companions. Gambal had exchanged his plain dark clothes for a suit of yellow, the Hump wore a cloak of black tabaret which softened his crooked outline and beside him Silvermane was dressed in a long gown of indigo which emphasised the bright silver of her hair. Only Ognam had refused to exchange his motley.

'It seems our little novice has discarded her habit,' murmured Alwald as Lorelle walked on to the terrace. She was dressed in filmy spider silk shot with delicate amethystine, and her raven hair, so long hidden beneath a cowl, hung down to her breasts in two thick plaited braids. Even her face, which had always been piously downcast, appeared to have lost some of its pallor.

'And she seems to have thrown away her doleful expression with it,' said Krispin.

From the far end of the terrace came the strains of a flute and dulcimer, and through the archway appeared a dwarf in a miniature suit of armour. His nose would have been far too large on a man of normal proportions but behind it his eyes had a shrewd glitter. Raising the emblems of his office, a toy mace and an antique lamp, in gloved hands, he cried in a harsh voice, 'Mesire Florizan, his consort the Lady Sylva and his heir Lord Ugo.'

Clad in deep purple adorned with river pearls, the tall master of the Domain strode on to the terrace. On his arm was a woman whose face was still youthful though her long hair, bound by a silver band inlaid with turquoise, was snow white. In contrast to the rest of the company, her dress of grey samite was simple and unadorned.

Behind them walked their son Ugo who, in his twentieth year, was a younger version of his father though perhaps lacking some of his elegant deportment. And whereas Florizan's expression was habitually benign, Ugo had a look of arrogance which the young women of the Domain found highly attractive.

Stalking beside him, and held by a chain fastened to its golden collar, was an animal the like of which was unknown to the travellers. He was a lithe cat-like beast standing as high as his master's knee; his mask and limbs were black, the fur of his underbelly was cream. His back was cinnamon but most remarkable were his eyes which shone like sapphires. Several ladies and gentleman, obviously members of the Domain's small court, followed the young man and his pet.

Mesire Florizan and his lady went to the head of the table and with a graceful gesture of his hand the prince invite the travellers to take places indicated by servants who, throughout the following banquet, stood behind their chairs ready to serve them from an amazing variety of dishes.

'My friends, be seated please,' he said in his melodious voice. 'I am delighted to welcome you to the Domain of Olam. Naturally we are curious to learn how you managed to reach us – as no doubt you are curious about this enclave in such a remote region. Now: I shall exercise my prerogative as host to hear of your adventure first, after which I shall be happy to answer your questions about the Domain. While we begin our first course – a pâté of carp and cream and spice which is the pride of our fish cook, a well-deserved pride I think you will agree – you may care to elect one of your number to entertain us with a narration of your journey.'

He sat down and looked with satisfaction at the plate which had been placed before him.

'In Olam we endeavour to raise even the simplest of things to an art, and the preparation of food ranks high in our attainment of this purpose,' he continued. 'Now, who will speak for you?'

The travellers looked at each other, each with an expression which said 'Not me'. Then all eyes swivelled to Ognam.

'Now is the time to prove yourself, jongleur,' said Gambal but for once his tone to the jester was less critical than usual.

'So be it,' said Ognam. He stood up and bowed to the prince and Lady Sylva.

'It appears, my lords and ladies, that because of my motley I, a poor wandering buffoon, am elected to recount a tale of strange adventures and terrible events. Normally the fare I provide consists of jokes and ditties, so if I cannot rise to the heights of minstrelsy that such a narration deserves I crave your indulgence.'

Florizan inclined his head and, leaving his seat, Ognam took up a stance on the floor of starstone tiles.

Raising his hand in the traditional manner of the old sagamen, he said, 'Listen!'

He paused until he was certain that all attention was fixed

upon him, then he declared, 'For me this story begins when I was a guest of that most benevolent personage – that most compassionate and ever-wise of rulers – namely His Mighty Magnificence the Lord Regent of Ythan . . .'

At the last word the jester broke wind with the loudness of a trumpet blast.

Krispin coloured with shame that one of his companions could descend to vulgarity before such a noble company, then to his amazement he saw Florizan and his court dissolve into helpless laughter. Tears streamed down his face and the Lady Sylva buried her face in her napkin to stifle her hilarity and Lord Ugo hammered his fist on the table with such appreciative violence that his pet leapt away spitting. The courtiers held their hands to their mouths to retain the pâté they were in the process of eating, their eyes screwed tight with merriment which redoubled when Ognam continued somberly, 'Decorum, if you please.'

When the guffaws dwindled to spasmodic giggles, he described his incarceration in the Citadel comically, but as the narrative continued on to the Wilderness of Gil his tone became compelling and the food in front of the guests remained untouched. The ladies paled at the description of the dhrul and Florizan leaned forward with his hand supporting his cheek as Ognam described their plight after the massacre of the drongs, yet his companions noted that he stuck to an agreement not to mention the mysterious fountains which saved their lives – they feared that there had been too much sorcery about it for comfort in orthodox quarters. Folk had gone to the cauldron for being involved in less spectacular marvels. Ognam adjusted the truth by saying that at the last minute they found a spring which enabled them to continue to Thaan.

When he described how they arrived at the city at the

same time as the Regent's army there were shocked exclamations from the courtiers who had no notion until then that the city had been endangered.

'Tell me quickly – the fate of Thaan?' demanded Florizan.

'Thaan is fallen, mesire.'

A sigh went up from the assembly.

'Forgive my interruption. Pray continue.'

Ognam did continue, describing the siege, the arrival of the Red Death and their retreat into the Drakenfel with the children, though he modestly made no mention of the part he had played as a piper.

'A truly remarkable tale, told in a manner worthy of your calling,' Florizan said when Ognam concluded the story of their subterranean voyage. 'There is as much untold, I think, as there is told – I would know more about the magical light that shone from your mast in the underworld caverns, and even more I would be interested to know, Master Jester, how your companions came to be imprisoned in the Citadel and why you found it necessary to make such a perilous journey to Thaan when there were easier havens to reach.'

Alwald and Krispin exchanged a glance of warning which was noted without comment by their urbane host.

'However such questions can wait,' he went on. 'It would be a great discourtesy to ask you to continue when doubtless your curiosity as to the nature of the Domain is eager to be satisfied.'

He paused as a procession of servants brought in a course of venison which they served with as much ceremony as priests performing a shrine ritual.

'I think you will find this a welcome change to travellers' bread,' said the Lady Sylva. 'It is a product of our deerpark.'

'An advantage of living in the heart of a desert land is that there is no shortage of sunlight to ripen the fruit of the vine and you will find that wine pressed from our black grapes goes with such meat tolerably well,' Florizan added as a servant went from guest to guest to fill their goblets with the ruby vintage.

'The story of the Domain goes back to the days of The Enchantment,' said Florizan reflectively as he held his wine up to the light to pleasure his eyes as well as his palate by observing its glowing colour. 'I must explain that my lineage is ancient and noble – as indeed is yours,' he added with a smile to Alwald, 'but while yours performed a useful duty by protecting the kingdom in marcher lands, my ancestors turned more to the scroll – and the wine glass no doubt – than the sword. They had an almost morbid interest in the curious, in exotic lands and fabled beasts . . . in that you can see my son is true member of his line by the sinister creature that he deems necessary to keep at his side.'

A long yowling cry from the animal, which sat beside his master on a chair, made everyone laugh for it seemed as though it had understood Florizan's words.

'Silence, Auzel,' said Lord Ugo, delighted at this display of his pet's intelligence.

'To resume,' said Florizan, 'my ancestors were learned, enquiring and, at the same time, hedonistic. This latter quality ensured their popularity at court in Danaak, especially with good King Johan. My great-grandame – before she married my great-grandfather who was Keeper of the Royal Vaults, and whose name was bestowed upon me in honour of his memory – my great-grandame was a close friend of the king's only daughter so on both sides my forebears were deeply royalist . . .'

'Pardon sir, but the king's daughter . . . was that the Princess Livia?' Krispin interrupted.

'The same.' Turning to the servant at attention behind his ebony chair, the prince whispered an instruction and the man departed.

Krispin felt a surge of excitement. Here was someone who could perhaps tell him something about the girl who was the object of his quest.

'Then came The Enchantment, the details of which have passed into myth,' Florizan resumed. 'Suffice it to say that Livia vanished, and King Johan spent the last few years of his reign in a search that was fruitless – as has been every search since then.

'My great-grandfather Florizan realised that without an heir to the throne the established order would change, and with his acute mind foresaw the evil that did come to pass in Ythan. He considered rightly that under a new regime the old nobility which been connected with the monarchy for generations would be endangered. Therefore he laid a plan to ensure that he and his descendants would continue to enjoy the family's traditional way of life . . .'

He paused as his body servant returned with a flat portrait case of carved ivory.

'Master Krispin,' he said passing the case to him, 'as you showed interest in the Princess Livia this may be of interest to you.'

Krispin released the catch and opened the case.

'Jennet!' he whispered.

THREE
The History of Olam

Florizan looked across at Krispin.

'You find something strange about that portrait of the Princess Livia?' he asked with deceptive mildness.

'For a moment the likeness reminded me of someone else,' Krispin replied, handing back the ivory case. 'It was a passing fancy for I can think of no one to match the princess in beauty.'

Florizan regarded the portrait reflectively.

'Some said it was her beauty that led to The Enchantment,' he said, 'but to me that has the ring of the folktale about it. But who can say after so much time has passed? To return to my great-grandfather, after the disappearance of this lady whose portrait is one of our heirlooms, he decided to create a refuge as far from Danaak – or even the humblest peasant village – as possible.

'As a young man he made a journey to this remote spot in the Desert of Akea when seeking fabled beasts, and he remembered it as a place where no man would willingly go and which had nothing to interest merchant or soldier. Working as secretly as possible he arranged for caravans to come here from Thaan, which is our nearest neighbour, carrying building materials and furnishings as well as artisans, gardeners, masons, sculptors and so on from his country estates where such movements of men were not likely to be noticed.

'The key to his enterprise was water, and the fact that a subterranean river made a brief appearance in the chasm suggested he could obtain a limitless supply. A man of immense practical ability as well as intellect, he sank several shafts through the rock to the river which were devised in such an ingenious way that water was constantly siphoned to the top of the cliff. The steps you ascended were cut by my great-grandfather's engineers.

'With abundant water the gardeners created a miniature countryside within the wall constructed by the masons, and right on the eminence overlooking the chasm my great-grandfather's builders raised this small palace.

'By the time King Johan was carried to his deathbed the Domain of Olam was complete, and in the confusion that followed my ancestor, his family, courtiers and many of his retainers disappeared from Danaak, and when the Witchfinders in their hunt for sorcery finally visited the family estates they found the grounds overgrown and the buildings empty. It was assumed that Florizan and his people had perished in the strife which followed the end of Ythan's ruling House.

'In reality Florizan and his people were continuing to live in the style they had always known in this secret enclave safe from the shadow of the Regency which darkened the rest of the kingdom. My grandfather and father were born here, and the people in the Domain are mostly descended from those who settled here a century ago.

'I like to think that like some beautiful butterfly set in amber, the Domain of Olam has preserved the art and elegance which flourished under Ythan's kings.

'You may wonder whether such an enclosed life in this inaccessible place did not breed both spiritual and emotional lassitude, but the mores of our House prevented that;

indeed, thanks to the philosophy of my great-grandfather, here in Olam we find life to be of remarkable richness. As I suggested earlier, we endeavour to raise everything, even the daily chores of life, to the level of art.

'Have you not noticed with what devotion the food you have eaten was served? I doubt if even the Regent has such dedicated servants or cooks who display their viands with as much care as they prepare it. And so it is with everything. Our gardeners strive to make the grounds of the Domain a paradise; our vintners never cease trying to find a wine that is equal to the legendary wine which came from vines watered by the Wells of Ythan in the ancient days. So, in our pursuit of perfection, and in savouring what we achieve, we pass our days in contentment. I hope that while you remain our guests you will share our harmony.'

Florizan spread his beringed fingers to indicate that his speech was at an end, and the musicians who had remained silent while their master spoke now resumed softly in the background.

'I find it hard to believe that the Domain has remained isolated for so long,' said Alwald. 'Surely over the years fabrics would have worn out, implements would need replacing.'

'Isolated we may be but we have never been out of touch with the outside world,' Florizan explain. 'During the cool season each year a small caravan sets out from Thaan with such supplies as we might need – and news of Ythan which year by year becomes blacker. Such is the loyalty of the merchant family who, since my great-grandfather's day have arranged the annual journey across the desert, and the caravaneers who travel with it, no hint of our existence other than the most ridiculous rumours has spread.'

'Such loyalty!' said Lorelle. 'I have lived all my life in

Thaan and no word did I ever hear of your Domain.'

'It is loyalty that reflects the shine of silver,' responded Florizan with a worldy smile. 'Alas, from what you tell us, the caravan will never come again. It is something to which much thought must be given in due course.'

'But should word of your Domain reach the enemies of the ancient regime and the Regent dispatch a force against you, you have no way of defending yourselves,' Alwald persisted. 'I speak with feeling, for it was the treachery of the Regent which brought down the happy rule of my father.'

'We are not as vulnerable as you may think at first sight – we have terrible allies. But we have had enough serious talk for now. Let us enjoy the words of Ronal my poet while we finish our repast. Then we shall dance and, with wine and song, celebrate your remarkable arrival.'

'But, mesire, there are things pertaining to your hospitality that we must discuss,' said Alwald.

'No doubt, but not now,' replied Florizan sternly. 'You will learn that time in the Domain of Olam does not flow so fatally fast as it does beyond our walls. Like the other good things of life we savour leisure, we revoke the bondage of the passing hour – and consequently life stretches out for us. The most youthful-looking members of this company have known many more seasons than you would imagine. Indeed, by the reckoning of the outside world I would be a very old man.'

He laughed deeply, showing perfect teeth.

'Now let us enjoy ourselves,' he said, 'and fear not, you will gradually become accustomed to our ways. Now hark to my poet, I understand he has written some stanzas on the love of a rose for a nightingale which I am sure you will find to be a delightful allegory.'

Alwald returned to his venison.

Later the first dance began. Led by Prince Florizan and Lady Sylva, men and women in sumptuous velvets and brocades wove intricate patterns to the measured strains of the musicians. Being accustomed to such dances in River Garde Alwald joined in, and the rest of the travellers, with winecups in hand, watched with the other onlookers. Silvermane suddenly felt the Hump's hand tighten on her wrist.

'Come away,' he said quietly and obediently she walked with him to the distant end of the terrace which seemed to hang over the chasm.

'Dear heart, what is the matter?' she asked.

'I felt I had to get away from folk,' he said, his hand surreptitiously feeling for the sooma seeds he carried in a box of auroch horn.

'That was . . . a pity. It reminded me of . . . old times. In Arkad my people . . . used to dance.'

'I am sorry,' said the Hump. 'Go back if you wish.'

'You . . . not well?' she said with sudden concern when she saw sweat bedewing his face.

'I shall be all right shortly. My accursed back has been troublesome of late.'

He did not tell her that since they had arrived in Thaan there were times when the usual ache became sheer agony. Sometimes it felt as though nerve and muscle was knotted by a force that was independent of his body, and it was only by taking more and more sooma seeds that he was able to free himself from the pain.

'That was not the only reason I brought you away,' he continued as he leaned heavily on the balustrade and gazed into the depths. 'I suddenly felt trapped. There is something here that I do not like.'

'Yet it is beautiful . . . and Florizan . . . is kind.'

'That is true. I cannot explain it but I wish to be away from here.'

'But here . . . we rest. You will . . . feel better with rest.'

He shook his head, angry with himself for not having the words to explain his presentiment. He changed his stance and suddenly felt a stab of envy as, looking up, he saw the silhouette of an eagle beneath the moon. To have such freedom as that great bird! To drift lazily on the currents of air which flowed over the desert or hurtle with the wild winds which blew high across Ythan! To wander at will wherever fancy took him!

The Hump realised that, apart from the short time he had spent with Silvermane, he had only known happiness when he was high in the saddle of a drong leading a caravan over some remote trail, especially in terrain that was new to him where his keen eyes roved over fresh landscapes and there was always an unknown horizon ahead. He was a wanderer. Nothing could alter that and he felt panic as for the first time he wondered whether he would be able to settle with Silvermane if ever they reached Arkad.

A groan escaped his lips.

Silvermane laid her arm across his curving spine and her anxiety showed in the way that she was unable to use the words that she had learned only latterly.

'Just my back,' said the Hump with an effort. 'Perhaps when I was beaten in Danaak some damage was done – had it not been for Krispin and Alwald I would have probably been killed.'

He smiled at her as the spasm of pain eased as the seeds took effect. 'I used to think that I was just a joke of fortune but there are times when luck has favoured me, and meeting those two was one of them.'

'And Gambal,' said Silvermane as she regained control of her tongue.

'And Gambal.'

Florizan's Time Warrior – an automated figure in armour – swung his mace against a bell to send the chimes of midnight echoing through the palace. Gambal left the revelry and walked to the apartments which had been assigned to the travellers. There was a slight smile on his young face as he thought of what the night would bring. The transformation of Lorelle the previous night struck him as almost miraculous; she had clung to him as though his body offered some answer for which she thirsted. Her lips which he had so often watched moving in silent prayer had sought his with a passion that made up for their inexperience. It seemed the fervour once devoted to the precepts of the All Father had been reawakened in physical desire.

On reaching her chamber, the young man tapped on the door and walked in. Moonlight streamed through rose-tinted panes and standing as still as a statue in the pinkish light was Lorelle – dressed in her familiar grey habit.

Gambal halted and gazed at her in silence.

His first thought was that she now saw the previous night as a moment of madness and the robe was a sign of repentance. For a moment his hopes were dashed – then a sensuous smile replaced the calm expression which she had assumed with her habit.

'You must take me as I am,' she told him.

'But . . .' began Gambal and then realised that she was inviting him to join her in some ritualistic game. As he crossed the floor she began to untie the cord which fastened about her waist as she had done the previous night.

'Kneel,' she said.

Gambal obeyed.

'Worship,' she commanded and once more her fingers teased his hair cruelly.

Later he carried her to the fur-covered bed and laid her gently upon it, and then he began to undress. As he removed his doublet a soft leather case fell from the pocket to the floor. With a curse he snatched it up, feeling if the mirror it contained had broken, but it was as solid as ever and he returned it to his pocket with a sigh of relief.

'What was that?' Lorelle asked.

'A mirror – I use it for shaving.'

She laughed.

'I knew you were particular about your appearance, but is it necessary to carry the implements about with you?'

'Only a mirror . . .' he began, then said, 'Lorelle, I want your word that you will never look at it.'

She stared at him, then laughed – how she had changed!

'Am I so ugly that I should shocked by the sight of myself?'

'I cannot explain, but to humour me please promise.'

'I am used to making vows. One more cannot hurt.'

'But unlike your pledge to be chaste, this vow must be kept,' said Gambal.

'I promise not to look at your silly mirror. Satisfied? Was it given to you by some woman in Danaak?'

Gambal smiled his innocent smile.

'Shall we say – I acquired it.'

Naked, his pale body almost as slender as hers, Gambal lay beside her on the fur and felt her hands slide across his skin, and his panic over the mirror receded.

FOUR
The Hunting Party

Krispin awoke with a dry mouth and a head which echoed painfully. Someone was knocking at his door.

'Enter,' he called as he screwed up his eyes against the sunlight streaming into the room.

'You look dreadful,' said Alwald when he walked in and, removing Krispin's tangled clothing from a chair, seated himself upon it. 'Just as you did the morning we set out from Mabalon.' He used the word easily, without thinking, but once he had uttered it his expression became thoughtful as it brought back memories of the Lady Demara.

'Could you pass me the pitcher of water,' said Krispin. 'The wine of Olam is much stronger than I guessed.'

'If you are only used to apple ale wine can be potent,' said Alwald handing him the pitcher. 'I woke up feeling perfectly well some hours ago.'

Krispin drank gratefully, long draughts with the water trickling down his beard and over his naked chest. When it was empty he placed it beside the bed and lay back, his hand across his eyes.

'Did I – did I behave indecorously?' he asked.

'Well, you did not vomit over our hostess so that was all right, but you would insist on telling everyone about some automaton you had made and how its movements were superior to those of Mesire Florizan's automaton.'

'Florizan's automaton?'

'Yes, you seemed to have the idea that his dwarf was an automaton, and you offered to improve his performance . . .'

'Serene Mother!' breathed Krispin. 'I did not try to adjust him, did I?'

'You wanted to tighten his spring but he kept you at bay with his little mace.'

'And Florizan?'

'He laughed in that tolerant way he has. I explained that you were unused to courtly revels.'

'And the dwarf?'

'He was more worried by Ognam. He was a great success last night and the dwarf was potton sick with envy, afraid that Florizan will offer him employment. They have been so cut off from the rest of the world that even Ognam's jokes have a fresh ring about them.'

For a while neither young man spoke. Krispin suffered what was known in Toyheim as 'drunkard's remorse' and Alwald gazed moodily at Woundflame which stood in its shabby scabbard in the corner.

'Did you have a reason to visit me so early?' said Krispin finally. 'Or is it early? You did say you were up hours ago.'

'It is noon. I had wanted to talk to you – privately, but I doubt if your wits are in order.'

'My wits are all right, it is my head that pains.'

'I care not about your head,' said Alwald. 'I care that we continue our journey as soon as possible.'

'That could be difficult,' Krispin said. 'Although our host gave us a short history of the Domain last night – that I do remember – it seems to me that there was much that he left out. Certainly he said nothing that could be helpful to us.'

'He was right when he said that time flows differently here. Everything is spread out, there is no hurry. This morning I tried to arrange an audience with him through Gifon, but I was told that he and his courtiers are spending the day in one of the gardens where a rare tree is about to flower. From a distance I saw them sitting about it on chairs and divans while musicians played, watching to see the buds burst. I can assure you that there is no chance of obtaining Mesire Florizan's attention today.'

'Is it wise to tell him about the nature of the quest?' Krispin asked.

'If we are to look to him for help we have no choice, and I cannot see that it would do any harm. His family has no love for the Regency, and such is his lively mind I think it would be intrigued by the thought of the search for Livia. In any event, there is no way he could betray us to the Regent or the Witchfinders in this forgotten spot.'

'So, at some moment when he is not savouring perfume or waiting for a flower to unfold we may be granted the opportunity to beg his aid.'

'The sooner the better. Having come so far, I feel that the final part of the journey lies just ahead, and if we can achieve that we shall discover where Princess Livia lies – or if we have suffered a fool's errand.'

'I agree. The sooner we reach The Mage, supposing there is truth in the report that he still exists, the sooner I can make my way back to the Wald.'

'And I to Mabalon.'

'Mabalon? It would not be possible to sail through the rapids without a Fey boat.'

'I should be able to find my way back over the mountains. I – I owe it to my father's memory, once I am no longer tied to the quest, to see to the comfort of the Lady

Demara and the child that she will soon be birthing.'

'That is your real quest,' said Krispin.

Alwald turned away, not wishing his companion to see that his eyes had misted.

'Put on your clothes,' he said gruffly. 'Let us seek the Hump. Mayhap his knowledge of the stars will enable him to relate our position to the map which Brother Mias gave us.'

'Where is he?' asked Krispin sitting up painfully.

'I expect he is mooning with his horsemaid in some secluded spot.'

Half an hour later, with Krispin manfully plodding behind him, Alwald entered a romantic grove in the southern part of the Domain. The tall oaks provided a leafy canopy through which bright shafts of sunlight pierced the warm shade. The air was filled both with the song of birds as they swooped among the century-old tree trunks, and the scent of wild flowers. As in all parts of the Domain a brook gurgled to keep the soil damp enough for plants to flourish.

As Krispin had predicted they found the Hump seated beneath the shade of a great oak while Silvermane trod daintily over the daisy-starred grass picking tiny pinkish mushrooms which to her were a delicacy. It was obvious that she was relishing the feel of turf beneath her hoofs after suffering the unnatural hardness of floor, street and boatdeck for so long.

With natural courtesy the Hump climbed to his feet as the two approached, aware as he did so of the clumsy figure he cut in comparison with the grace of the horsemaid. Yet again he felt astonishment that someone who, in his eyes, was so exquisite could find it in her heart to love him.

Beauty and the beast! he thought with a touch of sardonic humour.

'Master Guide,' said Alwald, 'have you yet observed the night sky above this place?'

'Last night on the terrace I watched the stars in their courses,' the Hump replied.

'And did they tell in what part of Ythan we find ourselves?' asked Krispin.

'Far north of the place where I last looked upon them – Thaan.'

'We know that,' said Alwald impatiently. 'The prince told us that much. But could you relate the constellations to the star signs drawn on the map?'

At these words Krispin felt beneath his shirt of green linen and from the flat leather bag he wore he produced the folded piece of parchment which had been given to him in the Great Library.

When the Hump had reverently unfolded it he gazed at the faded sepia marks upon it without comprehension.

'I am without letters,' he explained. 'Perhaps if I knew what was written here it might be possible to work out the position.'

'Of course, we need Lorelle,' said Krispin. If his head had been clear he would have brought her, remembering that it was her ability to read the Old Ythan characters inscribed upon the chart which had been the excuse for her joining the quest. 'Then let us meet tonight when the stars are brightest and she will tell you how to read the symbols.'

It was agreed and thankfully Krispin was free to trudge back through the glades and gardens of the Domain to sink back on to his bed and in fitful sleep dream strange dreams about the faraway Wald.

Alwald watched Krispin depart with a tolerant smile. The fellow had many good qualities and there was no denying his valour; yet there was still much of the peasant about him and it was obvious that he had not the stomach for noble wines.

He turned to the Hump.

'Once we know the direction in which the tower of The Mage lies I am sure that with your talent for way-finding you will have no difficulty in piloting us there.'

'Lord Alwald, I was hired by Master Gambal to lead you and your friends across the wilderness to Thaan. My engagement ended there. While it is a fine thing for you to travel on your quest like a knight errant it is something that holds not a scrap of interest for me. From here Silvermane and I shall go our own way.'

'You mean – you mean you are deserting us,' cried Alwald as anger surged within him. 'You were happy enough to save your skins by coming with us from Thaan but now it seems the danger is over you have no gratitude.'

'Gratitude!' said the Hump with a bitter smile. 'Gratitude for what? Why, I have not even been paid my promised fee for guiding you to Thaan yet.'

'*Silver* – you talk of silver, when the future of the kingdom could be at stake.'

'Lord Alwald, the future of Ythan is no concern of mine. To have a person of royal blood once more sitting on the Empty Throne might some day be a fine thing – if it were to come about! – but it would make little difference to the likes of me or Silvermane. We must seek our own destiny wherever we can find it.'

'But without you the journey will be impossible,' muttered Alwald. 'Is it more money you want?'

As he said it he realised with inward dismay that even if the Hump named a price for his services his own position was such that he personally could not raise a silver crown towards it.

The Hump smiled his bitter smile again.

'Money,' he said thoughtfully. 'I think there is little use for that in these parts, but I shall do all that I can to make sure that you will be able to travel in the right direction, though how you expect to cross such a wasteland I do not understand.'

'We will find a way,' declared Alwald. 'If we could travel through the Land of Blight we will certainly find a way here.' And with anger smouldering in his heart he left the grove.

That night the plan to relate the constellations that shone above the Domain to the map was abandoned when clouds rolled across the sky from west to east, an endless river of swirling vapour which flowed without letting fall a single raindrop on to the desert's face.

'I never expected to see clouds in the desert,' said Ognam when the travellers sat together for supper in one of the palace's minor halls. 'But as there are clouds why is there no rain?'

'There are no trees to pull it down,' replied the servant. 'It is told among the gardeners that centuries ago this land was clothed with forest and rain watered it in due season. Then men came and destroyed it by ring-barking and fire so that the ashes made good pasture on which they could run great herds of tamed aurochs, but before many seasons had passed the pastures became yellow with drought and the soil became so dry that the winds carried it away leaving only the sand which you see today. The men went away to cut down other forests and the beasts died so that even today when we venture outside the walls of the Domain we find horned skulls of the long-dead aurochs.'

'Do you often go outside the walls?' asked Alwald.

'Only to hunt,' replied the servant. 'Tomorrow will

be one of the days when my master leads the chase.'

'Hunt?' said Ognam. 'What is there to hunt out there?'

'Sandharts,' was the reply. 'They are rather like deer, and they can race and leap and zig-zag as though they were flying over the ground rather than running upon it.'

'What do they live on?' asked Alwald whose interest had quickened as hunting had been a favourite pastime at River Garde. 'Where do they find water?'

The servant shrugged.

'I do not know. To survive out there they must be magical beasts. Tomorrow you may find out because I understand you are to be invited to take part.'

Next morning the travellers awoke to find that hunting costumes had been provided for them, and when they assembled to break their fast they were informed that they would be conducted on the tenth hour to select their mounts.

When they walked along a rose-bordered path to the stables they encountered Mesire Florizan with his party.

'Here we hunt on drongs,' he told them as they entered the compound. 'They come from a strain which my ancestors specially bred for the chase.'

As usual he was gracious and amiable, yet to Alwald's chagrin he showed no interest in discussion other than that relating to the sport which lay ahead.

They waited on smooth emerald turf while the hunt-master led out a procession of saddled animals.

'*White* drongs,' cried the Hump in amazement.

'Since we came to the Domain my family has taken pride in breeding these animals,' said Florizan who had overheard his exclamation. 'Not only are they handsome to look upon, but they travel like the wind. You will not be disappointed in your ride today, Master Guide.'

Servants brought gilded steps for the ladies to climb to the side-saddles on which they would ride behind their menfolk who carried nets used to bring down the fleet-footed quarry, and razor-like knives for their ritual dispatch. When all were mounted the huntmaster led the cavalcade along a gravelled track to the open gates of the Domain.

'It is our custom not to hunt in one party,' Florizan explained to his guests. 'Sandharts are very rare and the more territory that is covered the greater the chance of raising one. My son will lead one party and I the other. Master Guide, I suggest you follow Ugo if you want to see how well our drongs perform as he has the daring of youth.'

When the two parties were drawn up the huntmaster blew a rising note on his horn and they rode through the gates; Ugo's riders turned their mounts to the west while Florizan set out northwards. As the steady loping stride of the drongs began to increase outriders unfurled silken pennants from their lances which, when they floated in long bands of colour, gave a hint of a masque to the proceedings.

Thanks to the Hump's tuition when they were riding across the Wilderness of Gil both Krispin and Alwald felt at ease on the speeding beasts; the warm air of the desert rushing past their faces gave them a sense of exhilaration. For a brief period they were released from all thoughts of the quest and the hunt became a race between the two of them.

Laughing with the joy of youth and speed they overtook the other riders and Alwald continued to forge ahead until he was abreast of Florizan who led the hunt on a silver caparisoned mount which was the pride of the stables.

'You ride like a man of gentle birth,' cried Florizan as the wind teased his long locks and billowed his cloak of purple velvet. 'Let us see if you can race like one.'

He pointed with his goad to where a distant ridge was outlined against the sky.

'You are on, mesire,' responded Alwald.

'I'll show you a marvel when you catch me up,' laughed Florizan and on a whistle of command his drong surged forward.

Behind them Krispin urged his mount to greater efforts and soon the three riders were well ahead of the main party, their drongs flying up the slope as easily as if they were on a flat road.

Perhaps it was because Krispin was not of gentle birth that he came a poor third. When he reached the top of the incline Florizan and Alwald were reined up and gazing over a vast expanse which hitherto had been hidden by the swell of the ridge.

'Serene Mother!' he exclaimed as he halted beside them. 'What are they?'

Half a league away there were what appeared to be formations of rock rising from the plain, yet even at this distance they were strikingly human in form.

'Giants,' said Florizan. Turning to Alwald he added, 'I promised you a marvel.'

FIVE
The Giants' Circle

The Hump watched the party led by Florizan speed away and then heard Lord Ugo saying, 'Today let it be us who return with the spoils. It is time we offered my father competition or he will become bored with the chase. Too many harts have been caught in his net of late, so away my friends.'

Laughing, the hunters urged their drongs forward while horns sounded and soon the walls of the Domain shrunk behind them. Most of the riders following the graceful Ugo were of his age and dressed as flamboyantly as he – the younger element of the Domain's small court. Aware of the contrast he made to these courtly young folk the Hump was content to ride at the rear of the column with Silvermane's hand on his shoulder as she sat side-saddle behind him.

'You like . . . white drong?' she asked.

'He is magnificent,' he replied. 'His gait is perfect and there is so much power in his limbs. On such a beast it might be possible to cross the desert . . .'

Her hand tightened on his shoulder at these words.

Looking at the undulating terrain about him the Hump wondered how any creatures could survive in it – the Wilderness of Gil was certainly barren but it did have some straggling vegetation; here there was only rock and sand.

It seemed wrong to him that if some creature did

manage to survive in such surroundings, these hunters on their specially bred mounts should be added to the hazards nature had already provided for it.

Someday the last sandhart will be killed and then the hunters will mourn the passing of their sport, he thought, not knowing that this eventuality had been forseen and in a remote corner of the Domain a small breeding herd of sandharts were kept to ensure that the joy of the chase would continue.

They had been riding for half an hour when suddenly Ugo raised his goad above his head and shouted, 'Hart! Hart!'

The notes of hunting horns rolled eerily across the parched landscape and the hunters goaded forward, no longer in a column but in an ever-changing formation, each eager to be the first to be in at the kill.

As the riders raced away the Hump forgot his wish to remain in the background as he was seized by the desire to prove that when it came to riding he was as good if not better than any of them. He had ridden drongs since, as a small runaway boy, he had hidden in the pannier of one on a caravan journey. Leaning forward, he began to mutter into the large furred ear of the animal and was rewarded by feeling the beast leap forward.

'Hold tight,' he shouted to Silvermane. 'We shall race the wind.'

Sand sprayed from the spreading feet of the drongs as they entered into the spirit of the chase; breath whistled through their dilated nostrils, and as the mane of the horsemaid streamed behind her she laughed with the pure joy of experiencing speed and space once more.

One by one the Hump overtook the other riders who looked sourly at his bent figure as he crouched forward in the saddle so his weathered face was close to his drong's head, his lips moving constantly as though he was actually *talking* to the animal.

'He must have the knack of beast talk,' muttered one rider, who, despite his work with the goad, saw the Hump surge past him.

'He probably learned it off that creature behind him who they say is not wholly human,' responded his lady love in his ear. 'Will you allow these uncouth outsiders to beat you!'

'No, by the Mother!' he replied, and he drove the sharp point of the goad into the drong's flank so deep that its wail of pain sounded louder than the hunting horn accompanying the wild chase.

Soon the Hump had caught up with the little group of hard-riders surrounding the elegant form of Ugo who led the hunt on a drong second only to his father's for speed and stamina. It was then he and Silvermane caught their first glimpse of the quarry which was bounding a couple of hundred paces ahead.

A deer-like animal as far as its shape and running power was concerned, the sandhart had adapted to desert conditions. It was covered with the lightest fur imaginable to protect its skin from the desert sun – fur which the Hump recognised as that used for the rugs on their couches – and instead of the spreading antlers of the deer kind it had a single spiralled horn which it used for burrowing in the sand for the underground fungi on which it survived.

The appearance of this graceful beast put the Hump in mind of tales of unicorns told in wayside inns on the caravan routes. And he marvelled at its agility as it tried to distance itself from its pursuers by frantic swerves and flying leaps over dangerous outcrops of rock.

'You ride well, sir,' shouted Ugo as the Hump came alongside him. 'It is between us now, but that hart has the cunning of his kind. Look at him.'

As he spoke the sandhart turned towards an area of tumbled rocks and jagged outcrops of reddish stone which was known to the hunters as the Maze, and with a flash of his feathery tail he vanished between a pair of boulders which stood like massive gateposts. Ugo took the lead and hurtled between them with the Hump's drong only a couple of paces behind, then they were flying up a long depression which might have been a waterway when the land was fair. Of the sandhart there was no sign, nor – when the Hump glanced over his shoulder – was there one of the hunters which he and Ugo had outdistanced.

Ugo slowed, his eyes making a practised sweep of the ground about them. He saw some stones sliding down a patch of scree and immediately set his drong scrambling up it. The Hump followed recklessly to keep up with the young man who was now twisting and turning among the rocks.

Suddenly he gave a shout of triumph.

Ahead the Maze opened out into a natural amphitheatre and in the centre stood the sandhart, its flanks trembling with exhaustion and its chest heaving as it panted for breath. From his saddle Ugo drew forth a weighted net and urged his mount forward. The sandhart began a stumbling run and as the drong raced beside it the hunter flung down the net with the graceful skill of long practice. As the sandhart became enmeshed he rolled over and over and then lay struggling to free himself. As the Hump reined up Ugo swung down with his knife like a shard of dazzling mirror in the sunlight. From over the rocks came the sound of the horn but for the moment they were alone. Looking down on the netted animal the Hump became aware of its large, limpid eyes gazing up at him in what appeared to be a mute plea for mercy.

The young man knelt over it. Holding the single white

horn with his powerful left hand he forced back the head so that the throat became taut – ready to be slit by the blade in his right hand.

'No!'

Silvermane screamed the word.

Surprised, Ugo paused and Silvermane leapt from the drong and threw herself on to his back. He sprawled forward on the burning sand while, released from his grip, the sandhart redoubled its efforts to escape the net.

Without a word Ugo reached up, caught Silvermane by the arm and sent her reeling so that she tripped backwards. He turned and cut the sandhart's throat through the netting.

Bright blood spurted in all directions as it thrashed in agony. It made its final defecation and the luminosity faded in its eyes.

The moment Ugo had seized Silvermane the Hump's hand vanished beneath his cloak to reappear with his drong-rider's spike and he slid from his saddle with it outstretched.

'By the Mother, I shall teach you to draw steel on me, hunchback!' Ugo cried.

There was a sudden crackle of applause. Riders appeared at the edge of the amphitheatre and, misreading the nature of the tableau before them, were congratulating Ugo on his kill.

While he smiled and bowed in recognition, the Hump sheathed his spike and crossed to Silvermane.

'Are you hurt?' he asked as he saw her tears.

'Not I . . . the hart.'

As he helped her to stand a hunt servant decapitated the still-twitching sandhart and held up the head in token of his master's prowess.

'That horn must be six handspans,' declared one of the hunters in admiration. 'It will be one of the finest heads in the trophy room.'

'On with the chase,' shouted Ugo gaily as he climbed back into the saddle. 'Its mate must be hereabouts.'

The horn sounded, the pennants swirled and Ugo led the cavalcade away through the rocks while a swarm of brown flies began crawling over the bloodied fur of the sandhart.

Without a word the Hump lifted Silvermane to the saddle – her hoofs were unsuited for stirrups – and after mounting himself they retraced their way out among the outcrops. Once clear of the Maze he turned the drong's head in the direction of the Domain.

Meanwhile, several leagues to the north-east, Mesire Florizan's hunting party lined the edge of an escarpment and gazed down at the life-like rock formations which lay before them. The hunters from the Domain, to whom the Giants' Circle was a familiar landmark, were gratified at the awe with which their guests regarded the group of enormous stone figures.

'When were those statues carved?' asked Alwald whose drong stood panting beside Florizan's after the long race from the Domain.

'If one is to believe a legend which was old when my ancestor founded the Domain, they were never carved,' said Florizan. 'They are said to be the magical work of the Mage Ysldon before The Enchantment.'

'Ysldon?' mused Krispin who had reined up on the other side of their host. 'That is a name I have heard before.'

Into his mind came a mental picture of a fowler in his boat in one of the waterways in the dreaded Shallows through which flowed the River of Night. He had been telling an old tale of necromancers who had earned the wrath of a great sorcerer of that name.

'In the old days many were the stories about Ysldon,' said

Florizan. 'He used gramarye for the good of men against the forces of evil, but most of the lore regarding him was suppressed by the Witchfinders after The Enchantment, along with anything else which showed sorcery in a good light.

'The story of those fellows is that they were a band of giants who somehow reached Ythan from their dark homeland beyond the Cold Sea. Wielding clubs the size of treetrunks they marched through the countryside in a delirium of destruction. With one stroke a giant could bring down the spire of a shrine or flatten a villager's house, and it seemed there were no weapons which could halt them. If an arrow or javelin struck them it caused no more annoyance than the sting of a marsh fly. Soldiers who were sent against them by the king of that day turned and fled before them.

'Some said they had been unleashed on Ythan by wicked enchanters, others believed they were part of the evil which came upon the world when the All Father fell from grace.

'As in other tales about the Mage Ysldon, he was prevailed upon to come to the aid of the suffering peasants. By using a magical lure, he led them away from the populated countryside to this remote spot and here he enspelled them into stone.'

'A grand story, but could it be true?' Ognam asked.

Florizan laughed.

'Who can say what is true in the old myths?' he said. 'I like to believe that every myth sprang from a seed of truth, but perhaps the giants you see yonder were really the work of forgotten sculptors. But come and see our stony monsters close to.'

At the touch of his goad the drong moved forward and the rest of the party followed towards the distant group. As they drew closer Krispin and his companions saw that whether the giants were petrified flesh or merely carved rock, the elements had softened their outlines.

They stood in a rough circle, each the height of four normal men and each holding a tremendous club. Their nakedness, which revealed the proportional size of their phalli, caused merriment among the ladies of the party. And, though wind-driven sand grains had over the centuries blurred the sharpness of their features, there was still an expression of malign ferocity about them. From under low bony brows their stone eyes glared in the direction of the Domain – apart from one, who as the result of some accident, had lost his head which lay with closed eyes several paces away from his massive legs which, like those of his fellows, were now buried calf-deep in sand.

There were eight in the circle, and they reminded both Alwald and Krispin of mysterious rings of standing stones to be found in certain forest clearings in the Wald.

While the others joked about the huge figures and urged their drongs round them, Krispin sat still in his saddle and gazed at them with fascination. Although there was something crude about their over-muscled shapes in comparison to living men, they retained an aura of menacing power.

'How the Regent would like to have a company of such . . .' Gambal was saying when Krispin began to feel a curious warmth in the region of his breastbone. For a moment he was alarmed, wondering if he had somehow caught the firepox which ranked second only to the Red Death in Ythan's most feared sicknesses. But he was reassured by the fact that the warmth appeared to come from outside his body rather than within, and he realised that it was emanating from the leather pouch which he wore beneath his shirt. Something strange was taking place within it.

The Esav! It was as though the crystal gem was coming to life. Hastily he unfastened his shirt buttons, ready to throw it from him if it should begin to scorch his flesh but the heat did not increase. Curiously, he felt there was something strange but not unpleasant about the sensation.

'I know it is utterly ridiculous – and you will say I drank too deep of the stirrup cup before we set forth – but I could vow that I saw that stone brute move,' said a lady sitting side-saddle on her husband's drong.

'You were always fanciful, Tana,' he said, adding with a mock sigh, 'Mayhap you think wishfully,' which raised a laugh from their friends.

'It is the effect of shadow,' said Florizan. 'When I was a child I used to come and watch the giants, pretending that they were stirring . . .' His voice trailed away.

Then he said in a quieter tone, 'I, too, just had that impression, Tana. For a moment it seemed that the stone *rippled*.'

'There is something strange here,' said Lorelle who was seated behind Gambal. 'The air feels as it did in Thaan when thunder was gathering over the city.'

'And that noise,' said Ognam. 'Do you hear it? It is like the far-off drone of bees.'

'Enough,' cried Florizan. 'We are all becoming the slaves of fancy. Stone cannot ripple, there is no lightning in the sky and the nearest bee is in the gardens of the Domain. Come, let us continue the chase. I would take it ill if that over-proud son of mine were to bring back the head of a hart while we were to return with our nets still folded . . .'

A scream cut through his light-hearted words.

'The eyes!' cried a young woman. 'The eyes!'

The rest of the party looked round wildly and she added, 'That head on the sand.'

'Serene Mother preserve us!' muttered several voices as it was perceived that the stone eyelids of the fallen head were slowly parting.

Florizan leapt to the sand and ran to it, his ivory-hilted dagger in his hand. For a moment he looked down on the huge face, then drove the point of the dagger against the eyeball which was appearing. A tiny spark flew upwards as steel struck stone, yet the lids continued to open until the huge eyes glared in unwinking anger at the headless body looming above.

For a minute the hunters watched in frozen silence but nothing more happened, then Florizan said, 'We have witnessed something marvellous but I . . .'

Yet again he was destined not to finish a sentence. There was a thud that made the earth beneath their drongs shudder, and turning to another of the statues in the circle they saw that his tremendous club had dropped from his petrified grip.

'We may be in hazard here,' Florizan said coolly as he remounted his drong. 'Let us return to the safety of the Domain. I want several men to keep watch until sunset and report if any more witchery occurs.'

'I shall, mesire, if it be your wish,' the huntmaster said.

Alwald caught Krispin's eye and Krispin nodded.

If we do this for him at least we shall get an audience with him, he thought.

'I beg you to allow my friend and I to remain here in appreciation of the hospitality you have heaped upon us,' said Alwald.

'So be it,' said Florizan, and he led his courtiers away in the direction of the Domain.

'A strange business, young sirs,' said the huntmaster as they hobbled their drongs at a safe distance from the circle of stone figures. 'In my time I have seen more marvels, including a city which appears to float over the desert, but I must confess that watching those stone eyes open made my blood run chill.'

'Mayhap we all suffered from an illusion,' said Alwald.

‘It could be that we only imagined the movement.’

‘That we will soon find out,’ said Krispin as they approached the circle on foot. Beneath his shirt he felt the warmth of the Esav waning.

‘If we all had an illusion that would be equally marvellous,’ said the huntmaster when they seated themselves on the sand thirty paces from the nearest giant. ‘It is like a phantom: it does not matter whether it is really there or not if you believe that it is. All we can tell of life and the world is what we believe.’

‘It was no illusion that the club dropped,’ said Krispin. ‘It still lies on the sand and . . . and I am certain the giant has moved. He has started to reach for it.’

For half an hour they concentrated on the figure. Its movement was so slow that it was imperceptible, yet at the end of that time the fingers of the huge hand were closing on the terrible weapon which had once wrought such havoc – if Florizan’s story was to be believed.

‘It seems to me that as time passes its movements are speeding up,’ said Krispin.

‘And it is not the only one that is coming to life,’ said the huntmaster. ‘I have marked them with my eye in relation to each other and there is no doubt that they are shifting. Serene Mother, protect the Domain if they get the power of walking.’

SIX
Star Signs

Mesire Florizan rose with his usual courtesy from his chair of carved ivory when his huntmaster, Krispin and Alwald were ushered into his apartment. Next to the Lady Merlinda's house of pleasure in Danaak, Krispin had never been in such luxurious surroundings. The walls were hung with tapestries depicting scenes of the chase, rugs of rare glowing colours lay on the floor of inlaid marbles and the gilded furniture, while suggesting comfort, appeared too fragile to one who was used to the solid wooden tables and chairs to be found in the cottages of Toyheim or in the hall of River Garde.

Through arches in one wall the sky appeared to be a dark velvet blue dusted with early stars; from the chasm below came the murmur of the river. Scented candles in horn lanterns threw a soft glow on the table where the master of the Domain had been reading a scroll.

'First be seated and refresh yourselves,' said Florizan pleasantly, 'and then we can talk of today's happening – and of other matters.'

He poured sparkling wine into three goblets and handed them to the men before him. The huntmaster's face showed his appreciation of the honour.

'It may be that what you will tell me is not for the ears of servants,' Florizan continued. 'Fear can be as contagious as the Red Death. Tell me, Brund, what happened at the Giants' Circle after we returned to the Domain.'

'Mesire, there was movement in the figures yet it was so slow that we could not see it happening. We could only judge it by noticing a limb in a different position after a lapse of time.' And the huntmaster went on to describe how one of the giants had reached for his club.

'Passing strange,' murmured Florizan thoughtfully at the end of his recital. 'We all saw the eyelids of the head move quite quickly.'

'My lord,' said Alwald, 'what is the quickest movement of the human body?'

'Ah yes, the blink of an eye. Yet the giant's eye opening must have taken half a minute at least.'

'It seemed to us that the figures are in a different time to that of this world,' ventured Krispin.

'That is obvious,' said Florizan. 'The questions are, what will happen if their time increases its speed to match ours and, if so, what could we do to defend ourselves?'

'Perhaps we could bind them with heavy chain,' suggested the huntmaster.

'I think not, Brund. In the Domain there was no need for such chains so we have none nor do we have metal or furnace capable of making them. Besides I doubt that the mightiest links could bind those hoarstones; there is more than a whiff of gramarye about them. What puzzles me is why at this moment in our history should they become animate?'

Krispin moved his head in the shadow cast by the sweet candles, afraid that his expression might hint at his belief that it was he, or at least the Esav which he carried, that had in some mysterious way altered the enchantment which had lain so long upon the colossi.

'Tomorrow we must keep watch on the circle,' said Florizan. 'Measurements must be taken so that we can estimate if they are increasing in speed. I shall put you in charge of that, Brund, for of all the retainers in the Domain I regard you as the most resourceful. Go and sup now, for there are other matters still to be discussed with our guests.'

Smiling at the compliment, the huntmaster inclined his head and left the apartment with a light step; now he welcomed the giants' stirring for it brought him favour in Florizan's eyes.

When the door closed Florizan poured more cool wine into their cups and tapped the parchment before him.

'I have been reading through what scrolls we have on ancient lore,' he said, 'but I can find nothing that throws any light on what we have witnessed today. What a coincidence it is that this marvel should happen after the arrival of the first visitors we have the pleasure to entertain for years . . .'

His words hung in the air; neither Alwald nor Krispin spoke.

'No doubt the next few days will tell us more,' he continued briskly. 'Meanwhile I should like to learn more about you. Of course that very amusing jongleur spun a fine tale about your adventures, but what interested me more than what he said was what he left out.'

'Mesire, we have been seeking an audience with you on this very point,' said Alwald, 'but it appeared that your time was taken up.'

Florizan smiled at the unintentional note of resentment in the young noble's voice.

'I try to understand your impatience,' he said looking at them over interlocked fingers, 'and you must understand our attitude to time. Here in the Domain we have no need of haste except in the hunting field. We have learned to savour everything, from journey of a spider across a web to a new epic from our storyteller, but to achieve such savouring requires time. My curiosity about you is intense but I had no wish to lose the pleasure of that curiosity by hurrying its satisfaction. Little by little I should learn about you, assess your natures, follow your histories, but this without hurry for time is the commodity of which there is no shortage in the Domain, and, after all, it is not as though you will be journeying from here . . .'

'But we must . . .' began Krispin.

Florizan's long fingers released their hold upon each other and became fan-shaped.

'The events at the Circle of Giants have upset the tenor of the day,' he continued. 'Normally at this hour I should be in my observatory tower studying the motion of the planets but it is in my mind that tonight is the time for you to relate that which Master Ognam omitted.'

Krispin and Alwald had already agreed that their only chance of continuing their quest was to trust Mesire Florizan with a full account of it – without his assistance they had scant hope of finding their way across the desert.

'Our quest started in my homeland known as the Wald, far, far from here,' began Alwald. 'A horde of nomads who worship the Wolf-in-the-Sky gathered on the bank of the River of Night opposite our castle of River Garde and when my father Lord Grimwald went to parley he was murdered by a werewolf . . .' And he continued the story until the hour candle on the desk guttered and during that time Florizan made not a single interjection.

'I had sometime heard of the Pilgrim's Path from those who came with the yearly caravan from Thaan,' he said at length, 'but it never occurred to me that I should meet anyone who followed it. I am heartened that in Ythan there are a few who dare to dream of better days.'

'Mesire, we do more than dream,' said Krispin boldly. 'And now we look to you for aid in our search for Princess Livia.'

'Alas, I cannot see what I can do to help you. We are surrounded by countless leagues of desert and you do not even know where to find this mysterious Mage.'

'In Thaan Brother Mias gave me a map of the region surrounding The Mage's tower,' said Krispin. 'And on it constellations are marked which would give its location to those who recognised them, though so far our guide says they do not fit in with the stars as seen from here.'

Florizan's face lit up.

'This sounds a pretty puzzle, and one that I shall delight in trying to solve,' he declared. 'Tomorrow night the moon moths are due to leave their sheaths to become imagos in the butterfly pavilion but for once I shall forego the pleasure of that vigil. Bring your guide to the observatory tower and we shall attempt to find where in Ythan your Mage is hidden.'

Next morning a large cavalcade rode out with Krispin, Alwald and the huntmaster for although there was a feeling of unease about the Giants' Circle, the marvel of it bred great excitement among those unused to excitement. On arriving at the spot it appeared that the giants had made no move during the night; they still stood with their legs deep in sand which showed no sign of having been disturbed.

While the courtiers watched from the ridge where servants had laid out portable breakfast tables, the trio who had stood watch over the giants the previous afternoon busied themselves tying cords to accessible parts of the figures, pulling them taut and fastening them to stakes with the idea that they would snap if there was any movement.

By midmorning all the cords had been broken yet no one could claim to have seen any perceptible stirring. By noon the furrowing of the sand made it clear that the giants' tremendous legs had borne them several handspans in the direction of the Domain.

When Mesire Florizan arrived on his white drong the huntmaster said, 'My lord, from measurements I have taken it would seem that movement is coming to them at an increasing rate. Look, mesire, that cord to the club has just parted, yet Master Krispin only tied it in place a few minutes ago.'

Florizan gazed at the figures festooned with broken cords.

'Try and calculate, if their speed of movement keeps increasing, how long it will be before they can move as quickly as living men.'

'I shall try, mesire, by use of measuring rods and an hourglass.'

By sundown many of the watchers declared that they could actually observe movement in the figures by aligning them with static points in the landscape. Each giant had left several huge footprints behind it and all had turned their heads in the direction of the Domain. Krispin believed that there were new expressions on their faces; mouths had tightened cruelly and – he wondered if it was his imagination being too fanciful – was there now a hint of evil intelligence in their stone eyes?

As dusk thickened over the plain measuring rods were laid by the colossal feet and several large lanterns were hung from their appendages with the idea of alerting watchmen if by any malign chance they should suddenly gain the ability to move normally.

After supper in the palace Gifon conducted the travellers

up a circular staircase to the top of a tower where Florizan was awaiting them. Vellum star charts lined the circular walls, astrolabes and similar instruments were mounted on stands and the domed roof was constructed so that curved panels could be slid back to reveal sections of the night sky.

'This lady bravely accompanied us because of her ability to read Old Ythan in which the directions on the map are written,' Alwald said to explain Lorelle's presence. Florizan nodded and led them to a large table covered with star maps, and all looked expectantly as Krispin produced the map which Brother Mias had given him.

'It is of a great age,' said Florizan as he unfolded it delicately and smoothed it on the table. 'As you said, it is a map showing a stretch of coastline and an island on which there is the symbol for a tower; but to what stretch of water does such a coastline belong? Let us look at the configurations of star signs drawn above it. What can you tell us about them, young lady?'

Lorelle bent over the faded writing.

'It says that the stars appear thus at midnight on the night of midsummer,' she said, and she continued to translate what seemed to be bewildering formulae and geographic directions, all of which Florizan noted with an inkstick upon a large tablet.

' "Beware the early tide when the Griffin is in the House of the West" is the last notation,' she said finally.

'Good,' said Florizan. 'Mysterious as it sounds, it does at least tell us that it is sea coast and not the margin of some great lake. Now, my friends, be seated and we shall explore the heavens in search of your Mage's island.'

As he spoke he went to the centre of the chamber where stood a large and complicated device of rods and gears above which was mounted what appeared to be a globe of opaque glass on which was fitted a concave cap of fine copper.

'This was devised by my father who spent much more time in the study of the celestial bodies than I permit myself,' Florizan told them as he busied himself placing a bright light in the base of the globe. 'Please extinguish the lamps.'

Licking their fingers, the travellers snuffed out the candles in the glass holders and as darkness filled the chamber they gave exclamations of surprise. Light from within the globe shone through minute holes in the copper cap and threw star-like flecks of light on the curved ceiling above them.

'Witchcraft,' muttered the Hump. 'You have captured the stars which shine above the Domain.'

'Not magic, my friend,' laughed Florizan, enjoying the effect his father's instrument had upon his guests, 'just a star map cut in metal. My father made such caps from charts which had been collected from different regions of Ythan before The Enchantment when men still studied such non-profitable things out of the joy of adding to their knowledge – and, of course, for predicting the future.'

'You are used to travelling by the stars, Master Guide, so I think you would be the most likely to recognise the constellations drawn on the map if they appear on the ceiling.

'I can try,' said the Hump simply.

Florizan removed the copper mask from the lamp and replaced it with another.

'I recognise the groupings of those stars,' said the Hump. 'I once led a caravan in a region – east of the Silver Ranges – where they appear thus, but they are not the star pattern of the map.'

After several more changes the Hump said, 'Wait, I

believe this might be what you are looking for. See, the Constellation of the Archer is only just above the horizon while the Star Bridge is no longer directly overhead.'

Florizan passed him the map to compare the drawn star plan with the bright specks above his head.

'What you show us are the stars above the island on the map,' said the Hump.

'That is excellent,' said Florizan. 'Tomorrow my scroll clerk can seek out the map of the region where the original star chart was drawn and that should tell us where your island lies.'

At dawn the next morning the Krispin and Alwald rode out with the huntmaster to the Circle of Giants to relieve the watchmen who had remained there during the night.

'There has been no movement, not a single string has snapped, Master Brund,' reported one of the men.

'Strange,' muttered Alwald. 'Before sunset yesterday the cords were breaking almost as soon as we tied them.'

They gazed at the huge nude figures with their half-raised clubs in the increasing light.

'They may not have moved in the night but it seems to me they are stirring now,' said Alwald after a minute. 'I am sure that one nearest to us is dragging its foot forward – you can see the sand round it is agitated.'

'Do you remember something the soldier Emon told us one night when we camped on an island in the River of Night?' asked Krispin thoughtfully.

'He had many stories, that one.'

'Yes. The one I am thinking of was about stonelings – he said they are stones shaped in the form of men which come to life when the moon is full.'

'But these are not stones that turn into men – they are men, or giants, who have been turned into stone and besides . . .'

'It is just that the stonelings gave me the idea that perhaps there is similar law that governs these giants, that nature only allows them movement when there is light.'

Alwald was about to say something when there was tremendous thud and the headless giant crashed full-length amid a shower of sand.

All through the morning they watched the giants while the huntmaster busied himself with his measuring rods. They no longer bothered to tie strings to the figures for it was now possible to discern their continuous movement which, even though it was painfully slow compared to that of ordinary humans, did appear to increase as the hours passed.

At noon Mesire Florizan accompanied by Lord Ugo, all the men of his small court and a number of servants, arrived to gaze at the giants which were now on a snail's-pace march towards the Domain with expressions of blind ferocity on their worn faces.

'I have made my calculations, my lord,' said the huntmaster when his master climbed down from his drong. 'Just after dawn they travelled at the rate of four handbreadths a minute. Now that is doubled and – allowing for the fact that they do not appear to walk at night – it means they should be walking at a normal rate the day after tomorrow.'

'Then may the Mother help us all,' said Florizan. 'For I can think of no way that we can halt them.'

'I did hear you say, when you were telling us the history of the Domain, that you had terrible allies,' said Alwald. 'Could you not call upon –'

'Terrible they are to creatures of flesh and blood,' said Florizan, 'but even they could do nothing except perhaps knock a few chips off the giants. Would that my house had a tradition of gramarye for I believe only magic can prevail against them, but my forebears were interested in the natural order rather than the supernatural.'

For a while the men stood about trying to think of ways of blocking the inexorable advance but no suggestions emerged other than the digging of huge pits for the stone giants to fall into or the use of pickaxes on their feet before their speed of movement increased.

'It would be impossible to dig pits deep enough in this sand, they would fill as quickly as they were shovelled, and besides how could we force these monsters to fall into them,' said Florizan. 'As to the other idea, remember that the point of my dagger hardly scratched the monster's eye.'

'Mesire, look out!' cried several voices.

Florizan turned and looked upwards. Slowly . . . slowly the giant's club was descending towards him. He calmly watched it for a while and then walked back to his followers.

'In a couple of days I should have been flattened like a slug beneath a gardener's boot,' he said. 'In a couple of days they will be battering down the walls of the Domain.'

He turned to the Hump who, swathed as usual in his long black cloak, stood on the edge of the group.

'Master Guide,' Florizan cried. 'You have had more experience in your wanderings across the kingdom than any of us and seen more strange things I do not doubt – tell me, how could we stop the march of the giants?'

'I should blind them,' he replied. 'I know it would be impossible to destroy their granite eyes, but they could be painted over with tar.'

'Here is a man who thinks,' cried Florizan. 'Bring ladders and paint from the Domain. We may defeat them by darkness.'

'Or by light,' Krispin murmured and he climbed into the saddle of his drong.

SEVEN
Krispin Underground

The night breeze, warmed over desert sands and perfumed by the flowers which grew in such profusion within the Domain, sighed dolefully in the colonnades of Florizan's palace. From within came the sound of solemn music as befitted the mood of its inhabitants.

Having lived so long in this peaceful spot – like those of us who lived in remote Toyheim – these people are unused to hazard, thought Krispin as Gifon let him leave by the gate and then bolted it behind him. *Even Mesire Florizan is at a loss what to do and seeks an answer in his old scrolls. I pray the Mother that my idea may work, for it seems to me that unwittingly I brought this curse upon them. It must be the nature of the Esav to undo ancient spells.*

At noon that day he had watched as one of Florizan's huntsmen attempted to put the Hump's suggestion into practice. A long ladder had been brought from the Domain. Several men took it to the front of the leading giant and raised it to rest against his shoulder. Climbing swiftly, for the giants were in constant if slow movement, the huntsman carried a wooden pail filled with melted tar. When he reached the top rungs he steadied himself and prepared to throw the black liquid into the huge face looming above him.

But before he could act the giant's arm swung ponderously across his chest and sent the ladder spinning away. The huntsman fell with it, striking a cruel crest of rock. For a long, hideous moment the air vibrated with his death scream followed by an equally terrible silence as the onlookers gazed at his broken-backed body.

Apart from work or hunting accidents, violent death was rare in the Domain and the sight of the giant killing a man with no more effort than a gardener brushing away a troublesome fly filled everyone with horror. The menace approaching the Domain was suddenly a reality rather than a bizarre phenomenon.

All through the afternoon the giants trekked across the sand, and those detailed to watch their pace saw that it was increasing hour by hour. By the time the sun carried her beams below the far rim of the world and the giants once more froze into motionless statues, it was seen that they had travelled half a league from their original circle.

'If my figuring is correct they will be moving as fast as us by this time tomorrow,' said the huntmaster as once more lanterns were strung from the petrified limbs.

Now, as Krispin walked along the wall towards the chasm, he could see these lights twinkling like far off festival trees which he had loved as a child in the home of Father Tammas. Although they were pretty, they were reminders of the danger which threatened them all.

Unless there is a chance that my plan might succeed, the walls of the Domain will soon be crumbling beneath the clubs of the giants, thought Krispin. *Mesire Florizan's folk will be scattered like ants across the waste without shelter or drink while the giants hunt them*.

His resolve firmed by this thought, Krispin squared his shoulders and hurried on to a task which filled him with apprehension.

On reaching the point where the wall ended, he began to walk carefully along the edge of the chasm in the direction of the rock-hewn stairs up which they had escaped from the river. Although the moon was on the wane it was still bright and that – with the lanthorn he carried – he prayed would provide enough light to enable him to descend those six hundred steps in safety.

At last he found the cleft where the steps began and as he looked down the rocky wall with its splintered crags and sheer drops he drew back as though the very sight of it would draw him over the brink.

For a long while he stood, trying to summon up the courage to put his foot down to the first step, but, with his inborn terror of heights, each time he tried he pulled back again. In the end he resorted to childhood practice. He would count and on the word *ten* nothing in the world would prevent him taking that first downward step. He began to count and as in childhood the space between each number lengthened as he approached the fatal double figure.

'Ten!' he said aloud and forced himself to move.

Krispin soon realised that while it had been an ordeal climbing up the stairway, it was doubly bad descending. Fearful of looking down into the depths, he kept his eyes fixed on the rough rock a few fingerbreadths from his face while his free hand became raw as it desperately scrabbled for some crack or protuberance to grip.

When he finally reached the bottom and stood on the bank of pebbles his limbs were atremble and the cold sweat which soaked his shirt made him shiver. Yet he had made the descent! Pray the Mother he would find that it had been worth it.

Carefully picking his way over scree and stone, he followed the river whose rush and roar echoed endlessly between the cliffs. Again he visualised how the *White Dragon* had been carried into it and how the wandlight dimmed as it went further and further into the earth's bowels, yet *it had not vanished!*

Was it possible that the craft had run aground or been trapped in rocks and the wand could still be seen like a fire-worm in the far darkness? Placing the lanthorn behind a rock to screen its distracting glow, he peered into the darkness. As his eyes adjusted he saw a tiny spark.

At midnight Krispin was admitted to Florizan's apartment to find the master of the Domain seated at a table with sheets of vellum before him. He exclaimed at Krispin's appearance, torn clothing and hands and face bloodied from grazes collected on the cliff-face.

'If you are wondering whether my scroll clerk discovered a map showing your magical island the answer is yes,' said Florizan wearily. 'But you must give up any idea of reaching it from here. It is on the coast of the Cold Sea, beyond the Ranges of Dono Kara.'

'I have not come to enquire about that,' said Krispin. 'It is about the stone giants . . .'

'Who approach us as relentlessly as death. What can one do against such beings? My men prepare what defences they can while I uselessly search through ancient manuscripts in the hope of learning something by which they may be halted.'

Florizan rose wearily and walked to a latticed window outside which a night bird sang sweetly.

'Of course we can load our drongs with food and treasure and flee – but to where?' He made a hopeless gesture. 'Only thirst and death await us out there.'

'Mesire, there is a faint chance that I have the answer,'

said Krispin and he quickly described his descent into the chasm and his reason for it.

'You shall have all you ask for,' said Florizan when he concluded. 'At dawn my carpenters will be waiting at the steps with timber and all the rope that can be found in the Domain. If you succeed you will have no cause to regret your bravery, of that I promise.'

When the sun rose the watchmen in the desert saw the giants resume their march while at the rim of the chasm Krispin and Alwald watched as a number of Florizan's men lowered balks of timber down the cliff. One length slipped from its sling and was smashed to splinters on the rocks so far below.

'Have you told the others of this mad notion?' Alwald asked.

Krispin shook his head.

'It would be unfair to give them false hope,' he replied. 'Like you, I have no great faith in the attempt but I can think of nothing else.'

'Then why tell me?'

'Because, Lord Alwald, I trust you,' Krispin answered with a grin that had been long absent from his face. 'After all, we do share the same quest, and I shall feel a lot happier if you are in charge of those fellows when they are paying out the rope.'

'That rope will fray on the rock and you will be whirled away to the earth's fundament,' said Alwald. 'What worries me about that is that you are wearing my sword.'

'The sword you gave me because it was tarnished and blunt and did not have a begemmed hilt like your noble weapon,' retorted Krispin good-naturedly slipping into the old argument.

'Have it your own way, toymaker,' said Alwald. 'But

take every care in the river cavern. If aught happened to you I . . . I should miss the sword.'

Soon the last of the timber had been lowered and the party – each man weighed down by coils of rope – descended the steps to the river. Here in the dim light with the sound of the river ringing in their ears the master carpenter set his men to work binding the balks together to make a sturdy raft.

'How will I know when to tell them to haul you back?' asked Alwald.

'Look,' said Krispin pointing to the opening in the rock into which the river raced. 'Do you see that tiny point of light? That must be the wand – it has to be the wand. When it is extinguished it will mean that I have secured it and that will be the time to heave in.'

When the raft was completed a short mast was fitted at one end on which was hung a lanthorn, and at the other the end of a rope was securely tied. With the assistance of Alwald and Krispin the men dragged it down a pebble bank and launched it into shallow water where fierce eddies tugged at it. Seeing it float so low that wavelets rippled over it, Krispin wondered at his own sanity in starting this venture but, not wishing to appear reluctant in front of Alwald, he waded to the raft and knelt in the middle. At his weight the timber sank even lower and water welled up between the balks.

'Fear not, master,' called one of the workmen. 'She may ride low but she will not sink. You will just have to change your hose when we pull you back.'

There was laughter and Krispin retorted, 'Be careful with that rope or it will be you who has to change hose.'

'Ready?' asked Alwald.

'As I shall ever be.'

He nodded to the master carpenter who loosened the rope. Thus freed the raft drifted with the eddy until it was caught by the current and swept away so fast that for a moment the men holding the rope almost lost their balance and Alwald feared to see it torn from their hands.

'Loop it round that rock and it will take the strain,' he shouted. They did so and from then on they were able to pay out the rope steadily, to the relief of Krispin who had nearly been thrown into the water. Soon he found himself being carried into the cavern mouth and memories of his subterranean voyage returned.

The lanthorn shed feeble rays on the glistening rock on either side and when he looked up he saw the occasional gleam of stalactites. Ahead the wand light grew brighter, but he began to wonder if there were enough ropes joined together to allow him to reach it. Then as it increased, he saw the *White Dragon* like a phantom ship.

When it had been borne into the cavern without steersman or steerage it had been a plaything of the currents and now it rested at an angle against the cavern wall with its bows caught in the jaws of a rock formation.

Steadily the raft drew nearer until it finally nudged against the side of the stranded craft. Krispin seized a mooring line attached to a grapple and managed to hook on to the *White Dragon's* bulwark. After that it was a simple matter to haul himself aboard and climb the rigging to unfasten the cord he had used to bind the wand in place. As usual there was no heat at the tip from which the shadowless light flowed and, holding it carefully in one hand, he returned to the deck. Next he went to the cabin he had used and retrieved the leather tube he'd had made in Mabalon as a case for the wand.

Krispin was filled with a sense of exhilaration as he lowered himself to the lurching raft – at least this part of his plan had worked without a hitch. Once he had taken up his position on the wet balks of timber he slid the wand into the case.

He knew that, with so much slack to be taken up, it would be several minutes before the raft would start to be hauled slowly back to the outside world, and he hoped that having come thus far without accident the rope would stand the extra strain imposed by the current.

Suddenly the raft tilted at such an extreme angle that only by a frenzied grab at the edge of the outside piece of timber did Krispin save himself from being hurled into the black water. Then, with an echoing splash, it fell back and to his horror he saw a grotesque horse-like head, its tusked mouth agape and its white eyes fixed on him with murderous intent. It was a waterhorse, a loathsome creature like the one he had seen seize the hapless merman in the underground lake.

The head vanished beneath a surge of bubbles and again one end of the raft reared up. Clearly the waterhorse was endeavouring to throw him into the water in order to devour him. Krispin shuddered with the knowledge that its powerful jaws could bite him in half.

Holding on desperately with one hand, he retained enough of his wits to slide the leather tube into his shirt and, this done, his hand closed on the comforting grip of Woundflame.

Again the raft crashed back on to the surface; water covered it briefly as it bobbed up and down, and then Krispin realised that the motion was not entirely the result of the creature's lunge – the slack had been taken up on the rope and the raft was being towed to the distant half-circle of light which marked the entrance to the river cavern.

'Serene Mother! Let it not sever the line!' Krispin cried aloud.

Fearfully he gazed about him in the light from the wildly swaying lanthorn. For a minute all he could see was swirls of foam flowing past, then there was a surge of bubbles and the dead-white horsehead broke the surface ten paces away. Water spouted from its flared nostrils, it exhaled with a trumpeting sound and oily breath rolled towards Krispin to bring bile to his throat.

Then it furrowed through the water, its jaws clamped on the outside timber which cracked and splintered as teeth the size of a man's fingers bit into it. If the waterhorse could not dislodge its victim from the raft it clearly intended to destroy it.

Krispin had rolled to the opposite side but was still within an arm's stretch of the monster's head. Timber groaned and he knew that if one balk was dislodged the rope holding the others in place would slacken and allow them to drift apart.

He pushed himself up into a kneeling position, and as he pulled Woundflame from its scabbard he saw its blade gleaming. With its eyes upon him, the waterhorse backed away from the nearly severed timber and then, with its head reared on its long thick neck, it hurled itself once more at the raft. As flippered forelimbs pawed at the raft's timbers, Krispin drove Woundflame's point into the pallid throat which had become exposed beneath the equine head.

Dark ichor gushed from its nostrils as it hurled itself back; a whinnying cry of agony issued from the open mouth and it went into a frenzy. Small whirlpools spun away from the blood-seethed spot where it twisted and dived and flailed. Then, summoning its still mighty strength it bore down on the raft once more.

This time Krispin knew that unless he did something desperate the demonic creature would smash the raft and wreak its vengeance among its scattered timbers. Struggling to keep his balance, he rose to his feet with Woundflame raised above his shoulder.

The raft rocked as the creature's bow-wave lifted it.

Head, pulsating throat, heaving chest reared out of the water; reared so high that for a moment man and monster were eye to eye.

Krispin had an impression of teeth about to close upon him and he swung his sword in a singing stroke from right to left, a blow so fast that it appeared for an instant that the sword had melted into a blur of silver. The edge of the blade, which had been tempered with spells as well as blood, had taken on a razor sharpness with its battle lustre. It sliced into the neck of the waterhorse, sinking deeper and deeper until the head was half severed. It sank beneath the blood-slicked surface.

Krispin reeled off balance with the momentum of the blow and fell overboard with a shout of fear. Icy water poured into his throat – evil-tasting and evil-smelling with waterhorse blood – as he reached out with his free hand and felt the raft sliding past. His fingers fought for a hold on the wet wood, hooked into a split left by the creature's teeth, and for several minutes he was towed with the raft before he summoned the energy to haul himself aboard. Then he lay face down with his hand still locked on Woundflame's grip.

'Here he comes,' cried one of the men heaving on the rope a few minutes later. As the raft neared the pebbled bank Alwald laughed and called, 'You lazy pottonson! This is not the time for resting!'

The men waded out into the shallows to haul the raft in.

'Lord Alwald,' shouted the master carpenter, 'he is not resting – he has fainted.'

EIGHT
The March of the Giants

All through the long day the stone colossi marched tirelessly over sand dune and bare rock. By noon the huntmaster's calculations were confirmed as their rate of progress became that of mortal men, and it was obvious that by sundown they would be close to the walls of the Domain.

Their march was watched at a respectful distance by a nervous group of courtiers and retainers on the fast white hunting drongs but the giants took no notice of them, their stone eyes remaining set on the shining roofs of Florizan's palace. Only once did they acknowledge the mortal presence. At mid-afternoon Lord Ugo, fired by rash courage and the chance to win esteem, set his drong racing towards the trudging line until he was within a dozen paces of the leading figure. Rising up in the saddle he flung a javelin which splintered against the petrified heart of the giant who immediately swung his club down on the manikin who dared make such a defiant if futile gesture.

The club, which had been fashioned from the trunk of an oak in the days when its wielder was flesh, struck the ground within a pace of Ugo's drong. As sand and rock fragments showered the youth, the giant again raised the weapon with the same ease as a human lifting a stick. Ugo drove the point of his goad into the drong's flank and with a convulsive leap the animal sped to safety as the earth trembled from the giant's second blow.

This demonstration of titantic agility lowered the spirits of the spectators even deeper, and many of the courtiers rode home to superintend the packing of food and their most treasured possessions in preparation for flight from the Domain.

In the later afternoon Mesire Florizan and Lady Sylva entered the sleeping chamber where Krispin lay on a couch with the horsemaid keeping watch over him.

'How do you feel now that you are awake, Master Krispin?' His melodious voice held a note of concern.

'I shall be fit for my task tonight,' replied Krispin struggling into a sitting position.

'My chirurgeon is mystified, for he could find no hurt with you.'

'I believe my faintness was caused by the water I swallowed when I fell from the raft,' said Krispin. 'There was much blood in it from the water creature and it is likely that it poisoned me. But I have been well cared for' – he smiled at Silvermane – 'and the strenghtening draughts your chirurgeon prescribed are restoring my strength.'

'You will be fit to go through with your plan tonight? Or should I command another to carry the wand? Ugo perhaps.'

'I took it from the eidolon – I must carry it,' said Krispin emphatically. He lowered himself back against his pillows.

'Yet you look so wan,' said Lady Sylva.

'Just a spell of dizziness,' Krispin assured her. 'Such moments have lessened through the day. Tell me, mesire, what of the giants?'

'We see them clearly from the walls,' replied Florizan.

'We are sending up prayers that your ruse works, for tomorrow they will be at the gate,' added Lady Sylva.

'If it does you will be rewarded with anything I can offer,' said Florizan. 'Indeed, it may be possible that I could help you on the journey to the Cold Sea but it would be at some risk. It is pointless to discuss it now – by this time tomorrow we may all be fugitives. Now I must leave you for I have much to arrange. Tonight, if you succeed, there will be a banquet the like of which has not yet been seen in the Domain.'

'Then it will be a truly amazing feast,' said Krispin with a brave attempt at a laugh.

The rays of the low sun shining almost horizontally through Lorelle's latticed window filled her sleeping chamber with the warm light that preludes the dusk of the day's end. With a sigh the girl opened her eyes and then her heart was filled with deep joy as she felt the warmth of Gambal's body beside her beneath the sandhart fur.

Since she had taken him for a lover the pleasure of love-making had come as a revelation to her. It was as though the spiritual plane she sought so fervently when she was a novice had been replaced by the worldly. When she thought of her time wearing the novice's habit it seemed unreal to her, another life – as indeed it was. Now, instead of theology, which had failed to satisfy her questioning mind despite her every effort to have faith, her thoughts turned often to the erotic acts which never failed to give her ease. Instead of wanting to learn wisdom at the feet of Brother Mias, she now only wished to please the young stranger to whom she had entrusted her heart and given her body.

Moving back the cover, she looked down on his pale form – the body which had wrought such a sea-change within her being – with a smile of affection. She looked to where her habit still hung on the wall – she should have thrown it away as it meant nothing now! – and although it had been replaced by clothing provided by the Lady Sylva after her arrival in the Domain, she wished with all her heart that she had gowns such as those worn by the great ladies of Thaan in order to make herself more attractive for her beloved.

As the sensual sleep which had followed their last love-making cleared from her mind, she remembered the threat of the stone giants and was surprised at how little it perturbed her. If they could not be averted she would flee with Gambal. As long as they were together!

Gambal's eyes were closed and in repose his face looked more innocent than ever, and she wondered how it was that it showed no mark of the dreadful life he had been forced to lead. Perhaps it was an indication of the self assurance which had first attracted him to her.

She ran her fingertips across his chest and as she felt a breathless heat rise within her she bent across him . . .

Gambal lay with his eyes closed and tried to come to terms with the perverse thoughts that ran unbidden through his mind. When he had met Lorelle in Thaan her remoteness had been a challenge to him. She was so chaste and so out of his reach that privately he had named her the Lily Maid. Unused to love in his self-oriented life, he had cursed himself for allowing her to unconsciously exert such a hold upon him; at times he almost hated her because of it. Yet her tranquil expression, downcast eyes and slender body which was only allowed to hint at its femininity beneath her novice's robe haunted him. As time went by and his obsession increased he sometimes had a dream-fantasy in which he stripped that symbol of inaccessibility from her.

It was like such a dream come true when they met on the moon-seared terrace – his body sang as she gladly gave herself to him.

And each time they lay together afterwards her eagerness to please and be pleased increased. She was shameless in her desires and for a time this excited him.

Only . . .

Only one night what had been an expression of passion became lewdness in his eyes; he realised with agonising clarity that the girl who lay spread before him murmuring the brothel words she had forced him to teach her was not the girl who had bespelled him in Thaan. It was her enigmatic expression, her unworldliness – her *chastity!* – that had drawn him to her. It was ironic that in quenching the immemorial male ache for the unattainable he had quenched his dream. Now when they lay together he was no more excited by her than by the ambitious females he had bedded briefly in the Citadel, yet she seemed to have no idea of what he thought behind his youthful mask, had no inkling of his sense of loss.

She is in love with coupling – not with me, he thought in crude anger and then even he felt shame at the untruth; what had become lewdness to him was to her an expression of love. But this did not give him back his vision of the Lily Maid.

Now he continued to pretend sleep as he felt her fingers glide over his ribs; she moved beside him and then there was the sensation of her hard nipples caressing his skin as she drew her breasts across his breast – a trick of affection that would have fired his loins a few nights earlier.

'Wake, Gambal,' she whispered in his ear. 'Awake my love.'

Rebelliously he kept his eyes closed, and treacherously behind the lids he had a fleeting glimpse of Lorelle as she had been in Thaan, her head inclined in silent prayer and an aura of sanctity about her like the statue of the Serene Mother in Danaak's greatest shrine.

Perversely it was this mental picture which began to arouse him rather than Lorelle's caresses, but he continued to lie supine as though the languor of their earlier love-making was still upon him.

'My poor sweetheart, do I exhaust you?' teased Lorelle. 'Do you find me like those beings in folk tales who steal the sap of men – the lamia?'

Gambal said nothing.

'Fear not, my love, I shall make it easy for you.'

She knelt astride him and he heard her sigh as she lowered herself upon him, and as he felt her warmth he knew it was like an old fantasy becoming reality, *only* . . .

'The worst evil to befall a man is for him to achieve his dearest desire,' ran an old Ythan proverb which, until that moment, Gambal had thought to be ridiculous.

His lack of response did not affect Lorelle; perhaps to her it seemed like a game for her to take the dominant role, and when she reached the climax of her solitary ride she rolled beside him with an expression of gratitude on her flushed face.

'My forever love,' she murmured.

When she opened her eyes again the room was filled with dusk and Gambal was standing over the couch with his cloak about him.

'I am going to watch Krispin challenge the giants,' he said.

'Sweetheart, I shall join you on the wall in a little while,' she said dreamily.

He nodded and left the chamber.

After some minutes Lorelle arose and dressed. Already she was missing her lover and, besides, she felt curious to see what Krispin could do against those monsters. At the thought of Krispin she smiled; he must have been attracted to her at first – he was so protective! – but he soon gave up and resigned her to Gambal when he realised how her affections lay . . .

Dear Gambal. How lucky she was to have a lover so devoted. With pleasure she remembered the ardent looks he had given her when she wore that shapeless habit – and had a demeanour to go with it. Now at least he did not have to suffer her holiness. He could take his pleasure with her however he wanted which was the fitting reward for his devotion.

Tendrils of her black hair hung over her face and as she reached for her comb she saw that, in putting on his warm night cloak, Gambal had not thought it necessary to wear his jacket as well. He had left it thrown over the back of a chair and she remembered that in its pocket there was a mirror, a mirror which for some foolish reason he had forbidden her to see.

But now she needed a mirror.

With her hair so disarrayed everyone could guess how her afternoon had been spent and, besides, she wanted to look presentable for Gambal.

'He is like the noble in the nursery story who forbade his wife to enter a certain room – though I cannot think that there can be anything wicked about a little mirror my vain love uses when he razors his face each day,' she said aloud.

It took only a moment for her to put her hand into the pocket and remove the flat leather case which held the mirror. She took it out and, sitting on the bed with her comb poised, she gazed into it and uttered a word of annoyance. No doubt due to the fading light she could not see herself properly. The mirror appeared to be clouded and when she peered into it closely she saw swirling smoke, yet there was no smoke in her chamber for it to reflect.

'All Father save me!' she screamed.

From the smoke two malignant eyes stared out at her.

Terrible eyes which held hers, would not let her drop the mirror; eyes that seemed to seek the very depths of her being.

She had no idea how long she had held the mirror in her hand when the smoke faded and she became aware of her own terrified face.

'Oh Gambal, what are you?' she moaned. 'Oh, what have I done?'

When darkness raced across the desert after the setting of the sun the giants were less than half a league from the crowded walls of the Domain. As before, when the light left them they froze mid-stride with their clubs either resting on their shoulders or trailing behind them.

'Are you sure you are fit enough after your ordeal in the cavern?' Florizan asked Krispin.

'Yes, mesire,' he answered. 'My legs are still a shade weak but I am not going to do combat with them like the giant-killer in the legends.'

The gate was opened and there was a murmur of talk from the walls as he set out with Alwald accompanying him.

'Are you so hungry for glory that you will not let anyone else carry the wand,' demanded Alwald in a low voice.

'Such as you?' answered Krispin in equally low tones.

'Why not? You are still shaking from your ducking.'

'I cannot explain properly but I want to do it because I

feel that it is I who has brought this calamity upon the Domain. I am sure it was the Esav that animated the giants when I went near the circle in which they stood. It seems to me that its power must be to remove spells – or at least partly so. The giants may not have returned to the flesh but the sorcery that held them motionless has been lifted.'

'Except during the hours of darkness.'

'Do not look to me for explanations. I do not understand the workings of gramarye.'

'Gramarye! I am heart sick of gramarye! Life at River Garde was straightforward, everything was natural and a man knew where he stood. And if it had not been for gramarye there would never have been The Enchantment. Sometimes I think the Witchfinders are right to seek it out.'

'But they seek out more than that,' said Krispin. 'Do you forget the Witchfinder who had us arrested in Danaak? If it had not been for Gambal . . .'

'I know, I know. I shall go to the chasm now. Every man will be needed there.'

For a moment they stood awkwardly, then Alwald slapped Krispin on the upper arm. 'Good fortune, toymaker!'

'And you, my lord.'

Krispin set off towards a light which, having been lit by one of Florizan's men who had kept pace with the giants, now indicated their position.

When he reached the lanthorn, which merely illuminated the colossal feet of the leading giant, Krispin took the tubular case from under his cloak and from it withdrew the wand. Immediately the tableau of graven figures was flooded with cold white light; to those watching from the Domain it appeared as though the enemy were enveloped in a brilliant halo.

'Awake, awake,' muttered Krispin as he stood holding high the wand. For a moment he feared that the light would have no effect on the giants who towered above him as stationary as they had been when they formed the age-old ring. The feeling of nausea which grew within him was not entirely due to the blood of the waterhorse which had entered his mouth that morning – it was also a physical reaction to the knowledge that if his plan failed the Domain would be despoiled before the next sundown, and with it any hope he might have of assistance in continuing the quest.

'Awake, awake!' he repeated, rubbing his knotted stomach hard with his free hand.

There was a sighing sound.

He knew it could not be the giants for in the state of petrification they needed neither breath or heartbeat. Then he realised that it was caused by the disturbance of sand. Those huge feet, extra huge because of the weight they supported, were moving – the light flowing from the wand was reanimating the giants.

Krispin began to walk backwards, and only just in time because the giants resumed their march as though it had never been interrupted by the setting of the sun. They moved so quickly that Krispin could no longer keep backing but had to turn and break into a series of runs to remain ahead.

The next question to be answered was whether the giants would follow the wand when he moved away from the Domain or would come to a halt and wait until the dawn showed them their objective. Gradually he turned from the Domain and headed towards a beacon which was to guide him to a spot further east. Looking over his shoulder he was relieved to see that the giants were following as, unable to see the Domain, they were drawn by the light moving ahead of them.

As he ran at a safe distance in front of them Krispin regretted his determination to carry the wand alone. Alwald had been right, he was still shaking – more than ever with this exertion – and he reproached himself for not giving him the wand. He had half a league to go, and he prayed to the Mother that he would be able to summon up enough strength to reach his destination.

As he came closer to the chasm the sand drifts became less numerous and most of the time there was rock underfoot. This had the effect of enabling the giants to travel faster and Krispin noticed uneasily that the distance between them was gradually lessening.

Suddenly another spasm of nausea gripped him. He doubled up, missed his footing and stumbled full-length to graze his hands and face on rough rock. In trying to save himself he had let go of the wand which fell to the ground several paces away. For a moment Krispin lay pain-racked where he had fallen, then as his wits returned he rolled over to see the giants looming up behind him. Desperately he tried to get to his feet and then he saw a figure race into the light cast by the wand.

'Lorelle!' he shouted.

As she passed the fallen wand he could see that she was wearing her grey novice's robe with the hem held up to enable her to run. Its hood had fallen back to reveal her face crumpled with grief and as pale as ivory. Her mouth was open as though in a perpetual shriek.

He called her name again but she did not hear or even notice him as she ran on towards the ponderous figures. He caught her words as she dashed past, and they were to ring in his ears for a long time afterwards: 'I have sinned . . . I have sinned . . .'

He watched in horror as she reached the leading figure. Its great arm swept down, its enormous hand grasped her and lifted her high. Her hysterical chant ceased. There was a sickening crack and her limp body plummeted to the ground.

The giants continued their march.

The brief diversion gave Krispin enough time to get to his feet, snatch up the wand and run as if the demon Omad was behind him. He knew not whether the girl might still be alive but on the slender chance that she might be he wanted to lure the enemy away from her. Pain, nausea, fear were forgotten as he sprinted over the rock towards the beacon gleam.

The race seemed to be endless. No matter how fast he forced himself to run the giants kept pace with him with long strides which made the very rock shudder. At last he could make out details of the lanthorn which had been mounted on a post to mark the point where the steps leading down the cliff-face began.

Krispin slowed to let the giants come closer and then, holding the wand high, he went on again keeping just out of range of the foremost giant's club. On reaching the lanthorn he scrambled drunkenly over the rocky lip of the chasm and down several of the steps into Alwald's arms.

Above them the giants loomed over the edge of the chasm, the light of the wand showing in detail their ferocious expressions and while Alwald still clutched him, Krispin flung the wand far into the abyss.

NINE
The Lily Maid

The sun was at her zenith when Alwald carefully made his way down the cliff-face steps. Like those in the Domain his spirit was heavy. Although, thanks to Krispin, the threat of the stone giants had been lifted, sorrow over the death of Lorelle pervaded the air.

There had been no triumphant banquet after the giants had followed the light to the edge of the chasm and then toppled to their destruction after it; no minstrels played, no perfumes scented the air – only a single bell tolled as Lorelle's body was borne back to Florizan's palace. As she lay on the flower-strewn bier her delicate face wore such an expression of repose that ladies who sat through the night in the death vigil found it hard to believe that the Dark Maid had taken her.

At first men said in hushed voices that she had died in an attempt to save Krispin when he fell, but soon it was realised that for her to have been at the spot suggested some other motive. When a parchment with lines of shaky writing was found in her chamber with the ink on it still fresh it was decided that for some reason known only to herself she had sought immolation.

'I am puzzled as to why she penned her last message to the world in Old Ythan,' said Florizan as he gently replaced the parchment on the table. 'In the morning I shall order my scroll clerk to decipher it and then mayhap we shall learn what so troubled her mind.'

But in the morning the mystery was increased by the disappearance of the parchment, and though it could have been wafted through the open window of the deserted chamber by the night breeze several strange theories were whispered in the corridors of the palace.

As was the custom in the Domain, Lorelle was borne to her grave while the dew still sparkled on the grass. Her resting place had been prepared in a grove of weeping evergreens where a column of stone was set up as her monument.

'What shall I inscribe upon it, mesire,' asked the mason when the flowered turf had been replaced and the mourners were dispersing through the trees.

'Lorelle . . .' said Florizan, and he looked inquiringly at the ashen Gambal nearby.

'Write *Lorelle – The Lily Maid*,' he said in a muffled voice.

'So be it,' said Florizan.

Now Alwald continued down the rock wall of the chasm, reflecting what a fool Krispin had been to insist on carrying the wand himself. To be just, the Toyheim apprentice had managed to lure the giants to their doom, but at what cost to himself? He lay in a fever which resulted from a combination of exhaustion and the noxious blood of the water-horse he had swallowed in the river cavern.

The trouble with fellows who have backgrounds like Krispin is the compulsion to prove themselves, Alwald thought, *whereas those of us who are fortunate enough to belong to the old families are not cursed with this compulsion*.

When he was half-way down the steps he cautiously

leaned out and gazed down at the shattered remains of the giants. They lay on the rocky bank and in the river shallows like dismembered dolls. On a scree of black pebbles Alwald saw the object of his descent – though eclipsed by the bright rays of the sun which at this time shone directly into the chasm, a steady point of light marked the position of Krispin's wand.

If ever I have children, especially sons, I shall have some tales to tell them, Alwald thought, and then it seemed the possibility of him enjoying fatherhood was remote.

On reaching the bottom the shattered bodies of the giants impressed him with their size more than when he had actually seen them marching abreast across the desert. Nearest to him lay a forearm with an outstretched hand. Out of curiosity he lay down beside it to measure it with his body and found that it was longer than he was tall.

Several torsos and limbs piled upon each other made a rugged island in the river, while further along the bank lay the headless body of a giant. When Alwald went to inspect the colossus he saw that it was cracked right through in several places so that if some power were ever to animate it again it would fall apart. A comforting thought.

Its gigantic head lay on the margin of the river, half in water which gurgled through the mouth which was wide open as though frozen in a soundless shriek when it had suddenly plunged into the void. The hair hung down over the low forehead like a petrified tangle of serpents and beneath it the stone eyes were closed.

Alwald sat on a nearby rock and gazed at it. Strange to think that yesterday it was filled with the power to smash its way through the walls of the Domain and now it seemed no more than a huge fragment of ancient statuary – the sort of forgotten relic to be found among ruins in the Land of

Blight. Unusually for him, Alwald drifted into a reflective reverie . . .

And the eyes of the head opened.

With a bound Alwald quitted his rock, ran along the bank with the round black pebbles rolling beneath his urgent feet, snatched up the wand and raced up the steps.

Only when he had no more breath did he stop. With his chest heaving painfully, he pressed back against the rock and slid the wand into its leather tube, then forced himself to look down. The debris - like that in the yard of some careless sculptor - was strewn just as it was when he had descended. It would lie like that forever but - he wondered as he resumed his climb - would the eyes stare with malign life forever?

That afternoon Krispin awoke from fevered dreams to see Florizan seated beside his bed. He appeared distinguished as always in dark green hose and silver-worked doublet and a silver grey fur cap adorned with a black plume. To Krispin he looked like a king in a folktale.

'Your pardon, mesire, I was sleeping,' the young man said.

Florizan brushed aside the apology with a wave of his hand and asked him how he felt.

'Weak,' Krispin admitted.

'No doubt. My chirurgeon tells me that he will not allow you to rise for several days. When time hangs too heavily I shall send you my story-teller - ask him for "The King of the Golden Mountain", his latest tale and most amusing. I shall not tire you with my talk, suffice to say that I do not have the words to express my gratitude for the deed you performed last night. I shall express it in another way. If you wish to continue your journey you will have the means even though it entails revealing the greatest secret of my House.

'On the other hand, if you and your company wish to remain here safe from the ever-darkening world you will be ever welcome.'

'For the others I cannot speak but for myself I must perforce go on,' answered Krispin. 'Once before I had the temptation of abandoning the quest but it would have meant breaking a vow; now I am tempted again, and again I will continue and this time it is not because of a promise made to an old woman but because I believe in the quest. Mayhap the Princess Livia will never be found but while there is the slightest chance that the kingdom may be restored to its former freedom that chance must be taken.'

'Ah, the idealism of youth!' exclaimed Florizan. 'I salute it – and envy it. Get your strength back. If you insist on following the quest you are going to need it.'

Florizan rose to leave.

'One question, mesire – Lorelle . . .?'

'Dead.'

Alone Krispin turned his face to the wall.

'And I promised Mias to guard her,' he muttered and shameful tears wet his cheeks.

In the days that followed gaiety returned to the Domain. Each night there was a banquet or entertainment presided over by Mesire Florizan and Lady Sylva to celebrate the deliverance from the stone giants, at which Ognam became a great favourite as an entertainer. He had a knack of making Florizan roar with laughter – usually by telling earthy tales which were something of a novelty in the Domain – but even when he was well into his act he was aware of a pair of glittering eyes watching him with undisguised hostility. Florizan's dwarf feared that his master would pervail upon Ognam to become his jongleur-in-chief, and his mind seethed with malicious schemes to discomfort his supposed rival.

As well as Ognam, who was overjoyed to have an audience again, Alwald found this period much to his liking. Like the jester he too was transported back to happier times as Florizan's masques reminded him of nights of courtly revels in River Garde, especially after his father had married the Lady Demara. And it was pleasant to be among those of gentle birth again just as he was sure Krispin would be happy to mingle with apprentices again or the Hump with caravaneers. To each his own!

But Ognam was not the only one to be the object of malice. During the festivities the Hump and Silvermane kept in the background except when Florizan insisted that they attend his banquets and sit at his table – having an inherited interest in unusual creatures, he was fascinated by the horsemaid. Such marks of favour were something that rankled with his heir. Despite the fact that the ill-assorted couple – nicknamed Beauty and the Beast in the palace – spent most of their time alone, often walking in the gardens and groves when Silvermane would lay myrtle flowers before Lorelle's monument, Ugo managed to find them and shoot them venomous glances.

'I have not forgotten you spike, crookback,' he hissed on one occasion. 'Before long you will pay for that insult. And you, half-horse, you will weep for the day you laid your hands on me.'

The Hump said nothing. With luck he and Silvermane would soon be far from the Domain and its hedonistic inhabitants.

Another who wandered the grounds of the Domain was

Gambal. He had spoken little since the death of Lorelle, and he was allowed his solitude as it was considered he was nursing a broken heart. Perhaps he was. But having found his mirror where Lorelle had dropped it, he guessed what had happened and he brooded on revenge. And what revenge that would be! Yet in one way he was solaced. The Dark Maid had made Lorelle unattainable once more so the memory he now cherished of her was of the Lily Maid to whom he had lost his heart in Thaan rather than the harlot lover in the Domain.

After a week Krispin was able to leave his couch, and being young and of a physical fitness enchanced by the rigours of his journeying, he told Mesire Florizan a few days later that he felt ready to continue the quest.

The two strolled in a walled garden. A sundial stood in the centre, statues posed in corners between flowering trees, crimson roses made the air heavy with their fragrance and, although it was not yet summer, vines hung over the walls heavy with fruit. At the far end sparkling spouts of water splashed into a bronze basin beneath the benign eye of a marble faun, a reminder to Krispin of the mystical fountains which had saved them in the wilderness.

Florizan said, 'You really wish to leave this . . .' a languid wave of his hand took in the garden as a symbol of the Domain '. . . to seek the unknown in perilous lands?'

'To you it must seem like madness, mesire, but . . .' Krispin raised his shoulders and let them fall.

'In the old sagas it is oft repeated that it is necessary for a man to perform what a man must perform. I never quite understood the phrase until now. I only hope you do not regret your decision when you reach the Cold Sea.'

'In Toyheim we learned little of the outside world, and the Cold Sea was only mentioned in fables. Is it so forbidding?'

'In the winter its shores are ice-bound and even the bears seek underground lairs to escape the cold – or so I believe,' Florizan answered. 'By now the ice will have melted but there are frequent tempests which hurl mighty seas against rock-girt shores. Here, in this pleasant garden, it is hard to picture such bleakness as the coasts of the Cold Sea where the wind is often of such strength that the malformed trees which manage to survive there cannot grow upright but writhe on the mossed earth like serpents.'

He spoke with such conviction that Krispin wondered if it could be possible that the master of the Domain had himself visited that far region at some time in his earlier life.

'Few ships venture into such waters,' Florizan went on, 'and then only during the summer to seek the fur of sea creatures which live along the barren coasts, and amber which is washed up on the shores of black sand. Both commodities are keenly sought in the marts of Danaak because of their excellent quality and rarity.

'It is said that less than half of the desperate captains who set out bring their vessels back to their home ports because of tempests and krakens, and corsairs who lay in wait to relieve them of their hard-won cargoes.'

'A bleak place for The Mage to live.'

'Bleak indeed, but far from the ken of Witchfinders.'

Florizan seated himself on a marble bench and plucked a fruit as purple as his robe from an overhanging branch.

'For your sakes I hope your Mage still lives,' he continued, 'for while I can arrange for you to reach the tower marked on the map I can do nothing about your return.'

Krispin gave him an enquiring look.

'I cannot tell you more until the time comes for your departure. Tell your companions to be prepared within the next two days. I understand that you and Lord Alwald will be accompanied by Master Gambal. Your guide and the horsemaid have asked for a drong and provisions to cross the desert in search of her homeland. To me it appears a forlorn hope, yet it is probably for the best. It would be impossible for him to settle in the Domain for he is a born wanderer. And for some reason I cannot determine, I sense there is bad blood between him and Ugo, who, I must admit, can be hot-headed at times.'

'The Hump has a remarkable sense of direction,' said Krispin. 'I shall miss him for though he is misshapen and says little there is great strength and virtue in him, as I found in the wasteland. Has our other companion spoken to you?'

'The jongleur? No, but I have spoken to him as I wish him to remain here as court fool. He never fails to entertain me. And I understand that, like Master Guide, he is not dedicated to the quest.'

'That is true. Yet I shall regret the parting – there seem to have been so many partings since Al . . . Lord Alwald and I left the High Wald.'

He sighed as he thought of those who had shared their dangers, especially the girl nicknamed Rose Red who had remained in Mabalon with the Lady Demara.

The next night light streamed from the rose windows of the palace and gay music filled the air as the most lavish banquet yet was held to farewell those about to leave the Domain. The most savoury food was served on the finest silver, the rarest wines served in the most sparkling crystal and the most exotic of perfumes made the evening one to be remembered and relished in the hard days that lay ahead for the travellers. As goblets were raised in toast after toast they looked upon each other with a cordiality suggesting life-long friendship rather than brief comradeship resulting from happenstance.

Even Gambal wrung Ognam's hand emotionally when they finally parted for the night.

At dawn Gifon roused Alwald, Krispin and Gambal and, bleary-eyed, they were escorted to the stables where Florizan and Brund his huntmaster waited with saddled drongs, the travellers' packs already stowed in the panniers.

Mesire Florizan, as urbane as ever despite little slumber, apologised for starting out at such an early hour but the secret of their destination was known only to a handful of the most trusted inhabitants of the Domain and the fewer who witnessed the direction of their departure the better.

As the sun rose in a glory of gold and cerise they set out northwards over the sands. For some minutes they rode in silence and then the huntmaster cried, 'Someone follows.'

They turned and beheld a figure running wildly after them, arms waving and bells tinkling.

'Ognam!'

They drew rein and waited until the gasping jongleur caught up with them. When he did so they had to wait again until he had got enough breath back to gasp, 'Must . . . come . . . with you.'

'What is the quest to you, jester?' demanded Gambal. 'Stay and amuse mesire's court safe from the agents of the Regent.'

Still unable to speak properly, Ognam merely shook his head vigorously which caused the bells sewn to the hood of his motley to tinkle louder. Then he turned from the riders, pushed down his green and red hose, and bending forward gave them a view of his shining bottom.

'If this is a joke . . .' began Alwald in outrage.

'I see nothing there that attracts me,' remarked Florizan drily. 'Pray, sir, spare us . . .'

'There! There!' interrupted Ognam in a strangled voice. With his forefinger he pointed to where two blue dots marred the marble whiteness of his left buttock.

'He has been bitten by a snake,' said Krispin.

In confirmation Ognam held up a small yellow reptile whose head showed unpleasant signs of having been dashed against a wall.

'A sand viper,' said Florizan. 'Not usually deadly but our friend will have a red-hot rump ere long. But why should such a mishap make you want to leave my employ?'

Ognam hauled his hose back into position and managed to say, 'It was put in my bed. Next time it may be firewort in my drink or ground crystal in my pottage . . .'

A look of understanding crossed Florizan's face.

'My dwarf! I shall have that misbegotten turd boiled in oil.'

'Please,' said Ognam. 'Slowly.'

'His office will be changed for that of dung-shoveller in the drong stables, and you can take on his ceremonial duties.'

Ognam shook his head.

'I thank you, Mesire Florizan, but I would rather travel on with my comrades here . . .' He looked up at them hopefully and Gambal snorted. 'I understand the hurt felt by the manikin after I had the honour of your favour though I deplore his method of expressing it. My reason for leaving is not due entirely out of fear of what trick he might try next – I realise that I am not suited for life in the Domain. One has only so many jokes, and after you had heard them several times, my lord, you would weary of me. In my trade I have made people laugh with my repertoire and then passed on to others to whom it was new. I was destined to be a strolling player rather than a court entertainer.'

'What do you say – will you take this ungrateful wretch with you?' asked Florizan.

Alwald and Krispin nodded.

'So be it,' said Florizan. 'You will live to regret your decision,' he continued to Ognam, 'but I force no man against his will.'

'I thank you, mesire,' said Ognam as he climbed up behind Krispin, 'but I have a very deep-seated reason for making it.'

A groan greeted Ognam's attempt at a joke, and the drongs moved forward. Before long the jester's gasps of pain proclaimed the fact that the toxin of the sand viper was having the effect that Florizan had predicted.

The day was drawing to a close when the cavalcade halted on the edge of a steep-walled valley and Florizan pointed into it with his goad.

'There,' he said in a solemn voice. 'There is the secret of my House.'

A series of small spring-fed pools were spaced along the valley floor with fringes of palms ringing them, but what astounded the travellers were the fabulous beasts basking in the last sunbeams on shelves of honey-coloured rock – six golden-feathered griffins.

TEN
Night Flight

Krispin's knowledge of the shining griffins was limited to childhood tales, and the fact that the first constellation to appear in the evening sky took its name from these fabled creatures.

'A griffin is half lion and half eagle,' Father Tammas had told little Krispin and the equally wide-eyed Jennet. 'They have beaked heads and huge wings with golden feathers, but their bodies are covered with fur, and like lions they have four legs with clawed feet and a long tail. They lived long ago in the Golden Age . . .'

In folktales these beasts may have lived long ago, but here they were before his eyes.

'Are they not magnificent?' said Florizan, his eyes agleam with admiration.

'Mesire, why do you refer to them as the secret of your House?' asked Alwald. 'Surely out here, away from the world, there is little need for secrecy.'

'On the contrary,' Florizan replied. 'Imagine if some member of the yearly caravan from Thaan – or one of my retainers who hungered for the outside world and the silver to enjoy it – took word of the griffins to the Citadel in Danaak. The Regent, with his passion for the bizarre, would send an army to capture them, and that would mean farewell to the Domain as well as these survivors from a more majestic age. Imagine them imprisoned in that foul menagerie of his. They would die within a season.

'It was the hope of finding such fabulous creatures that brought my great-grandfather to the Desert of Akea in the first place, and when he found that griffins dwelt here for part of the year he made their protection a family duty. Only the head of the House and his heirs, and a few of the most trusted servants such as Brund here, ever come to this valley. Each heir must come to converse with them and fly . . .'

'Converse with them?' Krispin exclaimed. 'You mean you can talk . . .'

'Not as you and I talk,' said Florizan, 'but my Great-grandfather Florizan devised a way by which communication is possible. It is not so difficult as you might imagine as griffins are the most intelligent beasts the All Father created, as you will doubtless discover.'

'Very honoured I am to have seen such wonders,' said Ognam, 'but –'

'Ah, you are anxious to continue. I shall go down to inform the griffins of your journey and solicit their agreement to carry you.'

'You mean – we are to fly?' cried Alwald.

'Of course. How else could you reach the Cold Sea from here?'

'Will you reconsider me for the post of court jester?' asked Ognam.

'The griffins spend the summer half of the year on islets in the Cold Sea where they hunt the kraken,' Florizan continued. 'When the sea turns to ice they fly here to spend the winter in warmth and safety. It is fortunate for you that this is the month when they return to their hunting.'

From his saddlebag Florizan extracted a frame of black

wood to which were attached a number of silver bells, then, while the huntmaster held the reins of his drong, he slid to the rocky ground and walked to the edge of the valley. Here he held up the frame and with a bronze hammer attached by a chain struck the largest bell. It gave forth a chime both pure and clear, and below the griffins twitched their pointed ears and turned their mighty heads to see the line of intruders against the skyline.

As Florizan walked down the steep slope towards them they rose on their legs and greeted him with a combination of grunts and whistles which sounded meaningless to the onlookers. When he stood before them he spoke in a gutteral tone, interspersing each sentence with a varying sequence of chimes from the silver bells.

As they listened the griffins stretched as voluptuously as hearthside cats and briefly unfolded their wings. In comparison to the figure of Florizan they appeared enormous.

Their chests and wings were feathered while their backs, bellies and legs were covered with white fur which was marked with reddish patches. Like their feathers, their claws and the wicked arrowhead barbs at the ends of their tails were the colour of gold.

'And he expects us to ride on their backs,' muttered Gambal. 'I would much rather trust myself to the subterranean river again than those monsters.'

'Hush, good sir,' said the huntmaster. 'One should never refer to the noble griffins in such a fashion. Though I doubt if they could know the meaning of the actual words they can tell much from the tone of them and their hearing is remarkable.'

'It seems to me that we have no choice but to ride those most noble creatures if we want to continue the quest,' said Krispin.

'At the moment the quest is losing its attraction,' Gambal muttered.

They sat in silence for many minutes and then Florizan trudged up the slope towards them.

'They will carry you to the Mage's island as a favour to my House,' he said. 'They will fly at dusk, for they do not like showing themselves in the daylight except when hunting over the Cold Sea. You should arrive at your destination within an hour of sunrise, though this can depend on the strength of the winds.'

'May I ask, mesire, have you ever flown on one of these most splendidly graceful creatures?' asked Alwald.

'Indeed I have,' Florizan answered. 'When an heir of my House comes of age it is a tradition that he comes here to the griffins and flies with one. To view the world from so high above must be one of the greatest experiences a man can enjoy. You are indeed fortunate - you will look down on the Dono Kara Ranges in the moonlight. But come, soon the sun will be gone. Fear not the griffins, they can be frightful in conflict but you have their goodwill.' Turning to the huntmaster, he added, 'Bring the straps, Brund.'

As they approached the griffins the four companions had to remind themselves of Florizan's reassuring words; emerald eyes in slanting sockets followed their approach, hot breath hissed gently through nostrils set in golden beaks, tails twitched and left runnels in the sand, and from the feathered throats came a low rumble which they hoped signified welcome.

They halted in a line in front of the creatures who, when they straightened their necks, gazed down upon them while Florizan rang his bells and spoke strange words. In response the griffins advanced upon the men until they could feel the heat of their breath.

'They greet you,' said Florizan. 'Put out your hands and touch them in return.'

Uncomfortably aware that one ill-natured snap of a beak could sever a man's wrist, Krispin did so. His fingers touched the feathers on the chest of the nearest griffin, and he was surprised at their metallic quality.

The griffin gave a whistling cry.

'Excellent,' said Florizan. 'She will carry you.'

Krispin smiled and nodded at the griffin.

The huntmaster now came forward with long straps which he buckled girth-like round the bodies of four of the griffins just behind the wings. Stirrups were fitted to each, as was a belt of leather which, Florizan explained, when looped round their waists would prevent them falling off should they succumb to drowsiness during the flight.

'You mount them just as a horse or drong and grip the girth or hold on to their fur, which you will find quite comfortable to sit on.'

'Not me,' Ognam muttered.

Violet shadows heralded night across the desert. Grunting to each other the griffins walked on lion feet to the nearest pool where they stretched out their long necks and drank deeply.

When they returned Florizan said, 'It is time. We made our farewells last night but again I thank you for overcoming our enemies. May the Serene Mother protect you and may you find The Mage.'

The huntmaster helped them on to the backs of the griffins where they hastily fixed the belts. Krispin was pleasantly surprised at the softness of the white fur which, as Florizan had said, made a comfortable covering in place of a saddle. Nervously he watched as the great wings unfolded

– larger than windmill sails – and began to rise and fall with increasing speed.

Faster and faster they beat, their wind teasing his long auburn locks, until the griffin gave a harsh cry and leapt into the air. With her pinions moving so fast they appeared like blurs of gold, she rose straight up. Forgetting his dislike of heights Krispin looked down past his knee at the shrinking figures below. Such was his terror at the sight he flung himself forward on the griffin and, clinging desperately to the strap, buried his face in the soft fur and kept his eyelids pressed tightly together.

One after another the griffins soared into the sky with their riders. Ognam was too much in pain to care what happened but Gambal gazed about in near disbelief as the world seemed to shrink below him. Alwald looked ahead into the sunset, his eyes bright with excitement as the wind roared past him and he felt the throb and surge of the magnificent creature's heart and muscles.

Alwald had always loved the chase, and now to be sweeping through the sky on a winged mount was something that would stay in his memory as a sublime moment for the rest of his span.

Once the griffins had reached a certain height the rhythm of their wings slowed considerably and they instinctively used them to take advantage of the airs which rose from the heated face of the desert. At times they merely held them rigid and glided like windhovers and eagles.

After many minutes Krispin cautiously opened his eyes and, raising his head slightly, saw the Desert of Akea rolling to the horizon like a petrified sea, its shadowy dunes in ranks like waves driven by a constant wind. Daring to rise a little more and glance over his shoulder, he saw that the griffins were flying in line as he had seen wild geese fly over the Wald, and like geese their wings made a pleasant swishing sound. The two griffins – the youngest of the group he guessed – who did not bear a traveller flew with lazy wings at the rear of the line.

Ahead the sun was dropping rapidly into the abyss at the end of the world against a backcloth of smouldering colour and despite his fear he could not help be heart-touched by the sheer beauty into which he was flying. Soon the sun was gone, taking away the glory in exchange for a brief fan of luminous shafts.

Below the face of the desert was covered by the cloak of night and soon the griffins were flying in darkness. This helped Krispin to lose some of his apprehension and he looked up. Never before had he seen so many bright and beautiful stars, with the pearly glow of the Star Bridge flowing from north to south.

Later the moon rose so that when the travellers looked down they saw that the desert had given way to barren foothills which were the beginning of the Dono Kara Ranges whose jagged snow-silvered peaks reared up far ahead of them. The sight of mountains in moonlight reminded Krispin vividly of the ranges which had protected the Wald and in particular he recalled the beauty of the White Virgins who guarded the pass which led to the outside world.

The wings of the griffins beat faster as they rose to clear the mountains. Even so they were not able to surmount the highest peaks but flew between them, sometimes so close to walls of rock stippled with ice that their riders instinctively closed their eyes and raised their forearms to their faces. But the griffins never faltered as they sailed through dizzy passes, round cliffs and over snow-shrouded saddles with their green eyes glowing in the dark.

Then the ranges were falling away to foothills covered with fir forests, and soon clouds carried by a high wind from the west extinguished the moon and the flight continued in pitch-darkness. Krispin lay forward on the griffin's back and, exhausted by the exertions of the day, slept with his cheek resting on the musky fur.

When morning light came it came dimly through cloud. Opening his eyes, Krispin tightened his hands on the girth strap in a spasm of terror and he heard a deep surging sound below which he guessed must be the sea breaking against rocky shores. Could it be that they were over the Cold Sea and would soon reach their destination? Shuddering with cold he looked down but could see nothing in the opaque mist below; he looked behind for his companions but again there was only clammy white vapour that had a curious salty smell.

The rhythm of the griffin's flying had altered. Frequently it held its pinions rigid and glided in gentle descents. Soon there were breaks in the mist. The rider had a fleeting view of a gigantic wave crashing in a welter of spume against black rock; a moment later his heart thudded with excitement as another gap in the mist showed him a tower-like castle poised on a mount of sombre basalt whose natural pinnacles and buttresses were mirrored by the tall grey keep, turrets and central tower crowned with candle-snuffer roofs which rose above it. Next moment the mist had hidden it again.

It could be naught else but the home of The Mage!

The griffin gave a mournful cry which was answered faintly by her invisible fellows, then Krispin saw a stretch of wetly gleaming sand materialise ahead of them. The griffin slowed, hovered a moment and then landed on her feet. Her head turned on her long neck and, regarding the young man with her jewelled eyes, she uttered a series of high pitched sounds.

In response he patted her back and said, 'My thanks, my lady, for bearing me so far and so safely through the night.'

He knew the words would mean nothing to her but he remembered Florizan saying that they understood the tone in which things were said. He freed himself from the belt, slid down her side and unbuckled the girth. The moment she was freed from it the griffin gave a cry of farewell – or so it seemed to Krispin – and soared up into the mist.

Alone on the sand, Krispin stretched his cramped limbs, adjusted his pack and tried to peer through the mist in hope of seeing his companions. With relief he saw a figure materialise.

'Ognam,' he cried as the jongleur limped into view. 'Well met. Have you seen the others?'

The jester shook his head and rubbed his hand over his buttock to which life was returning painfully.

'They could be anywhere in this fog. Have you any idea where we are or which way we should go?'

'I fear not, though I did get a glimpse of The Mage's tower two or three minutes ago. The trouble is I have no idea in which direction it lies.'

'How cold it is after the Domain,' muttered Ognam, pulling his travelling cloak closer about him. 'Perhaps we had better call out.'

For a minute they shouted but the vapour had the effect of deadening their voices and all they heard was the continuous noise of the unseen sea.

Suddenly Ognam gave an exclamation and pointed to the sand. A froth-flecked ripple was spreading across it followed by another, and then another to splash coldly over their feet. They were followed by a small wave that creamed out of the mist and left the two companions ankle-deep in water. Each of the following waves seemed to be deeper and flow with more power than the last.

'It occurs to me that we should be moving,' said Ognam. 'Or soon we shall have to swim for it. At least these waves tell us which way to . . .'

His words were interrupted by another wave which soaked their hose up to their thighs.

'Run!' cried Krispin, remembering the words that had been written in Old Ythan on the map Brother Mias had given him: *Beware the tide* . . . Both broke into a shambling trot with legs still cramped after the night flight. Breakers caught them more and more frequently and the level of the salty water continued to rise higher and higher.

Suddenly a gust of wind rolled away the mist about them as though a curtain was being drawn. Ahead they saw a vast stretch of black sand which was rapidly vanishing under the rising sea. Behind them they were horrified to see leaden combers with spindrift smoking from their crests surging remorselessly towards them.

'Faster!' cried Krispin who suddenly felt the ironic possibility that the quest might end with them being drowned under the shadow of The Mage's tower.

'I am doing my best,' shouted Ognam over the hiss of foaming water that buffeted them so hard they nearly lost their balance. Ahead they could now see where the shore ended against a black precipice in which a flight of steps had been cut. They raced towards it with wet sand sucking at their feet.

'Mother preserve me!' cried Ognam as an increasing roar made him turn. Far out ranks of huge rollers smoked towards the land, and both knew that their survival depended upon climbing the steps ahead of the moving walls of water.

The next minutes were the stuff of nightmares. Floundering waist deep they hardly seemed to make any progress while the thunder of the great waves grew deafening in their ears. But they were unexpectedly helped by the increasing slope of the shore as they neared the cliff; the water through which they were struggling became shallower until for the last few paces they were actually running over dry sand.

Reaching the shell-encrusted steps, they climbed frantically and were half-way to the top when the send of the sea burst below them in cascades of foam and made the very rock tremble with its impact. Pausing to get their breath, they saw that now the whole shoreline was hidden beneath the surging waves.

'This must be what they call the tide,' said Ognam. 'I have never seen the sea before but I have heard tell that it rises and falls each day.'

When they neared the top of the steps they saw that a high wall of rough stone blocks had been built along the clifftop with an archway set where the steps ended. Krispin had hoped for another sight of the towering castle but everything above the wall was obscured by sullen cloud.

Ognam was about to walk through the arch when he cried suddenly through chattering teeth, 'Lord Alwald and Master Gambal! Do you think they were somewhere down there? Do you think . . .'

'I pray the griffins put them down in some safer spot,' answered Krispin who was filled with fear for his companions at Ognam's words. 'Mayhap we will find them on the other side of this wall.'

'Mayhap,' said Ognam dully and went through the arch.

They found themselves in a narrow passage between high

walls of stone which, unlike the clifftop wall, had been dressed so that the surface was smooth.

'Strange,' muttered Ognam.

'Perhaps it is part of the castle's fortifications,' Krispin suggested. They followed the curving passage to a circular courtyard with equally high walls from which radiated seven passages.

'Let us take this one,' said Krispin indicating the central one.

'Be careful,' said Ognam, 'there is something about this place that I greatly mistrust.'

Privately Krispin agreed with him. An air of menace hung about them. The only sound to be heard was the sad serenade of the sea.

'This reminds me of a labyrinth I saw on Lord Odo's estate which I visited once with a company of entertainers,' the jester continued, 'though that was formed out of clipped hedges rather than unclimbable walls.'

'You could be right,' said Krispin looking round the courtyard. 'Each passage looks exactly the same. To be truthful I am not sure which one we entered by.'

'Surely it was that one over there – in the middle.'

Krispin looked doubtful.

'How can we say which is the middle passage when we are in a round courtyard?'

'At least we can try it,' said Ognam, leading the way. 'If it is the right passage we will be back at the cliff steps in a couple of minutes and then we will know for sure.'

Krispin followed him. In a couple of minutes they had not reached the steps but another courtyard with more passages leading from it.

'Sorry,' said Ognam.

'We must keep on trying. No one can be lost in a maze for ever.'

Ognam opened his pack and began to fumble through it.

'I have a stick of red cosmetic,' he said. 'I used to use it to colour my nose for my drunken priest act – very popular until word of it reached the shrines.' He sighed. 'Now I can use it to leave marks on the walls so that we can always find our way back.'

'At least the snakebite has not addled your wits,' Krispin told him. 'Let us set off.'

With the jester leaving a scarlet arrow on the stonework every few paces, they returned along the twisting alley they had followed – or had they? For instead of returning to the circular courtyard they suddenly found themselves in a quadrangle with a lancet archway set in each of its four walls.

Bewildered, they walked to the centre of the paving and then Ognam said in a hoarse whisper, 'Keep calm but something rather unpleasant has followed us.'

He was staring at a shining black shape, vaguely human, which stood motionless in the archway.

'Keep calm,' said Krispin, 'but there is also one ahead of us.'

ELEVEN
Magic Casements

The figures standing motionless in the archways were identical. Neither had a face in the portion of the body that corresponded to the head; a lack of clothing revealed no sexual characteristics but exteriors that were hard and gleaming black like the carapace of a beetle.

'Serene Mother! I used to have nightmares about things like that when I was a child,' whispered Ognam.

'Quick, down this passage,' cried Krispin turning to an archway in the side wall but as they took a pace forward a dark figure appeared out of its shadow.

'Surrounded,' muttered Ognam.

As though animated by a common impulse, the four faceless figures took a step forward simultaneously, then another, and another. They held no weapons but there was something so menacing about these dummy-like beings that Krispin's hand was shaking as he reached for the grip of Woundflame, and as the blade was drawn from its scabbard its battle gleam was bright in the pale light filtered by the vapour flowing over the walls of the labyrinth.

Another step, and as one they raised their arms as though reaching blindly for the two companions.

'What can they want?' Krispin asked.

'Us!' replied Ognam simply.

'Be ready to run.'

'Believe me, I am.'

Krispin raised his sword and then brought it hissing against the side of the beetle-body nearest to him. The blade bit into it with a sound like tearing parchment, and to Krispin's astonishment it fell apart in two halves. For a moment he stood staring, then Ognam tugged his arm and they pelted down the passage from which it had emerged.

When they reached a corner they looked back and saw that swarming from the sundered body were scores of small black imps – reproductions of the slaughtered original. Like a pack of rats dislodged from a sewer, they *flowed* vengefully down the passage.

Ognam whimpered, a terrified child, and turned away but Krispin, his face a mask of disgust, stepped forward with Woundflame and steel rang on stone as he chopped wildly at the scuttling horrors. Each time one was struck even smaller replicas poured from the wound.

'Run!'

Krispin did not need Ognam's urging and they raced along the curving passage until at length they had to stop, bending double as they fought for breath.

'I am spent,' gasped Ognam. 'I seem to have been running all morning and my backside is still ablaze thanks to the dwarf's pet.'

'At least we have left those *things* behind,' Krispin managed to say reassuringly. 'The little ones could not keep up with us.'

'There may be more of the big ones waiting for us.'

'Woundflame will take care of them . . . Hush, what is that?'

Both listened but all they could heard was the racing pulse in their ears.

'What is what?' Ognam asked anxiously.

'I thought I heard a cry . . . more of a bellow, such as a beast would make.'

He shuddered.

'My soaking breeches are cursedly cold,' he explained.

'Of course,' said Ognam. 'We may as well carry on as shiver here.'

As they walked along the passage the jester continued to leave his grease paint marks on the stone blocks until they saw another of the labyrinth's archways. Suddenly a long-drawn roar reverberated between the walls; inhuman, full of menace, yet possessing a mournful quality beyond the comprehension of an animal.

Krispin and Ognam were transfixed, and then – for a moment that was long to haunt their memories – they beheld a grotesque shape pass the arch. Its body was that of a deep-chested man but the head was that of a beast, a blunt-nosed beast with a pair of horns curving forward from its broad brow, large bovine eyes that shone with malign intelligence and a mouth open hugely as it gave tongue to another wild cry.

'The Bull Man!' muttered Krispin when the apparition had gone past. 'When I was small . . .' His voice trailed off.

'I am getting a strange idea about this place,' said Ognam.

'There is a pattern about it – the maze I mean – that reminds me of something,' Krispin went on. 'It is the way these passages all curve and run into courtyards of different shapes. Remember we went through one formed like a cross?'

'So?'

Sheathing Woundflame, Krispin felt inside his shirt and brought out the Disk of Livia. He looked at the tiny runes set in a spiral which had been engraved on the yellow metal.

'I believe this maze is copied from the disk,' he said. 'The curving passages are like the spiral, and the courtyards represent the runes. See, if we take each right hand passage we will cross the spiral until we reach a gateway in the outside wall.'

'Perhaps it might have amused an enchanter to set out his maze like a huge amulet,' said Ognam doubtfully. 'But at least we can try your idea – anything to get out of this place of nightmares.'

They set out and each time they reached a spot where there was a choice of passages they took the one on the right. After what seemed an age, during which ears and eyes were strained for some new and ghastly denizen of the labyrinth, they came upon a gate of corroded bronze set in a wall. It was partly open and, pushing through the gap, they found themselves on an expanse of dark rock which sloped at an increasing angle to the mount on which the castle stood.

'At last,' said Krispin. 'The Mage's Tower.'

It should have been a moment of triumph – a goal reached after travelling half across the kingdom – but now they were safe from the dangers within the labyrinth concern for their companions was uppermost in their minds.

The tower, too, was not as Krispin had imagined. He had expected the home of a sorcerer to be rather like the watchtowers once used by the wayside knights in the Wilderness of Gil, but the bulk of this rivalled that of River Garde. Unlike the castle of the River Lord it was redolent of gloom. There were no banners straining in the salty breeze, no men-at-arms in bright armour, no merry clang of farriers' tools or snatches of song from servant wenches. The Mage's Tower was as grim as the basalt from which it rose.

The dismal effect was heightened by the melancholy

boom of surf and the cloud which streamed so low overhead the conical roofs of the turrets shredded it. This sickly vapour hid the upper part of the central tower from view.

'I hope The Mage is a mite more cheerful than his residence,' muttered Ognam as they trudged over the wet rock towards a ramp which curved steeply to the castle entrance.

Suddenly Ognam gave a joyful cry and pointed ahead. Two small figures stood in the open gateway set in the barbican.

'Lord Alwald,' he cried, adding less enthusiastically, 'and Master Gambal.'

Within minutes the companions were united.

'Our lion birds landed us right below the gate,' explained Alwald. 'When we did not see you we decided to wait here because it would be the place you would be sure to make for.'

'You had better fortune than us,' said Krispin. 'We came down on the shore with the tide raging in.' And while he and Ognam changed into dry breeches and top garments from their packs he gave a brief account of their adventures.

'Tell me, Krispin, do you sense anything weird about this place?' asked Alwald as they passed through the gateway into a deserted courtyard.

'The maze was certainly strange enough. I felt it was somehow out of time – the frightening things we saw were like mirrored images of childhood fears. But what do you mean by weird?'

'It is hard to put into the right words,' said Alwald uncomfortably. 'It is not like me to fanciful as you know, but I must confess that I do not feel that this is real. It is as though there is something of a dream mixed up in it.'

Krispin nodded.

'Perhaps it is because this island belongs to a master of gramarye.'

'And this tower depresses my spirits,' Alwald continued. 'Have you noticed that there is not a single watchman? I have the feeling we may be a century too late.'

As with the castle gate, the huge double doors of the keep were unlocked and they opened with screeching hinges when the four put their shoulders to the worm-pitted wood. Inside they found themselves in a long hall dimly lit by light beamed through stained glass set in mullioned windows. Down the centre a double row of massive pillars supported a hammer-beam ceiling.

'It is like a shrine,' said Gambal in a hushed tone. 'A shrine that has been abandoned for many a year.'

The companions moved slowly over the deep-dusted floor, stepping through sombre splashes of tinted light cast by the stained glass – purples, blues and viridian which were the only colours to be seen in the hall of grey shadows. Their hearts were heavy that their journeying had led them to such a dismal place.

They climbed a broad staircase, guarded by grimed statues which once held flambeaux, and found themselves in what might once have been a banqueting chamber. The tapestries on the walls hung in tatters like ancient battle flags, the furniture was rotten and when Ognam lowered himself wearily on to a divan it sank beneath him in a cloud of throat-drying dust. All that could be seen through the windows was a wild sea rolling endlessly to fountain against the fang-like rocks guarding the coast.

They moved through other chambers, along passages and across halls and everywhere they were oppressed by the same sense of desolation and decay.

'To think we have followed the quest so far, over wilderness and under the earth and through the air, only to find this . . . this mausoleum!' Alwald cried with a sudden flare of anger. 'I just wish the old dame who started us on the quest was here to see how it has ended – in an abandoned ruin at the world's end.'

No one else said anything though their thoughts were similar.

'Still, we may as well finish exploring it,' Krispin said moodily.

They ascended a spiralling staircase which led up to the main tower. As they climbed higher they had more glimpses through lancet windows of sea which separated the island from the forbidding mainland. Like the island, it was bordered by basalt cliffs.

At the top of the staircase they explored in different directions and soon Krispin found himself alone in a dim gallery with a row of damask-draped windows rising from floor to ceiling along one wall. This long chamber did not appear to be as neglected as the rest of the castle and, curious to see it better, he went to the first window and drew back the heavy curtain.

Krispin expected to see low cloud and grey waves but to his amazement there was smiling countryside with a river along which a white barge was being pulled by a large horse on a towpath.

For a moment he believed it was a trick picture painted to give the effect of a scene through a window, but when he reached up and felt the cold glass and lead strips he knew it was not the work of an artist.

Mystified, he pulled aside the next drape and through the casement saw a great spiral of stars – hundreds of them! – against a void of ultimate blackness.

He leapt to the next window, wrenched back the damask – and a sob of anguish rose from his heart. He found himself gazing through the diamond panes at forest slopes leading up to a range of magnificent snow-capped mountains. In the foreground was a village of brightly painted houses with decorated woodwork, high gables and thatched roofs. Smoke coiled peacefully from chimneys – a gust of wind made it dance as he watched – and he could even see the Jack-in-the-Box sign of the inn . . .

Toyheim!

But all that remained of Toyheim was ashes.

Something made Krispin drag the curtain across the scene before he could see any more.

Magic Casements.

The two words swam into his mind as though he had just recalled them, and he wondered if they had been hidden in his memory by the Lady Eloira.

Magic Casements.

He looked along the row of windows but he dared not draw another curtain. There was high sorcery here and through his confusion the thought came to him that The Mage must still be alive. Then he was struck by another idea: What if he opened one of the casements and walked through into the world on which it looked? Where would he be, what would he find – the Toyheim of his dreams? Secret lands? The Princess Livia . . .?

Magic Casements.

The words rang in his brain like an incantation.

With a shudder he hurried from the gallery in the direction of Alwald's voice. He found the young noble and Gambal in a small antechamber, Ognam having wandered off on his own.

The room was hung with mildewed tapestries which had exchanged their patterns for the webs of spiders who once may have spun in hope but succumbed to starvation. In the opposite wall was a door of polished wood which appeared less time-spoiled than the rest of the woodwork they had so far seen and it was with a flicker of hope that Alwald turned the grotesque handle and pushed it open.

The chamber beyond brought exclamations of surprise and relief. In one wall was a fireplace where logs blazed brightly in a wrought-iron fire basket so that the air was free from the salty dampness which pervaded the rest of the tower. The hangings and carpet, though of ancient manufacture, were without holes, and there was no patina of dust on the furniture which comprised a massive chest carved with leering images of woodwoses, a chair and a table on which lay a black broad-brimmed hat. Against the far wall was a four-poster bed with its curtains drawn.

Alwald crossed the floor and parted the hangings to reveal an old man lying beneath a cover of soft fleeces which almost hid the line of his frail body. His emaciated hands lay crossed upon it. A bolster covered with samite supported his head with its profusion of silver locks combed neatly to each side of his face which, sharpened by age, had an almost transparent quality. His thin bluish lips were curved into the hint of irony but his eyes were hidden behind veined lids perhaps for ever, for he lay as motionless as an effigy on a tomb.

As Krispin gazed upon him he had the feeling that he had seen that ironic expression before but when the face had been animated and the eyes twinkled with life.

'The Mage,' murmured Alwald.

'He has gone with the Dark Maid,' said Gambal. 'We are too late.'

TWELVE
Metamorphosis

The day after Mesire Florizan had taken the four travellers into the desert to continue their mysterious journey the Hump, with Silvermane sitting side-saddle behind him, rode out from the Domain on a white drong that had been given to him. A second drong, its panniers loaded with waterskins and provisions, followed on a lead. Using his instinctive sense of direction, the guide hoped to cross the desert and then travel through remote but more fertile terrain until they reached the Arkad woodlands from where the horsemaid had originally been taken. The pair had made their farewells to Florizan and his courtiers the night before as they wanted to begin their journey in the cool of the dawn. Apart from the watchman who opened the gate there was only one other who observed their departure.

It was a relief to both when they felt the rhythmic gait of the drong bearing them over the sand. Although the Domain had been pleasant enough, especially after their subterranean voyage, neither had felt at home there. They had always been conscious that they had been the objects of politely-concealed curiosity – good manners were the hallmark of the Domain – and this sense of being outsiders had sharply increased with the departure of their fellow travellers.

If it had not been for that, the Hump would have been

tempted to delay setting out. For the past few days the pain in his back had been increasing and this was accompanied by alarming sensations of movement within the spinal curvature which bowed him. Not wishing to alarm Silvermane he kept this to himself and tried to hold back the spasms which literally shook his body by taking more and more sooma seeds.

Now as the walls of the Domain dwindled behind them he felt the pain increasing and the sweat that beaded his face had little to do with the warmth of the sun. Surreptitiously he slipped yet more seeds into his mouth and rode on with his teeth clamped on his lower lip. Anger boiled within him. From the moment he had been found as a babe beneath a thorn bush he had known little peace . . . He remembered the jeers that had filled his childish ear – the jokes about him being hatched from an egg, the beatings his foster mother gave him for not being straight like the others, the pain that had been a daily companion ever since he could remember . . .

And the jest was that having finally won the chance to quit the world of men and share his life with Silvermane he was likely to be betrayed by his own body. As another spasm clenched the nerves along his back he knew it was foolhardy to continue into the desert yet he could not bring himself to turn round.

They rode on for an hour, and then the horsemaid gave a cry of alarm.

'Dearheart . . . you bleed.'

He reached behind him and when he looked at his hand he saw that she was right.

'What is it?'

'I am not sure,' he answered. 'It feels as though something is breaking. I . . .' But nausea robbed him of further words.

Silvermane pointed to where a rare hill of jumbled rocks rose from the dunes.

'Go there . . . you can rest . . . in the shade.'

He nodded and urged the drong towards the hill. Once they were close to the rocks he climbed from the saddle and managed to drive the long iron tethering stake into the sand.

'Come,' said Silvermane and with her arm round his waist they reeled towards a spot where a shallow cave was formed by a natural slab of rock resting on boulders. He fell forward and lay on his side in the cool shadow with relief. Silvermane rolled up the cloak he invariably wore and laid it beneath his head, then she unsheathed his drong-rider's spike and with its point deftly ripped open his shirt.

She failed to bite back an exclamation of shock and – to the Hump's ear – disgust.

'What ails me?' he asked.

'Your skin . . . it tears . . . you need physician . . . I ride back to Domain.'

He tried to argue and then decided that she was right.

'I bring you water . . . then go,' she told him.

She left the cave and he took more sooma seeds and thanks to these, combined with the shade and the fact that he was resting, the intense pain begin to ebb and he fell into a light dose. It was the thought of Silvermane that brought him back to full consciousness. She should have returned with the waterskin by now. He sat up and then, as a scream came to his ears, his hand tightened on the spike which lay on the sand.

Ignoring his weakness, he hauled himself to his feet and went into the dazzling sunlight.

There, a hundred paces away Silvermane was surrounded by four young men led by Lord Ugo; a grinning servant stood a short distance away holding the reins of their drongs.

One of the gallants waved Silvermane's long-skirted gown like a victorious flag. She stood naked, the mane of silver hair which grew down her neck and her graceful equine limbs exciting remarks and laughter from her tormentors.

'Have you ever seen such paps on a horse!' shouted one of Ugo's companions.

'And have you ever seen such a crotch on a woman?'

'Who is going to get her in foal?'

Ugo stepped up behind her and tripped her forward on all fours.

'I shall play stallion,' he cried. 'And that will reward her monstrous mate for drawing steel on the son of his host.'

Silvermane tried to regain her feet but he seized her viciously by the shoulders and flung her down on to the sand.

The young courtiers were so engrossed in the sport that they had not heard the Hump approach nor did they see him hurl his spike.

It struck Ugo in the thigh. With a curse he climbed to his feet, his hand gripping the steel whose point was embedded in his flesh. His companions drew their swords and began to advance on the guide.

'No,' cried Ugo as he jerked the spike from his flesh and flung it to the ground. 'I wish their deaths to come slowly – and in a manner that will not bring a blood sin upon us. Drive off their drongs and leave them.'

With his hand pressing his wound he limped painfully to his own drong and was helped into the saddle by the servant who then untied the Hump's two animals and sent them racing away with his whip.

'You, crouchback, are used to desert places,' called Ugo. 'Tell me, how long will it be before her young tongue swells with thirst? Will you suck your own blood to cheat the Dark Maid of an hour? Which of you will live to see the other's corpse bloat with the heat?'

As they sped away shouting curses the Hump raised Silvermane and then helped her into her torn gown.

'Curse my weakness,' he said. 'With my usual strength and aim I could have sent the spike through his black heart.'

'It matters not,' she said. 'They are gone . . . we are together . . . when the Dark Maid comes . . . we meet her hand-in-hand.'

'We have some time yet. If only I could recall the drongs. Help me climb to the top of the rocks and I may see them.'

For the last few minutes anger had submerged his pain but as he toiled from rock to rock it returned and several times he would have slipped as a spasm gripped him and dimmed his sight had not Silvermane been there to seize his arm.

By the time he neared the summit of the natural pyramid he felt the blood which oozed over his back baked into a black crust by the ferocity of the sun. It was only with difficulty that he could form words, and perhaps it was merely the suggestion of Ugo's words but he began to suffer pangs of thirst. Yet the determination which had saved him before on hazardous caravan trails did not desert him, and finally they reached the summit where both collapsed on a slab of burning rock.

After a minute he knelt up and scanned the horizon in the hope of seeing their drongs.

'To the south . . .' he began and then a cry of agony burst from his throat.

Silvermane gazed at him in horror and pressed her hands to her mouth.

The hump between his shoulders appeared to swell. From it issued a creaking as though the bones beneath it were in conflict. Skin parted under the pressure so that his body was glazed with blood and lymph. And Silvermane watched mute as her lover's back appeared to split. From the opening which ran the length of his spine two bloody bundles of membrane were thrust forth and immediately began to unfold. As they did so the flexible bones within them widened into predetermined formations, and in a serious of jerks the wet tissue expanded to become as thin as sail cloth between them.

'Wings!' exulted Silvermane. 'You have wings!'

The Hump's moans died away. He was still on his knees but his back was no longer bowed. The graceful pinions which grew out of it stirred gently above his shoulders as though they had life of their own. He reached up and pulled down the tip of one to examine the texture of the creamy membrane. Then, with an expression of wonderment on his face, he stood upright, the wings shifting to balance his new position.

'Do you still pain?' asked Silvermane in a husky voice.

He shook his head.

'It went when they burst forth, though it did feel strange as they unfolded.'

'Can you . . . fly?'

'Yes. I shall fly the moment they have dried and toughened. I do not know how to explain it, but it is as though I have always known what to do but have only just remembered it. See, I can fold them.'

As he smiled down at her the great hawk-shaped wings retracted and folded upon themselves until they were flat against his back.

'If you wore a cloak . . . no one see,' said Silvermane. 'Now stretch.'

'Watch,' he said with a touch of boastfulness.

The wings unfolded and spread to their full extent and for a moment a hot gust of desert wind almost caught him off balance.

He sat down beside her and she was shaded by one of the wings which he kept outstretched.

'Dearheart . . . do you know . . . what you are?'

'No.' He laughed, a deep happy gut laugh. 'But there must have been truth in the story that I was hatched.'

They sat for a long while in silence until he said, 'They are strong now. We can be on our way.'

For a moment fear crossed her face.

'You are going to . . . now?'

'Yes. We still have the drongs to find. As yet I do not feel capable of flying with you right across the desert, though some day . . .'

He stood behind her and clasped her beneath the arms.

'Fear not, Silvermane, *they* know what to do.'

His wings began to rise and fall, and as he willed it their speed increased and the heated air sang about them and his body seemed to lose its sense of weight just as it had lost its deformity. And suddenly the hill, the desert, the world – all were plunging beneath them and they were soaring.

Soaring!

More Fantasy Fiction from Headline:

ROGER TAYLOR

THE FALL OF FYORLUND

The Chronicles of Hawklan

The darkness of ancient times is spreading over the land of Fyorlund and tainting even the Great Harmony of Orthlund. The ailing King Rgoric has imprisoned the much-loved and respected Lords Eldric, Arinndier, Darek and Hreldar; he has suspended the ancient ruling council of the Geadrol; he has formed his own High Guard, filling its ranks with violent unruly men; and Mandrocs have been seen even in Orthlund. At the centre of this corruption is the King's advisor, the evil Lord Dan-Tor, who is determined to destroy the peace won by Ethriss and the Guardians eons ago, and surrender the land to his Dark Lord, Sumeral.

The people look to Hawklan to make a stand against Dan-Tor. But he is a healer and not a soldier – though, deep within himself, Hawklan has felt an ancient power, and when threatened has been seen to fight like a warrior out of legend. Hawklan knows he must confront Dan-Tor before the land falls forever to the encroaching, eternal night . . .

Also by Roger Taylor from Headline
THE CALL OF THE SWORD
The Chronicles of Hawklan

FICTION/FANTASY 0 7472 3118 4 £3.99